# OFF TO THE RACES

ELSIE SILVER

Bloom books

Published by Bloom Books, an imprint of Sourcebooks
P.O. Box 4410, Naperville, Illinois 60567-4410
(630) 961-3900
sourcebooks.com

Cataloging-in-Publication data is on file with the Library of Congress.

*Off to the Races* and *Out of the Gate* were originally
self-published in 2021 by Elsie Silver.

Printed and bound in Canada.
MBP 10 9 8 7 6 5 4 3 2 1

*For my parents, who spent hours upon hours driving me to and from the barn.*

"I don't like people," said Velvet. "...I like only horses."

—ENID BAGNOLD, *NATIONAL VELVET*

# PROLOGUE
## Billie

TEN YEARS AGO

LIGHTS FLASH ALL AROUND ME, FORCING ME TO COVER MY eyes with my forearm. I can still hear the camera bulbs popping as I surge forward. The thrum of bodies around me is oppressive. They threaten to close in from every side.

*I just need to get to the car.*

"Wilhelmina! Wilhelmina!"

I move faster, butting up against security guards as I flail blindly toward the waiting town car, a beacon where I might finally relax. Where I can let the facade slip. Where I can put my head in my hands and cry.

I can see the open door beckoning me to slide in and escape.

*I'm so close.*

I'm jostled against my shoulder and feel cool crosshatched

metal press up against my lips. Dropping my arm, I face eager eyes and too-white teeth.

"Wilhelmina, can you tell us if you've seen the videos of your father?"

All I hear is the steady beat of my heart pumping in my ears. I feel borderline feral in my need to disappear into the waiting car. The one I can see just beyond her perfectly coiffed blond hair.

I'm functioning on instinct. It's fight or flight now.

All I hear are gasps around me when I look right into the camera and say, "How about you go fuck yourself?"

I choose *fight*.

# CHAPTER 1

## Vaughn

I MOAN, HANGING MY HEAD IN MY HANDS, DEFEATED. "JESUS Christ."

The emails won't stop coming. The inquiring reporters. The never-ending questions.

I've been sitting at this desk for hours every day listening to the nonstop pinging of messages coming through while I turn my grandfather's office upside down looking for *something*. Scouring page after page of farm financials, digging through filing cabinets, looking for a clue. I've even gone so far as knocking on the inner walls of his desk drawers, like this is a movie rather than real life and a hidden compartment will pop open and show me exactly what I am looking for.

What am I missing?

I have to prove he's innocent. I can't let this be his legacy.

As the family business marketing whiz, I know I have a heaping pile of shit to clean up. That's what I should do right now. Paste on a winning smile and smooth things out. Nail down a plan to move forward. Reassure the media, apologize to fellow industry members, and rub our shareholder's backs.

I can't let the scandal here at the ranch seep into anyone's trust about how Gold Rush Resources operates. Sure, they're both our businesses, but one makes all the money while the other basically just continues to break even. And deep down, I know the only way to inspire confidence in the mining company is to throw my grandfather, one of the most important and influential men in my life, under the proverbial bus.

On a heavy sigh, I click the mouse to open my inbox.

Statement Request Re: Race fixing

Stubble rasps under my fingers as I scrub at my face. I don't want to make a statement, but it's been two weeks. I need to stop hiding out at the farm, banging my head against the wall.

Two weeks ago, our grandfather, Dermot Harding, the man who practically raised me when everyone else had tapped out, died from a massive heart attack. He keeled over right here in this office, and a day later, newspapers across the country splashed our family name and his photo on the front page, accompanied by a story about how he'd been the ringleader behind one of the biggest race-fixing scandals in thoroughbred racing history.

A fucking disaster, to be sure.

Rationally, I know the man was in his eighties—not an unusual time to die. But somehow his sudden loss has shocked me to my very core. Maybe his death hasn't hit me yet, because all I can think about is clearing his name. He's been slandered—his entire legacy—and he isn't even here to defend himself. There's just no way the man who practically raised me would have done this. I can't wrap my head around it.

My phone vibrates, drawing my attention away from the email in front of me as I watch it dance across the desk's surface. The name *Cole* flashes on the screen with a picture of a G.I. Joe toy—an image that usually makes me smile. But not today. Today, I'm not in the mood to talk to my big brother.

I can't peel my eyes away from the phone but can't bring myself to pick it up either. I let the call ring through to voicemail, and within moments of the screen going black, it lights back up with another call. Cole is relentless, and I'm too obedient where my family is concerned to ignore two calls in a row. Something could be wrong.

I swipe the answer button and lift the phone to my ear. "What?"

"You done playing *Little House on the Prairie* yet?"

I roll my eyes. Cole is such a dick.

Everyone has their own idea of how I *should* act in the wake of my grandfather's death and the exposure of the scandal. My brother. My mom. The board of directors.

"Is there something you need that doesn't involve mocking me?"

"You need to get your ass back here. There are expectations, Vaughn," he grumbles, knowing this won't go over well.

I'm accustomed to being the face of the company, but

they need me to put on a totally different show than usual this time, and I guess I'm not quite meeting their expectations for marketable grief. They want that devastation, sprinkled with a hint of shame, and they want it where everyone can see it.

And this time? I'm not buying.

"I know what the expectations are, Cole. I just don't care."

I can hear him groan on the other end of the line. I'm the one thing he can't check off his to-do list, and that's probably keeping him up at night. He's not worried about how I'm doing; he's worried about keeping things clean and tidy. Just the way he likes them.

"How long is this little stint going to last?"

I feel my jaw tick as I consider the best way to answer that question.

It makes him and everyone else involved uneasy that I shut them down and fled Vancouver for the tranquil mountains and valleys of Ruby Creek. I'm not mourning solemnly, toeing the company line about being shocked and disappointed, and "acknowledging my feelings" appropriately. Which is apparently achieved by holding press conferences, parading around with an appropriate date, like I'm some sort of glorified escort, and then penning an emotional editorial for the newspapers to print.

Too bad for them, I'm not sad yet.

I'm angry. Angry that the man I love more than almost anyone died alone in his office after being delivered such a shocking blow that his heart gave out.

And that anger? It makes the people around me uncomfortable, and if I've learned anything in my twenty-eight years on this earth, it's that most humans will do almost anything to salvage their own comfort. They'll grasp at it with white knuckles and sweaty palms and hold on to it with absolute frantic desperation. Destroy relationships with family members, endure shitty marriages, stab friends in the back—you name it. Comfort is king.

And for now, I care little about how I appear to the media or how my lack of comment reflects on the company. I've been their darling for years. I got the right education and then let them trot me out and parade me around like a fancy show pony.

"As long as I need it to," I bite back before hanging up. I'm done bending over backward to accommodate everyone else. I need some time for *me.*

I've suffered the company of people I can't stand, laughed at jokes that aren't funny, and rubbed shoulders with some of Vancouver's most influential people to satisfy my obligations to the family business. I've been the poster boy and most eligible bachelor of the elite scene in this city for years now. Without complaint. So as far as I'm concerned, they can all just buck up and deal with me feeling edgy for a few weeks.

The world won't stop turning if I take a break from smiling. Or if I take a step back from Gold Rush Resources to salvage the ranch.

Even just floating that idea went over like a lead balloon though. Cole hit the roof. Something about flushing my career and future down the toilet, followed by some advice about how perseverating on the farm isn't healthy or productive to the *main business*. According to Cole, in the wake of my grandfather's funeral, I should focus on my job and take some time with family. *Grieving.*

I snort. That was rich coming from him, the man who took off last time tragedy struck. Which I told him just before adding that I was in fact going to be taking a leave of absence to run the ranch. Then I'd spun on my heel and stormed out of our lavish downtown offices.

Good fucking riddance, concrete jungle.

I packed my bags and moved into my grandfather's farmhouse that very day, comforted by the closeness I felt here. Full of happy memories from my childhood.

Gold Rush Ranch has been in our family for generations. Once my grandmother Ada's family cattle ranch and now one of western Canada's premier racing facilities. This place had been my grandmother's dream—or at least that's what Dermot always told me. She died when I was younger, and my memories of her are less vivid. But I know that she's why my grandfather stayed out here and focused on the ranch while letting other people run the downtown offices for the mining company. And I know their love was one to rival a fairy tale.

So just because my brother and mother don't understand my attachment to the place doesn't mean it isn't true. Neither of them know me that well anyways, haven't ever really tried. Haven't ever gone out of their way to be there for me. Sure, we talk. But unless we're talking about running the family businesses, it's brief and superficial. I only tolerate my mother's meddling because it's the only attention I get from her. Which sounds pathetic—*I know* (hello, abandonment issues!).

Plus, if Cole can duck and run to the army in the wake of our father's death, I can duck and run to the ranch. Fair is fair.

I don't care what he thinks about it. Unlike everyone else, I'm not afraid of him. His holier-than-thou asshole attitude doesn't scare me. He never stuck around to take care of me before, and I will not let him do it now.

My grandfather spent decades building his empire from scratch. I owe him this.

Between the two companies, his blood, sweat, tears, and a little luck glued our entire family legacy together. Grandpa Dermot turned his full attention to the ranch in the depths of his mourning. And it has garnered accolades, prestige, and a hell of a lot of wins under his management. This whole place is a living, breathing ode to his late wife and son.

Reminiscing about my family history...I shake my head and stretch my arms out in front of me. *That* is not a productive rabbit hole to fall down.

Pity parties are for chumps.

Giving each sleeve a tug and adjusting my cuff links, I lean back and sigh deeply. I've been doing a lot of that lately. Big, heavy, hopeless sighs. The sound annoys me.

Looking out the office window, I feel...overwhelmed. I admire the perfectly arranged white fences in precise squares, each square a home to one horse. I appreciate the organization of the layout. One object arranged into one tidy box. So uncomplicated. So logical. The simplicity soothes me, and I repeat my grandfather's words to myself like a mantra. "You can only control what's right in front of you, Vaughn."

*God.* I sound like I've been reading lame self-help books. Something that my mother, bless her, has recommended. Right before she offered to set me up on *another* date. Like getting married off and pumping out grandbabies will make me as happy as it would her. She's a rich city girl through and through, one who fell in love with a farm boy, and I think Cole and I have never quite known where we belong. She loves me, but she doesn't understand me at all—doesn't even try.

"Well meaning. But so goddamn misguided."

"What was that, son?" Hank barks breathlessly, making me spin quickly in my chair. He's grasping the doorframe to pop his head back in, like he almost made it past without hearing me.

I really need to stop talking to myself.

"Nothing," I respond, more dismissively than intended. Kind of the norm for me these days, to be honest.

"You sure you're doing all right?" It's hard to sneak anything past old eagle eyes.

"Yup. See you at eleven." I try to make up for my tone by offering him a wave and a forced smile, but I'm not sure it works. It probably just makes me look feral. It doesn't feel natural. I'm just...numb.

Hank grins, winks, and continues on his way, completely undeterred by my shitty attitude. How the man is always in such a good mood is beyond me. He's so unflappable that it's borderline unnatural.

I need a few of whatever he's on.

The first thing I did when I got to the farm was clean house. Some people might say I burned the whole house down, but I couldn't rebuild this place's reputation surrounded by untrustworthy people or even people who were happy to look the other way.

Gold Rush Ranch is under new management, and that comes with a new moral code too.

I made it my mission to track down and hire Hank Brandt, the man who'd been Dermot's best friend when he moved to Ruby Creek all those years ago. A man who knew and loved this valley but who also knew racehorses. He went on to manage one of the East Coast's most successful racing and breeding programs before taking an early retirement and moving back out this way.

When I reached out to him about stepping out of that retirement, he'd been keen to return to the place where it all began, and to his credit, he wasn't even put off by the farm's declining success at the track and now tainted reputation.

He said he was "looking forward to the challenge" and flashed me his signature megawatt grin, like he knew something I didn't.

Hank and I agreed to a partnership where he would take the reins, so to speak, on all the horse-related tasks while I manage the business side of things. We agreed to hire everyone together. I wanted to ensure we were creating a work environment that we could both live with. I wasn't ready to relinquish control of my grandfather's legacy.

At least not before properly restoring it.

Which is why we're interviewing a new trainer this morning. Some guy named Billy Black who Hank met and worked with out east, who he raved about being young and cutting-edge. Trained in the United Kingdom under the tutelage of someone renowned over there who I didn't know at all and "brimming with new ideas and strategies," he said.

The guy didn't sound like the safe and reliable choice I'd like in place for this shit show, but I'll humor the old man. An interview can't hurt, and a person completely unknown to the industry in this area may just be the fresh start we need.

That *I* need.

Out the front window of my office, I can see the perfectly paved circular driveway. Just beyond the driveway, a fountain shoots arching streams of water in front of a bronze statue of my father in his jockey silks, poised over a galloping horse.

There are so many memories here. So many places for my mind to wander, to trip and fall into a daydream. So much to reminisce about.

The sound of rubber quietly rolling over sticky asphalt jolts me from my reverie, which is good because I don't have time to let myself turn into a sentimental sap right now. We are interviewing the new trainer in twenty minutes, and I really don't need any interruptions.

I watch the black SUV pull into the parking lot and feel frustration burn in my chest. I don't feel like dealing with people right now.

The driver's side door opens, and one polished black loafer steps out. It has interlocking horse bits across the top, accompanied by a long slender leg in slim-fit burgundy dress pants. My gaze travels up that leg, taking in the woman as she exits the vehicle. Bright spring sunlight glints almost blindingly off the thick chestnut braid that hangs down her back.

Standing to both feet, she gently smooths the collar on her black blouse before propping a hand over her brow and rotating slowly to take in the scenery. I can't help but let my eyes linger on the spot where her waist nips in between her curves.

A wistful smile touches her shapely lips as she stands there, all doe-eyed and serene looking.

She looks like a doll. She also looks altogether too smug. Like she knows she's here for her chance at bagging Vaughn Harding. I've seen that look a thousand times before, social climbers in their element. Gold diggers ready for their kick at the can. Women are constantly looking at me like that, and it has lost its appeal.

She's *beautiful*. Of course she is; they always are. But this woman is attractive in a classic and wholesome kind of way—a change in strategy, apparently.

I shake my head, feeling frustration bubble up in my chest, fast and hot. These games and charades are the last thing I need right now. Why is nobody *listening* to me? My fuse is short, and I'm ready to blow.

This time, I will not smile and nod. This time, I'm going to send a message. Loud and clear.

This time, my mother has gone too far.

# CHAPTER 2
## Billie

*This.*

This is my happy place.

No drama. No faking it. Just me and horses.

No human as far as the eye can see. Just the way I like it.

Anywhere with horses has always been my sanctuary, and this property is no exception. It's *immaculate*. Idyllic white fences outline the perfect green grass stretching out before me. And within each wooden square, a home to a beautiful shiny horse.

All layered with that comforting horse farm aroma I love.

I close my eyes and take a deep breath. No matter how pristine a farm is, you can't escape it, even outdoors. You can spend all the money in the world to keep your over-the-top, swanky facility spotless, and it will still smell like horse shit.

Makes me smile every time. Horses—1, humans—0.

I'm reveling in that score when a door slams behind me.

I jump and turn around, hoping it's Hank, coming to wrap me in the best bear hug in the world. I peer through the fountain, centered in the driveway, expecting Hank's familiar frame, but it's not him. I'm met with an absolute vision far better in person than any of the pictures I found online.

Tall? Check.

Dark? Check.

Handsome? Check.

Looks like he wants to kill me? Also check.

I run my teeth over my bottom lip as his tall lithe body, wearing the hell out of a dark fitted suit, stalks toward me. Dark chocolate hair, longer on the top and a little disheveled, like he's been running his fingers through it, frames his annoyed face. Stubble blooms below razor-sharp cheekbones as he stops in front of me and peers down a straight nose almost too masculine for the shapely frowning lips beneath it.

Good thing I'm not one to cower, because at what has to be at least six foot three, this man is imposing.

Fiery mahogany eyes bore down on me. "You need to turn your sweet ass around, get in your car, and leave. Now."

*Wow, what a greeting.*

I tilt my head and search his face for some trace of humor. Finding none, I bark out a laugh. Because who talks to a person they've just met this way?

Okay, it was really more of a loud snort, but snort laughs make normal people laugh. Right? I even giggle a little at myself and think, *Hey, maybe he'll join in!* But no, not this fire-breathing dragon. He crosses his arms over his broad chest and continues to glare at me like I'm dirt beneath his expensive shoes. *Typical.*

"Pretty and slow to follow directions. Seems on par with every girl she's been serving up to me on a platter lately. This whole natural look is a fresh angle," he says, waving one arm up and down me like I'm a broodmare, "so I'll give her that. Do pass my kudos on in that regard when you report back to my mother about your failed attempt to lock me down into some breathtakingly boring arranged relationship. I'd rather date a blow-up doll."

I rear back slightly at that last bit. Date a blow-up doll? Oof. Did he really just say that? The man practically handed me an alley-oop. I could make so many jokes here, but I remind myself to keep it professional. Steeling myself, I take a deep breath, because this is about to get awkward. He clearly does not know who I am, but I've done a bit of homework and know exactly who he is.

Vaughn Harding.

I've missed Hank like crazy. When I showed up on his doorstep looking for a job ten years ago, he took me in and gave me a lot more than employment. Work, advice, a place to live, even a good talking to when I needed it. He was the father figure I always dreamed of. So when I heard I could be working beside him on the West Coast of Canada, I couldn't get on a plane fast enough. I mean, my working visa was up so I had to leave my training position in Ireland anyway. At least I knew where I was going and the name of the farm so I could do some research.

My internet stalking skills are so next-level I almost added them as a bullet point to the skills section of my résumé. In putting those skills to good use, I found two types of photos of this man populating the internet. Half of the images were Professional Vaughn, looking suave and serious in relation to his family's business ventures. The others were of Party Vaughn, looking charming and polished, usually at some glitzy event with a beautiful woman beaming on his arm.

Never the same woman from what I could find. And trust me, I *looked.*

An animalistic growl pulls me from my thoughts. "I said leave."

Is this fucking guy for real? As a general rule, my brain-to-mouth filter is a little relaxed. I've been an agitator since childhood and am well-versed in navigating situations where someone is ticked off. But this? This is new. Which is probably why I'm standing here silent and dumbfounded, staring like an idiot.

Before I can say something polite to defuse the situation, he holds his arms out and widens those molten eyes at me as if to say, "Hello? What the fuck are you doing?"

And then… He. Stomps. His. Foot.

Like a toddler.

A soft giggle bubbles up out of my chest. I don't even try to hold it in. I am well acquainted with men like Vaughn Harding. Few truly dependable things in the world exist, but trust fund babies being douchebags is one you can count on.

Holding one hand up to stop him, I launch in. "Okay, first of all, I am downright fascinated by your blow-up doll preference. Can we table that for now but revisit it someday?"

A sneer touches his lips. Ha. Didn't like that one.

"Second, I'm a grown-ass woman. Don't call me a girl. And third, when you're finished having this epic man-child meltdown"—I wave my hand up and down his body like he did to me—"can you please let Hank know that Billie Black is here for her job interview?"

And then I beam at him with a big old cheesy smile.

In his defense, he visibly pales while smoothing his suit jacket down and standing straighter.

He repeats back to me, "Billie Black?"

"That's me."

"I..." He shakes his head. "But you're not a man?"

"An astute observation, Mr. Harding," I reply with a smirk.

This is familiar territory for me. My name frequently confuses people; it doesn't bother me. It's a nickname, and I could go by something else if I wanted, but I kind of enjoy people's confusion over my name. And this encounter is no exception.

"Hey, Billie girl!" a familiar deep voice calls from over my shoulder. "You made it!"

Hank Brandt. Man, just hearing that voice makes me smile. I turn immediately, leaving Vaughn there gaping, to take in the face of the warmest, gentlest man I know. Broad shoulders, close-cut sandy hair, and a ruddy, deeply lined face, a face that's spent decades working out in the sun, rush toward me.

I've missed him. Sometimes you're born into a family, and other times you choose them. And when you choose them, you know in your bones that they're right for you. And that's Hank for me. The family I've chosen.

Almost jogging, Hank goes right in for a big old bear hug. And I soak it up. "You're even more beautiful than the last time I saw you," he says, holding me back by my shoulders and taking me in.

I go pink in the cheeks and roll my eyes at him. "Stop sucking up, old man. You already got me here. Now, show me around."

Hank has been a pillar of support in both my childhood and in my professional career: a friend, a father figure, and hopefully now an employer.

Assuming I haven't completely blown it with moneybags back there. Anxiety flutters in my stomach. I have my work cut out for me and will have to rise above that awkward introduction if I really want this job.

"Never lose that spunk, kiddo," Hank says, shaking his head and slinging an arm over my shoulder.

Hank leads me back toward Mr. Handsome and Crazy, who appears to have regained some composure.

"Billie, meet Vaughn Harding, the new owner and operator here at Gold Rush Ranch. He's a busy man, between this farm and the family mining business, but he'll be around for the foreseeable future managing our business operations."

Vaughn stares down at me now with an unreadable expression.

"He's going to sit in on the interview today to provide a second opinion. Hope that's okay with you."

I feel my throat bob as I swallow. *That's great. Just great.*

Stepping out from under Hank's arm, I extend my hand forward into Vaughn's strong grasp. I search for any signs of embarrassment on his part and find none. His face is stony and locked down now. All traces of the fiery passion he spit mere moments ago have completely disappeared.

Naturally, I test the waters by tossing him a quick wink while reciprocating his firm handshake. And by *handshake*, I mean *death grip*. I squeeze the hell out of his hand right back. Years of handling and riding powerful horses means I'm stronger than I look. I think I might even hear him grunt under his breath when I clamp down around his fingers. "The more the merrier," I say. "It's a pleasure to meet you, Mr. Harding."

He nods as he drops my hand abruptly and then switches his focus to a spot over my head. "I'll be in my office when you're ready," he says to Hank before spinning on his heel and walking away, head held high, like he didn't just embarrass himself.

When I glance back at Hank, I see a twinkle in his eye as a slow Cheshire cat grin spreads across his face. Tutting and shaking his head, he says, "Billie, Billie, Billie. What did you do to that poor boy?"

At that, I throw my head back and laugh. Poor boy? I'm well acquainted with men like Vaughn Harding. I grew up immersed in that culture. Rich and spoiled men like him never outgrow their arrogant entitlement. Instead, they wear it like some sort of badge of honor.

My dad is exhibit A in that kind of behavior, followed by all the boys at boarding school and the men who mingled in our circles. Carbon copies of each other, the lot. Polished, calculated, and unfeeling.

Not to mention boring.

And fake, fake, fake.

Fake smiles, fake friendships, fake family. And that last one is the real kicker. I felt my pretty, perfectly curated life crash down around me the day that scandal broke.

Surprisingly, being a shitty, misguided person isn't enough to make a little girl stop loving her dad. But it is enough to make me lose respect for him. And that is a heart-wrenching combination…loving someone you can't respect.

Even a decade later, years into adulthood, it hurts in a way that has the power to take my breath away.

My father's word might not mean anything anymore, but mine is still good. I kept the promise I made to myself—leave and never darken the door of that lifestyle again.

I went out in a real blaze of glory, and I've been in rebuilding mode ever since. My sole focus has been my career, and this opportunity is the perfect next step.

As I watch Vaughn, the embodiment of everything I ran away from, enter the building, I admire the physique within his tailored suit pants. Trim waist. Incredible ass. Ten out of ten, would grab.

But I won't. Because I know this type of man. An absolute nightmare to interact with, dangerous to get involved with. But still fun to ogle. I am only human after all, and the man is hot as sin.

Yes, I will enjoy the hell out of this view, but from a safe distance. Because men like Vaughn are a trap I will never fall into.

# CHAPTER 3

## Vaughn

What a fucking disaster.

I flop down in my desk chair and stare at the ceiling, wishing the floor might swallow me whole.

I can't help but shake my head at myself.

Marching out there like I had no self-control? Flying off the handle like a petulant child? What was I thinking? My mother's increased meddling in my love life is turning me into a goddamn wrecking ball.

She keeps dropping women on me like it's my birthday and they are perfectly wrapped presents for me to unwrap. I know being married to my dad made her happier than anything else, and she just wants that for me. I also know my brother, Cole, is a lost cause in that department, which means I get to play all her silly dating games alone.

Lucky me.

Even if it *had* been a woman my mother sent over with

her insane scheming, my behavior would have been out of line. The way I acted was so much worse because of Hank's excitement about the possibility of hiring this girl…woman.

One side of my lips quirks up at the way she bit back about being called a girl.

*Whatever*. She looked young and definitely nothing like the man I expected to interview.

Billie, not Billy.

Who would have guessed?

I suppose if I'd actually looked at her résumé, I might have noted that minute difference. Not that Hank really threw me any bones in that regard. He could have warned me. Instead, he was all, "I know this trainer who I think we should interview. Good international experience but not stuck in a rut. Might be a nice fresh option. Managed to take a stable in Ireland from relative obscurity to a mainstay in the winner's circle over there."

He seemed so excited, and his description sounded good to me. Most of all, I trust him, so I just gave him the go-ahead to set up an interview without asking much more.

Thinking back, I almost feel like he intentionally left out mentioning if we were discussing a he or she. Not that it matters. I have no problem hiring a woman. She's just young. Which means inexperienced. Too inexperienced for this high-stakes game.

And too mouthy.

That mouth. Sultry, soft, heart-shaped.

Yeah. *That* is not what I need.

I need someone dependable and organized who I can

count on to take the success of Gold Rush Ranch seriously. This isn't a game.

The way she let me carry on like an idiot when she probably knew exactly who I was…

And then she had the gall to laugh at me.

*Unbelievable.*

I can feel myself getting worked up just walking back through the moment in my head.

I've elicited a lot of responses from women over the years: desire, lust, moans and whimpers, and even anger when our time together inevitably ended. No one ever looked me in the eye and laughed at me.

No, this is new.

Her glowing amber eyes widened so expressively when I told her to leave. Her full pink lips lifted at one side as a few stray pieces of dark chestnut hair blew gently across her cheeks in the breeze.

She looked wild and untamed at that moment. She looked like a challenge.

Under different circumstances, I'd have liked to grab that challenge firmly by her heavy braid and show her who is really in charge here. I'd tilt her head back and drag my teeth along the bottom of her jaw while whispering all the filthy ways I planned to wipe that condescending smirk off her face.

I huff out something that resembles a muffled laugh and adjust myself in my briefs.

Something tells me the only thing that scenario would get me is a swift kick in the balls. She has chutzpah; I'll give her that.

And she's a wild card, which is the very last thing I need in my life right now.

Racing season is about to be in full swing, and they have forced us to pull all the horses from the track. To retreat here to the farm in disgrace, suspended from all sanctioned events for three months. We won't be racing any of our string until halfway through the season at least.

I don't need a wild card; I needed a fucking miracle.

Light, feminine laughter filters through the hall outside my office door, pulling my attention from the full inbox in front of me. I've spent the last hour here staring at the screen, achieving nothing, and living in my head.

A place that no one wants to be right now.

"Ladies first," Hank announces as Billie rounds the corner.

I roll my eyes. Talk about laying it on thick.

I turn around to grab the files we'll need for the interview, assuming they finished with the grand tour.

"How'd it go?" I ask as I rifle through the drawer of folders.

"So good," Billie responds enthusiastically. "Your facility is truly world-class, Mr. Harding."

My cock twitches against my will at the way she says *Mr. Harding* with such admiration.

*Vaughn, you're a fucking mess, bud.* I manage not to chastise myself out loud this time—a minor victory for the day. But when I look at her now, she almost takes my breath away. She is positively glowing and so full of excitement she's almost vibrating in her seat.

I stare at her, struck by how genuine she is. So open and honest with her feelings. What must that be like?

I scour my brain but can't remember the last time I felt as happy as Billie looks in this moment. I feel like I'm looking at the sun, blinding but so deliciously warm that I just close your eyes and bask in the glow anyway.

"Yes, well, thanks. My grandparents transformed this place from a cattle ranch into everything you see here. Lots of family history," I say, dropping my gaze quickly.

"I want to extend my condolences about your grandfather. What a terrible loss," she says, hitting me with her best doe-eyed expression.

"Thanks. Let's carry on," I reply, brusquer than intended.

I'm prepared for battle with this woman, not decorum and innocent looks. She's giving me whiplash. Thankfully, Hank chooses this moment to jump in and save me.

"Okay, Billie. Let's get started."

Leaning back in my seat, I steeple my fingers and watch them interact. Hank asks pointed questions, and Billie responds eloquently even though she flaps her hands around like she's trying to take flight.

Of course, she's a hand talker.

They discuss training techniques, racing strategies, bloodlines, and god knows what else. To be frank, it's mostly Greek to me. As a child, I hung around the stables talking to people, lending a hand with farm chores, and doing schoolwork in the lounge, but it was more of social setting than anything—a way for my grandfather to keep me close, especially after losing my dad.

That's why Hank is here. I need his expertise. He's one of the best in the business with stable management, and I can tell by the proud look on his face he has practically already hired this woman.

I'll have to play this right. Anything short of diplomatic will be like taking away a kid's toys on Christmas morning. I'm not stupid. It's clear to me I can't afford to piss Hank off by raining on his Billie parade. I obviously missed the memo about how close they are. Come to think of it, I've missed a few memos from Hank where she's concerned, but that's a conversation for another time.

Either way, I'm not about to let this situation slip through my grasp. If Hank thinks he can pull a fast one on me and this woman thinks she can laugh in my face and still waltz into a cushy new job, they're both mistaken.

It's still my farm. I make the final decision.

"Why do you want this job?" I bark.

She gazes at me with intensity, a tinge of pink on her pale cheeks. I can see her thinking. I wait for her to scold me for interrupting her so that I can send her packing for a good reason.

Instead, she leans forward, rubs her hands down her slender thighs, and chews on her bottom lip. Fuck, I wish she wouldn't do that.

"To be frank, Mr. Harding…"

And now that again. How am I supposed to lead an intimidating line of questioning with her calling me Mr.

Harding while innocently biting her damn lip? "Call me Vaughn."

"Okay, Vaughn. To be frank, I've earned a head trainer position."

I scoff. Talk about entitled.

"No. Listen, I don't mean I deserve one. I mean, I've *earned* it. I started on my own, with absolutely nothing, and I've taken every opportunity that has presented itself to me with a smile." She sighs and starts flapping her hands around again as she carries on. "I worked my butt off at low-end farms with low-end horses until I was good enough to work at mediocre farms with mediocre horses, and I kept my nose to the grindstone until I landed an internship as a working student at a world-class farm I had planned to apply for since I was fifteen years old. I made it happen. I worked with the best of the best in the United Kingdom. I learned the ropes and then got good enough they wanted to keep me around for actual paid positions. I've poured my blood, sweat, and tears into becoming one of the best so that I could apply that knowledge here, on home turf." Her hands land across her chest, and she looks at me so earnestly that I almost can't hold her gaze. "Give me a shot. I can turn this around for you. I know I can."

I have to hand it to her. That was an excellent answer. Not even a little contrived the way the story spilled from her lips, brimming with pride and grit.

I tap my pointer fingers together, assessing her from my position. She doesn't shy away from holding my eye contact in the moments that follow. My plan to trip her up has backfired because she blindsided me with so much confidence in her hard work, in her own ability, when initially she seemed like this was all some big joke to her.

Confidence and dedication are two things I probably respect the most in another person. I've worked my ass off too. I won't be the one who has to work with her every day, so if she's good at her job, what does it matter if she's also irritating?

"You're young," I say.

"I have energy," she counters.

"You're inexperienced."

"And I'm hungry to prove myself." She grins.

Is she intentionally filling her answers with innuendo? This woman is certifiable. Leaning forward, I toss the file folders I put together across the desk at her. *Last hoop, honey.*

"Okay, Billie, I've got five folders here, one for each horse that will make their debut at Bell Point Park, the track here in Vancouver, next season. Why don't you look through them and pick a favorite?"

She eyes me with suspicion. "I mean, I'd have to see them run to make that kind of call. Despite what some people think, stats and bloodlines aren't everything. A horse needs a lot of heart to win. The right mindset."

*Smart girl.*

"For the sake of this exercise, just pick based on what you can see on paper."

She meets the challenge in my eyes with her own. I know she has an inkling I'm leading her to slaughter here. I see it written on her face. She's suspicious, but she's going to follow me anyway because if I can guess one thing about Billie Black today, it's that she's stubborn as fuck.

Hank starts in on me, not completely oblivious to what I'm doing here either, "Vaughn, I think that..."

Billie holds a graceful hand up in his direction while pulling the folders toward herself. "Hank, please. I can manage."

She leans over my desk and opens the first folder.

Each one contains a horse's Canadian Racing Club registration that breaks down several generations of their bloodline and notes physical information, like height and sex. I've also included information on each horse's dam and sire, which is often important in predicting a prospect's aptitude for success. Genetics and all that.

The part I've left out is each horse's report card in Hank's initial assessment. I had him take a small team through the barn and create a profile on each horse for me. If I'm being honest, the information I've provided her with is pretty bare bones. I know I'm making an unfair request.

But that's all part of my plan.

I examine her. Brow furrowed in concentration, eyes flitting back and forth, absorbing each line in each folder. Dark lashes frame golden irises with darker flecks throughout, like one of those tiger's-eye stones. The color gives her an almost feline look. I can spot mascara and maybe a little blush; otherwise all she's sporting is a smattering of freckles across her nose that you only get from time spent in the sun.

Studying her now, I'm not sure how I could ever have confused her for one of the women my mother handpicks. No chance they would go out with visible freckles on their nose.

Billie Black isn't a done-up kind of hot. She's just...naturally alluring. I'm sure men stop and stare at her but can't quite put their finger on why. At the risk of sounding like some sort of new-age chump, there's just an energy about her. Something gravitational.

She's now humming to herself and organizing the folders into three different piles. I realize that I've moved forward in my chair, trying to see what she's doing. With my elbows propped on the desk, I'm leaning toward her like a total creep.

She calls me out on it without even sparing me a glance.

"Trying to steal the answers off my test, Vaughn?"

I clear my throat and sit up straight. When I chance a look over at Hank, he just lifts an eyebrow at me as if to say, "What are you doing, you absolute loser?"

My nostrils flare on a heavy breath, but Billie remains focused. She's lost in thought, tapping a pointer finger over her lips.

But I'm done waiting.

"Okay. Time's up," I bark.

Billie gives me the same lifted eyebrow look that Hank just did, and I already know that having these two working together is going to be a pain in my ass.

"Okay," she begins, "I've got these organized into three categories. This first stack, these three are all great high-quality horses ready to get started this year. They'll succeed, and we can probably get a few good races under their belt and then sell one or two as prospects for good money without pouring a bunch into them."

Yup. I like the sound of that.

"Second category is this mare, Brite Lite. I like her physical characteristics; she's young and has a nice early birthday, which will lend her a little extra maturity come race time. She's also beautifully bred, has a few famously consistent producers in her background, and could easily be a nice foundation mare for your breeding program in the future."

Hank nods his head and pipes in with, "I agree."

Her eyes flit from his back to me. "She *might* be my favorite."

I stare at her blankly, not wanting to give anything away.

Without breaking eye contact, Billie taps two fingers on the final folder. She hits me with a steely look and asks, "What's wrong with Double Diablo?"

I give her a deadpan look. "I don't know what you mean."

Hank groans audibly. *Fucking traitor*.

"I mean that he's three years old with zero starts under his belt. His pedigree is drool-worthy. Looking at his papers is like reading a list of the world's most famous racehorses. I know what breeding a horse like that costs. You must have at least a quarter million dollars invested in him already." Billie grunts and shakes her head, like she can't quite believe it. "Even with only a moderately successful racing career, he'd be your golden ticket to collecting big money on stud fees one day. He should have been running this year already, but he's done nothing." She flops back and pins me with her intelligent eyes. "So...what's wrong with him?"

*Smart woman.*

She looks at me like she expects an answer. But this is

my test, and I refuse to give anything away. "That wasn't my question. I said, on paper, which one is your favorite? From what you've just told me, the answer is obvious."

She peeks back down at that final folder, nervously tucking loose strands of hair behind her ears.

"Is he injured?" she asks softly while flipping through the pages in front of her again as if she looks hard enough, more information might magically appear on the pages.

"No," I reply honestly.

I'm thoroughly enjoying watching her squirm. She looks so uncertain, and I know I'm taking far too much pleasure in knocking her down a peg.

She blows a dramatic breath out like I'm exhausting her and meets my gaze with a determined set to her face. "Okay, he's my favorite," she declares, tossing the folder back at me, like I had done to her, and then crosses her arms like a suit of armor.

*Game. Set. Match.*

I can't stop the sly smile that slowly spreads across my face.

"Excellent choice, Ms. Black."

Hank is now shaking his head at me. I know I'm going to hear from him about this later, but I don't care.

My farm, my rules.

"I'm assuming I have Hank's blessing when I say I'd like to offer you the position of head trainer here at Gold Rush Ranch. You can start as soon as you like. Take a few days to get settled. I'm including accommodations in the offer. There is a cottage down the road with your name on it. Our three-month suspension from competition ends on July first, and that gives you…" I trail off, assessing the calendar on my desk. "About three months."

Head tilted, she asks, "Three months for what?"

"To get Double Diablo in shape to win his first race of the season. He wins, we extend your contract to a permanent position. He loses, and you receive a glowing reference and an extra paragraph to beef up your résumé."

Billie blinks at me.

"Maybe we should talk about this first, Vaughn." Leave it to Hank to rush in and try to save her.

I understand this isn't the joint choice we agreed to, but this is the best way for me to appease him while also ensuring I won't have to deal with Billie Black's unpredictable attitude and boner-inducing face for long. It also gives me three months leeway to vet my own candidates and find the perfect fit for when our ban ends.

She'll do fine until then.

"No, Hank, it's a fair enough offer. I'm still untested in a lot of ways, and this will be the perfect opportunity for me to prove what I can do," she says with a determined set to her jaw.

Hank sighs audibly, and I grin triumphantly. A genuine grin.

*God, I love winning.*

"Well, it's settled then. Welcome to the team, Billie. Swing by tomorrow morning, and I'll go over the contract with you." I stand, rolling my shoulders back. The high of tying up a good business deal never fails to make me feel like a million bucks.

Billie looks me in the eye and takes my hand, just as firmly as last time. "Thank you for the opportunity, Mr. Harding."

"Billie girl, you have no idea what you've bitten off here," Hank warns.

She turns to shake his hand next. "Hank, I'm not an idiot. I can piece enough together here to assume that the horse is going to be a challenge."

Ha. A challenge is an understatement.

As they filter out of my office, I watch Billie go, sassy little thing that she is. I have to admit, the view from behind is equally as alluring as the front. The thrill of victory has me all worked up, and I can't help but let my mind wander to how good that perfect round ass would look with a pink handprint on it.

My handprint.

I imagine bending her over my desk, in complete control, yanking her pants down around her thighs, bunching up the back of her shirt, holding it in one fist, and giving her a few good smacks all while she moans and writhes beneath me.

She'd enjoy it; I'd make sure of that. My cock swells in my pants. *Good god.* What is wrong with me? I need to get my head in the game.

I turn back to my computer screen, resolving to do some actual work when out of the corner of my eye, I see that caramel mane pop back through my door with a mischievous glint in her eye.

"Sorry to interrupt, Boss Man," Billie says. "Forgot my purse!"

Boss Man? I roll my eyes and shake my head.

*So annoying.* My cock doesn't seem to care though.

She grabs the offending handbag and turns to leave but pauses at the door and looks over her shoulder, hitting me with a cocky smirk. "I also wanted to mention an amendment I'd like to make to my contract."

I scrub both hands over my face. This woman is going to be a lot of work.

"Go on."

"How do you feel about an extra ten percent on my base salary for my, what did you call it…sweet ass?"

Fuck my life. This is going to be a long three months.

# CHAPTER 4

## Billie

THIS IS GOING TO BE FUN.

I strut out of Vaughn's office, squeezing my lips together, trying to contain my laughter. The guy is too easy to rile. And no, I probably shouldn't be antagonizing my new boss. But I couldn't help myself. Stuffy rich dudes like him practically beg for it.

What dawned on me in that office is that our relationship here is rather symbiotic. He needs me as much as I need him. He needs a trainer who is new to the scene, and I need a job as head trainer where I can prove myself to be as good as I know I am.

*Think* I am.

I suppose I could fail. But believing that will get me nowhere. Best foot forward. Clear eyes, full hearts, whatever the fuck, can't lose—right? At any rate, I'm stoked. The facility is outstanding. Hank is possibly my favorite human. My boss is uptight eye candy. And my horse, from what I gather, is probably totally crazy.

Life is good.

I squint into the bright spring sun. It's low in the sky this time of year, so I hold my hand up over my brow and peer out into grounds looking for Hank. I haven't lived in Vancouver's Lower Mainland before, but what I know of it is that I should expect a lot of rain. But on days like this… man, Ruby Creek is breathtaking. Fresh air mingles with the aroma of pine and the mineral scent of the river rushing nearby, and lush green valleys butt up against the start of British Columbia's North Cascades mountain range. I feel like I'm standing in a picture book.

Someone nudges my shoulder, and I turn to see Hank standing with me, squinting out into the sun too.

"Beautiful spot, eh?"

I tilt my head slightly and raise one shoulder in agreement. The property itself is immaculate, tree-lined, and manicured. It almost looks like a golf course. All of which doesn't really matter if their actual racing program is in shambles. So yeah, it's beautiful, but troubled.

"Well," I say, gazing ahead, "why don't you introduce me to the new man in my life?"

He turns toward me slowly with a grave look on his face. "He's going to be a lot of work, Billie."

"Of course he is, Hank. Men always are."

At that, he snorts and shakes his head.

We walk through the lines of paddocks where Hank points out many of the horses to me. Some retired, some breeding stock, some just babies still. Most of the racing horses stay in their box stalls but exercise daily, sometimes even twice daily.

"When they handed down the suspension, it forced Vaughn to pull all the horses they had stabled at the track, so it's busier around here than usual."

I nod. There are a lot of horses on-site right now. "I read the gist of it all in the news. Is there anything else I should know?"

Hank sighs raggedly. "Dermot Harding was one of my best friends when I was younger. This was his wife Ada's family ranch. Never seen two people quite so in love as those two. Dermot was a good man who got embroiled in something he shouldn't have." He trails off. "Vaughn is struggling. His father was a jockey, you know. A good one."

I shake my head as we continue our stroll. "No, I didn't."

"He died on the track. His horse went down in the middle of the pack. Vaughn was only ten years old."

All the air leaves my lungs on a single exhale. This sport is not without its risks, that's for sure.

"Dermot practically raised him," Hank continues. "He was recently widowed at that point. I would have thought the loss of his son would be more than he could bear. But when everyone abandoned Vaughn, Dermot threw himself into giving that boy the best life he could. This is more than just a ranch for Vaughn. It's a legacy."

I blink rapidly, not wanting to feel bad for the man who just accosted me. "Gotcha," I say, grateful when Hank adds nothing more.

We make it to the far end of the paddocks where there is one larger pen tucked into the rolling green fields behind it. My new project is there, head down, grazing on perfect emerald grass. He looked impeccable on paper, but in person, he looks a little unkempt. Especially compared to the perfectly tended horses around him.

He's solid black. Classic looking. Not a single speck of white on his face or legs. He looks healthy, if lacking a little fitness. He also looks like he's been rolling in the dirt. Dust covers what could be a shiny coat.

As we approach, I click my tongue at him, a noise we often use with horses to get their attention or signal that it's time to get going. He startles, head flicking up at me instantly, and I'm met with the most angelic little face. Dishy forehead, big innocent eyes, long lashes, and ears so pointy that the tips turn in toward each other.

All those features framed by a thick, unruly forelock, with a heavy tail at the other end to match, almost make him look like an oversize pony rather than a lean, mean racing machine.

I sigh. He is *adorable*.

I'm not sure he feels the same about me though, because those charming little ears whip back flat on his head, his soft little nose wrinkles up like there's a foul smell, and that big, luscious tail whips back and forth angrily. Then he drops his head and charges at the fence like a little warhorse.

Hank takes a step back from the fence, even though we aren't standing close enough to be in the line of fire. The horse isn't stupid; he's not going to bust through the fence.

He's trying to scare me off or intimidate me. Sadly for him, it will not work.

I stand my ground.

Sure enough, he slams on the brakes as soon as he comes close to the fence and lunges his neck over, showing me the whites of his eyes and a nice set of pearly teeth as he bites at the air in front of me.

Charming. The men of Gold Rush Ranch are a lot of bluster.

I don't shy away, but I also don't want to threaten him by making eye contact, so I pull my phone out of my purse and start scrolling through my social media accounts, not giving him an inch.

Double Diablo stands there, staring at me, snorting so heavily I can feel the damp heat of his exhalations across my down-turned forehead. He eventually stomps his foot, which makes me chuckle. Seems to be an ongoing theme.

The young stallion eyes me warily as I say, "You remind me of someone else I met today."

He snorts again and then turns his butt to me. Yup, a total drama queen.

"And that," Hank says, pointing at the little black horse, "is why no one wants to deal with him. He's built and bred to be one of the best, but no one's put the time in to earn his trust so far. I haven't been here long enough to assess him, but the word among the staff is that he's just plain mean. They don't even bring him into the barn at night."

I snort and roll my eyes. "How much work has he had?"

"Not much. From what I gather, they started trying to

get his training going early for his two-year-old year. People have tried intermittently since then. Apparently, he spends all his energy going straight up rather than straight forward, and he's proven to be dangerous in the starting gates. Throwing himself against the sides to the point no one wants to risk sitting on him in there."

I hum and tap my pointer finger against my lips. "So the poor boy is scared, and no one has taken the time to listen to him."

"Bingo." Hank points at me with a finger gun. "But don't underestimate him. He's a smart horse who's had a couple years of learning that he can get his way."

I scoff at that.

"I'm serious, Billie. You have to be careful. You need to create success for yourself, not end up in the hospital."

"Hank, the horse isn't some sort of evil mastermind." I sigh. "He's terrified. I clicked my tongue, and he jumped out of his skin. I'd be willing to bet my first paycheck that he hasn't had many positive interactions with humans. He needs a fresh approach. We both know traditional training techniques don't always work. You can ruin a sensitive horse and eventually injure an otherwise great one." Just thinking about the unfairness of it all agitates me. I cross my arms and shake my head, looking back at the beautiful animal before me. "He needs patience, confidence, and a new name. I mean, really. Double Diablo? It's like some shitty self-fulfilling prophecy."

I meet the incredulous stare of someone who clearly thinks I'm nuts. Hank barks out a laugh.

"You think his *name* is the problem?"

I smile sheepishly. "I mean, it doesn't help his case."

Eyes twinkling with mirth, Hank shakes his head. "I don't know about that. But the one thing I am sure of is that if anyone can bring this guy around, it's you. This horse needs some love. He just hasn't met anyone brave enough to give it to him yet."

Pride swells in my chest at his affirmation. Hank has never failed to make me feel like the world was mine for the taking. Sometimes all you need is one person's unwavering faith. Support that is absolute.

Looking back at Double Diablo, who is still sulking like a big baby, I decide that I'm going to be that person for him.

I pull a smooth white peppermint out of my purse and toss it over the fence to land beside him. Even at that one little movement, I see him flinch and flick one ear to the side where the mint lands. Other than that, he doesn't budge. *Tough customer.*

I turn to Hank, who is regarding me with those signature sparkly eyes. "Okay, what next?"

"Do you have all your stuff with you?"

*What little I own, you mean?*

"Yup. Figured I'd get a hotel out in the valley where all the farms are anyway. I'll have to deal with the rental car at some point though."

Hank nods decisively. "Let's get you settled in at your cottage. Then if you want to get anything, I can take you into the closest city to get what you need. Tomorrow, I'll introduce you around and see what we can do about the car."

I earn a head shake when I loop my arm through his to lead him away and respond with, "Sounds good, old man. Let's go check out my new digs."

We start back up the pathway toward the stables in a companionable silence. On one hand, I have so much I want to talk to him about, so much to tell him. On the other, I'm jet-lagged as fuck and just happy to be here with him.

A little way up, I sneak a look over my shoulder at the little devil horse, just in time to see him sniffle the mint on the ground. He stares at it for a moment, inhaling the minty scent, and then snaps it up quickly like he's stealing something and doesn't want anyone to catch him.

Then he turns his neck while chewing and looks back at me with ears pricked forward before storming off again.

The inside of my SUV is dead silent and awkward as fuck as Vaughn directs me down the back roads to a long gravel driveway that weaves through the trees. Why he insisted on showing me the place when he clearly can't stand me is beyond my comprehension.

"Left." He barks out directions like I'm his limo driver or something.

I take the left, biting my tongue, and come around a slight bend to see a charming pine A-frame house with a red tin roof.

If I'm being honest, it's more house than I need. It's definitely not what I was expecting when I heard "cottage," but I suppose this facility isn't really what you think of when you hear "ranch" either. People above a certain tax bracket enjoy doing this thing where they pretend they're just one of the commoners. Growing up, my mom loved to talk about our cabin like it was some sort of rural nature experience. Spoiler alert: it's a mansion on a lake.

Vaughn steps out once I've parked, every movement graceful and athletic. He strides up to the front door, taking every other step up the short staircase, and unlocks it before heading back to the rental vehicle. I move to the back hatch of the SUV to grab my bags only to feel his hand clamp down on my forearm.

The warmth of his palm, the firmness of his grasp—it has me thinking about things I shouldn't be.

"I've got these. You go ahead."

*Cute.* Now *he's going to be a gentleman?*

I just scoff and grab one anyway, walking past him with a smile so big and cheesy it makes my cheeks ache. I'm more than capable of carrying a bag. Haven't needed a man so far, not about to start falling over myself for this one, mind-numbingly sexy as he might be.

The inside of the house is beautiful and cozy. Open concept with exposed wood and vaulted ceilings, a kitchen island overlooking the dining table and living room. To the right is a staircase that I take up into a large loft bedroom and drop my bag.

From up here, the view is truly outstanding. Lush and green and so peaceful. This side of the house is almost all windows. It's built to face out over the farm's rolling fields. I'm fairly certain that if I headed straight out the back door and over the hill, I'd end up at the horses' paddocks.

I pinch myself. And I don't mean that as a manner of speaking. I literally pinch myself, thumb and finger gathering the skin on the side of my forearm. I've been rooming with other grooms and trainers in a male-dominated sport for years now, and the thought of having my own space feels downright luxurious. No stepping over questionable single socks or doing other people's dirty dishes. *Heaven.*

I let out a big breath and blow a loose piece of hair off my face. I want this so badly. This is what I've been craving my entire life. Roots. Family. A quiet setting. A secure job. A place to call my own.

"Billie. I'm ready to go," Vaughn hollers from downstairs.

My eyes roll so far back in my head they're at risk of staying there. "You can just walk yourself back to the farm, right?" I shout as I turn to head down.

He meets me by the door, chest all puffed out in some sort of *National Geographic*–worthy show of dominance that makes me giggle. Vaughn doesn't look quite so amused though. Instead, he looks pained. Like he's short on air, like he's holding one breath in and can't bring himself to let it out. He looks *uncomfortable.*

I quirk my head. "You all right?"

"Yup," he says brusquely, popping the *p* sound loudly. "Need to get back to work."

A ghost of the past flickers across his face as he spins on his heel and leaves. Good lord, this man is a puzzle I don't have the time or patience to figure out.

After a couple hours spent buying some basics, I pull back up to my new home. I drop my head back against the headrest and close my eyes for a moment. My eyelids are heavy. I momentarily wonder if driving in this condition was really my best move. Exhausted doesn't even cover it. But I know I have to keep pushing if I'm going to make jet lag my bitch.

I count to sixty and then force myself out of the car.

First, laundry. I'm looking forward to crawling into a fresh, cool bed at the end of this long-ass day. Nothing better than fresh sheets, that clean laundry smell wrapping itself around you like a comforting cocoon. One of the greatest feelings in the world, if you ask me.

Next most important point of business: coffee. I start a pot, hoping it will give me the boost I need to get settled in. Then I throw on some old torn jeans and a tank top, twist my hair up in a messy knot, and get to work cleaning and unpacking.

Upon closer inspection, I'm finding that the place isn't just dusty—it is plain gross.

I really have to put some elbow grease into scrubbing the stove top and cleaning out the unidentifiable sticky pools in the fridge. After finding mysterious yellow splatters around the porcelain toilet bowl, I close my eyes and spray bleach everywhere. Living in my filth is one thing; living in someone else's is downright scary.

I rifle through a couple closets and cupboards until I find a vacuum and all the mopping supplies I need. I mop myself right out the front door and stand on the front mat, looking around, feeling accomplished about what I've gotten done around the place.

With all the windows open, a breeze wafts through the house and slowly but surely pushes the stale odor out. Instead, it now smells overwhelmingly like cleaning products. Either way, it's a far cry better than bunking with other people, never mind the palatial dungeon I grew up in.

Amusement dances on my face as I imagine what my mother would say about this place, let alone her reaction to me scrubbing a stranger's dried piss off the toilet. Satisfying.

I take another step outside, looking over my shoulder at the still-wet floors that separate me from the coffeepot. I planned this poorly. Oh well. Onward and upward.

I turn away reluctantly and do a quick perusal of the property. Trees line the driveway heading up to the cottage. On the other side, the property opens up and faces toward the grassy rolling hills. A large wraparound deck juts out off the back door, overlooking what appears to be a hay field, and situated just to the left is a single empty paddock.

I'm trying to be as upbeat as possible, but I admittedly get grumpy when I'm hungry and low on sleep. Super grumpy. Hangry. Slangry? Where sleepiness, anger, and hunger collide into one terrible mood. And the more I stew, the more slangry I become.

Letting myself wander down a path to extreme agitation, I find a broom in a small shed and angrily sweep at the debris-covered deck.

Would it have killed Vaughn to have one of his million staff members come out here for a couple hours and make it even a little presentable? The lawn is mowed, so it's not like no one has been out this way. He knew he'd be hiring *someone*, so my arrival wasn't a total surprise. I don't need the red-carpet treatment, but a quick wipe-down and a roll of paper towels wouldn't have been overkill.

I try to imagine his reaction to arriving at a place this grungy. He strikes me as the type who probably expects a swan towel on the bed and a chocolate on his pillow. I envision those dark almond-shaped eyes narrowing to slits, those pronounced brows dropping low on his face, and the nostrils on that strong nose flaring in indignation.

I also imagine there would be foot stomping.

Which, to be fair, is how I feel right now. He didn't hire me to be a maid. I didn't work my ass off for years to become a trainer so I could do free favors for one more entitled rich prick in my life.

I got my fill of these types of guys at private school as a teenager and during obligatory owner meetings for certain horses at past farms as an adult. That's part of the allure of working somewhere with one owner rather than starting up my own stable full of independently owned horses. One owner to deal with, more horses to spend my time with.

The prick-to-horse ratio is favorable.

I've said it before, and I'll say it again: people suck.

I trudge back inside and kick my checkerboard-printed slip-ons off toward the mat. In my agitated state, I flick one more forcefully than intended, and it bounces off the wall, landing on the clean floor and dropping bits of grass and dirt around itself. I glower, like the shoe has somehow wronged me. Standing there, staring at the offending shoe, I force myself to take a few deep breaths.

In through the nose and out through the mouth.

"Let it go, Billie," I mutter, chastising myself for getting so worked up. I need to not let my temper get the best of me.

I know I fly off the handle too easily. I often feel like the ballerina in a music box, every irritable thought twisting inside me like another crank of the key. I know I do it to myself, and in the end, I'm the one left twirling around like an idiot with no way to turn that obnoxious twinkling music off.

On top of that incredible skill, I'm also a gold medal–level grudge holder. Forgiveness doesn't come easily to me. And right now, I'm acutely aware that leading myself down this path on day one of the most exciting job opportunity of my life isn't the best way to get started.

Luckily, I know exactly how to turn this frown upside down. I toss a bag of carrots and a wheel of brie into my backpack. I eye the loaf of French bread on the counter. It gets jammed in the backpack too. A girl's gotta eat, right?

My phone dings right as I'm about to pack it up. A text message from an unknown number.

**Unknown Number:** Billie, this is Vaughn Harding. Tomorrow morning we'll go over your contract. 7 a.m. Be there.

I can't help but laugh. This man has all the charm of a toad. How the hell am I supposed to respond to that kind of demanding bullshit?

I start typing.

Yes, Master.

Nope. *He's your boss*. Delete, delete, delete.

I settle on Or be square! ;)

Because Vaughn Harding is nothing if not square.

Smirking to myself and feeling very pleased with my level of wit, I swing a single strap of the bag over my shoulder with one hand while reaching for the bottle of red wine sitting in the middle of the island with the other. I march straight out the back door and into the buttery evening light with my eyes set on the hill ahead of me.

I need a glass of wine and some good company.

# CHAPTER 5

## Vaughn

*Reaching out for comment…*

*Would you be willing to talk about…*

*Looking for confirmation that Dermot Harding was no longer involved at Gold Rush Resources…*

I STARE AT THE PRESS RELEASE I'M ATTEMPTING TO DRAFT in response to the endless requests from reporters until my right eye twitches with the strain. I don't know why I even continue to open the emails, to subject myself to this drivel. I have no intention of talking to anyone. The minute we present anything other than a united front is when these leeches will latch on and suck more out of us for a story than they already have. As it stands, the businesses have a good chance to recover, provided nothing else goes wrong.

"Like the loose cannon you hired today," I mumble, shaking my head while shuffling papers to clear off my desk.

Billie Black.

Probably not my most business-savvy hire to date. Unpredictable. Fiery. *Inappropriate.*

Not at all what I imagined for a nice, reliable trainer who could get us back on track. But I also know I had to find someone who has no connection to the questionable side of this industry, and Billie certainly fits that bill. Not only geographically, but I am almost positive that if anyone ever tried to solicit her in any way, she would tell them exactly where to stick it.

One side of my mouth quirks up at that thought. I can already imagine how that encounter would play out.

Pulling up the browser on my laptop, I do something I probably should have done several days ago. I google her. I know Cole will do a thorough background check when I hand all her paperwork over to him, but I'm still curious.

The first page of web results consists of news articles and racing results where she's mentioned or interviewed. I swap the top tab to only show photos and am met with a large picture of a bright chestnut horse wearing purple and white silk blinders over its face, with its head and neck tilted affectionately toward Billie's stomach. She's holding the reins in one hand, resting across its nose. Her face is barely visible, nuzzled in toward the horse's ear.

It's a sweet picture. Almost looks like they're giving each

other a hug. The headline accompanying the photo reads *The Future Is Female: Young Trainer Taking the Track by Storm.*

I look for more photos, but that's the only one. "Huh," I mumble to myself.

"Huh, what?"

I jump a couple of inches out of my seat and slam my laptop shut like a guilty kid who just got caught doing something he shouldn't be.

Billie stands in my office doorway, shoulder propped up against the doorframe. She crosses her arms over her chest, pushing her breasts up toward the neckline of her white shirt.

I slowly drag my eyes up her delicate neck, outlined by loose wisps of hair that have fallen from the mess twisted atop her head. A light shimmer of perspiration glistens over her collarbones, and a faint frown touches her full, pouty lips. She's sporting a big black smudge of dirt across her forehead. She looks fucking edible.

I work to maintain a blank expression, trying to keep my eyes from straying back down over her body as she crosses into my office uninvited.

"Talk to yourself often?"

"Why do you look like you've been playing in the mud?"

My shot must land because what was already a pouty face darkens into an angry one. Precious as it is, if I keeled over every time someone frowned at me, well, I wouldn't be where I am today—running a multinational company that makes money hand over fist.

"Well, Vaughn," she muses, "that's because you provided me a pigsty to live in."

*What?*

"I probably would have preferred to sleep in a stall with the horses than with the ants and piss splatters at the cottage."

I wish I could say I know what she's talking about, but I don't. And I'm not in the habit of apologizing to people for things I had no hand in. I haven't stepped foot in the place since I took over. Maintenance was low on my list of pressing things.

Shrugging, I say, "I have no objections to you doing that."

Now she's gone from glowering to gaping at me, mouth open like a fish out of water. I lean back and steeple my fingers, watching her lips move like she's saying something but can't get any noise to come out. I'll concede that I'm probably being too hard on her, but her level of insubordination and boldness irritates me. *Nobody* talks to me like this. And bad as it sounds, women are usually especially accommodating of my moods and opinions. I'm not sure what's wrong with this one, but it feels like she's intentionally trying to set me off.

"You are something else," she continues. "I spent all night on a plane to come help *you*, all morning dealing with *your* games, and now I've spent all afternoon playing maid and cleaning *your* house."

Images of Billie in a skimpy maid costume dance through my sex-starved mind.

"I am exhausted, and I am starving. Can you please just point me toward a knife so I can leave before I do something I'll regret?"

Short lace-trimmed skirt. Garters wrapped tight enough around each thigh that they create a slight swell at the top of the elastic. A feather duster in one hand. I imagine her quietly going about her job without disrupting and provoking me and realize *that* might be the real dream.

Her hostile attitude is a real boner killer. I lean back and take in her full form, standing here looking all sassy with both hands gripping her slender hips. Upon closer inspection, I realize she looks exhausted. Smudges of light blue are painted beneath her golden eyes, and where she carried herself tall and proud earlier today, her shoulders now sag with exhaustion.

No one informed me she came straight from the airport. *You haven't been informed of much where she's concerned.* Maybe I can throw her a bone, attribute a bit of her poor behavior to jet lag. I'm not a completely unreasonable man.

"Are there not any knives at your house?"

She sighs, shoulders slumping even further. "I walked back with a picnic to have out there and forgot to bring the one utensil I need."

I make my way around the desk in silence, striding toward the cabinet beside the door that is home to piles of Gold Rush Ranch promotional gear. I'm certain I saw a box of monogrammed Swiss Army knives in there when I tore the place apart looking for clues.

They don't jump out at me immediately, so I crouch down to rifle through the lower shelves. Still coming up empty-handed, I end up kneeling, trying to reach the very back of one of the lowest shelves. Leave it to this woman to come up with something colossally inconvenient for me to do.

In my annoyance, I chance a look up and see that Billie has switched back to leaning against the doorway and is watching me intently. Even though I've caught her staring, she doesn't drop eye contact. It's almost as though she's refusing to blink. I pause and stare back at her. Her throat moves up and down as she takes a big swallow. But unlike most people, she still doesn't look away.

Nah, Billie Black is a bit nuts and more than a little bold.

Two can play that game. "Enjoying the view, Miss Black?"

She tilts her head to the side and rests it against the doorframe. An almost imperceptible smirk touches her mouth. She lightly taps her pointer finger against the indent along her top lip. "Yeah, Boss Man. You look good on your knees."

I thought my comment would embarrass her, throw her off, wipe that obnoxious smug look off her face. But she comes back swinging. She was reaming me out not two minutes ago, and now she's back to spouting off inappropriate comments.

*Absolutely nuts.*

Dropping my chin and shaking my head, I grab the small box I can feel against my fingertips. Lifting one foot and pushing to standing, I roll my shoulders back. Billie is taller than most women, but I'm taller than most men and tower over her.

I hold one knife out toward her. She reaches for it, and her dainty fingers rasp lightly over mine as they wrap around the hilt. But instead of letting go, I yank it toward myself, causing her to stumble a couple of steps closer.

Uncertain eyes shoot up to meet mine, and I puff up a little at seeing her so off balance. I much prefer this look on her face.

Acting quickly, I run the pad of my thumb across my tongue and then reach forward to swipe it across the smudge of dirt on her forehead. Her golden eyes grow wide, like two glowing moons staring back at me. But not for long. No, if I hadn't been watching, I'd have missed that one uncertain moment before she reverts to shooting daggers at me.

She jerks the knife from my hand, spins on her heel, and storms out of my office into the darkened hallway, but not before muttering, "Fucking gross!" just loud enough for me to hear.

"You're welcome!" I call back as she propels herself out of my view.

I roll my lips together and swallow the chuckle bubbling up in my throat. God, I haven't laughed in weeks—maybe longer. Toying with Billie Black is *fun*.

I have to put up with her antics for three months before she'll be hitting the dusty trail, so I might as well enjoy it. If she thinks she's going to waltz in here, all alluring and sharp-tongued, and play this game unchallenged, she's in for a wild ride.

I don't roll over for anyone.

Fucking my employee is off the table. The farm is in too much trouble. But fucking *with* my employee…now that's another story altogether.

*Off to the races, honey.*

# CHAPTER 6
## Billie

WHAT. A. PRICK.

Who does that to a woman they've basically just met, let alone their employee? The guy's gumption is absolutely out of this world. Typical for a guy with a face like that and more money than sense. They're all the same. Altogether too confident, knowing there are no real repercussions for their inappropriate behavior.

As I head toward Double Diablo's paddock, I replay our interaction in my head. I'd be lying to myself if I pretended that his proximity didn't shake me. He stood close enough for me to know he smells like almonds. That alluring amaretto sort of smell, but not over the top, just the right amount. I expected something harsh and obnoxious—just like his personality. It didn't match up. I couldn't reconcile it.

It obviously muddled my brain. Because while I sniffed him like a bloodhound in heat, I couldn't help but check him out more closely. I blame the jet lag and the wine I already slammed back on an empty stomach before dragging my ass up there to find a knife. Like a brainless sap, I savored the way he filled out his suit. It was honestly criminal.

I've always had this theory that there are two types of men: the ones who look edible in a suit and the ones who look edible in their birthday suit. Suit guys are a little more slender than I like, naked guys a little too bulky to pull off that GQ suit look. I'm not saying I'd kick either out of bed if they knew what they were doing. It's just an observation. Like Goldilocks, my ideal man is somewhere down the middle. And Vaughn Harding is right down the middle.

I stood over him, gawking like a teenager, purely for research purposes, of course. I analyzed the way his suit sleeves bunched up around his broad shoulders and then let my eyes trace the line from his briefs on his firm ass in a completely clinical fashion. After collecting data, I can now conclude that under different circumstances, I would climb the man like a tree.

Reaching my spot in front of Double Diablo's gate, I sink onto soft grass, so thick it feels like a rug beneath me. I've opted to call him DD, like Deedee, because I really can't handle his name. He needs something as cute as he looks that I can whisper soothingly into his pointy little ears when he finally lets me close enough. His initials are short and simple and good enough for now.

I startled him when I came over the fence behind his paddock earlier, but he didn't race at me like a fire-breathing dragon charging out of its cave. Instead, he watched me walk to where I'm now sitting, gave me a suspicious look, and then turned his butt to me.

Upon my return, he's still facing away from me. The only recognition he gave me was a sulky little foot stomp and the flick of his right ear, pointing it back at me as a way of hearing what I'm doing.

Sitting cross-legged on the grass, I break off a piece of a carrot and toss it into his paddock. I cut myself a few slices of cheese with my shiny new Gold Rush Ranch knife and lay them on top of a freshly torn piece of French bread. I sip my red wine from the bottle because I also forgot a glass. The small victory in this day is that this bottle has a screw top, no corkscrew required.

Leaning back on my elbows, I stretch my legs out and try to relax while I watch day turn to night, twilight laying itself over the farm like a blanket. All in the good company of one grumpy little black horse.

A few small sandwiches later, DD finally turns his head toward the carrot I threw. Stubborn little bugger. He turns a little farther so I can spy his eyeball stretching in its socket to see me without giving away that he's actually looking at me. He looks like one of those guys who's trying to check you out discreetly but failing miserably. Except when he does it, it's cute.

The stallion looks back at the carrot and takes one small step toward it, drops his head, and brushes his lips across the bare patch of dirt where it landed to pick it up. Crunching away, he eyes me more openly now. I casually toss him another piece, enjoying watching the way his mind works.

He startles and flips to face me head-on while I take another sip from my wine bottle. After a moment of glaring, he continues crunching, a bit of orange-colored drool frothing on the sides of his lips. With brief hesitation, he drops his head again to pick up the piece of carrot.

"Good boy," I murmur gently, which earns me another flick of his little elf ears. I look up, taking in the white glow of the stars against the darkening sky. "DD, I don't think I'm off to a very good start with the boss man."

Big black doe eyes stare back at me with the strands of his thick forelock falling around them.

"You kind of remind me of him. You both have nice hair."

More staring and crunching.

"You know." I sit up straight like we're in the middle of an engaging conversation. "I raged all the way down here about what a prick he is. But with some food and wine in me, I feel like I'm ready to admit to you I haven't exactly been on my best behavior either. It's possible that I provoked him a little."

DD appears to have finished chewing, so I toss him another carrot, closer to the fence this time.

"Smart boy. Admit nothing. You'll only piss the girls off that way."

I watch his nose wiggle as he shifts his eyes back and forth between me and the carrot a couple feet ahead of him. One step. Two steps. And then he cautiously lowers his neck and stretches out the very tip of his top lip to pull the carrot toward himself.

"Good boy, DD," I tell him softly before continuing. "So, you know, the polite part of me thinks I should apologize for prodding at him so much. I know it wasn't very professional of me. And it's definitely not the ideal start to a new working relationship."

A slow blink. More contented chewing.

"He just ticks me off, you know? I'm painfully familiar with his type. All the same."

I marvel at what good listeners horses are. I can lay it all out, my deepest darkest secrets, and they never judge me or think less of me. In fact, the more I talk to DD and feed—ahem, bribe—him, the more he likes me. His eyes soften and the muscles along the top of his back relax.

"But then there's the childish part of me"—I toss a piece of carrot closer again—"that feels like he should apologize first. I mean, he's the one who flew out of there first thing accusing me of being some sort of paid date or something."

I watch the silhouette of the dark horse move ahead, with less apprehension this time, to claim his treat.

"You guys really are like the same person, DD. You can't continue to greet people that way either. It's unbecoming, you know? People will mistake you for being a mean boy rather than just a sensitive one."

We sit there staring at each other, no longer needing to avoid eye contact. I roll him another piece of carrot, which brings him right up to the fence line.

I smile and sigh with satisfaction.

"Guess I just answered my question, didn't I, big guy?"

The sound of footsteps on pavement has me shooting

up and whirling around with speed that does not match my current level of sobriety. Looking up the slope of the hill, I see Vaughn standing beside his expensive black car. It's too dark for me to tell if he's looking at me or just pausing to admire the view.

My confusion clears quickly when he reaches one hand up to wave, his keys jangling in the quiet as he calls out to me, "Good night, Billie!"

I freeze and feel a flush creep up my neck and across my cheeks. *Fuck my life*. Had he just heard me talking about him? To a horse?

The parking lot is probably too far away for him to have heard me, or at least that's what I tell myself. Maybe he could have caught some general mumbling but not actual words. *Hopefully*.

Worst-case scenario, he'll think I'm a little nuts, and I can live with that.

I raise a hand up in his direction with an awkward "Night!" before bringing it down to scrub over my face when Vaughn drives away.

Facing DD's pen, both hands now covering my face, I peek through my fingers at him. Much to my surprise, in the time that I'd been facing the other way, he moved closer, bringing his chest right up to the fence with his neck and head now hung over the barrier.

I hum happily at our progress in just one night. "Are you laughing at me, DD?"

Bending down, I retrieve a whole carrot from the bag, the longest one I can find. I hold the thick end in my hand like a wand and reach out slowly toward his face, holding the carrot toward his flared nostrils. I stand stock-still and watch those big dark globes stare down his dishy forehead at the treat I'm offering him. It feels like minutes crawl by, even though it's probably only mere seconds.

In trying to stand still, I realize just how inebriated I am. Whoops. But I am no quitter. I stick it out, and it pays off in spades.

I watch as the whiskers on his nose twitch, his lips wiggle and smack against each other as he reaches out toward the tip of the carrot, making a hollow little popping noise. I feel the heat and moisture of his exhale as he stretches his face toward my hand and gently grabs the carrot.

He pauses for a moment and then pins his ears while stepping away from me. A sure sign he is unimpressed with what I just talked him into doing.

Baby steps with this one. Just like Vaughn.

# CHAPTER 7

## Vaughn

I ROLL OUT OF BED THIS MORNING, NOT FEELING RESTED AT all. *Again*. This seems to be my new normal. Work. Stress. Poor sleep. A vicious cycle. It isn't helping my mood either; I know I've been a cranky bastard. The overwhelming pressure I feel to succeed and the ever-present memory of my grandfather are combining to bring me down. To paralyze me.

Taking over at Gold Rush Ranch isn't just another challenge; it's downright daunting. I love the farm in a special from-my-childhood sort of way, but I was *thriving* in my role at the family mining company. I felt like I'd really found my stride. I liked the board meetings, the anticipation of drilling for new deposits, and managing something that was fiscally booming. Talking to the media about Gold Rush Resources was easy. It was *exciting*.

This? This is depressing. An absolute clusterfuck. And I'm not above admitting how grumpy I've been at having something my conscience won't let me walk away from dumped in my lap.

On my drive back to the ranch offices this morning, I replayed the events of the night before. Billie Black, talking way too loud as night fell over the quiet farm. I didn't mean to listen in on her, but the way the sound traveled up the hill made it almost impossible not to overhear. The gist of it was that I'd been such an ass that I drove a woman I hardly know to drink wine straight from the bottle and hash her day out with a horse in the dark.

That's a new low, even for me.

I knew she was a little nuts, but that scene was really just more depressing. And standing there listening, I felt a creeping sensation of shame swirling in my gut. I'd never tell her that though. Even if she was one of the trophy wife prospects my mom liked to send around, my outburst was a shit way to talk to a person. I've been told I can be cool or hard to get a read on but not downright rude. That's not who I am.

Apologies aren't really my strong suit either, but weaving down the back roads this morning, I know I'm going to have to extend some sort of olive branch. I should try to start fresh. I'm stuck in this small town working with the woman, and I know she's going to be grating, but I also know a business runs best when everyone is on good terms.

I can't afford to be on bad terms with her.

After pulling up to the farm, I step out of my Porsche, feeling the invisible pressure of running behind. Although for what, I'm not sure. It's only seven in the morning, so a light misty haze hangs over the back fields, contrasting against the vibrant green of the grass. I breathe deeply, feeling that cool, humid West Coast air slip past my lips and coat my lungs. It smells like spring.

I can hear the clip-clop of hooves on concrete around the corner. The farmhands and grooms will already be a couple hours under way. Horses don't much care about business hours.

Turning to head into the office, I catch movement out of the corner of my eye. Down by Double Diablo's paddock, Billie sits facing him, in a lawn chair this time, reading and flipping through sheets of an open folder on her lap while the horse happily munches his hay out of a feeder right next to her. I stretch my left arm out to check the time again, almost in disbelief that she's already here. And that she's sitting so casually beside a horse that everyone has told me is crazy.

A match made in heaven, those two.

I stride into my office to get the coffeepot going, because I really need the caffeine boost this morning. I slam the glass pot back into place a little too hard, agitation lining every movement I make. Luckily, it doesn't break. I fire up my computer and am met with what had me storming out of here last night.

The cursor blinks on the blank page of my Word document. Yesterday, I got as far as opening it and titling it *Gold Rush Ranch Statement*. That is what I have to show for all of yesterday. I shake my head, disappointed in myself.

"Big win, Vaughn. You fucking sad sack," I mumble to myself.

I've always been a hard worker, a high achiever. Not being able to buckle down and focus is messing with my head. I lean forward on my elbows, willing myself to type, but end up staring at the blank screen with my chin resting on steepled hands. Maybe what I need is scotch rather than coffee.

Or maybe just a change of scenery.

***

Five minutes later, I stand in front of Billie with a cup of peace-offering coffee in hand. She's either totally absorbed in what she's reading or ignoring me, because she hasn't acknowledged my approach. Even standing here, facing her, she doesn't glance up.

She looks cozy and relaxed. Natural. Like she belongs here, all curled up in the great outdoors on a lawn chair with one jean-clad leg folded underneath herself and a light blanket wrapped around her shoulders. There's a small bucket of crunchy horse treats in her lap, and her worn black Blundstone boots lie discarded carelessly beside her.

"Did you sleep out here?"

She snorts and quirks one eyebrow without looking up at me. "You said you wouldn't object."

I sigh. "Is the house really that bad?"

Feline amber eyes shoot like lasers to mine. "Not anymore, it's not."

I stare at her, honestly not sure where to take this now. "Do you like coffee?" I mumble.

Her gaze shifts down to my hands. "Is water wet?"

I reach one mug toward her, and she eyes me with suspicion.

"I'll take the other cup."

I roll my eyes. "They're both black coffee, Billie."

"Yeah, but I feel you might be offering me the poisoned one," she deadpans.

"I—you…what?"

She presses her lips together, eyes twinkling with mirth. "I'm joking, Boss Man. If you wanted to kill me, you missed your chance with that knife last night."

I don't even know how to respond to her, so I just stand here, floundering. Like he can smell weakness, Double Diablo's head shoots up out of his feeder. He pauses before lunging toward me at the fence.

*Little prick.* Just because I've spent years wearing a suit doesn't mean I forgot how to be around horses. I give him an unimpressed look; his pinned ears and angry face are nothing new to me in the world of business. If nothing else, I feel like his angry face is just a reflection of mine these days. I lash out just like that too.

Billie gawks at me with a big smile on her face. "Not bad, fancy pants. You didn't even squeal."

Is she kidding? "I grew up on this farm, Billie. Horses aren't completely foreign to me, and I deal with assholes every day." I motion my cup at Double Diablo, who snorts and goes back to eating.

"Good boy, DD," she murmurs, tossing a small crunchy horse treat beside his feet.

I blink and shake my head at her. "What did you just call him?"

"Deedee. Like, his initials. His name sucks."

Inclining my head toward the little devil, I ask, "What would you name him instead?"

She wraps both delicate hands around the mug and takes a cautious sip of her coffee, looking over the rim to assess the horse. "I don't know." She snorts in a completely unladylike way. "Maybe Mister Black. Humans suck, so he's pretty much the perfect man for me. You'd take my name, wouldn't you, DD?"

I cough out a laugh. "My grandfather named him, you know."

She says nothing but pulls her lips back as if to say *yikes* and then promptly changes the subject. "Thanks for the coffee, but I take cream in mine."

Is she kidding right now? I must give her an incredulous look, because she smiles at me like the Cheshire cat.

"You know, for next time."

"You're incredible," I say, shaking my head at her.

"Thank you." She points behind me. "Grab a chair and chill out for a second. You're all uptight. It's making DD and me nervous."

"Did he tell you that?"

"No. He told you that when he snapped at you."

I shift my eyes to the horse. He stops munching and looks at me suspiciously, out of the corner of his eye, without lifting his head. Maybe she's right. I take a few strides toward the other lawn chairs she has leaned against the fence and fold one out beside her, facing the paddock. A breath I didn't realize I was holding whooshes out of me when I sit.

This is nice.

I attempt to look at Billie's profile without openly turning to stare at her. She's so unusual, so alluring, like a piece of art in a gallery I want to analyze, get lost in. She's like a splash of red in a sea of gray.

I realize she knows I'm checking her out when her cheek closest to me quirks up before her lashes shift my way. A mischievous look takes over her whole face as she says, "Hello, and welcome to my crib."

I can't help but laugh, and a low rumble rolls across my chest. "You're nuts. You know that?"

"Ha! I've been told they really broke the mold with me." Sadness flashes across her face but disappears as quickly as it showed up. She turns and looks at me, a small smile touching her full lips. "Thank you for the coffee. I'm jet-lagged as all get-out, and I may or may not have enjoyed a little too much wine last night after not eating properly all day. I really needed this."

She lifts her mug in a silent toast and appears so sweet and sincere. The carefree, sarcastic woman is missing right now, and I realize she's actually easier to take when she's being obnoxious. I don't know how to respond to this almost melancholy version of her.

I grunt and return the gesture with my mug.

*Smooth.*

We sit in silence, sipping our coffees and watching Double Diablo, or DD—insert eye roll here—as she's now calling him. The soft sound of him munching on hay mingles with snorts and whinnies from around the farm. The whole sensory experience brings me back to my childhood summers spent here. I close my eyes and tip my head back to rest on the chair. I'm not sure when I last sat outside and just enjoyed nature.

Life got too busy. Skyscrapers and busy traffic, the sound of phones ringing and printers pumping out warm sheets of paper usually fill my day. I have to admit, this is almost therapeutic. Extending an olive branch has been bearable so far. And Billie is being quiet now, which makes it even better.

But of course, she can't let it last.

"Are you okay, Vaughn?"

"What?" From this angle, I can really analyze her profile, lit by the early morning sun. She sniffs, and the end of her straight, upturned nose does a little wiggle. Thick caramel hair tucked behind her ear cascades straight over her shoulder like a waterfall.

"You heard me," she says, looking back out to the paddock.

She looks almost uncomfortable. Too still, like she's avoiding looking at me.

No one has asked me how I'm doing in the last few weeks. Not in a way that makes me feel like they *actually* want to know and aren't just asking to be polite. Billie doesn't strike me as the type of woman to ask me something just because it's the polite thing to do. It's unnerving to have someone I barely know—and barely like—reach out to me in this way. It throws me off balance, a feeling I'm not fond of. I don't want to share my inner turmoil, my inner shame, with *anyone*. Least of all Billie Black, who would probably find some way to mock it.

My goal of being passably nice to a new employee today is complete. I stand and shoot her a wry grin. "Peachy."

Her response is to stare at me and tip her head to one

side. Her gaze makes my spine tingle, like she can see right through my charade.

I depart with a "Good luck today" from over my shoulder.

Yeah, I duck and run.

# CHAPTER 8

## Billie

THIS MORNING, THE FOLD-OUT CHAIR HAS BASICALLY TURNED into my throne, and I'm not complaining.

After my date with a grumpy black horse and a bottle of red wine last night, I quickly showered and fell into bed. I was dead to the world until about 3:00 a.m. when I jolted awake feeling totally disoriented. I tried to fall back asleep, but jet lag was still a bitch and wouldn't let me sleep anymore. After all, it was 11:00 a.m. in Dublin. I rolled out of bed, chastising myself, and let the shame spiral begin. How old am I? Draining a bottle of wine on a work night? Telling my new boss he looks good on his knees?

Cringe. Cringe. *Cringe.*

When I crawled out here for some fresh air and to peek in on how the farm runs in the morning, Hank walked up to me and said, "Billie girl, you look like death warmed over."

I grumbled back something about, "No, *you* do." Because I am very witty and mature like that.

He laughed and scrubbed my hair like I was a little kid. Then he sent all the other staff down to introduce themselves and have a little chat.

I feel like a lazy queen.

DD seems pretty comfortable with me, the human vending machine, sitting here. So long as I don't move too suddenly and keep tossing the odd cookie his way, he's happy. I watch his reaction to each of the five men who came down to visit me. He ignores a couple, makes faces at one, and throws a total tantrum over the other two. I'm thinking he's a better judge of character than I realized.

None of them come very close except to shake my hand, after which they back away slowly. Or quickly, depending on how badly DD is behaving. It makes me chuckle inwardly. I feel like Daenerys sitting here with a dragon behind my back. Everyone is scared to come too close. Some more than others.

I think they're all being ridiculous. Sure, DD comes across as a real grumpy little bitch, but he's still just a horse. You work with them long enough and you get to know their different behaviors. And in my books, DD isn't that alarming.

I think he's kind of charming. I appreciate he doesn't have a silly, dopey little persona. I know that if I can channel his intelligence and spunk into a competitive instinct, he'll be winning Gold Rush Ranch an awful lot of races.

I just have to come at him from a different angle.

I'm still sitting on my throne making notes on each of the horse's files when I hear footsteps approaching. Looking up, I see a young woman with a serious look on her face walking toward me.

"Hi. I'm Violet Eaton," she says quietly, getting close enough to shake my hand.

"Hi, Violet." I give her a warm smile and look her up and down.

"I'm one of the grooms here. Hank has me assigned to the young horses, and I just wanted to come introduce myself." She stares past me at DD, wringing her hands.

"It's really nice to meet you," I say back. "It's also really nice to see some estrogen around this place."

At that comment, her round blue eyes shoot back toward me in shock. Her cheeks tinge light pink on her porcelain skin while she tries to bite back a smile. "It's kind of a sausage fest, isn't it?"

I bark out a loud laugh. "Welcome to the sport of kings, my friend," I reply with a wink.

She chuckles while nodding her dainty little head. She looks like a doll. Petite everything, topped off with a shock of icy blond hair rolled up into a tidy bun on her head. I feel like a slobby Amazon next to her.

"Tell me more about yourself," I say, waving a hand toward the chair beside me.

She hits me with a surprised look and then plops down.

My eyes immediately shift to DD, who startled at how abruptly Violet sat down. He stares at her with intelligent black eyes, then looks at me and pricks his ears forward.

*Forward!* Which is basically the equivalent of a smile. Then he snorts and goes back to his fresh pile of hay.

I look over at Violet and bulge my eyes. She quirks one side of her mouth and shrugs in response.

"I don't think he's as bad as everyone makes him out to be. The rumor mill here is vicious, and so was the old trainer."

My mouth twists as I shake my head at her assessment. Pretty much what I figured all along.

"Sorry," she adds quickly, "I shouldn't speak poorly about someone who isn't here to defend themselves."

I roll my eyes at that. "Don't be. My responsibility is to the horses here, not some person I've never met before. Plus, I already came to the same conclusion."

And I mean it. A horse can't speak for himself. It's my duty to be his ally. Other adults can be accountable for their own actions and reputations. That isn't my job. I'm not here to hold anyone's hand and rub their back over how they trashed their own reputation. Either way, I like this girl. She's adorable, honest, and DD approved too.

I also need a friend. Everyone I met this morning was polite enough, but I could tell there were a couple exercise riders who might be a harder sell on their new boss. Older guys who've probably been around a long time, maybe friends with people caught in the cross fire of the scandal here.

As the new girl on the block, still only in her twenties, I know I'm going to be subject to some scoffs and silent treatment. Maybe even a little mansplaining, if I'm really lucky. That's my favorite. *Listen up, little lady. I been at this for a long time.*

I inwardly roll my eyes and look next to me where Violet still looks guilty for saying too much. Breaking our moment of silence, I ask, "Are you only assigned to the two-year-old horses?"

"Yes."

"Perfect. They're my main projects right now, which makes you my groom." I brush my legs off as I stand and stretch my hands above my head. Violet gives me another wide-eyed look. "You've really got that deer-in-the-headlights face down, huh?"

A shocked giggle escapes her lips as she grazes one hand over her cheek and stands. "I've been told I don't control my facial expressions very well."

"Ha. You don't, but I like it. It means you aren't full of shit. Join me for lunch at my house? I'm starving. Then we can get the horses out for some work this afternoon."

After enjoying tuna sandwiches on the porch swing, Violet and I walk back across the field to the farm. We had a nice lunch. The more relaxed she became in my presence, the more she talked.

"So where are you from originally?" I ask.

Violet rolls her eyes. "A small town you've probably never heard of. Chestnut Springs. It's just south of Calgary, Alberta."

"Sounds like a town in a cowboy movie."

"Looks like one too."

"Yeah? Hot cowboys and everything?" I waggle my eyebrows at her.

The apples of her cheeks bloom pink and she shakes her head, amusement dancing in her eyes. She's only a few years younger than me, but she comes off so innocent. For a farm girl, she's remarkably demure.

"Hang around with me long enough and you'll loosen up a bit, Violet."

"I'm a little scared by that statement." She giggles.

"I'm willing to bet that if I get a few drinks into you, you'll be swearing like a sailor and riding the mechanical bull topless at the local country bar. The quiet ones are always the craziest."

A strangled noise lodges in her throat as she turns her wide eyes on me once again.

I throw my head back and laugh as we round the corner back into the barn. But my amusement is ruined by Vaughn "the wet blanket" Harding when I crash right into his rock-hard chest and hear him say, "Why are you so loud then?"

He looks down his straight nose at me smugly, feeling all high and mighty about having overheard us no doubt.

*What a dick.*

I just roll my eyes and strike back, "Why? You hoping to catch me riding topless, Boss Man?"

I swear he growls as he shoulders past me, and I can't stop the small smile that tugs at the corners of my mouth. Antagonizing the boss shouldn't be this fun.

# CHAPTER 9

## Billie

THE NEXT WEEK PASSES EASILY, AND I FALL INTO A COMFORTable rhythm. I'm kept busy working with the exercise riders who breeze the established horses first thing in the morning. Violet and I are becoming fast friends, having lunch together most days. Hank gives me the best hugs, and working on the day-to-day aspects of the farm with him has things running like a well-oiled machine. Even the most standoffish staff members are coming around. Sometimes, rather than speaking to me in grunts, they use words, which I'm counting as a win. Boss Man is still sex in a suit but also a typical crabby rich bitch who hides out in his office all day.

Now I'm doing what all the cool girls do on a Friday night: kicking back with my main man.

A horse.

We've come a long way in the last week. I walk over the crest of the hill every morning to find him waiting for me at the back corner of his paddock. I coo at him in a mushy baby voice as I approach, and he doesn't even startle or pin his ears. He just looks at me expectantly because he *knows* I have the goods.

Apples, carrots, the odd peppermint. Yeah, he knows the drill.

He now allows me to sit on the top rail of the fence beside him, where I can pat his neck and scratch his ears. I sit by him and have one cup of coffee every morning, letting the early morning damp air wrap around me while watching the sun come up over the mountains. We sit in companionable silence as the farm bubbles to life. When I finish my coffee, I give him a kiss on his soft nose, and he stands there happily watching me walk up to the stables. It's honestly the best way to start my day.

The evenings at the farm are quieter. Everyone heads home, either to the bunkhouses on-site or into the small town of Agassiz nearby. I volunteered to do night check because, well, I have nothing else to do. So nobody knows it yet, but DD and I are making even more progress in the evenings when no one's watching. I can now walk right into his paddock and get up close with him. Consistency and cookies were key.

Tonight, my plan is to enjoy a few beers and groom DD to a perfect shine. After months of being untouched, the poor guy is looking worse for wear. Dusty black rather than shiny black. Tangled mane and dreadlocked tail. No wonder he hid at the back corner of the property. He looks like a lot of things, and an expensive racehorse is not one of them.

This time, he willingly dropped his head into a halter and let me tie him to the fence post. I grabbed a box of brushes from the stables and plan to groom him to a perfect shine. Plastic combs, rubber combs, soft-bristled brushes, moisturizing spray, special oil to paint on his hooves. Yes, DD is heading to the spa tonight. I take a swig of my cold beer and then get to work.

I zone out, departing into a happy place where I've always been able to lose myself, even as a child. I savor the sounds of his contented sighs and make sure I tell him what a charming boy he is. Standing by his shoulder, I peek at him out of the corner of my eye, watching his topline relax and his eyelids go heavy. I marvel at how far he's come in such a short amount of time—the ultimate validation that what I'm doing is working.

"Who is the prettiest boy?" I coo at the horse.

DD's head shoots up abruptly, knocking me out of my trance. I look over my shoulder to see Vaughn standing at the fence, arms resting across the top, looking pretty comfortable. And smug. Yup, he has that obnoxious, smug look on his face.

"Should I be concerned about how much you talk to this horse?"

I glare at him. No, I drink him in. He's been a hermit in his office, and I almost forgot how blindingly beautiful he is. I hate the way my body instantly responds to his presence. The uptick of my heartbeat, the hairs standing on my arms. "No, but you should probably be concerned about ruining your fancy suit leaning on that dirty fence."

He waves me off. "I can afford a new one."

Yup. Obnoxious. Comments like that are why I've vowed to stay away from trust fund babies. "Charming." I turn back to DD, starting with a soft-bristled brush to dust off all the loose hair I rustled up. "Can I help you with something, Vaughn?"

"I can see you down here from my office window and wanted to come check how this week has gone for you."

Great. So he's been watching me out here every night. It should creep me out, but my chest warms at the thought. *Don't act like an airhead, Billie.*

I continue brushing, moving around DD, who isn't helping me at all by ignoring Vaughn's presence. If he throws a fit, maybe Mr. Moneybags will feel uncomfortable and leave. Then I wouldn't have to continue staring so hard at the short black hair in front of me to keep myself from gaping at the handsome face beside me.

Admitting that I'm attracted to Vaughn Harding is annoying. Unsettling. But a fact all the same. A fact I am acutely aware of after barely seeing him all week. It almost seems like he wanted to avoid me after our last conversation. I've gazed up at his office now and then, wondering if he was going to bring me a cup of coffee again one of these mornings.

He's been out of sight and mostly out of mind. But now my brain isn't connecting to my lips because it obviously forgot he is insufferable. I realize I've been silent for an awkward amount of time and chance a peek up at him.

His cheekbones are still high and sharp, shoulders

still broad and powerful, and those eyes are still dark and stormy—and trained on me. Boring into me with such intensity that I inadvertently lick my lips under the pressure of his attention.

His gaze narrows and drops almost instantly to my mouth. I swear the air around us crackles with unspoken tension. Yup, Boss Man and I have some crazy volatile chemistry. *Dangerous* chemistry.

"Good," I reply, in a much more strangled voice than I intend, dropping my chin and brushing DD more forcefully. It's safer to keep my focus on the task at hand. Obviously, my ovaries don't know what my brain does. Men like Vaughn are bad news.

*Knock, knock, ovaries! It's brain here. Let me in.*

"That's it? Good? Care to elaborate on how my horses are doing?" His voice is like velvet on my skin, like a soft caress in the low early evening light.

I stop brushing abruptly, shaking my head at myself, and sigh dramatically. "Can't this wait until Monday? I'm off the clock right now," I say, pointing at my beer, wanting him to leave now and stop interrupting what has been a splendid night so far.

His eyes follow my finger, and he looks back at me with a wicked glint in his eye. "No, you're not. You're doing night check," he responds while picking up my can of beer and taking a big long swig.

His gaze stays trained on mine, challenging me. And against my better judgment, I let mine slip and admire the way his Adam's apple dips with every gulp. His tan throat and dark stubble move against the crisp white collar of his dress shirt, sending a strike of electricity through my core.

I swallow in response. *Billie, what are you doing? This guy is a nightmare.* Tossing the brush back into the bucket and dusting my hands against each other, a little more forcefully than necessary, I turn to face him.

"Hope you can afford to treat the cold sores you'll be getting for the rest of your life now too."

"Nice try," he replies with a stupid smirk on his face.

"Guess you won't ever really know. From here on out, you'll wake up in the morning wondering if today will be the day you look in the mirror and see one marring your pretty face. You'll just be in a constant state of not knowing, and you'll forever regret stealing my beer."

One side of his smug mouth hitches up. "You think my face is pretty?"

I roll my eyes and grab the spray bottle and a rag, and resume grooming DD, who is dozing happily with one back hoof cocked and resting on the ground, somehow oblivious to the surrounding tension.

"Everything has been good this week." I launch into my explanation of what I've been working on and mention specific horses and staff. I tell him how impressed I am with Violet, and his only response is, "Who?" because the asshole is making me describe a bunch of strategies and people that he doesn't even understand or know, all while standing there looking breathtaking and enjoying his stolen beer.

The upside is that I'm ticked off enough to throw some good elbow grease into polishing DD, and when I finish my monologue, I stand back to admire my handiwork. The sunset gleams on his shiny flanks.

He'll probably go roll in the dirt as soon as I leave, but grooming him has been satisfying and therapeutic nonetheless.

"Sounds like it's been good then," is the very intelligent response Vaughn comes up with while also looking at DD. I'm so glad I gave him a ten-minute rundown of the week all for him to repeat back to me that everything was "good."

Removing DD's halter, I give him a kiss on his cheek and a good rub behind his ears, and then set him free before turning to climb the fence. I sit on the top railing like I do every morning, except tonight I'm right beside Vaughn. I like the height advantage this position gives me. From here, I can be the one to look down on him.

I feel DD popping his lips gently around my pockets, shaking me down for more treats, no doubt, as I take my beer from Vaughn's hand. Thinking I must look cool stealing it back, I take a long swig before I realize that what's left is basically just a warm mixture of our backwash and flat beer.

"Blech," I gag, shaking my head as if to dispel the taste and tossing the can toward my backpack lying on the grass.

I grip the fence and look down at Vaughn, whose eyes twinkle like he's at some sort of live comedy show. He intrudes on my peaceful evening, drains my beer, and now he's laughing at me for drinking his warm saliva? *Cool.*

That hot familiar fire licks up my throat, and I feel my head buzz with agitation. My will to play nice flies away into the pink twilight sky. "Has anyone ever told you what a smug dick you are?" is what I get out just before DD loses patience with his treat-thieving attempts and takes a more forceful shove at my waistband, sending me sailing headfirst toward the ground.

Except I don't hit the ground. Strong hands break my trajectory. Long fingers splay firmly around my rib cage, and before I know what's happening, I'm pushed up against a fence post with one of Vaughn's knees pressed between my legs to keep me from dropping like a stone.

Pinned.

Looking down at where his hands are resting on my thin shirt, I see his thumbs just crossing the boundary of my soft sports bra, grazing the side of each breast. I see the veins popping in his hands, somehow so masculine and alluring.

In his grip, I feel like my shirt could burn into ash, curl up, and float away on the evening breeze. Being surprised by my tumble has left my chest rising and falling more heavily than usual, and I'm completely entranced by his hands moving up and down with my ribs as my lungs heave.

His amaretto scent wraps around me like the softest silk. I feel like I've been dropped into a glass of him, all honeyed and manly. I drag my eyes away, chin tipping up slowly to meet his face. Bad choice. Very bad choice.

Under the thick dark fringe of his lashes, his eyes are hot molten chocolate, utterly focused on my body. He's staring, taking in the way his hands possess me, so big that they almost wrap right around my rib cage. His head snaps up to meet my gaze, his expression downright dangerous as he breaks our tense silence.

"No, Billie." His voice is dangerously low as he angles his head so close to my ear that I can feel his breath fan across my throat. "Women usually go out of their way to endear themselves to me. Not piss me off."

*Time to teach this prick a lesson.*

His words set me off, and without thinking, I reach out toward him and hook my index finger into his crisp white dress shirt, right between the buttons. I can feel the muscles in his abdomen clench under my touch as I gently trace the tip of my finger across his hot skin, feeling the firm ridges I knew would be there.

To anyone loitering at the stables, our silhouettes would almost look like he was a vampire going in for a quick taste with the way he towers over me. I send up a silent prayer that no one can see us and close my finger around the fabric that's brushing against my hand, pulling his torso closer to mine so that I straddle his thigh.

I hear his sharp intake of air and feel a familiar ache just below my hip bones. *This is such a bad idea.*

I look up, taking in the dark shadows falling across his brow and his almost pained facial expression. We hold each other in this limbo, facing off for a few seconds before I move so close I can feel the scruff on his jaw lightly scratch my cheek. His hands squeeze my ribs, trying to hold me in place.

At the increase in pressure, my nipples harden and goose bumps bloom across my arms unbidden. *This is fine.* A totally typical reaction to absolutely anyone touching me like this.

Disturbed by the way my body responds to his, I opt to up the stakes, fingering the collar of his shirt with my opposite hand and gently running my teeth along the lobe of his ear. I'm pressed so close to him I can feel more than hear the grunt that breaks loose from his chest.

For a moment, I let myself imagine us together under different circumstances, all the delicious noises he would make as he moved above me, pressing into me so hard that our bodies would sink right into the mattress beneath us. Coming completely undone, just for me.

It's with that image in my mind that I slide my fingers up his neck and through his hair before grabbing a handful firmly. He stands stock-still, frozen.

"Well then, let me be the one to deflower you on this one, Boss Man," I whisper against his ear. "You are absolutely insufferable." I bite down on his earlobe again, a little harder this time, which causes the air to leave his lungs in a loud hiss. "Now get your hands off me. I'm not one of your playthings," I finish, essentially dousing us both with a bucket of cold water and firmly pushing him away.

I lick my lips as I watch him jerk his hands off me like I burned him. His absence leaves an arctic chill over places that had just been so hot, and I can feel my heart crashing around in my rib cage uncontrollably as we stand there staring at each other.

Shocked eyes bore into my wild ones. He looks stunned, and I can't help but notice how painfully beautiful he is standing here in the dim light with his hair all mussed. I did that to him. My chest pinches, and that ache snaps me out of my trance.

*My god.* I took this too far. Way too fucking far.

I think about all the goals I haven't yet achieved, all the shit men exactly like him have put me through. I remind myself of all the sacrifices I've made to get to where I am, and feelings of shame wash over me. Why even give him the power to make me feel like this?

The sensation of my embarrassment is so intense, it spills down my backbone like molten lava and hardens into rigid but brittle rock, lending strength to my frayed nerves. Strength enough to shove past a completely immobilized Vaughn, our arms brushing against each other one last time, as I scoop up my backpack and sling it over one shoulder.

"Recycle your beer can," I bite out, nudging it in his direction with the toe of my boot but not daring to look up.

He still hasn't said a thing or moved an inch.

I take off into the night, willing my feet to walk gently, my hips to sway confidently, and my shoulders to drop serenely, all to portray a level of confidence that's not at all a reflection of the conflict raging inside me.

# CHAPTER 10
## Vaughn

It's been exactly two weeks since Billie and I faced off. Not that I'm counting. Women throw themselves at me all the time. Either of their own fruition or at my mother's behest. It made no difference. One hundred percent of those encounters did nothing but irritate me, and I treated the lot of them with respect but a general lack of interest.

That night, with Billie pressed up against me, shouldn't have felt different—but it did.

I wish I could say I hadn't thought about the way she touched me. So confident and indifferent all at once. I'm not sure she even realized she had been slowly rocking herself on my leg as she brushed her soft lips against my jaw and bit down on my ear like the little vixen I hadn't seen coming.

No one has ever made me that hard and then pushed me away. She's a challenge now, and I am completely fixated.

I shouldn't be.

God, I really shouldn't be. It's like she's infected me with her recklessness, because I certainly should not be giving that interaction any thought at all. But I have been. That she can effortlessly rattle my grip on control is driving me crazy.

That night has been keeping me up. It's what runs through my head while I give in and grip my throbbing cock in the shower, spilling myself all over the tiles. I feel the swell of her breast against the pad of my thumb and her dainty fingers taking a fistful of my hair with a level of authority that does not befit her happy-go-lucky personality. But I can't stop and continually promise myself that each time will be the last as I jerk myself off angrily.

I hate it. I'm self-controlled and meticulous. I always have a plan, and now one of the most annoying women I've ever met has me shaken. I've been in a foul mood since our family scandal hit the papers, and I've been running on fumes trying to save my grandfather's crowning achievement, the farm he loved given to him by the wife he cherished. But this encounter has really pushed me over the edge. I know I'm snapping at people who don't deserve it. I'm distracted and agitated. I'm tired, and I'm tired of constantly thinking about bending my employee over my desk and having my way with her.

It's beneath me, and it's not even something I can just get out of my system and move on from.

Our family doesn't need more scandal. I'm aware of how I'm portrayed in the media. The Harding family heir with a new woman on his arm every time he steps out in public. I'm the playboy and my brother the cold recluse. Ask Page

Ten (or whatever page it is). They would have an absolute heyday writing about me banging the new help.

I shake my head. Prime example. I know Billie isn't just the help. She's accomplished at her job. Despite what I initially thought of her, she's proving to be perfect for the position. At our management meetings, both she and Hank report to me that all the horses are running better than ever. It doesn't take a rocket scientist to see that all the staff around the farm love her. Some have even told me as much. I can hear the upbeat and playful way she interacts with everyone. That boisterous laugh constantly echoes down the barn alleyway and floats into my office like some sort of cruel joke.

She doesn't even give me the cold shoulder, like she's on some sort of holier-than-thou mission to be the bigger person. Every day, she waves a hand through my door as she walks past and gives me a "Hey there, Boss Man" as she continues past, completely unaffected by the fact that she almost ate me alive the other night. I can't even bring myself to tell her to stop calling me that ridiculous name. If only her professional facade would crack again, just a little, it would give me a good reason to get even with her.

I see her playing My Little Pony, or whatever it is she does with Double Diablo, who so far just looks like a shiny black hole that we've thrown almost a million dollars into for shits and giggles. Every morning, she has coffee by his fence, and every night, she brushes him until he shines like an oil slick. I can hear her talking to him every time I walk to my car, and I try to convince myself she's probably unstable, but truthfully, I can't help but admire the way she's turned the horse's attitude around. Even the grumpiest horse in the world likes her.

She is inescapable.

Which is why I'm here, pulling up to the farm late on a Saturday afternoon. The junior trainers do most of the training work early on the weekends, so it'll be a ghost town. And Billie doesn't work on the weekend at all right now, which means I don't have to hear her voice or breathe in that sunshine and lemon scent I associate with her now.

I worked out hard all morning and burned off my angst, and now I need to deal with month-end spreadsheets and compose an email to our public relations firm about how we should best approach rejoining the very public racing circuit in a few months. I need to focus.

Afternoon bleeds into evening as I hole up in my office, working. I take a break to eat the protein bar I packed for my dinner. It's not appealing at all, but cooking alone isn't either. I spin my desk chair around to face out toward the window, half expecting to see Billie down at DD's paddock.

I chide myself for feeling disappointment at not seeing her down there. What would I do anyway? Just sit up here like a stalker and watch her?

"Yup, pretty much," I murmur to myself. "It's what you do most days, Vaughn."

I shake my head at my foolishness and continue to gaze out the window. The longer I stare, I realize I can't see Double Diablo at all. I stand and peer out the window, hoping a higher angle will help me see him standing in the far corner of his paddock, probably chewing on company cash and swatting flies with his tail.

But it doesn't. He's not there.

I stride out of my office, calm but admittedly feeling a little concerned. I jog down to his pen, making that kissing noise that horses seem to love. It sounds sweet when Billie does it and just kind of lame when I do it. But it makes no difference. Here at the fence, holding the post I had Billie pushed up against, I can see that he is not in his pen. Not in a corner, not in his shelter, not lying down.

Blood roars in my ears, and my pulse thumps heavily against my sternum. Horses don't just go missing.

I scrub my hands through my hair and stare at the empty paddock. The gate is latched and all the fences are intact, which means he hasn't left on his own. But no one has been foolish enough to risk taking him out of that paddock in the time that I've been here, so I turn in a circle, hoping he might just be chilling in a neighboring paddock.

He's not.

A vise constricts my throat, because I don't know what to do in this situation. I work with files and papers. They don't have a mind of their own, and they usually just stay where you leave them. I'm out of my element here.

So I do the only thing I can think of—I run.

In a full sprint, I race back to my car, hop in, and speed down the back road to Billie's cottage, rounding the corner into the driveway with a spray of gravel. I'm driving like a maniac, and I know this. Unfortunately, I realize it a little too late as I come to a screeching halt by the front porch.

To the left of the cottage, I see Double Diablo standing up on his back legs, wildly showing the whites of his eyes. Billie, legs wrapped around his ribs with no saddle to hold her in place, gripping his mane in her hands, leans forward to meet his vertical motion, almost hugging his neck. She's glued onto him like a little fly on his back, gritting her teeth in concentration.

The pause at the top of his motion almost makes time stand still, and the surrounding sounds bleed into nothingness. Before I know it, his front hooves are lowering to the ground, and she has one rein away from his body, turning him in a tight circle. The sound of her murmuring to him in a low, soothing voice filters into my awareness.

I lean my head back against the headrest and close my eyes, running both hands through my hair. The breath that's been a hard knot in my chest for the last several minutes leaves my lungs in a shaky exhale. Relief flows over me like a cool shower on a hot day. The horse is here, and I didn't accidentally kill an employee in my moment of panic.

Lifting my head to glance out the window, I see Billie sitting securely on Double Diablo's back. His flanks heave with the weight of his breaths, and his head turns toward where her foot hangs at his side. She leans down to his face, rubbing his neck with gentle caresses.

*Thank fuck.*

I open the door and step out of my car. The inky black horse startles at the sound and swings his head up to look at me. Billie's head follows, but slower. Like a predator.

Beneath the shadow of her wide-brimmed black riding

helmet, her lavalike eyes narrow. I know her well enough now to recognize her angry face. But two can play this game, so I stand in place and give it right back to her. I refuse to let her make me feel bad. She shakes her head and turns her attention back to the horse, slowly flipping onto her stomach to slide gently down his side, constantly running her hands over him and talking to him reassuringly.

Facing away from me, she takes the reins of the bridle and slowly lifts them over his head, like he's made of porcelain or something. I try not to check her out, but as usual, I fail. The thick brown braid hanging down her back is like an arrow directing my eyes straight to the way she fits in her skintight jeans. *Start here!* it says, pointing my focus to her slim waist, then the feminine curve of her hips, and finally to her firm round ass. It isn't one of those skinny flat asses either; she's sporting some curves. She isn't willowy and weak; she's slender and strong. I assume working on a farm and spending long hours in the saddle are to thank for that.

It cuts my perusal of her body short when she spins around and spits fire.

"What the fuck do you think you are doing? Flying in here like a bat out of hell? Scaring the bejesus out of my horse?"

"You must be confused," I bite back, resting one elbow on the roof of my car and trying to look more casual than I feel. "That is *my* horse. And you removed it from *my* property without *my* permission. I came to work to find one of our most valuable assets missing, and now I probably have dings in my Porsche from having to race around on gravel roads looking for him."

She sniffs haughtily and tips her chin up defiantly at me.

"Sounds like you should look into a more practical car. Minnie Mouse's slipper isn't exactly an ideal farm vehicle."

"I feel like I've said this to you before but…that's your takeaway here?" I reply, raw disbelief bleeding into my tone.

"Yeah, Vaughn, it is," she continues, absentmindedly holding a cookie out to Double Diablo, who is watching us intently with wide black eyes. "I have a phone. Presumably you know how to call and text people. That would have been a good place to start."

She has a point.

"This is still your property. I rode him through the pastures up to the house so I could work with him. *On my day off*," she emphasizes.

I cross my arms and look at the ground. "Okay," I grumble and give a pebble a swift kick.

She looks at me like I've grown extra heads and then launches back in, "Incredible! And now you've got the gall to stand here and sulk about your stupid car while accepting zero accountability for almost killing me?" She scoffs. "Typical trust fund baby behavior."

I. See. Red.

I hate that implication. It's one I've grown up having to shoulder. In my mind, I've worked my ass off to get where I am. I'm not completely naive though. I'm aware of the boosts my privilege has bought for me. The doors my family name has opened. The struggles I've bypassed. But I haven't sat back and coasted either. I don't need a participation medal for showing up, but I despise being lumped in with my peers who spend all day golfing at the country club and collecting interest payments on their investment accounts. I've put myself to use.

I can feel the heat of the ruby stain crawling up my neck. I hate that I'm offended, that her words have landed in the worst way possible. Full of tension, I turn to take a few clipped steps back to my impractical car when I feel something thump me right between the shoulder blades.

I freeze, facing away from her, and hear muffled giggling.

"Billie," I bark out, "did you just throw something at me?"

The giggling morphs into a loud snort.

I turn around in slow motion to find her laughing into the hand plastered over her mouth, reins drooping in the other. Her saucer-size eyes glitter with unshed tears.

"You are unstable." She is unbelievable. "Did you seriously just throw something at me?"

She nods her head, lips pressing together, obviously trying to hold back laughter.

"It was a treat," she chokes out. "Throwing them seems to have brought DD around."

I want to say I don't find this funny, because I shouldn't, but her amusement is infectious. And the aftereffects of all that tension make me feel giddy.

I smirk. "I'm pretty sure you haven't been throwing them *at* him."

She shrugs. "He doesn't make me as mad."

Point taken. Giving her a curt nod, I turn to leave.

"Vaughn," she calls out, "stop."

I keep going, opening my car door.

"Good lord, don't be such a bitch baby."

I can't help it. I bark out a harsh laugh against my will and turn back to take her in.

"Billie Black, did you just call your employer a bitch baby?" I say, giving her an incredulous look.

"Yeah, yeah." She grins as she walks toward the small pen beside the house. "Turn your fine trust fund ass around, and come have a beer with me. I owe you an apology."

This woman is absolutely astonishing.

Almost as astonishing as the fact that I am turning my "fine ass" around and waiting for her by the front steps. *What am I thinking?*

# CHAPTER 11

## Billie

AFTER SETTLING DD INTO THE PADDOCK JUST OUTSIDE MY back door and tossing him some fresh hay, I make my way back out front to find Vaughn sitting on the porch swing. He looks almost too big to be sitting on it, too broad, too tall, too *much*.

I've always thought he looked edible in a suit, if a little ridiculous on the farm in the middle of nowhere. But this jeans and a T-shirt look definitely tops the office candy one he usually has going.

A heathered gray V-neck leaves a lot less to the imagination than a dress shirt. I can almost see the lines beneath the fabric that I traced that night with my finger. The outline of his pectorals is square and stands out over his flat stomach and tapered waist. I wonder if he'd lift it up just a few inches so I could actually see what's under there. My working hypothesis is that there's a six-pack. Eight-pack is also possible. Those last two abs might just pop out because he's so uptight he's constantly clenching.

I breeze up the steps. "Come on in, Boss Man," I say, holding the door open for him.

He looks at me like I'm a grenade that could go off at any moment but follows anyway. Smart man.

I chuckle to myself. It makes sense Mr. Uptight would be nervous around me. I haven't exactly proven myself as cool and collected where he's concerned. But it's like he knows where my secret switchboard is and knows exactly which switch to flip to make me fly off the handle.

Waltzing into the kitchen, I open the fridge and grab two frosty glass bottles before turning back to face him across the island.

"Lager or pale ale?" I ask, holding up both options.

"Lager," he replies, pointing at the amber bottle.

I turn toward the cupboards. "Excellent. Bottle, glass, or sippy cup?"

I don't even need to look behind myself to know he is shaking his head since I seem to provoke that response from him frequently.

"Sippy cup it is." I wink over my shoulder with a sly smile.

"Bottle is good." He sighs and, sure enough, shakes his head.

I twist the cap off and slide the beer across to him before leaning against the opposite counter and taking a swig of my beer.

He looks tired. Like, exhausted. Hot, always stupid hot,

but honestly a little haggard with disheveled hair and a tense set to his mouth. He sits on the barstool, shoulders slumped over the island. Guilt niggles at me, and I press my palm just above my breasts to push it away. With a dark lock flopped over his forehead, he looks like a lost little boy.

He stares at his beer bottle, silently picking at the label. I don't know what to say to him, so I let my typical instinct take over. I'm going to feed him.

"Do you have any food allergies?"

Dark chocolate eyes shoot up to mine. "No."

"Are you a picky bitch about eating anything?"

"No." He focuses back on his bottle again but quirks up one side of his sinful mouth.

I've been up close and personal with that mouth, so it's hard to forget. Some nights, when I'm alone in bed, I relive our interaction against the fence that night and kick myself for not just kissing the colossal idiot. My mind plays out what it would have been like, where we would have ended up. And then I usually flash to the hundreds of pictures of him on the internet with some new and expensive-looking woman draped on his arm, and I give my head a shake. No distractions and no rich playboys. Nope. No sirree. Not for this gal. Career goals and nice normal dudes are the winning ticket.

Without a word to him, I pull out a couple steaks from the fridge and walk out the back door to fire up the barbecue. I check in on DD. He looks happy in his new special digs, and I like knowing he's out there. The weekends have been lonely at the house all by myself, so I cleaned the pen up specifically hoping I could get him over here at some point. We'd been having a nice leisurely walk over until the man-child had to burn in here and ruin it. The good news is DD rebounded quickly; he didn't stay worked up. The little chicken pulled himself together. He's trusting me.

When I rejoin Vaughn in the kitchen, he hasn't really moved, except now he's tearing up the label and leaving little torn pieces in a pile.

I season the steaks and wash and chop the vegetables for skewers right in front of him, but he says nothing. His pile continues to grow until I can't take it anymore. "Are you building a baby bonfire there, Boss Man?"

He stops.

"Sorry. I kind of zoned out. I didn't really even realize what I was doing." He sighs and leans back.

"Something on your mind?" I probe, not looking up from cutting the zucchini into perfect coins.

"Too much," he responds on an audible exhale, piercing me with his dark eyes.

He's looking more and more like a storm cloud. It's easy to forget he's really my boss when we're being so combative with each other. My filter falls to the wayside, and I say regrettable things, often just for the sake of riling him up. Super mature, I know. But now his silence and contemplative looks are getting me worried. I chance another look up at him as I move on to boiling the potatoes. He's still staring at me.

"Look, I'm sorry. I owe you an apology. Maybe more than one apology, actually. I haven't been my most professional around you. I'll be the first to admit that you have a super special ability to just completely set me off. And I know I have a temper. It's not my best character trait," I ramble on, "but I love working here. The staff, the horses." I sigh wistfully. "The whole place is a dream."

He says nothing.

"And look!" I exclaim, pointing out the back wall of windows. "I'm even riding your devil horse with a modicum of success. He'll be ready to race this season! I promise you—"

"Billie," he cuts me off, "stop rambling."

"You just looked like…I don't know. Like you were coming up with ways to fire me or something."

Vaughn blinks slowly and massages his temples. "Some days, you're a lot of work. But no. I was trying to come up with a way to apologize to you," he grumbles.

Oh. Well, that's a relief.

"Is that why you looked so constipated?"

*God, Billie, really?* Yup. That's what I come up with. Even I impress myself sometimes.

He holds both hands up in front of himself and drops his mouth open as if to say, "Seriously?"

"Where did you learn your manners?" he asks.

"Private school. Where rich kids get away with behaving badly." I turn to get our steaks going on the barbecue.

"And here I could have sworn wolves raised you," he says to my back.

To be fair, he's not far off.

"Just call me Mowgli," I toss over my shoulder as I head out the door.

The rest of our dinner passes in peace. We sit at the antique dining table and make polite small talk as the evening sun slowly descends behind the mountains. He compliments me on dinner and even takes seconds. At one point, I tell him I accept his nonapology apology, which earns me a dramatic eye roll.

When I offer him another beer, he merely grunts and shoos me away while he takes over cleanup. While he does the dishes, I perch on the kitchen counter, enjoying the way his corded forearms flex and ripple as he scrubs the dishes. Has any man ever made doing domestic chores look this good?

Vaughn's frame is so large that even though I try to move away from the sink, we're not that far apart. Maybe a foot separates my thigh from his waist. And yeah, I'm looking. No man with a face like his should also be able to fill out a pair of jeans the way he does. It's almost criminal. All sharp masculine planes and dark brooding eyes paired with these powerful toned legs.

It's not fair. At least I can take comfort in the fact that his personality sucks. Or at least that's what I tell myself.

"I think we should try to be friends," I blurt out.

He snorts and continues scrubbing the plate in his hand.

"I'm serious. I'm tired of being combative. I don't want to walk on eggshells around you anymore. Water under the bridge and all that," I say, waving my hand dismissively. "Sitting here with you is better than sitting here alone all the time."

Okay, maybe that was taking it a bit far. But deep down,

I know that even in his weird mood and with his sucky personality, having some human company is a pleasant change of pace.

"Okay, Mowgli," he replies with a faint smirk, still avoiding eye contact.

I swat his chest playfully and then dramatically pull my hand back to myself as though I'm cradling an injury. "Are you wearing a bulletproof vest under there?" I tease.

He finally graces me with a wry but forced smile. "Gotta be ready for anything around you, Billie."

We sink back into silence. He's unusually contemplative tonight. I haven't been able to find a single trace of smugness. And trust me, I've spent all night looking. I just gave him a perfect opening to lay a cocky remark down on me, and he let it sail right past his head.

After a few beats of total quiet, I sneak a peek at him out of the corner of my eye. He looks very serious. I can't help but wonder what's going through his mind. I lean closer, like I'll be able to see his thoughts floating around somewhere down in his ear canal. (I can't.)

I drink him in from this proximity. Dark stubble peppers his cheeks and neck, and a dusting of chest hair peeks at me from the lowest dip of his V-neck. The fresh smell of laundry detergent is a new addition to his sweet almond scent. He's intoxicating, and I breathe him in against my better judgment.

"Do friends sniff each other?" he asks.

*Fuck*. Busted.

I clear my throat and shift back away from him. "No, but

they check in with each other when they can tell something is wrong," I reply, picking at something on my sweater that isn't there.

I think I've struck a nerve because he leans forward, gripping the counter, and drops his head.

I sigh. "Vaughn, are you okay?"

A strangled *no* escapes his full lips. Like it physically pains him to even respond to me at all.

My heart cracks a little at his broken tone, his defeated posture. I might not like him very much, but he sounds borderline distraught. He's been strength and confidence since I met him, and it feels just wrong to see him like this.

A tight lump forms in my throat, and I can't help but reach out to him. I pause when my hand gets close to his face. He shows no signs of distress at my proximity, so I push my hand closer, stroking a loose lock of his hair between my thumb and middle finger before reverently combing it back into place, dragging a few tips of my fingers against the scalp of his bowed head.

He doesn't move, and I'm emboldened to repeat the motion a couple of times. His eyelids flutter shut. The shadows from the porch light play across his profile, and I lick my lips. This brooding schtick is dangerous.

*Get your shit together, Billie.*

"Want to talk about it?"

He shakes his head.

My hand rests softly on the back of his neck when I whisper, "Do you need a hug?"

The silence in the house is deafening, and I shift

awkwardly on the counter, already regretting my offer. I'm mentally chastising myself so hard that I almost miss his quiet, "Yes."

Vaughn rises and with one large side step moves between my legs. When he almost instantly wraps his steely arms around my waist, I can't hold back the sigh that escapes my lips. He feels so warm and solid pressed up against me—soft and vulnerable.

I snake both my arms around his neck, and we melt into each other. I've never hugged a person who needed to be held so badly. It should feel strange, hugging your boss like this, but wrapping myself around Vaughn Harding in the middle of my kitchen feels like the most natural thing in the world.

The air thrums between us as he burrows his face in my neck. My skin prickles with awareness at the feel of his stubble. I wish I could pry him open and figure out what's wrong, but I also know we only talk about our darkest thoughts when we're good and ready. God knows I have enough of my own secrets lurking beneath the surface.

Sometimes silence is what a person really needs.

I don't know how long we stand there holding each other. I'm zoned out until I feel Vaughn's thumb draw soft circles on the small of my back, just beneath the hemline of my sweater. Skin on skin. Arousal races up my spine, and my relaxed heartbeat crescendos. I don't want to ruin the moment, but I also can't help the way my body reacts to his touch. It's something deep and undeniable, a chemical reaction. Like pouring vinegar over baking soda.

I sigh and arch into his chest, feeling the hardness of his body rasp across my erect nipples.

"Billie." His voice is raw when he whispers my name against the shell of my ear. When he draws back to look at me, his eyes are hazy, more lidded than usual. Apparently, our embrace wasn't wreaking havoc on only my will.

I know I shouldn't, but I reach up and drag one hand through his dark hair. Vaughn's chest rumbles, and he drops his forehead against mine. My inner thighs clench his hips as I press myself closer. This is altogether too intimate, and I know it. He knows it too. But neither of us seem able to stop ourselves.

When he gently feathers the tips of his fingers up the side of my neck, goose bumps pour down between my shoulder blades. He strokes the bottom of my chin, and I tip my face up to bask in the heat of his gaze. My body follows the lead of his, like it's the most natural thing in the world.

And when his warm lips descend onto mine, I sigh, like we've done this a million times before.

The kiss is chaste. Reverent.

But my body doesn't care. It reacts like this is the most passionate kiss in the history of mankind. My breath stutters in my lungs, my stomach drops, the arches of my feet ache, and my core goes damp all at once.

*This might be the best kiss of my life.*

I pull away on a gasp. *What the fuck am I thinking?*

Vaughn steps back instantly, holding his hands up like I'm a scared animal. "I'm sorry."

"No. I'm sorry."

I press the tips of my fingers onto my lips, trying to erase the feeling of his imprinted on mine. We'd been yelling at each other not two hours ago. What is wrong with us? I slip off the counter, needing some space from his body—from *him*. Like space is what will somehow dull the intense tug I feel toward him now.

"Water. Want some water?" I offer as I round the island to grab a glass.

"Fuck, Billie. That was so out of line. I'm all fucked up. The hug was..." He combs his hands through his hair. His chest rises to full height and then falls on a whoosh of air, almost vibrating with tension. "I needed the hug. Thank you. But I took advantage." Dark, sincere eyes dart to mine. "I'm so sorry. It won't happen again."

I stare straight back at him. "It *can't* happen again. But you did not take advantage. We can chalk the whole thing up to temporary insanity."

The corner of his mouth tips up, but he looks melancholy as I move to sit at the kitchen table.

"Why don't you sit down?" I point to the opposite end of the rectangular table. "At that end, so there's no funny business, and tell me what's going on."

He groans and shakes his head. Apparently too fucking macho to talk about his feelings.

I hold one hand across my heart. "Vaughn Harding, I solemnly swear that I will go back to relentlessly taunting you effective Monday morning. No one keeps a secret better than me." I look up at the ceiling momentarily. *If he only knew.* "Trust me."

His dark eyes dart around the house before landing on me. He looks like DD, avoiding eye contact. Scared of making a connection.

He sits across from me, hands flat on the table, and says, "I don't know where to start."

Less is more in a situation like this, so I say nothing. I know I won't be able to solve whatever is eating at him, but I also know that being able to tell someone, anyone, is cathartic. For me, that someone is horses.

His fingers trace the grain of the wood tabletop, swirling around every knot, gliding down every line. It's almost hypnotic.

"First, I was angry." Vaughn's voice is so soft that I barely hear him. "Now..." He looks away, out the dark window. "Now, I just feel overwhelmingly sad. Helpless. And I don't know how to get out from underneath it. I don't know how to stop."

Sounds familiar to me.

"Everyone keeps telling me how I *should* feel. What the proper stages of grief are," he scoffs, "or whatever. But it's not a fit, you know?"

I nod. I do know.

"I was only ten when my dad died. Of course, I was devastated, but it just didn't hit me the same. I didn't understand it the same. My brother up and left, my mom struggled, and my grandfather stepped in to fill that void through the most memorable years of my life. And now, I'm just..." His voice cracks, and he clears his throat to bat it away. "Really fucking sad. I keep hoping that I can prove him innocent, clear his reputation, but I don't think I can."

I trail my finger down the outside of my glass, watching the condensation trickle in its wake. "Maybe he's not innocent."

Vaughn's head shoots up to look at me.

"Maybe he's not, and, you know, that's okay. People aren't black and white; they're just shades of gray. Maybe he did some bad things, made some bad choices, but that doesn't make him *bad*. It doesn't negate all the wonderful things he did for you or the important role he played in your life. He can be both." I huff out a breath. This is a conversation I've had many a time. Except with a horse. Best listeners in the world. Telling another human is new, but I forge ahead. "You can feel disappointed and angry and sad and whatever the fuck else you want to feel. You can feel whatever you want. There is no right order or right way. You're entitled to it all. Because at the end of the day, he's not here to explain things to you, so it all just comes down to how much you can forgive. How much you can accept. And there's not a single other person in the world who can tell you what that threshold is." I look up at him now. "But you need to keep searching for it, no matter how much it hurts, because otherwise it will eat you alive."

"Jesus." Vaughn drops his head into his hands and mumbles, "Never thought I'd be getting good advice from crazy Billie Black. How do you know all this?"

"Because I'm still looking for that threshold."

# CHAPTER 12

## Vaughn

ONE MONTH LATER

I STAND AT THE TOP OF THE BLEACHERS, STARING THROUGH the set of binoculars Hank just handed me. At the far corner of the track, I can see a little black bullet breezing around the corner, head and neck stretched out long, legs moving like a blur across the dirt track. Billie, long bronze braid flying out in the wind behind her, hunches down low on his neck, keeping herself light and aerodynamic.

I lower my hands and glance over at Hank. My look of disbelief meets his look of pure joy. I mean, the man is positively beaming. His smile threatens to crack his sun-worn face right open. I shake my head, like what I'm seeing is an illusion I can clear away with the motion. Once more, I lift the binoculars and peer back through the lenses to drink in the pair out on the track. They move as one. Like what they're doing together is as natural as breathing.

That's how Billie felt in my arms. She felt *right*.

I'm entranced by their faces when they turn down the home stretch and barrel toward us. DD—I've accepted he is never going to be called Double Diablo by anyone other than me and the track announcer—looks relaxed and determined. I'd almost say he looks like he's having fun. And Billie, my *friend* Billie, has a satisfied smirk on her face. She looks wild and free…and beautiful. Like she belongs up there. I can't hold back the genuine smile that takes over my face.

"Astonishing, isn't it?" Hank asks as I continue to watch them.

"She—they—yes, they are." I absently hand him the binoculars back and watch Billie stand up in the irons to draw DD up, slowing him down. He flicks one ear to her, in tune with every movement—the shift of her shoulders, the drop of her hips. He responds to the directions her body gives him almost instantly. No fighting at all.

The whole thing is impressive. Some horses take a good chunk of time to calm down enough to drop their speed and even more to relax after getting all hyped up. But DD seems perfectly amenable to all Billie's requests.

I reluctantly tear my eyes away from the dirt track to look at Hank again, standing in his signature jeans and polo shirt with that knowing sparkle in his eye. Like he knows something you don't.

"What? You want me to admit that you were right about hiring her?"

"No, son." His cheek twitches.

"Okay. So you're just taking pleasure knowing that my plan to get rid of her is looking like it might backfire?"

He lets out a booming laugh, slapping my shoulder on his way past, rocking me back on my heels with his old-man strength. Smug prick.

I hate admitting he was right, but this was a show of force on Billie's part. I can't deny I'm more than a little excited. And relieved. Gold Rush Ranch desperately needs something to put us back on the map. I don't want to get my hopes up, but god, I hope Double Diablo is that something.

I don't even think I'd be sad about Billie sticking around anymore. She's grown on me. Enough that I've continued showing up on her porch like a sad puppy every Saturday, even though she never really extended the invite. She looked a little surprised the first time I knocked on her door, but she didn't send me away.

I like her company. I like her wacky sense of humor. I like the way her hips sway while she hums and cooks me dinner. I like the person I've become around her—unconcerned with the drama of the media and the country club crowd. I like the taste of her lips too, the little sighing sound she made when I kissed her, but I've been able to restrain myself from crossing that line again. Because that is the line that neither of us needs to blur. The farm can't take any more drama, and Billie doesn't need me thinking with my dick.

Sounds cliché, but hiding out in Ruby Creek has been almost healing for me. Leaving behind the office, the city, the pressure, is refreshing in a way I couldn't have predicted. I understand why my grandfather loved it out here. Tracing his steps around the farm gives me solace. I think I'm even working toward forgiving him.

Finding that threshold.

Finding a new rhythm.

Like getting to my office early every morning just to watch Billie ride DD bareback over the hill. Then I bring her down a cup of coffee. I even put cream in it now. Although sometimes, I try to put not *quite* enough in it just to see if there's a point where she'll lose it and say something. So far, all it's gotten me is a little sideways glare I try not to smile at. We drink our coffee at the paddock and have a little morning meeting about the farm and plans for the upcoming season. Hank often joins us, shooting speculative glances, like Billie and I getting along is truly suspicious to him.

Everything isn't perfect though. I'm still nervous about the future of the farm. About stepping back into Bell Point Park and being able to hold my head high considering the shame I feel over the scandal. Nervous about proving my asshole brother wrong. He wants me back in the office working at Gold Rush Resources, not wasting my time "playing Farmer Joe." Just thinking about it all is a bucket of ice water over a good mood.

I scrub my hand across my face, trying to wash all my worries away, and look back down at the track to see Billie has dismounted and DD is following her toward the gate like a lost puppy dog. It makes me chuckle. That horse is a total goner for her. I take long strides down the benches of the bleachers and head toward the gate to give Billie a metaphorical pat on the back. If her constantly babying that black stallion can save the farm's future, well, then Billie might just be my greatest asset.

I round the corner to find her hugging a small blond woman, both jumping up and down squealing while they embrace. Billie is so dramatic. You'd think they just won the derby. The blond's head shoots up with startled eyes when I clear my throat. She tries to extricate herself from the hug, but Billie has her tiny body tangled up in her graceful arms.

"Shh. Just ignore him. He'll ruin it," she whisper-shouts.

I place my hands on my hips and look to the sky, a silent prayer for patience.

"Billie, I was watching you guys out there. I came to reinforce you with some kind words so I can get back to work. Stop wasting my time."

She giggles like she's drunk into the small woman's shoulder.

"Hi, Mr. Harding," the blond says in a shaky voice while reaching her hand around Billie to shake mine.

"Nice to see you, Violet. Please, call me Vaughn." I shake her hand and then grip the middle of Billie's braid and gently pull her head back from where she's burrowed, forcing her to look up at me.

She might be tall, but I'm taller.

Untamed amber eyes flash to mine from under the brim of her black helmet, and Violet can finally step away. She finds something interesting to look at on the ground as Billie and I stare at each other in a face-off. Excitement courses through me. I like to compete, and we haven't done this in a while. Her breathing is slightly labored, but I assume that results from galloping a twelve-hundred-pound animal around in the warm spring sun. My gaze drifts over her flushed cheeks and delicate collarbones sprinkled with freckles before landing on her perfect bow-shaped mouth. Her tongue darts out to wet her bottom lip. And in a matter of seconds, Billie, *my friend Billie*, has taken me from exasperated to aroused.

*God.* I am pathetic.

"Congratulations. Double Diablo looks great. Very impressive." My words come out rigid and stilted.

She watches me with a knowing smile and hits me with a saucy wink. "Thanks, Boss Man."

"I'm going to go and get started on cleaning some tack," Violet interjects before basically sprinting away.

"That's my awkward little Violet," Billie says affectionately.

"You're incorrigible." I shake my head in disapproval.

"Okay, you can drop the private school vocabulary now. No one is here to impress. Your name alone is already a big enough testament to how expensive you are."

"Excuse me?"

"Vaughn Harding," she announces, pronouncing it with an English accent and rolling one hand through the air, folding into a bow.

I attempt to bite back the unwanted smile that's threatening to take over my face. I fail.

"Whatever, Mowgli" is my response. "We need to talk about jockeys for Double Diablo. The suspension lifts in July."

"Stop calling him that. He's a sweet, sensitive boy, and that name is stupid."

I ignore her. "I have a guy with an impressive record lined up for when you think the time is right."

She turns away to remove the saddle from DD's back. "I'll look at him. We're going to need someone special, Vaughn. It's going to take more than a winning record to get this horse to run in an actual race." She hefts the tack onto the fence and adds, "I don't think he should stay at the track. It's too stimulating, and I wasn't joking about him being sensitive. He needs peace and quiet. I'll trailer him the day of and then bring him home after the race."

"Billie, he's a racehorse, not a puppy. You know that, right?"

She shoots me a withering look. "You gonna hop on and take over his training?"

I look at the horse. He seems pretty docile these days, calmer than most stallions I've known, but she has a point. I take a step forward and surrender. "Okay, okay."

Her shoulders climb high and then fall on a big relieved sigh before she completely changes the subject. "I have a killer meal planned for tomorrow night. The veggie stand had the most incredible-looking asparagus so I'm going to make—"

I raise one hand to slow her down. "Actually, there's a fundraiser they have asked me to attend tomorrow."

Her hand freezes midstroke on DD's shoulder, and her eyebrows pop up. "No problem," she says.

Her shoulders droop incrementally from their typical

proud spot, and she pastes a weird smile on her face. It's like watching a balloon deflate right before my eyes. *And you were the one to stick the pin into it, asshole.*

I take a step closer, wanting to comfort her without overstepping our tenuous boundaries. "Billie, I'm sorry. I should have mentioned it earlier."

She looks down and turns abruptly, horse in hand, to leave. "Have fun!" she shouts too brightly over her shoulder while hustling away to the barn.

Standing here, watching her leave, I'm tossed into a pool of total confusion. I didn't think our Saturday night dinners were so formal that I needed to let her know I wouldn't be there. I'm not accustomed to accounting for friends in my schedule.

My stomach hits me with a new flipping sensation, like I'm hurtling toward the ground on a roller coaster. A ride I want to get off. This doesn't feel good. I can't remember the last time I felt bad for letting someone down, let alone sick over it. But I sure as fuck do now.

# CHAPTER 13

## Billie

It's go time. I slam the door on the truck attached to the black trailer with the Gold Rush Ranch logo splashed across the side. Inside that trailer is the ebony horse that my career is banking on.

I'm nervous. Nervous as fuck. But I also *know* that DD is ready and up to the challenge. We have spent the last few months preparing for his first race. He's been on the practice track, in the fields and forest, and I've even let Violet breeze him a few times just to see how he'd handle a different rider. The last few weekends, I've trailered him down to the races just to desensitize him to how loud and busy it will be today. He's fit and mentally prepared.

Me? Not so much.

I know I shouldn't let myself think about it, but today's race is a qualifier for the prestigious Denman Derby. Go big or go home, right? I haven't vocalized my plan. That makes it too real—too ripe for disappointment. But I think we can do it. If we start off right, he only needs to win a couple races to qualify. I don't want to run him into the ground; he's not the type of horse to go out and make money every weekend. He needs to do *just* enough and then kick back and relax until the big day.

I secretly have it all plotted out.

I paid the extra fee to register him late, which means our competitors won't see us coming. He is literally the dark horse, and I have everything planned out to a T. The only thing that's a minor unknown is the jockey. Vaughn's brother, Cole, has apparently made a huge deal about being half owner and having to use this guy because he knows him or some shit. It borderline enrages me he's using this horse and me to foster family connections for the Hardings. This "I'll rub your dick if you rub mine" mentality pisses me off. It's the garbage I left behind for a reason. But I know there's a time and a place to smile and nod, and, well, this might just be one of those times.

Vaughn and I have been distant since he bailed on our Saturday night dinner. I have no right to be angry with him, yet I can't deny the intense disappointment I felt. Or the twinge of jealousy that flared behind my solar plexus at the thought of him out with another woman on what was meant to be *our* night. It seems like he doesn't quite know what to say either, so shit is awkward now. Snark has been the lifeblood of our friendship since day one, but neither of us seems to have the heart for it anymore. The truth of the matter is I like Vaughn. More than I should. He might be a tad smug and broody, okay; he sometimes borders on pompous. But I know he's a good person trying to do his best. Maybe I didn't see it at first, but he's worked hard in the face of immense pressure and grief.

Aside from our first misunderstanding and a little verbal sparring here and there, he's never treated me (or anyone else) in any way that wasn't plain gentlemanly. So it sucks that our friendship seems to have fizzled. After he canceled a couple of Saturday dinners in a row, I kind of got the hint. We've been nothing short of cordial and professional—if a little cool.

I drive along the major highway, pulling DD in the rig behind me. It's raining now, not ideal for his first race. My stomach flip-flops nonstop. The feeling pools in my gut and crawls all the way up my throat. I couldn't even eat this morning. I suspect I'll be living on coffee today. Who knows? Maybe I'll even take up smoking. Seems like a good thing to do with my hands when I'm nervous. Plus, I'd look so much cooler puffing on a cigarette than wringing my hands.

The drive passes by quickly, and I focus on deep breathing and letting the constant swing of the wipers across the windshield lull me into some semblance of calm. It's borderline meditative. And when I pull into the stabling at the track, I feel a little relaxed.

I had my freak-out in private. Now it's time to put my game face on. DD doesn't need to pick up on my anxiety, and neither does the staff around me. I want to say there is no pressure, that this race is just for practice, but it feels like so much more. The farm's first weekend back at the track. My debut. DD's debut.

*No big deal.*

I drop out of the big truck in front of our bank of stalls here at Bell Point Park to see Violet already waiting for me. She looks stressed too. Wide blue eyes. Pursed lips. Bun so tight I wonder if her face hurts.

I wave at her and call out, "Hey, Vi! You ready to show these amateurs how it's done?"

That garners me a small smile. "So ready."

A firm grip lands on my shoulder, and I turn to see Hank grinning at me. My big old comfort blanket. "They're not going to see the little black bullet coming. He's like a secret weapon that you ladies have under wraps. I can't wait to see the race and hear the buzz."

All three of us grin at each other like loons. Stress does weird things to people, and I am not immune to the effects. The only thing that breaks up our creepy anxiety party is DD's loud stomp and snort summoning me, his slave, to get him out of the trailer and provide him with some food. We unload him without incident, make sure he's set with food and water, and then I go in search of my very special jockey, leaving DD behind with Violet to ensure he's the shiniest version of himself for his big debut.

On my stroll through the stables, I soak up the hustle and bustle of race day. The sounds of horses snorting, their aluminum shoes ticking against concrete, the whoosh of grain being added to a bucket. It's almost sensory overload behind the scenes in the stables, but to me, it's comforting to be back at the track.

I live for this.

Within a few minutes, I reach the main administrative building that is all offices on the main floor and boasts skyboxes and meeting rooms on the upper levels. It's about two hours to race time, and I'm due to meet Vaughn and our fancy new jockey in the owner's lounge upstairs. Make introductions, talk strategy, get everything set just right. I would have liked to talk to the guy earlier, paid him for a few practice rides, really hammered out the details of how specific DD could be. But apparently he's too busy. He gets thrown on a horse just before the race and then hops off at the end to go back to hobnobbing it with the suits.

As I climb the stairs, I hear the dull hum of dry conversation and the clink of ice against glass. I breach the doorway and take in the large room. Everyone else is crammed onto metal benches, drinking Budweiser from the can, but up here, it's all luxury. Floor-to-ceiling glass provides a completely uninterrupted view of the track. Plush brown leather couches and armchairs with nailhead details look out through the windows.

I continue scanning the room. I swear I feel Vaughn before I see him. Like a tug right at the solar plexus. We've spent so many of our interactions in the last month tiptoeing around each other that I feel especially attuned to his presence. When I finally turn in his exact direction, I find him already staring at me, head turned away from the conversation he's a part of, his deep chocolate eyes lasered in on me.

I drink him in like frozen lemonade on a hot day. Except it's cool and pouring outside.

What a specimen. He looks so good in this setting. If he looked happier, I would say that it suits him perfectly. But he looks predictably detached. Not at all like the man who would have a beer at my kitchen counter while I cooked for him. His perfectly tailored dark blue suit and signature white shirt contrast beautifully with his inky locks. They're gelled into place flawlessly, and all that makes me want to do is run my fingers through it and pull a few tresses free. Loosen him up a bit.

Under the scrutiny of his gaze, an unconscious shiver racks my body. I can't prevent it, don't even really want to—don't even try. I know I'm admiring him openly and he's scowling back at me. Which is a positive in my book. I still get high from rattling his control. Watching him lose his cool is basically a drug for me, and I know this look. It's the "pull yourself together" look, and it's meant to intimidate me.

But the joke's on him. All it does is set me on fire.

I flash him my best beauty queen smile and a secret wink as I head his way, which garners me an almost imperceptible agitated sort of head shake. *Ha. I win.* He thinks he's subtle, but I've spent the last decade of my life studying body language and using it to my advantage with horses. People are no different. Same shit, different pile.

I stride up to the group of three men just in time to hear Vaughn introducing me. "Gentlemen, I'd like you to meet the resident head trainer for us at Gold Rush Ranch," he says, gesturing toward me amiably, "Billie Black."

I reach forward to take the hand of a small middle-aged

man with watery eyes and sandy-colored hair, who I'm assuming is our new jockey.

"Billie, this is Patrick Cassel, Double Diablo's new jockey."

"Nice to meet you, Patrick," I reply cordially, shooting Vaughn daggers as subtly as possible for still calling my horse Double Diablo. *What a dick.*

I shake Patrick's limp hand, the lamest type of handshake, and he gives me a flat smile. "How lucky for me. Canada's long-lost princess."

Panic suffuses me as I focus on schooling my features. I've always known this day would come. Someone was bound to recognize me eventually. After all, I've basically been hiding in plain sight. My plan all along has been to ignore it, and I will not deviate from that plan now. I see Vaughn's eyebrow quirk up out of the corner of my eye, but I just stare back at Patrick with a bored smile on my face.

I pivot to the other man in the group, wanting to move the conversation along. I would say I don't recognize him, except he looks an awful lot like Vaughn. Not as tall or refined, somehow coarser, more muscular. Cunning gray eyes rather than warm brown, but the same inky dark hair and the same facial features. If Vaughn is a soccer player, this guy is a football player. But the resemblance is unmistakable.

Vaughn's hand comes to rest on my lower back as he motions me toward who I'm sure is his older brother. "And this," he almost growls, "is Cole Harding. My brother and co-owner of Gold Rush Ranch."

Cole's icy gray eyes hit mine, and the differences between

the two brothers multiply by the moment. This guy is cold as fuck. Where Vaughn is detached and smug, Cole is downright glacial. If I were a wimpier woman, it would intimidate me.

His handshake couldn't be more different from Patrick's. His long fingers wrap around my hand in an absolute vise grip of a handshake. He would have pulled me off balance if I were less fit.

"A pleasure to meet you," he says in the most obnoxious, sardonic kind of voice. Aha. Another rich prick. Condescending by nature.

I put on my debutante smile, pinch my shoulder blades together, and squeeze the living fuck out of his hand right back. "Oh, the pleasure is all mine. I've heard so much about you!"

His eyes narrow at that, and Vaughn's hand slides around my waist to squeeze my hip bone. A silent demand to please not lay the smackdown on his shithead brother, which is fine, but I'm not letting go first. Cole and I stare at each other, squeezing each other's hands to dust. I handle horses for a living, and this guy goes for weekly manicures and holds gold-plated pens. I'm really not worried about winning this pissing match. So I hold on and continue to stare with a fake-ass smile plastered on my face.

That fake-ass smile turns to my jaw swinging in the wind when Vaughn grumbles, "Jesus Christ, Cole. Don't break my trainer."

My head swivels to him as the big brute drops my hand. Did Vaughn just come to my defense?

I turn back to the men, smiling brighter than the sun,

waving my fingers at them like jazz hands even though they hurt like hell. "Bah, nothing I can't handle."

The ice king continues to glare at me. What a riot. He seems like a fun guy. *Said no one ever.*

Vaughn clears his throat, eyes twinkling and lips pursed. I'm almost positive he's trying not to laugh. I can't stop winning today. That has to be a good omen?

"Okay, Billie," Vaughn starts back in. "Cole and I are going to leave you and Patrick to it. If you need me, I'll be in here. You're welcome to join us here for the race."

"No, I think I'll be good down at track level," I reply as Vaughn follows my gaze. "I want to be there for DD at the end."

He gives me the sweetest smile. Small but genuine. And it lights me up. It's like a balm to my nerves. A balm I'm going to need to talk to Patrick after that comment. Does he even know how lucky he is to ride on a horse like DD? Has no one impressed this upon him? He should be kissing someone's shoes in thanks. Instead, he's standing here smirking at me, trying to steer the conversation to places I don't want to go.

*Tool.*

"Okay, Patrick," I start off a little too brightly. "It looks like you have an outstanding record. I'm really excited to see what you can do with DD. He's a very special horse."

The brothers turn to leave, and I get a light squeeze on my elbow as they walk behind me, which I interpret as Vaughn telling me to behave. Does he have so little faith in me to conduct myself professionally? What a vote of confidence.

"Mothers always think their own children are special. I've been in this business long enough to know that a horse is just a horse until it proves itself," Patrick says. "Same can be said for a trainer."

Smiling in the sugariest way possible, because men like this are not a new phenomenon to me in this business, I say, "Well, call me Mother Hen then, Patty. Because you've never ridden a horse like this."

He sniffs and rubs his straight nose at that.

"It's Patrick, and I highly doubt that. I've ridden the best horses in the Pacific Northwest. I'm doing this as a favor to Cole, you know. Our families have been connected for years."

My fingers curl into my palms, nails threatening to puncture the skin.

"Congratulations. I've worked with some of the best horses in the world. You might be a big fish in a small pond, but I'm almost positive I didn't see any big-name derby wins anywhere on your record."

His eyes narrow. My aim for sore spots is exceptional.

"But this horse could actually do that for you. For *us*. So you're going to drop the attitude and listen to me. I don't really need you to believe he's special, but I do need you to execute my plan in a very precise fashion."

He lifts his hand, palm up, to peer down at his nails like he's found something interesting there. Avoiding eye contact he mutters, "I'm listening."

Relief courses through me. DD is depending on me, and I need this dick on board whether I like him or not. "Great. He's a nervous horse. So no whip."

"No whip?" he sneers. "It's just a tool. You are aware it doesn't hurt, right?"

"No. Whip. He doesn't need it, and it scares him."

He twists his face like I'm an idiot.

"Deal with it," I bite back, holding eye contact with him. "He doesn't like the gates. He's going to tense up in there, and I want to use that to our advantage. Off the start, hold him back. Let him own the back of the pack so that he can see the other horses running away from him, okay?"

A terse nod.

"Good. On the first straightaway..."

# CHAPTER 14
## Vaughn

The gates burst open, and the line of horses fly out. I can pick Double Diablo out immediately. Our yellow and black silks make it easy to find him. Under the amber glow of the overhead lights, the falling rain looks somehow suspended in motion, like this is a moment to pause and watch. Everything is about to be caked in mud, but still, DD looks outstanding. All lean muscular lines and gleaming coat. Even from here, I can tell that he's a cut above the rest of the horses out there. He's in his own class.

He leads the pack right out of the gate, surging ahead of the rest to take up an early spot on the rail. Keeping him on the inside of the track means less distance to run, making it a coveted position for a front-runner—which I didn't think this horse was.

They're on the first straightaway now, and Patrick has him absolutely flying. The other horses are eating their dust. I almost can't believe my eyes. To think that three short months ago, no one could get near this horse, and now he's leading the pack under the lights at his first race. It's bewildering.

I shake my head in disbelief and hear Cole beside me say, "Huh," as though he can't quite believe it either. He told me when we first arrived that he "couldn't wait to watch Patrick get dumped on his conceited ass by the crazy horse." It doesn't look like that dream will come to fruition.

Billie's unusual training regimen of trotting him up and down and around in the fields and over the hills and her unique approach of treating him like a lap dog really worked. The horse is spectacular and flourished under her hand. Pride wells up in me. It blooms in my chest and twines in my shoulders, flowing down through my elbows and fingers in a completely unfamiliar way. Like I am itching to hug her, to congratulate her. To tell her how wrong I've been.

I gave Billie what I thought was an impossible task. I believed I set her up to fail, and she gave me the middle finger in the most spectacular way possible. I'm not mad. She's an impressive woman. Smart, tough, kind, beautiful.

And maybe that's the most annoying thing about her. She doesn't annoy me at all anymore.

Watching the pack of horses come into the final bend, I feel a lump of nervousness in my throat. Double Diablo is slipping back. One spot. Two. Now he's lost position on the rail. I shove my hands into my pockets, jangling my keys, trying to give nothing else away with my body. On the final straightaway, I can see our team lagging, like they're losing steam.

Patrick reaches back and gives Double Diablo three hard thwacks with the whip, something I realize I've never seen Billie or Violet do in all the times I snuck around the back of the barn to watch them train.

But it works. It's almost as though the other horses drop into slow motion as Double Diablo flies past them like an avenging wraith. He drops his head and stretches out as far as he can, surging ahead with incredible power to cross the laser finish line a half a length in front of his next closest competitor.

I can't help but grin. I gaze down in wonderment at the little black horse. He's slowed down already, flanks heaving and body all splattered in mud. What a night. What a show. It was close, but a win is a win.

I turn my head slowly to take in my brother beside me. He's staring at the track, arms crossed, not a shred of emotion on his face. Typical. I get something right, and he can't even bring himself to grace me with a smile. I punch him in the shoulder playfully, just to irritate him, in the way that only a little brother can. He scowls at me.

"We did it," I say, smirking, nudging him with my elbow a few times.

He shakes his head and deadpans, "I would rather have watched Patrick get dumped in the mud."

I grab a glass of scotch and turn to lean against the bar, letting my gaze wander around the room in front of me. Cole is sullen, talking to some people he knows. He hates this shit. Always has. And lately I feel like I can't blame him. It's boring. But our dark horse was a winner at his first race, so I am on cloud nine.

A long swig of the amber liquid burns my throat. I feel content in this moment. I have to confess, the thought of this race made me nervous. I had pregame jitters, and this scotch feels both celebratory and soothing. I want Billie to come toast with me.

I see movement at the door and watch Patrick walk in like he's the king of the world or something. Some other owners in the booth who know him offer up light applause, and he takes an obnoxious little bow. As though he was the one who took that horse from zero to hero. The whole scene hammers a little crack into my contentment. I know he rode the horse, but I watched Billie slave over Double Diablo every damn day for months.

And now this tool is up here bowing like he's royalty, already changed out of his muddy silks and into his stupid khakis and polo shirt. Obnoxious little fucker. Billie is the one who deserves a round of applause.

The thought of applauding when she eventually walks in makes me smile. She would *hate* that, which is a great reason for me to do it anyway.

I turn back to the bar, tired of watching Patrick preen, and continue to smile privately over applauding Billie. The more I think about it, the more I really think it's a good idea. She likes it when I pick on her, enjoys the challenge. I know she does.

Zoning out at the bar, musing to myself, I feel the room

go quiet. I turn back to the door to see Billie, wild-eyed and muddy. Covered in raindrops, her bronze braid looks darker than usual. Loose pieces of hair plaster against her forehead, and her eyes look like burning coals. Wearing a black pantsuit, she looks downright scary.

I'm standing here, hands held out like I'm about to clap, but her intensity stops me in my tracks. Focused on where Patrick is standing, she starts her forward motion again, prowling across the room like a panther in her formfitting suit, quiet and deadly. He's facing away from her, gesticulating, like he's recounting the most exciting story in the world. He's clueless about what is coming up behind him.

And within a few moments, I realize I am too. Because Billie stalks up behind the small man, and my brain is obviously a little slow on the uptake, because I am downright floored when she winds up one arm like she's the batter up at a baseball game, racing whip in hand, and gives him one sharp spank smack dab in the middle of his tiny ass.

I spit my mouthful of whiskey out, full spray. And then I gape at the scene in front of me. She just walked up and absolutely whaled on the guy. That is going to leave a welt. He lets out a high-pitched shocked scream and spins around to face Billie. He has to look up to meet her eyes, which gives the whole interaction this funny dynamic where he looks like a little boy who just received a public spanking.

Shock and disbelief course through me. I wipe my mouth across the sleeve of my suit jacket, not caring about the mess. I'm more captivated by the scene in front of me.

"You gonna scream like that," Billie says, gesturing the

whip up and down his body in a condescending way, "and then try to tell me it doesn't hurt?"

Her tone is eerily calm and even. I'm impressed, because she is terrifying right now. I thought I'd seen Billie mad before, but now I feel like all I've seen from her mood is good-humored child's play.

Patrick's face is red. Red, like a dark cherry. Not a maraschino cherry with that bright vibrant dyed color. Like a black cherry. He. Is. Fuming.

"How…how dare you!" he splutters.

Pointing that whip right at his throat, Billie leans down just enough to be exactly at his eye level.

"How. Dare. You. You fucking rat bastard."

Patrick's hand falls across his chest in the most scandalized way. Every eye in the room is on Patrick and Billie. You could hear a pin drop.

"*You* work for *me*. I gave you explicit instructions. I brushed off your small-man-syndrome chauvinistic comments to forge a working relationship. And what did you do?"

"I will not allow you to talk to me this way, Wilhelmina. Though it shouldn't surprise me that Victor Farrington's daughter is just as trashy as he is."

Billie rears back as though someone has slapped her.

Wait. What? Victor Farrington. *Like former Prime Minister Farrington?*

Patrick huffs, puffing his tiny chest out and brushing his shoulder like there's dirt on it. He turns to leave, but she holds the whip out to stop him.

"I'm not done yet, Little Patty. I want to make myself clear, so look me in the eye before you run and hide." She bends even lower, her face coming within only a few inches of his, with the whip still resting on his shoulder. "You will never ride another one of my horses again. You will never come near Double Diablo again. The only view you're going to get of him is of his shiny black ass while you watch him cross the finish line." She lowers the whip and stands up tall. "And as for me? My family has no bearing on my professional life. I'm no mother hen. I'm a fucking mother bear. And you poked me. So when you see me around, I want you to turn and run the other way like the snively little bitch that you are."

From behind me, I hear a sigh and, "I think I'm in love."

I turn to see the bartender staring at the scene in front of her with absolute awe.

She shifts her gaze to me. Pointing over my shoulder, she says, "That lady right there is a stone-cold badass."

*She's not wrong.*

"And you…" Billie starts up again.

Oh god. Who's next? I spin around to see her pointing the whip at my brother, who is rigid like a statue. A soldier through and through. His gray eyes are cold and glacial, while hers are hot and molten. This will not end well for either of them.

"If you ever use me or my horses to win brownie points in your billionaire-baby sandbox, I will bury you there myself. Are we clear?"

Cole looks downright murderous. I move toward Billie to intercept the looming explosion.

"Ms. Black, that is not your horse," he says. "It's my horse. He's an asset."

"Give your head a shake. Before me"—she pokes her chest with her pointer finger—"he was an expensive lawn ornament, not a Denman Derby contender. He is a living, sentient being—not a pawn. And you put him in the hands of an asshole who has *your asset* so scared he can't stop trembling in his stall." She tosses the whip down at his feet, causing Cole to rear back ever so slightly, which is a bigger reaction than I've seen out of him in years. "I will *never* forgive you," she finishes, her voice breaking on the last sentence.

God, I need to get her out of here. Now.

In three long strides, I'm at her side, pressing my hand into her lower back, trying to guide her out the door.

"Don't fucking touch me," she bites out, shrugging me off and waltzing out of the room with her head held high. Like she's royalty. Like she fucking owns this place.

I follow her into the hallway. She looks around like she's unsure where to go and opts to head toward the fire escape at the end of the hallway.

"Billie, slow down," I call as she bursts out the door. She's like a tornado losing potency. I can see her facade starting to crack.

"Leave me alone, Vaughn," she shouts over her shoulder, blowing out into the dark rainy night.

I pause at the door. She's asked me to leave her alone, but I don't want to. I lean back against the wall next to the door, pinching the bridge of my nose. Trying to figure out what to do next.

"Is she okay?" I hear from down the hall.

"Hey, Hank." I drop my hand and look up at the ceiling, "I don't know."

"Did she put on a show at least?" he inquires with a smile in his voice.

A laugh bubbles out of my throat. "Did she ever."

"She's an impressive woman."

I roll the back of my head along the wall to look at him. "She is," I agree honestly.

Hank just smiles, that irritating, knowing smile of his, nods his head, and turns back down the stairs with a wave. I gaze back up at the ceiling, weighing my options, trying to figure out how best to approach her right now.

I reach my left hand up to the emergency exit door and knock three times. "Billie? It's Vaughn. I'll just wait here until you're ready for company."

"Man, you're like the clap. I can't fucking get rid of you" is her muffled response.

My lips quirk. Most women I know would be happy to have me following them around, but not Billie. Nope. To her, I am nothing but a painful STD.

"In that case, I'm coming out," I reply, pushing the bar across the door to open it.

She stands there on the landing of the metal staircase, holding the railing, looking out over the lit-up track. "Careful, Boss Man. I'm liable to murder someone tonight. And you're not exempt from my list."

I stand beside her, leaving a couple feet of distance between us. Just to be safe. I grip the railing and look out over the track. Silent moments stretch into minutes.

"Why didn't you go off on me in there?"

"Lost steam, I guess," is her quiet response.

"I have a hard time believing that."

"Because I know you well enough to know you'll be beating yourself up about it anyway. I don't need to say anything. You'll shoulder your family guilt and any guilt I give you like you're a modern-day Sisyphus or something. And you were probably too busy trying to bang the bartender to watch the race anyways."

That was a low blow, and my fingers clamp down on the metal bar. "Is that really what you think?"

"Sure is," she spits out while turning to rip the door open and head back inside. But not before I can turn and slam a palm down, forcing it closed from behind her. "Vaughn, I am so not in the mood for your trust fund baby temper tantrums right now."

"Billie, turn around."

She stands still, silent. All I can hear is the rain falling heavily on the metal stairs.

"Now." I use my boardroom voice.

She turns quickly then, one hand raised. "You know, go fuck yours—"

I capture her wrist in my hand, push her up against the cold metal door, and press my lips onto hers, interrupting her fighting words in one hard, punishing kiss. She doesn't respond or fight it, so I stop. I'm pinning one wrist above her head when I pull my face back to gauge her reaction.

Her molten eyes bore into mine. Absolute shock paints her feminine face. I cup the base of her skull, brushing the pad of my thumb across the high point of her cheekbone, and smirk back at her. The look on her face is endearing. I want to soften her up and work her up all at the same time. I've learned tonight that I like her like this, all feisty and wild and unpredictable. Her chest is heaving, and she looks cornered, a little bit scared.

"I'm sorry," I breathe.

I expect her to lash out, for more cutting words to fly past her bee-stung lips. Instead, she fists the lapel of my suit jacket and yanks me back into a kiss. Her lips move frantically against mine, so different from our first kiss, burning me up in a way I didn't think a single kiss could.

Raw emotions flow between us. Anger, frustration, tension, and yearning. So much yearning.

She turns from cold, hard stone to flowing lava beneath my hands. Her entire body relaxes under my contact. But our lips are still at war with each other. Nipping. Sucking. Sparring. How she and I have been since the day we met. I fucking love it.

I release her head and slowly trail my hand down to her neck and hold her there for a moment, giving her throat a gentle squeeze, making her whimper into my mouth.

"God. Billie. You drive me crazy," I rasp, desire coating my voice. Because it's true. In every sense of the word, she does.

She pulls back to meet my gaze, wet skin glowing in the low light. She looks beautiful. Painfully so. I watch a droplet of water fall from her hair and roll down to rest in the hollow just above her collarbone. I release her hand and bend down to kiss her there. Her eyes flutter shut and her head tips back.

She moans. And it's like an instant blood rush to my already aching cock. We're fully clothed, and I can't remember the last time I was this painfully hard.

"Vaughn," she whispers, running both her hands through my soaked hair, "what are you doing?"

"Shutting you up," I murmur against her skin as I drag my teeth and feather soft kisses up her throat before giving her ear a good hard nip.

"Mmm," is the muffled sound she makes in response. "You're going to regret this tomorrow."

I stop at that, bringing my pointer finger to the dip just below her bottom lip. I press it there to tip her head back, and her exotic eyes flutter open to meet mine.

"No, I won't," I respond, dragging my finger up toward the seam of her puffy lips.

Eyes glued to mine, she parts her lips and then sucks my finger, hot tongue swirling around it.

"Fuck," I mutter, watching her suck on my finger and stare me down in the most sinful way.

I shift my hips closer, pressing into her so she can feel what she's doing to me. My hard length lines up exactly right with her pelvis. The way she looks right now is fucking criminal. Wet and hot and smoldering. My finger in her mouth is an image I'll never be able to scrub from my mind.

I pull my finger out with a wet pop. She presses her lips together and drops her eyes, a shy blush staining her damp cheeks.

"Don't you dare look away from me, Billie Black," I say, gently tipping her head back up.

She looks down and to the side, all that brazen confidence seeping out of her now. I come back to cupping her head and kiss her gently this time, softly. Trying to coax her back from her retreat. Trying to tell her things through my touch that I've never said out loud. Our lips move together, slow and sensuous this time. Sweetly. Like waves lapping at the beach in a perfect rhythm.

She sighs into me, sliding her palms up the front of my dress shirt, exploring my body, running her nails down my back underneath my blazer. I open my eyes, like a total middle school creep, and watch her. She's pouring herself into our kiss, and the weight of it almost knocks the air from my lungs. Like a boy who's just been pushed off the playground equipment.

Eventually her hand comes up to my cheek, and she drops her chin, absently running her fingers through my tousled hair. She meets my gaze again, but not with the fire from a few minutes ago. Not the way I want. And in this moment, I know I'm not going to like what she says next.

She rests one hand on my chest and says, "Thank you, Vaughn," before turning and walking back through the door into the dark hallway.

I stand there at a complete loss to understand what just happened and adjust myself in my pants. The memory of her mouth on mine is burned into my body and something my aching dick is obviously not ready to let go of. And quite frankly, something my mind isn't prepared to let go of either.

And thank you? A fucking thank you? After we both just completely incinerated each other? With chemistry like that?

I don't think so, Billie.

# CHAPTER 15

## Billie

WOW. MONUMENTALLY STUPID. LIKE, SO FUCKING STUPID.

Did I seriously just suck on the finger of the man who signs my paychecks?

*Stupid, stupid, stupid.*

But also:

*Hot, hot, hot.*

My panties are ruined. So is my job, probably, but I'll focus on that later.

I jog down the barn alleyways, trying to get back to DD's stall. I've been away longer than I intended, and now I'm feeling guilty for leaving him.

When Patty the Prick hopped off his back and left him with Violet, he'd been all right, but as soon as he got into his stall, he froze on the spot and trembled. We whipped his tack off and started cleaning him, covering him up with warm fleece blankets. Hank ran to get the track vet to come check on him, worried that maybe he had an injury. The poor thing was in shock.

And I tore out of there like a bat out of hell with a major bone to pick.

I almost couldn't believe my eyes when I saw Patrick all washed off and changed into some fresh douchebag outfit while his winning mount was melting down in his stall. It enraged me. All I saw was red and his shitty, smug miniature face.

I was clear with him. Precise. Forceful but specific. And he outright defied me, and now an animal who trusted us enough, against his natural instincts, to do what we asked of him was the one paying the price. That fucker was lucky I only hit him once. I was ready to turn him into a spit roast on that whip. Especially after spilling everything about my sordid past in a room full of people.

But I can't focus on that right now.

I finally get to our aisle and see Violet and Hank standing outside his stall, looking in. When I get there, I'm huffing as I come to stand between them and peer into the stall. DD is hooked up to an IV, and a young woman with a thick dark ponytail is checking his legs over.

"Is he okay?" I blurt out, breathless.

"I think he's all right. Just had himself a bit of a panic attack, I think. Legs all seem fine." She rises and gives him a soothing rub behind his ears. "Didn't ya, big guy?"

DD lets his eyelids droop and neck relax under her ministrations. He's not shaking anymore. But he looks exhausted.

"I've got him hooked up to the IV for some extra

hydration. Nothing seems swollen or sore, but we haven't been able to get him out of the stall to see him move either. I think he just needs some TLC and rest."

A warm hand lands on my back, rubbing in small, sure circles. I peek over my shoulder and give Hank a watery smile, fighting the hot tears welling in my eyes. They threaten to spill out, but I'm not really a cry-in-front-of-other-people kind of gal. I'll save that for when I'm alone.

When I peer over at Violet, I expect to see puppy dog eyes and a tearstained face. But her eyes are like dark sapphires and her pouty lips are frozen in an angry frown. She looks like an angry little sprite, and it honestly lifts my spirits. She's such an enigma. There's still so much I don't know about her. But I like her. A lot. More than most people.

"Thank you so much for helping us out," I say, barely above a whisper, to the vet.

"Absolutely, any time. I'll give you my card, and I'll call for an update on how he's doing tomorrow." She returns a firm handshake and tries to force a comforting smile, but I can tell it's not really part of her natural persona. Her eyes dance with intelligence, but she's not the rub-your-back type of veterinarian. She's the facts-and-science type, which is fine by me. But I hug her anyway and she returns it woodenly, patting my back with quick slaps as she peels me off.

"All right then," she says, pressing her lips together.

"Thank you so much, Doctor…?"

"Mira Thorne. And you're welcome." She pulls a card from her pocket and hands it to me. "If anything changes,

I'm on call tonight." She unhooks the IV from DD's neck, packs up her kit, and heads out with brisk strides.

Hank, Violet, and I stand in silence awkwardly. Like we don't know what to say to each other. We won tonight, and it was a big win. The points from winning this race mean if we pick our next race carefully and win, he could qualify for the Denman Derby, the crown jewel of racing on the West Coast of the continent and the first leg of the Northern Crown.

But at what cost? Would DD want to run again after this? Would it even be fair to ask him to? He was supposed to have a fun night, play around on the track, and get some experience. Not be traumatized.

Just thinking about it makes me feel sick and ramps my heartbeat back up, heats my blood. I am terrible at letting things go, and I can already tell this will be a night that sticks with me for years to come.

In more ways than one.

"I'm going to kill that arrogant little fuck," Violet spits out.

Hank and I both turn to look at her with jaws unhinged and flapping in the breeze.

"Vi...did you just swear? Are you sure you're old enough to talk that way?" I ask, trying to infuse some humor into the moment.

"That's rich coming from you, B," she barks back. "You swear like a sailor daily."

"She behaves like one too," Hank adds with a chuckle. "Or at least that's word on the street around here."

Violet arches one dainty eyebrow my way, shooting me a questioning look.

"Patty may or may not be nursing a big old whip welt across his ass," I explain with a cringe.

"You hit him?" she shrieks.

I tip my head from side to side and pull at the neckline of my blouse. "Yeah. Hard. Like...I whaled on him."

Violet stares at me, blinking slowly like she can't quite process what I've just said. Hank covers his mouth and laughs silently into his hand, shoulders shaking and amused shock on his face.

"Billie! That's assault! They could arrest you," Violet squeaks out.

I pull her into a side hug. "They could. But it would be worth it. You'll bail me out, right, little Vi?"

Her laugh is strangled, but she hugs me back. "I love your wild side, Billie."

With the mood lightened and with Hank and Violet's help, I manage to get the trailer all loaded up and DD ready to ship. After a little pick-me-up of sweet feed, a molasses-covered grain, DD started moving around again. We confirmed he was not in fact injured anywhere and loved on him as much as we could. Hugs, pets, massages, cold boots on his legs—full spa treatment. He loaded up into the trailer quietly, probably exhausted from a trying day.

I make the long dark drive home on my own. Both Violet and Hank offered to ride with me, but I need some space. Some quiet.

When I unload him at the cottage, I walk him to his paddock like he might break. I unlatch his halter and he stays right in front of me, so I wrap my arms around his big warm neck and hug him. I stroke his shoulders, and he drops his neck down to rest his head along my back. Like I even still deserve his affection. I should have fought harder to pick my own jockey, someone I knew I could work with. I could put a chimp on this horse and he would win. I know it in my bones. And the weight of my failure makes me almost nauseous.

I stand there for I don't know how long and cry. I cry so hard I feel like I'll never catch my breath. I cry for more than just tonight. I cry because I miss my family. I cry because I'm sure Vaughn will have to fire me after everything tonight. And I cry because this beautiful soul who is standing here, letting me rub snot and mascara all over his perfect coat, still loves me despite it all, which is more than I can say for almost anyone in my life. No one has ever *chosen* me. It's always money, reputation, or work, and then I'm somewhere further down the line.

Except horses. Their love in my life is an unwavering constant.

And I've never felt so undeserving of that love as I do tonight.

My broken sleep is short. I set an alarm to check on DD every two hours, and when I finally decide to just get up for the day, I catch sight of myself in the mirror and startle. I look downright scary.

I shuffle out the back door and rest my forearms on the banister of the back porch where I have the perfect view of

DD's pen. I expect to see him standing by the gate, waiting impatiently for his breakfast, but he's not. My eyes dart around his pen until I finally find him in the back corner by his shelter. He's covered in mud and lying flat out on his side, groaning.

My heart jumps into my throat, beating wildly. Horses rarely lie flat on their sides, particularly nervous ones like DD. It's just not a good defensive position. When you've been around horses long enough, you know almost immediately what this kind of behavior can mean. Equine colic, which sounds silly and is common in babies, is emergent and deadly in horses.

My morning fogginess vanishes as I jam my feet into the slip-ons I leave at the back door. It's drizzling rain, but I don't bother with a coat and barrel down the few steps off the back deck, calling out to DD, trying to keep the panic I'm feeling from overwhelming me.

Grabbing his halter and lead rope off their hook, I duck through the middle part of the fence and am at his side in no time. He raises his head a few inches at my arrival before dropping it back down to the muddy ground with a groan.

"Hey, little man," I murmur, rubbing his big round cheekbone. "You gotta get up. You're gonna feel so much better if you get up."

Gravity doesn't work as well on their digestive tracts as it does on ours, based on shape. I drop my head to his stomach. Gut sounds would be good. Dead silence is not what we want.

But it's what we've got.

I gently lift his head into the black leather halter in my hand, attaching the buckle down beside his ear, constantly telling him what a good boy he is, rubbing him, patting him, covering myself in dirt and mud. I step away, gently tugging his head a few times before he lifts it and comes into more of an upright position. He's breathing hard now, uncomfortable. But I know the sooner I can get him up and moving, the sooner I can get him over to the farm for medication and veterinary attention.

Then we will walk. We will most likely spend the entire day walking. I'll walk him until I pass out if I have to. We just need to get that intestine straightened out.

I move to stand behind his back, pushing on his ribs and giving his haunches a gentle tap. "Up we go, DD. Come on, baby. You can do it."

He sticks both front legs out in an attempt but gives up and rolls back down into the mud. Sweat soaks his neck and chest, and I am having a hard time keeping my panic at bay. Worst-case scenarios race through my head. I want to keep a positive outlook, but I'm a realist, and this is not looking good.

I pull his head back up and get behind him again, pushing desperately now, pleading with him to get up. He's groaning and sweating but is stuck with his front legs out.

I'm wishing we were at the farm. There would be someone there to help me. The medication would be closer. He'd have a better shot. But I was emotional and selfish and kept him down here at my house instead.

Fear courses through me, and I give him a good poke between the ribs while shrieking, "DD, get up!"

And he does.

With a tremendous groan, he finally gets up.

I get moving immediately, opening the gate and heading straight toward the hills behind my house to cross the soggy fields leading to the stables.

I pull out my phone and dial as I walk.

"Hello?" a groggy voice answers.

"Hank, DD is colicking. Badly. I need you to call our vet and get him down here right away."

The sound of rustling sheets filters through the line. "Okay, Billie girl. Deep breaths. I'm calling him right away, and I'm coming to you. I'll be at the ranch in twenty minutes."

"Okay, great." My voice shakes.

"It's going to be okay. If anyone can take care of that horse, it's you. Just keep him walking. I'm on my way."

Hank hangs up, and we continue our slow walk across the field. Every time DD nips at his rib cage or kicks at his tummy, I urge him forward.

When we crest the hill, I see Violet in her pajamas, running toward us with a big syringe in hand. Obviously, Hank called her. The relief I feel at seeing her there ready to help makes tears spring to my eyes. My nerves are frayed, and my emotions are running rampant.

She reaches out to DD. "Hey, poor boy. Aunty Vi is here with your medicine," she coos, coming around to his neck with the needle.

I'm a tired, shaky, sad mess, and no one should trust me with a pointy object right now. Thankfully, Violet finds a vein, and I am so grateful for her at this moment.

"Hey, B." She turns to wrap me in a hug. "You look like shit."

I laugh, and it makes me cry. I drop my head into the crook of her neck and take a few centering breaths.

"Want me to take him while you go get some coffee or something?"

"No, I think I'll just head to the indoor arena and keep walking. I want to get him somewhere warm and dry. Could you bring some brushes and a fleece blanket though?"

"Of course," she replies, spinning on her heel and jogging to get our supplies.

We get inside quickly and begin our march. The more he walks, the better, so my plan is to walk in a big oval all day long.

"Billie!" Hank calls from the other end of the ring. "Dr. Thomas has been up all night with other emergencies. He's still in surgery and won't be able to get here anytime soon."

Anxiety wells in my throat. I feel like the edges of my vision are blurring. There are only so many vets out this far. *Fucking fuck.* I holler back at him, "Okay. Call Dr. Thorne from last night. I know she's in Vancouver, but just see what she says."

"Got it!"

"And, Hank!"

He stops to look back at me.

"I don't want Vaughn here. I know you have to tell him, but I'm too mad at the Harding brothers right now to deal with their shit. Please, whatever you can do to make that happen."

Hank gives me a terse nod before he spins on his heel to leave. He doesn't like my request, but I know he loves me enough to respect it.

# CHAPTER 16

## Vaughn

I've spent all morning cleaning out my grandfather's house. Or trying to. How the hell am I supposed to throw any of this stuff out? What am I supposed to do with it all? And how do I make my mind stop fixating on last night in the rain with Billie?

Wilhelmina fucking Farrington. How on earth did I miss *that*? Probably because at that age, I was holed up on the ranch with my grandfather, sheltered from the news, and far too fixated on my own family's bullshit to care much about politics or someone else's pain.

But still...another person I've come to trust. Another lie. I must be naive to be continually surprised by this.

At first, I didn't care about her past. I mean, I *don't* care about her past. But it niggles at me she wasn't forthcoming about it. People I care about keeping secrets from me seems to be a recurring theme. It bugs me more than I let on that she kept that hidden from me. On a personal level and on a professional level. She didn't consider how her past baggage might affect me or my family business. The farm's reputation is already in tatters thanks to my grandfather's dishonesty.

Which is really what this all comes back to. Dishonesty.

And that's when it hits me. Cole never overlooks background checks on employees. He would have known this from day one, unless he's letting himself slip in his old age. Cole should have been able to tell me about Billie's hidden background. I jam my finger against the screen of my phone, pulling his number up.

The phone rings twice before Cole answers. "Little brother. You snuck out early last night." Amusement sprinkles his typically cool and indifferent tone. Or at least as much amusement as I've heard from him in over a decade.

I ignore his comment and cut to the point of my call. "Did you run a background check on Billie Black?"

"Crazy Billie?" he corrects me. "I did. Yes."

"Care to elaborate on that?"

"In what regard? Don't beat around the bush, Vaughn. Passive aggressiveness is a tactic reserved for hormonal teenagers and simple-minded adults."

I press my lips together to tame the inner dread that's creeping up my spine as I come face-to-face with what my brother isn't quite saying here. "Did you know about her past? Her former identity?"

He's downright apathetic to what I've just said. "As the daughter of our most scandalous and infamous prime minister? That came up, yes."

Air lodges in my throat. Betrayal sears through me. Deep down, I know I'm probably overreacting, but I hate that I'm constantly left out of the loop. The little brother, the new kid, still at twenty-eight years old. An afterthought.

After an awkward amount of silence, I say, "Didn't think that was worth mentioning to me?"

"Well, I didn't expect you to fall in love with the psycho."

I rear back in my office chair. *What did he just say?*

I'm not…

He's trying to get under my skin, but he leaves me speechless. Am I in love with Billie Black? "I'm not—"

He cuts off my protest. "Her tracks were carefully covered. It clearly wasn't some rash decision on her part. I didn't feel like it mattered much if she was good with the horses."

I just blindly trusted that Hank brought me the best. *Hank.* He was the next person I'd be grilling about this. He must have known too. Basically, everyone around me who I care about knew, and not one thought to tell me. Talk about a dagger to the back.

I'm still silent on the phone, because I'm so angry I don't trust myself to speak.

Cole sighs, quieting his tone. "Vaughn, you're taking this personally. But, and I mean this as kindly as possible, get the fuck over it. It's time to be an adult. You need to stop holding the people you profess to care about to these idyllic black-and-white standards. It's unrealistic, and the only person you're hurting here is yourself. Humans are complex." His voice hitches uncharacteristically. "Sometimes a person needs a fresh start. This wasn't my story to tell."

It feels like my brother just slapped me. Deep down, I know he's right. But I'm not ready to admit that. I need to grapple with the bits of wisdom he just dumped all over me. I need to lick my wounds privately.

"Okay, thanks."

I hang up on him but only get a moment's peace before Hank's number flashes across the screen.

I answer with "I have a bone to pick with you."

"Pick it later." His voice is gruff and commanding. "DD's been sick all day with colic, and Billie is unmanageable. She hasn't eaten. Hasn't slept. But she doesn't want you here. Not yet anyway, so don't push your luck, son. I'm handling it, and I'll keep you posted."

# CHAPTER 17

## Billie

I PUT MY HEAD DOWN AND TRUDGE FORWARD. I DON'T KNOW how long I've been walking when I hear voices echoing through the alleyways that lead to the covered arena. Violet has brushed DD as he walks, at least enough to get the caked-on mud off him, and he's now wearing a yellow Gold Rush Ranch fleece blanket. Somehow Violet is calm and collected, and I'm the nervous wreck. She attends to him while I stare at my feet, watching each step and the imprint that it leaves in the sand. My shoe next to his hoof, in perfect sync. His head is low and sullen, but he's marching onward, trying his best for me.

Like always.

I don't deserve him.

"Billie girl, she's here."

I look up and see Hank with Dr. Thorne and what looks like a big toolbox. I head their way with a wave. "Dr.

Thorne, I'm just so glad you're here. Thank you for coming all this way."

She enters the gate, walking with precise movements toward me and DD. Her confidence is comforting. She's completely no-nonsense, and I love that. I feed off it, trying to leech some of her strength.

"Hey, big guy." She drags her hand down his neck a few times. "How we doing?"

She pinches his skin, checking to see his level of hydration. If the skin stays peaked, they're dehydrated. If it flattens back out quickly, then all is well.

It stays peaked.

"Billie, how are you doing?"

I stare at the spot on his neck as it slowly recedes into position.

"Billie, hon." She snaps her fingers in front of me. "You okay?"

"Hmm? Yeah. Just tired."

She gives my shoulder a tight, reassuring squeeze.

"And worried. I could barely get him up out of the mud when I found him."

"Okay, we'll take care of him. I'm going to grab some fluids. We're going to try to flush him out. We want to avoid surgery if we can. You just keep him walking." She looks me firmly in the eye, grabbing both shoulders. "You're doing great."

I nod my head resolutely and get back to walking.

I am beyond exhausted. My day moves along like one of those slow-motion montages from a movie, but a boring, shitty one. It's all cut scenes of walking in big circles, reassuring DD, and switching his fluid bags. Dr. Thorne has come and gone. She has set us up with all the medication and fluids we'll need, and she's of the opinion that if he isn't getting worse, he probably won't need surgery.

I want to be relieved, but I'll believe it when I see it.

She thinks his stress reaction triggered the episode, which makes me want to kill Patrick and Cole even more. And probably just maim Vaughn for being such a fucking pushover. Idiots, the lot of them.

I'm so busy staring at the ground, I hardly notice Hank walk up beside me and drop a hand on my neck in a fatherly way.

"Billie girl, it's been hours. It's almost dinnertime. You should go take a break. Let Violet and I walk him for a bit. Have some coffee, eat some food, take a nap, whatever you need. You look dead on your feet."

"I'm fine."

"I've known you a long time, and I know that you're blaming yourself right now. You shouldn't. You've always been too hard on yourself. None of this is your fault."

I scoff at that, sniffling and looking up at the roof, willing the pooling tears to leak back into my eye sockets where they came from. "Hank, I very much appreciate you being here. I do. But this is absolutely my fault. You should go home and enjoy your day off, spend some time with your family. I'm better off by myself right now."

And then, like he's trying to make me break down, he says, "You're my family too, you know."

I can't stop the tears then, and I turn into him, into the safety and comfort of his embrace, and rest my face on his chest. I'm engulfed by his large frame, his soft plaid shirt wrapping around me like an old blanket. One large hand holds the back of my head, and the other rubs up and down my back while he shushes me soothingly.

"Shh. It's going to be okay, Billie. We got this. Shh."

I allow myself a few minutes to seek comfort in his bear hug and to find solace in his words. I don't necessarily believe them, but it feels good to hear them all the same. When I pull back, I offer him a watery smile that doesn't reach my eyes. "I'm so lucky to have you."

He just smiles at me, rubbing my shoulders like he's trying to build me up, pull me up taller, shake me out of my funk. A soft nose nuzzles at my lower back, and I turn back to offer DD a kiss on his soft forehead.

"Stop crying. You're upsetting your horse." He winks at me. "You sure you want me to go?"

"Yes. I'll call you with any updates. I know you're just down the road if I need you."

"All right, all right," he replies, waving a hand my way. "Violet, it's your day off too, little lady. Go enjoy yourself."

Violet stares back at him, alarmed. "But that leaves Billie all by herself. What if something happens? What if she needs help?"

A conspiratorial grin touches Hank's lips. "She won't, but if she does, you'll be right upstairs," is his reply as he leads Violet off the benches at the end of the arena.

She looks back at me to confirm I'm okay with this whole scenario. I nod and wave a hand at her to skedaddle.

Finally alone, I look back at DD. He seems incrementally more chipper, like his head isn't hanging so low and like he's groaning less. Come to think of it, I haven't seen him kick at his stomach in—I check my phone—about half an hour now. He nuzzles at me, and I scratch his ears before moving toward his rib cage to listen for gut sounds.

And I hear them. Faint and fleeting, but definitely there.

Relief washes over me like cool rain on a hot day. I know we're not out of the woods yet, but this is concrete proof that his condition isn't worsening. That sense of relief is cathartic, and with no one around to see me, I burrow my face into DD's shoulder and let the tears come. I haven't cried this much in years. I didn't even cry when I left home. The fact that I have barely slept in two days is most definitely a contributing factor to the frazzled state of my emotional well-being. No sleep and a roller coaster ride of emotions have whipped me up and spit me out.

I'm a fucking mess.

I sob. Those bone-deep, body-racking kind of sobs. It's an ugly cry for sure. DD wraps his neck and head toward me, almost as though he's shielding me, as I rub snot and tears and second-day mascara onto his beautiful coat. Again.

"I'm so sorry," I weep into the little bubble we've created between us.

That's when I feel a hand cup my elbow, and a jolt of electricity runs up to my shoulder. A current that feels far too raw and far too recent for me to handle right now.

"Billie, come here."

I freeze in position.

"No."

"Yes. Now," Vaughn says, and it's a command, not a request.

He uses a voice that I've only heard him try to use a few times with me. Usually, it pisses me off. But falling apart here and now, it feels more like the direction I need. Like maybe all the strength in his voice means I can lean on him instead of propping myself up so poorly.

I turn around and look at him, biting at my lips to keep them from wobbling, wiping at my cheeks to try to cover up how hard I've been crying. Like he wouldn't have heard me or wouldn't be able to see what a hot mess I am right now. He doesn't give me a pitying look, and I could hug him for that alone. I don't want anyone to see me like this, and I especially don't want their pity. It's an affront to my pride, to my whole carefully concocted carefree persona.

He puts his arms out and glares at me. "Come here."

And I go to him.

Against all my better judgment. Against everything I know about him. Against everything my logical brain is telling me to do. I collapse into his arms. And he props me up, like I knew he would. He doesn't placate me or tell me it's going to be okay. He doesn't offer me fake words or try to console me, to fix me. He just lets me be. And as memories of all our quiet moments together bubble up in my mind, I realize maybe he cares about me more than I thought.

# CHAPTER 18

## Vaughn

WALKING IN TO SEE AND HEAR BILLIE SOBBING INTO THE horse's shoulder had been an absolute gut punch. Hank told me she wasn't in good shape, but he failed to mention the part where she was absolutely falling apart. Seeing someone as strong as Billie break down and sob her apology to a horse for something I am ultimately responsible for almost brought me to my fucking knees.

The guilt. The ache in my chest at the raw pain in her voice. I knew she was more sensitive than she let on. But this. This scene could crack my chest right open and leave my heart beating at her feet.

Yeah, this hurts.

She hiccups in my arms, head nestled toward my shoulder, arms resting low around my ribs. I'm holding her as firmly as I can without hurting her, trying to absorb all her anguish, letting it seep into me. I'm the one who deserves the blame. Her sobs slow as I run one palm over her messy chestnut hair. I glance behind her at DD. He looks tired, closing his eyes and dozing now. Like he was just waiting for someone else to get here and take care of her.

I'm not a spiritual guy or into any new age energy kind of shit, but even I have to admit there is a special connection between Billie and DD. A connection you don't see very often, the kind in books and movies.

Her very own Black Beauty.

A tiny childish part of me is envious. What would it be like to have a woman like Billie love you, trust you, and believe in you? For DD, transformative.

"Thank you," she whispers into my shirt and gives me an extra squeeze around the ribs as she burrows her head further into my bicep. Like she's trying to hide there or something. Knowing Billie, she probably is.

"Of course," I reply softly, resting my stubbly cheek on top of her soft hair.

"You probably think I'm unstable. I shouldn't cry this hard over a horse."

"I actually do think you're unstable," I deadpan, which makes her laugh but also earns me a firm poke in the ribs. "Billie, some people celebrate Mother's Day for being a 'dog mom.' *That's* unstable. Crying over a sick horse that you love isn't." I pause a beat, trying to decide if I want to profess my culpability out loud. Hating how wrong I'd been to ignore her warnings about needing the right jockey.

"Don't judge dog moms, you dick. I plan to be one someday."

I chuckle, but it's half-hearted. She's trying to redirect an otherwise uncomfortable situation with humor. Jokes are her armor, and I know she's feeling vulnerable right now. "You can't beat yourself up this hard. I'm the one who fucked everything up in the last couple days. I'm sorry. I let both you and DD down, and you both deserved better from me."

"Wow."

"That's your response? *Wow*?"

She hiccups a laugh. "Yeah. Wow. That must have physically pained you."

I shake my head, rubbing it across the top of hers. "See? Unstable."

"Thank you, Vaughn."

"There's a sandwich and a bottle of coconut water on the bench for you. Go sit and eat."

"I'm goo—" she protests, but I interrupt her.

"Billie. I said go." I point back toward the entrance.

"What about DD?" She looks back at the dozing horse, running her long fingers gently through his forelock.

"I don't know why you continue to not believe me when I tell you I practically grew up on this farm. I'm more than capable of walking a horse around in circles."

She looks me up and down with narrowed eyes. "He might not like you."

"He's falling asleep. Hank updated me on Dr. Thorne's diagnosis. Has he improved at all?"

"Yes," she says, shoulders slumping.

I take the lead rope from her hands while pointing back at the bench. "Good. Now go."

A deep sigh rattles through her chest, and she relents, turning on her heel to walk back to the doors.

I give DD a gentle rub and get his attention with a gentle clucking noise. "Wake up, fella. We need to keep marching."

He groans but follows me without much protest.

I walk, and Billie eats.

As much as I hate to admit it, I spent all night and all day thinking about her. Her warm cinnamon-scented perfume intoxicated me. It lingered in my nostrils, made me hungry for more. I replayed our kiss, her touch, the way she'd dragged my finger through her mouth. She'd been bold and then shy. Mostly, she was confusing.

She wants nothing from me, which is a refreshing challenge since my money or my clothes or my car are important requirements for the women I've spent time around.

*Should probably stop letting Mommy pick your dates, eh, big guy?*

I round the corner of the ring, and my eyes find Billie immediately. She looks beat, but at least she's eating. Hank called me again a few hours after telling me not to come, saying that Billie wouldn't listen to him and needed someone who could handle her when she was being a brat. I laughed and told him *no one* could handle her then.

I glance back at her, catching her looking me over.

"Thank you for dinner," she says. "I needed that."

"You're welcome."

"And…uh." She clears her throat and looks away. "Thank you for driving all the way out here to help me. I know you were staying downtown for the weekend."

"I followed you back last night."

She gives me an astounded look, like she can't believe I would do that.

"Wanted to make sure you both got back okay. You were pretty upset."

Her cheeks flush pink, and I look away.

"We should just forget about what happened last night." Her voice comes out raspy.

That will never happen. But I'll play along for now.

"I don't think I'll ever forget you cracking Patrick on the ass in a room full of owners and sponsors," I reply with a chuckle, coming to stand in front of her.

She groans, covering her face with both hands, and leans back against the bench.

"And then you went off on my brother." I shake my head in disbelief. "Best thing I've seen in a long time."

She spreads two fingers and peeks at me from behind them. "Tell me the truth. Is your brother a robot?"

A loud, genuine laughs bursts out of me. I turn to DD, who is dozing again now that we're standing still, and chuckle to myself.

"I'm serious. I thought you were an uptight prick, but you're downright sunny next to him."

That comment hits me in a way I didn't expect. Did she really think that? I look back to check if she's joking. Her cheeks twitch in an effort to hold back a small smile, and I raise an eyebrow to let her know she didn't get away with that one.

"Are we going to ignore what Patrick said?"

A shield clamps down over her features as she schools them into perfect indifference. "Which part?"

I look her dead in the eye. "The Farrington part. In all our conversations, you conveniently left out that your father is the former leader of our country."

"Ha!" Her voice bites with sarcasm. "Oh yes. That's a title I just *love* to wear like a badge of honor. I have such fond memories of being paraded around as the dutiful, gracious daughter on his national apology tour. I especially enjoyed answering reporters' questions about whether I'd seen the videos of my dad fucking hookers. Which I had, by the way, and there's not enough bleach in the world to wash those images from my mind. So I guess forgive me for not laying it all out. I ran as hard and fast as I could as soon as I could. I worked my ass off to start fresh. I'm not Wilhelmina Farrington anymore. I haven't been for a long time."

Okay. Sore spot. My mind reels all the same. From what I looked up, her name was splashed over every newspaper in the country, maybe in the world, for weeks on end. I suppose this makes a lot of things add up. Her lack of presence online, her loathing of anything she considers to be elite. I laugh as a memory springs to mind.

"What?" She sounds accusatory, defensive—laid bare in a way she doesn't like.

"Remember that time you made fun of me for having a rich-person name?" I try to hold back my laughter, but my shoulders bob, and my eyes water under the strain. "Wilhelmina fucking Farrington," I blurt out before dissolving into uncontrolled laughter.

She tries to look offended but can't hold out. In a matter of moments, we're both laughing so hard we can't even talk. Tears stream down our faces. This is the type of laughter that only comes in the wake of tension and exhaustion.

"Oh god." She wipes the tears from her eyes as our laughter subsides. "It's true."

She gazes at me, shaking her head, and I turn to look at a calmly dozing DD. "You could have told me, you know."

She clears her throat. "I know." She wrings her hands and stares at her lap. "Are you angry with me?"

She can't be serious. Maybe I was angry at first, but how could I ever stay that way when all she wants is something different for herself than all that?

"Why would I be angry with you? I don't care who raised you, Billie. The only people I'm angry with are the ones who made you feel you had to run and hide."

She looks up at me from under her lashes, nibbling nervously at her lips. Like she doesn't quite believe what I'm saying.

"I wouldn't have—I won't—betray your trust with this though. It doesn't matter. I'm all ears when you're ready to talk."

She sighs, the look of relief plain on her face. "Thank you."

"You're welcome. And also, next time, you pick the jockey."

She sits up at that, surprised by the sudden change of subject. "Seriously?"

"Seriously."

"What about Cole Harding, the 'half owner'?" She uses her fingers to make sarcastic air quotes.

"I'll handle him."

She rears back, amber eyes wide.

"Don't worry about it. Relax for a bit. I'll keep walking."

She doesn't fight me on it this time, just leans back on the bench, slides her phone out of her pocket, and huffs out a deep breath.

I walk. And I think. I think about what Billie grew up in. About everything I read this morning. Videos of her dad, the prime minister of the country, having sex and doing drugs with prostitutes blasted out all over the world. *Jesus.*

I guess she really had an idea of what I was going through with my grandfather's scandal. She didn't bat an eyelash when I told her. She didn't make me feel guilty or pathetic for holding on to hope that he might be innocent. She just… let me feel. When everyone else around me wanted me to be a certain way, she just let me be me.

DD stops, jolting me from my realization. He groans and…he poops. I never thought I'd be so excited to see horse poop. The blockage has moved, and I turn to celebrate with Billie. But what I see is Billie curled up on the bench, out cold. She has one arm under her head like a pillow and her long legs bent so that her knees dangle off the edge. The sun has set, and one of the overhead lights is shedding its neon glow over her sleeping form.

Even in this moment of excitement, I can't help but notice how young she looks right now. No jokes, no sarcasm, no fighting words. She looks peaceful but sad. Beneath it all, she always looks a little sad. A surge of protectiveness washes over me as I make my way toward her.

Coming to crouch down beside her, I run a hand through her hair, pushing it back away from her face. This close, I'm truly entranced. The light smattering of summer freckles, the perfect bow shape to that puffy top lip, so soft and feminine. Until you pair it all up with one of the worst cases of trucker's mouth ever. Yes, Billie is all dichotomies and surprises. Hard and soft. Happy and sad. Hot and cold. And I like her hot. I like her every which way.

Her unpredictability used to make me nervous. Now, the feeling of being on my toes around her excites me. She's a live wire, and I am the idiot happy to see what happens when I pick up the loose end. When those walls come down, and I know they will, she and I will light each other on fire.

Our banter went from grumpy to funny to intense. Images flit through my head like one of those flip books that make an image look like it's moving. Billie on top of me. Billie on all fours in front of me. Billie gasping my name from beneath me.

Yeah, I have plans.

I just need to get Billie up to speed.

My thumb traces her cheekbone, thinking about all the sinful things I plan to do to her, causing her eyes to flutter open.

"How long you been staring at me, Boss Man?" she mutters.

"Since day one," I whisper in her ear.

"Take the sappy shit somewhere else, Vaughn."

I snort. "There she is."

She closes her eyes and tries to wave me away. DD nudges her hip and looks at her quizzically.

"I'll take over walking. Just give me five more minutes, DD. I know you're probably sick of him."

"Billie. He pooped."

Her eyes fly open, and she sits straight up. "Come again?"

I point out into the arena where the physical evidence sits.

"Ah! Oh my god!" She bounds to her feet. "For real?"

"I mean, you can go look at it if you want?"

Her hands shoot up in the air like she's just scored an Olympic goal. And before I know it, she's launched herself at me, causing DD to jump, and wrapped her arms around my neck.

"Thank you, thank you, thank you!"

And it's the best feeling ever. Seeing her this excited? It's addictive. I want to make her this happy all the time. Okay, maybe not all the time, because I kind of like her surly side. But more often.

Definitely more often.

I smile into her hair and rest my hand over the back of her head before she pulls back to look at me, one hand resting on each of my shoulders.

"Vaughn Harding, I could kiss you right now."

Fire licks at my core almost instantly at hearing her say that. My look must change, because she's promptly walking her comment back, wide eyes trained on my predatory ones as we stand here, suspended in time and space, holding each other.

"But I won't. Because you're my boss."

"I am." I take a step closer.

"And because you're everything I promised myself I'd stay away from."

I quirk my head at her as I step again, but she surges on.

"And because Gold Rush Ranch doesn't need to endure any more scandal."

"Who says we'd be a scandal?" I inquire, inclining my head toward her and dropping my eyes to her lips.

"Are you joking? Every woman you're seen with is splashed across Page Six." She steps back from me, pressing one hand into my chest. "It's hard enough getting people to take a twenty-eight-year-old woman seriously in this business. But one who's banging her billionaire playboy boss? I'd never live it down. I've worked too hard. Given up too much."

Her words are like a bucket of ice water over hot simmering coals. The steam burns me, and the smoke chokes me. And she stands in front of me looking completely unaffected.

I never gave much consideration to how the papers portray me. Truthfully, it never really mattered to me. It certainly has never been a black mark against me. But Billie is different. It's what I like about her, and it is also what's killing me right now. I can't undo my past choices, and holding them against me stings in a way I'm not prepared for. She's right though. And that's what bites the hardest.

There's wanting something you can't have, and then there's this—wanting something and knowing you'll ruin it.

I care about her too much to do that.

I step away and watch her hand fall from my chest. When I catch her big amber eyes looking at me with sadness, I hate it. I hate the pity. But most of all, I hate that she's providing excellent reasons I can't have her.

I revert to Spoiled Brat Vaughn and shove DD's rope toward her, shaking it. "You're right. Here. Take it."

She takes it but tries to capture my hand too. I yank it away.

"Vaughn, I'm sorry," she whispers, looking stunned at my reaction.

To be fair, I'm stunned too. Twenty-eight-year-old men aren't meant to throw tantrums when they can't have something. And I'm not sure I realized how badly I wanted *her* until now. I want to hide and lick my wounds, but I also know that DD isn't completely out of the woods, and she's going to need help tonight.

Eyes trained on the ground, I turn to leave. "Don't worry about it. Glad he's doing better. Let's go." I wave over my shoulder.

"Let's go?"

"Yeah. Back to your house so you don't have to sleep on a cold, hard bench. He needs a rest, and I can keep watch at the paddock you have there."

"You really don't need to do this..." she starts.

I just shake my head and continue walking. "Keep up, Billie. It's dark out."

# CHAPTER 19

## Billie

It's pushing midnight when we leave the barn and head out into the dark fields. It smells like rain and fresh-cut grass, and I can't see a single star through the clouds overhead. The moon is just a lighter spot in the overcast sky.

I'm tired, but I'm fixating on the tension between Vaughn and me.

Shit is weird.

Maybe I'm not firing on all cylinders—sleeplessness and high levels of stress will do that to a girl—but I am confused.

When I told Vaughn I could kiss him, his whole face and body changed, morphed into someone a lot more dangerous. It took me aback. He looked like a predator who was about to have me as his snack. And the worst part is, in that moment, I wanted to be snacked on.

If he wasn't my boss, that is. I mean, has everyone seen that man in casual clothes? Because it's pretty much criminal. Fuck suits. Vaughn Harding wears casual clothes like one of those sexy, scruffy Calvin Klein models. Like he's just rolled out of bed and wants to take you back there with him.

*I volunteer as tribute!*

Maybe for one night? We could probably handle one night with no complications. We're both mature adults... Haha. Just kidding. We are not. It would ruin our working relationship, which is often tenuous at best.

I peek at him from under my lashes and admire his masculine profile. He looks mysterious, all dark features set against the blackness of the night. But I also know him well enough to tell he's simmering, a bit angry, like he could manhandle the hell outta me right now. I like that side of him, how he took control of my body in the rain last night. He walked that line of power so deftly when he waited for me to come back and kiss him. Such a turn-on. My ruined panties were proof of that. And he's obviously scrambled my brain enough that I did it.

And fuck. Last night was hot. *Worth it.*

But then his reaction to me today? That was downright dangerous. Doing it again would make things complicated. Much too complicated.

He idolized his grandfather, and this farm was that man's legacy. His identity is far too tied up in it to let it flounder. This I know. He'd resent me if I were the reason it did. So I'll admire him—and his ass—from afar. I lean back a little to take a peek, but black pants in the middle of the night aren't very effective for creeping.

I settle for his face and nibble hungrily at my lip. It's a close second in the looks department.

"Billie, you're staring." His growl cuts through my musings.

"Yeah. Sorry." Why even deny it?

He just grunts.

The night is quiet, and our sneakers squelch across the damp grass intermingled with the clip-clop of DD's feet. He's so tired. I can feel him lagging behind.

"I'm sorry," I say again.

"You said that."

"No, not for staring. Well, I'm sorry for that too, really. But I meant that I'm sorry for whatever I said before that upset you."

"I'm not upset," he snarls, shaking his head.

"Oookay," I mouth silently up to the sky.

After a few beats, he adds, "I'm sad."

Hearing him say that absolutely winds me. Like I've fallen off the swing at the park, and hitting the ground pushed all the air out of my body. What the fuck am I supposed to do with that? If shit was weird before, now it's awkward as hell.

Sad? I didn't want to make him sad. I was being realistic. I honestly didn't even think I had the power to make Vaughn sad. As his annoying employee, I pick on Vaughn, and he picks back. It's part of our game, part of our push and pull. And even if I know he's the type of guy I should steer clear of, I don't dislike him for it. I wouldn't be intentionally hurtful or spiteful because of it. He's just not what I'd *choose*.

I don't know what to say to that, so I just reach out, yank

at his wrist above where his hand is shoved into his pocket, and take his big warm hand in my own. He doesn't resist. In fact, after a couple minutes, his thumb rubs absently across my palm as we walk in silence, sending a wave of goose bumps up my arm that land right on my pebbled nipples.

*This is fine.*

After setting DD up in his paddock, I walk to the bathroom first thing and catch sight of myself in the mirror there. Wow. *Yikes*. The yellow in my eyes highlights dark smudges, and my hair looks like the little kid in elementary school who refuses to use a brush. It appears that I have cried off all traces of mascara (win!), but that win is balanced out by the fact that my entire face is puffy and pink from crying (lose!).

The good news is that this frightening look is an excellent way to deter Vaughn from whatever has been running through his head since last night. After seeing me in the light, he's probably already imagining all the fancy well-bred women he can invite on his next date. My raggedy ass just gave him the push he needed.

The thought twists in my sternum. Like that unending throb you feel when you hit your funny bone. Why the fuck do they call it that? There is literally nothing funny about it. Or what I'm feeling right now.

*This isn't funny. It's fucking insane.*

I brace my hands on the counter and take a few deep breaths. I almost feel like I could fall asleep right here, standing up.

I splash my face with cold water and rub vigorously before heading back out into the living room where Vaughn is waiting. He's rotated a chair to face out toward DD's paddock and is sitting quietly facing away from me.

"You could have told me I look like trash."

"You don't," he says.

I mean, yeah. But...harsh.

Walking into his view, I jut my bottom lip out. "This"—I point at myself, gesturing up and down my body—"is really bad."

He looks over at me, sighs, and closes his eyes. "You look like someone who saved that horse's life today. That's what matters. I already know you're beautiful."

If his eyes weren't closed, he would see my mouth hanging open. Does he realize he just called me beautiful out loud? Is he joking or not? I can't tell anything anymore. Down is up, left is right, and Vaughn Harding thinks I'm beautiful.

He cracks his eyes open a slit, his expression giving away nothing. "Billie, I can almost hear you thinking. Go to bed."

"Okay," is all I can muster as I turn and walk up the stairs, stunned. The word *beautiful* bounces around in my head, weaving between all the twisty lines of confusion.

I shower. And scrub and soap and shave off what feels like two days' worth of grime and emotions. It does nothing to lessen my confusion, but it makes me so dopey I crawl into bed and fall asleep with my damp towel still wrapped around me.

I startle awake at hearing my screen door close. Whatever time it is, it's still dark outside. I listen carefully and hear muffled footsteps downstairs. Logically, I know that it's probably Vaughn, but a seed of doubt lingers. As a woman who lives alone, there is always a level of fear about noises at night.

I drag my legs out of bed and plant my feet on the floor. Creeping toward the stairs, I ditch my towel and wrap myself in my thin black robe to combat the chill that runs down my spine. I peek my head around the corner as I tiptoe down the first few stairs.

Relief courses through me at the sight of Vaughn's dark form sitting in the same chair, illuminated only by the yellow glow of the patio lights. The phone he's scrolling through illuminates his silhouette. From here, I can see row after row of pictures I recognize of him smiling for the camera, looking painfully handsome, with a beautiful date on his arm. I scrolled through these exact pictures when he canceled dinner at my place several weeks ago. Different suits, different women, and different events for each one. And if I'm being perfectly honest, I may have looked at them once or twice since. As visual reminders of why I shouldn't ever think of Vaughn as anything other than my very nice-looking boss.

Being around Vaughn reminds me of window shopping. I'm a woman, and I'd have to be blind to not notice him. But that doesn't mean I touch him or…uh…try him on?

Yikes. Okay. Different metaphor. I appreciate art all the time, but you don't catch me rushing in to buy it. I admire it and carry on. *Ooh, aah, nice painting! Look at those brushstrokes! The colors! Oh, wow, look at the time. I better get going. The end.*

The beautiful painting in front of me tilts his head to the side and rests his temple in his palm, elbow wedged against the big cushy armrest of the brown leather chair, and exhales. His shoulders take on an angle I'm not accustomed to, like he's folding in on himself. A part of me feels like I'm intruding, but the other part of me with very few boundaries doesn't care. I pad down the rest of the steps, which catches his attention.

He locks his phone quickly and turns to look at me. "Can't sleep?" he asks with a tired rasp to his voice.

"I did for a bit. But I heard the door close and got a little freaked out." I round the corner, giving his shoulder a squeeze on the way past, and lean against the windowsill in front of him.

"I just gave DD some hay and checked on him. Seems like everything is moving well again." He pauses and inclines his head a tad to show his confusion. "Freaked out how?"

Relief floods through me at his update on DD's condition. "Like maybe someone was in the house or something."

"But you knew I was here?"

"I know." I wave him off. "Sometimes living all alone out here means my imagination runs away with things. That's why I like having DD outside, for company. My guard horse." I force out a laugh.

His brow furrows, and his eyes pinch. "I'll have an alarm system put in for you."

I roll my eyes. "Vaughn, that's overkill. I'm fine."

"I'm doing it, Billie. I don't want you feeling that way in your own home."

What a caveman.

We stare at each other, my bitch face versus his. But he gives up earlier than usual, shaking his head and looking away. He seems tense, and after catching him googling himself, I know something must be up. He's been looking away for an unnatural amount of time, like he's intentionally avoiding my eyes.

"Vaughn," I start quietly, "I can tell I struck a nerve earlier. I'm sorry if I hurt your feelings."

"You didn't." His reply is curt.

"Don't bullshit a bullshitter, Boss Man. I saw you googling yourself."

He groans and scrubs his face with both hands at my admission. "I will not dignify out-of-context photographs on the internet with a response. I know what kind of man I am."

His eyes flit back to me before dropping lower. Super great. Now I've hurt and embarrassed one of the proudest men I know.

"Talk to me. We're friends, remember?"

"No."

"No? To which one?"

"Both," he says, settling his gaze back on mine now.

"Both?" I shimmy my shoulders taller, standing to lean against the window frame, trying to shield myself. I don't want to be offended by what he's just told me. But I am.

He stares at me with no hint of a joke anywhere. This isn't our regular ribbing; he's being very direct right now. And I hate that it's making my eyes sting.

Determined not to cry in front of him, I push off the

window frame to move past him. "If we're not friends, then you don't need to be here. Go home. I'll see you at work tomorrow."

He grabs my wrist before I can escape past him, stopping me in my tracks. Memories of him pinning my wrist above me last night flood my mind.

I shiver, even though all I feel is heat. And when I look down at him, I'm hit with an overwhelming sense of desire. I hoped he wouldn't notice my physical reaction to his touch, but I know he did. It's so clear that we're both burning, and I don't know how to stop it. The look on his face takes my breath away—it hurts. Makes my chest ache.

Taking in all his hard angles, those intense eyes, I'm rooted to the spot. Frozen.

"I don't want to talk. We're not friends." His words are like a paper cut. They sting but don't produce any blood. "What I want is you, straddling me, and I don't let friends do that."

He's still staring at me, holding my wrist, rubbing small circles over my pulse point. All I can hear is my own shallow breathing and the rush of blood in my ears. I have no doubt my pulse is jumping wildly beneath his thumb, dancing to his tune.

"That's a bad idea, Vaughn," I rasp out.

"Tell me why."

"I already did. I gave you a whole list of reasons," I reply, panic seeping into my voice now. But my body is already moving to stand in front of him, responding in ways that my brain can't keep up with.

"Billie, I'm not the womanizer you think I am." He drifts his other hand up the outside of my robe, starting at my knee and landing on my hip. "I go on the mostly platonic dates my mother sets up to make her happy. Because I love her, and I know she means well." He pauses, pinning me with his glare. "And I have no reason not to."

His meaning hangs in the air between us like bait on a fishing line, shiny and undulating and enthralling. He looks up at me with eyes gone black with intensity. The question dangles between us, and all I can think about is how badly I want to run my hands through his mussed hair. Just one more time. *Don't give him a reason. Keep walking.*

I step closer to him and ignore the warning voice in my head. I reach out and drag my fingers across the hair at his crown, combing back that one dark curl that always flops onto the same charming spot on his forehead. The one that is always a dead giveaway for what type of day he's having. The one that always makes him look *just* disheveled enough to melt my panties.

His eyes never leave mine, that gaze holding so much promise. His hand trails across my hip and only stops where he can palm my ass and pull me closer. That hand travels farther down to my upper thigh where he squeezes his fingers. I can feel the tip of each one, wrapped around my leg, pressing into the delicate skin of my inner thigh just below where my panties would be if I were wearing any.

Those fingers send a jolt of electricity up through my pelvis and a rush of heat back down. And to make my body completely defy my brain, he leans his beautiful head forward and presses a kiss to that ultrasensitive spot just below my hip bone and whispers against the thin silk, "Give me a reason, Billie."

A whimper escapes my lips as he continues kissing me there, dragging his teeth along the bone, making me shudder. My aching body takes over, and before I even realize what I'm doing, I drop to my knees in front of him and pull frantically at the waistband of his joggers. I don't know much, but I know I want him in my mouth. I want to feel every ridge. I want to take back control, and I want him to lose his.

Firm hands grasp my wrists. "Billie, stop."

I look up, away from where his very impressive package is straining against his pants, and pull my hands back, scrambling away from him. "I'm sorry." The reality of what I'd just been trying to do to my boss hits me with full force.

His lips tip up at one side, and he beckons me closer with his hand. "Come here."

I take a tentative step toward him, and he holds both my wrists again.

"Sit," he says, dipping his chin toward his lap.

I comply, straddling him, exactly how he specified. His clothes are soft against my bare skin as I place one knee on either side of his trim waist.

We fit perfectly.

With both wrists still locked in his hands, I'm unable to adjust myself, and the front slit of my robe slowly falls open as I spread my legs around him, not leaving much to the imagination even in the blackness that surrounds us.

He groans, watching intently, eyes smoldering, and tongue darting out to tease the seam of his lips. Seeing him admire my body so openly is dizzying. I can feel the wetness between my legs, and I know he can see it too.

His quads are hard and unrelenting beneath me, but the erection pressing up into my ass is even harder. I grind down, rocking my hips against him, eliciting a growl from deep in his chest. He grabs my hips to stop the motion, and I let my hands come to rest on his pecs, whose solid definition I can feel through his thin T-shirt.

"Fuck," he says on a shaky breath while staring down at where I'm exposed before lifting his head to look me in the eye again. A look that smolders like hot black coals. Coals I'm probably about to get burnt on.

I bite at my lips nervously. "I'm going to regret this tomorrow."

"No, Billie." His hands stroke me. "I'm going to eat that perfect pink pussy and then put you back to bed. And tomorrow? Tomorrow all you're going to think about is how good you felt with my tongue inside you."

Breath hisses through my lips. Holy fuck. I am no virgin, but Vaughn just made my cheeks flame like one. Turned my entire body to flame, really. My brain too, since it seems to have melted into a puddle of poor decisions that I am about to happily roll around in.

Vaughn's hands slide sensuously up and down my back, leaving a trail of goose bumps and singed nerve endings in their wake. I can barely think. One hand moves up to grip a handful of my hair, and he pulls me into a kiss. A kiss I expected to be hot and rough, but it's soft and searching. He's masterful, playing my needy body like an instrument he's perfected over the years. And at this moment, I don't even care. Why mess around with a bumbling boy when I can play with an expert?

His tongue darts into my mouth. Teasing. Seeking. Asking for more this time rather than taking. His left hand has slogged its way up my stomach to my breast. His thumb rubs back and forth across my nipple while he grips my hair and explores my mouth.

I surrender, and not a single part of me objects to this right now.

"Say you want it, Billie," he rumbles against my lips with a nip.

So fucking bossy. Does he have to ruin this by giving me directions?

"Can't you tell?"

He tugs my hair so that I'm forced to look him in the eye. "No. I want to hear you say it. I want to be sure."

And with the way he's looking at me right now, I'd say anything. His eyes are like chocolate fondue. Hot and molten. I want to spread it all over my body and have him lick it off. His hair is wild and his five-o'clock shadow gives him that slightly rough look and feel I love.

*Not love.* Correction, that I'm a big fan of. I like rough Vaughn, more so than polished Vaughn. Actually, I like the dichotomy of his two sides and how quickly he can switch. Do I want it? Fuck yes, I want it.

"I want it." My body shudders at my admission.

"What do you want?" he muses with an evil glint in his eye and a knowing smirk on his lips.

I know he's trying to throw me off balance here. We're both constantly doing that to each other. I like the challenge, so I bat my eyelashes at him and lean in toward his ear, dragging my teeth along his stubbled jaw as I go. I try to speak low, but it comes out loud in the quiet early morning hours.

"I want your tongue inside me." I pick his hand up and drag it down my body, placing it right on the wetness between my legs.

His muscled chest rises and falls now, and his fingers move of their own accord, exploring my folds, brushing across my clit.

"I want you to eat this perfect pink pussy."

Almost instantly, he shoves one finger inside me. My body bucks as he curls it around to press right into that one spot.

My head falls back, and breath rushes out of my lungs. His hard cock presses into my ass as his firm hand coils in my hair, and that strong finger pushes inside me. The sensations collide. He overwhelms me. My nerve synapses sing. And before I know it, I'm wrapped into him while he grips my ass and carries me up the stairs, taking every second step.

I barely even have enough time to think. *What on earth am I doing?*

# CHAPTER 20

## Vaughn

I FEEL LIKE A CAVEMAN AS I CARRY BILLIE UP THE STAIRS. OR maybe a Viking who, after months of raiding, has finally gotten his hands on the treasure he wants the most.

I'm not even fighting this anymore. Fuck work. Fuck my family. Fuck what I thought I wanted.

I want Billie Black.

In fact, I've never craved a woman as much as I crave her. Her multiple personalities, her filthy mouth, her long legs and perfect round ass. I'm done pretending. Done holding myself back. Done sulking about it.

Tonight, I'm going to make her come harder than she ever has before. I'm going to own her body. Show her what she's missing. And then I'm going to tuck her in and make her yearn for more. I'll dole it out in pieces. Like little breadcrumbs on a path she'll have to follow. I will not rush and give her the satisfaction of thinking I don't take this seriously.

Because I do.

Those pictures? Those other women? They don't mean shit. And I'm happy to prove it.

I'm not stupid, and I know her well enough to understand that no matter what I do tonight, she's going to freak out tomorrow. I'm well prepared to get a different version of Billie in the morning. She won't be the molten, hungry, pliant version of her I have right now. But I'll enjoy this while I have it, and I'll prove to her this Billie should come out to play with me more often.

Because this is a game I intend to win.

I want to throw Billie down and ravage her, but I also want to treat her like porcelain. I don't want to break this tenuous agreement we seem to have arrived at. She puts up a tough facade, plays up her peppy personality, but I see the sad girl she hides under there. The shy, mistrustful one who's had to fight tooth and nail to get to where she is and will beat a stranger's ass with a whip.

I lay her down on the bed and move over her, resting my elbows on either side of her head. I kiss her again. Reverently. Her lips are putty beneath mine, open and eager. Her moans and sighs are like lightning strikes on dry grass. Fuel for my fire. I want more. I want to hear her lose control and scream my name. I want to imprint this in my mind. On my body…on hers.

I retreat from her lips to watch her face. Moonlight through the window showcases her delicate features, illuminating all the feminine angles and dips across her cheeks, at the base of her throat, and along her collarbones. I want to lick each one.

Her eyes glow amber, catlike in their color and shape, and they search my face with an openness I haven't seen before. Her full, heart-shaped lips are slightly parted, and I can't help but imagine pressing my cock there. Watching it slide between her lips. Watching those feline eyes go wide. Feeling her moan vibrate through me as she swallows my hard length.

Just thinking about it has me impossibly hard. She hasn't even touched me, and I'm about ready to explode. Across her face or those full tits. But I have a plan, and painting her with my come will have to wait for another time. Because I'm just getting started.

I stand up and look down, towering above her. Her beauty, the wanton look on her face, almost undoes me. My breath seizes in my chest. She's splayed out beneath me for the taking, all long lean limbs with that thick chestnut mane spread around her like a halo.

Like the most delicious dessert, ready for me to devour.

She doesn't shy away from my gaze as my eyes roam her body. The thin, black, poor excuse for a robe she's wearing doesn't leave much to the imagination. A deep V runs from her shoulders, just covering her nipples, to where it ties around her slender waist. From there, a mirrored V runs down her toned thighs, barely covering her.

I grab one end of the tie around her waist and yank. The knot unravels easily, and I hook a finger under each panel of the robe and drag it back, exposing her smooth moonlit body.

I know Billie is hard on her appearance. I didn't miss the

self-deprecating way she referred to herself as an Amazon or acted like I'd be horrified to see her with unbrushed hair and a clean face. But she couldn't be more off base. Spread out beneath me, naked and wet for me, all I can think is *mine.*

Perky breasts. Just a handful. All I need. Toned shoulders and arms, flared hips, firm stomach and thighs, all from years of riding and manual labor on a farm. I'm not sure how I haven't found her completely irresistible since day one.

Was I blind? She looks damn near perfect to me.

She looks like no other man should ever enjoy this view again. If anyone ever made her feel anything short of stunning and supremely fuckable, they are idiots.

I kneel at the edge of the bed, right in front of her, ready to worship at her altar, and I don't miss the way she wets her bottom lip as I do.

I drag my hands along her calves and rotate them under her ass, right between her bare skin and the soft, thin fabric of her robe.

"Scoot down, Billie."

She lifts her head to look at me but says nothing. Her eyes say it all. Her breaths morph into pants that rattle her chest. Her pelvis pops up much too slow, and my impatience takes over. I grab her by the hips and pull her down, eliciting a gasp.

With her ass close to the edge of the bed, knees folded up, and heels pressed into the mattress, I rub a thumb over each hip bone and hold her there, exposed. "Tell me what you want."

"I...I want you to keep going," is her stuttered, breathy response.

Hearing her say she wants it, wants me, makes my cock swell and my heart quake in my chest. Billie is so guarded, so untouchable, this admission feels like something else altogether.

I press a gentle kiss to the inside of her knee. "I can do more." Don't have to tell me twice.

I hook my hands beneath her knees and spread them, kissing my way up the inside of her soft thigh as I hook one leg over my shoulder. Her pussy glistens now. This close, I can see that she is soaked. *I did that to her.*

"Fuck, Billie. You look edible."

She turns her head to the side, covering her face with one hand to stifle the moan she can't hold back. *Sweet girl, you don't know what you're in for.*

I place her other heel back on the bed and spread her wider for me. Driving myself wild. I am truly torturing myself here. Both of us, probably.

I run one thumb up through her folds, brushing gently across her clit at the top of my stroke. Watching her velvet skin move around me. Her hips buck off the bed. I rub again and watch her squirm and writhe. So responsive. So sensitive. I dip the pad of my thumb into her pussy and feel the leg that's now slung over my shoulder tremble.

"Vaughn. Please." She moans.

"Please what?" I ask, watching the top joint of my thumb pump in and out of her, slick and tight.

She pushes up onto her elbows, the wild look in her eyes reflected in my own. "I need more. Give me more."

Without breaking eye contact, I slowly drag my thumb

back out of her and swirl it across her sensitive bud. Her head drops back as she cries out, pressing her round tits up into the air like the embodiment of ecstasy. I love watching her.

Focusing back down between her legs, I pull her closer and drag my tongue through her core. Slowly.

I faintly hear her: "Fuck, yes." Her entire body shivers around me.

That tremor is all it takes to snap the fragile grip on my control. And I'm pressing her legs open. Devouring her. Reaching up to manhandle her breasts. Rolling her hard nipples between my thumb and forefinger. She thrashes around me in pleasure. Her unfiltered words are a stream of consciousness, of desire, that stoke the fire burning inside me. "Keep going. Don't stop. Harder. More. I want you to fuck me, Vaughn."

I should have known she'd be just as vocal in bed as she is out. She's begging for it. And my cock is so hard. Harder than it's ever been. It hurts. And Billie tastes like heaven on my tongue. So I don't even care.

Both her legs curl around my neck, pulling me closer. Her hips gyrate, pressing herself into my mouth shamelessly. I fucking love it.

"Vaughn, I'm so close," she pants out at me, entranced by the show happening between her legs.

I stop and look up at her wickedly.

She whimpers. "I said, 'Don't stop.'"

I smirk and remove one hand from where it's been gripping her ass cheek. Then two fingers are there, and I thrust them in with one hard stroke.

Her head tips back again as she cries out, "Fuck."

Fuck is right. Fuck, I love watching that.

I focus back down on my fingers. Setting a rhythm. Pushing and pulling. Watching them move in and out of her wet heat.

"Oh god," is all it takes for me to add my mouth back into the mix, swirling my tongue around and pressing down on her bundle of nerves.

Billie's body is tight and writhing beneath my ministrations. She pinches her nipples. *Good girl.* I can feel the tension in her pelvis building. Like a coil waiting to release. To fire off. To explode.

And then she does.

"Oh my god. Vaughn! I'm—"

Everything around me clenches. Her legs. Her pussy. And her hands, which are now in my hair, pulling me into her. Vibrations rack her body as I pump my fingers and lap at her, drawing out her orgasm for as long as I can.

Eventually, her body relaxes around mine. And the enormity of what we've just done hits me.

Time stands still. I'm wrapped up in Billie—her heavy breathing, her skin, her scent—and I realize this time, it's different. With Billie, it's *more.* My cock is about to self-destruct, and all I can think about is kissing her, holding her, and making her come again. And again.

Watching her fall apart all around me must be the most beautiful thing I've ever seen. Months of buildup, months of feelings, all toppling over into the single most satisfying sexual encounter of my life.

*I am so fucked.*

# CHAPTER 21

## Billie

Looks like Vaughn and I were both right.

It's six in the morning, and I'm wide-awake, freaking out about last night but also very fixated on remembering his sinful tongue. We took turns checking on DD every hour, and every time one of us would crawl back into bed, he'd pull me into the curve of his body and press a kiss to my hair.

I push the heels of my palms into my eye sockets before I look over beside me where Vaughn is still sleeping. He is breathtaking. Literally. My breath hitches in my chest when I study him lying there, looking like a god in the filtered morning light. *The god of pussy eating.*

I can't decide what's better: dangerous-looking Vaughn in the moonlight last night, cocky and panty-melting, or peaceful-looking Vaughn in the golden glow of the morning light, all warm skin and hard lines. Soft breaths, topped off with that signature amaretto smell.

Maybe that's why I feel drunk right now. I'm drunk on Vaughn and poor decision-making.

I'm usually adept at separating feelings from sex, but this is new, and I'm panicking a little.

Okay. A lot.

Over the years, Hank has implied I may have commitment issues. And the nosy fucker might not be all wrong.

*Cheers, Mom and Dad! You sent me out into the world with something after all.*

Last night, Vaughn, the epitome of every man I've ever avoided, strung me up and flayed me. Ripped my chest wide open. Made me come like a freight train. We didn't even have actual sex—though I vaguely remember begging for it.

Oh god. I *begged* for it.

*Cringe. Cringe. Cringe.*

He will hold that over my head forever and ever once we get back to our regular working relationship—because that's definitely happening.

*One night only. Show's over, folks.*

One night that will not wash easily from my memory. The way he touched me. Licked me. Bit me. *Owned* me. That will be burned into my brain and body for years to come. I've had good sex and bad sex. I'll even say that I've had great sex. (Irish accents just take dirty talk over the top, ya know?) But last night was otherworldly. I squeeze my thighs together just thinking about it. My skin burns at the memory of his stubble grazing my sensitive inner thighs. He was masterful.

Which is why I didn't give him the boot. He tried to

leave, walk back to the barn and then drive home before dawn. Dumbass. I called him one too.

"Don't be a dumbass. You're not driving on dark country roads after pulling an all-nighter. Get in here." I held open the blanket and moved over to make space for him.

He seemed too big for a queen-size bed, but it worked. He looked at me suspiciously and said, "Okay, but I'm not going to fuck you," with a stupid cocky smirk on his face. *Prick.*

And then I watched him undress in the dark, with only the silvery light filtering through the windowpane. I knew his body was going to be good (I like to think that I'm a connoisseur of checking dudes out), and I copped a feel here and there.

But it was really something else.

He exceeded my expectations. I had ideas of what Vaughn did in his free time, which mostly involved boning every woman he comes across, but I'm thinking I might be wrong. Because no one looks that good without working out for at least a couple of hours every day. No. One.

Then he *cuddled* me. And I wasn't sure what to do. So I just lay there and took it like a champ. I expected him to just lie down and fall sleep. Not prowl into bed wearing skintight boxers, kiss me like we were exchanging souls, making me taste what we'd just done, and then wrap me in his arms while peppering soft kisses across my bare shoulder.

That part was a surprise. A pleasant surprise.

I soak him in again now, letting my eyes roam over his sleeping form. Trying to imprint the image in my memory. A fun story to tell my grandkids one day. Or whatever.

I'm overachieving. I bagged an Adonis for one night. Hard lines, impossibly broad shoulders, biceps I'd like to sink my teeth into, that V disappearing beneath the duvet, and a smattering of black curls. He is just plain masculine.

That growly, bossy voice rumbling between my legs.

*Fuck*. I am such a goner.

I drag myself out of bed, wrap my discarded black robe around my body, and pad downstairs. First, I check DD, who appears to be comfortably dozing standing up in a paddock with a couple poops in the corner.

Excellent news.

Second, I make coffee and plan out what I'll say to Vaughn when he wakes. While I am prepping myself to be cool and not just awkward as fuck, I hear vibrating and look around for my phone. Of course, I've misplaced it. I am a fucking mess after all.

Having checked over the kitchen, I end up in the living room, eyes landing on the offending chair from last night. Where my whole debacle started.

The black butt end of my phone is sticking out from between the seat cushion and the arm. *Hallelujah.*

I pull it up and go to open the screen, planning to send out a flurry of update texts. But my thumbprint doesn't work. Neither does my code. And as I reset to the phone screen, I realize this isn't my phone at all. It's Vaughn's. Makes sense that it might have fallen out of his pocket while I mauled him last night. I mean to leave it on the counter, but his waiting text message is staring me in the face. And when I tap the screen, the entire text pops up.

**Mom:** Good morning, honey. Just wanted to remind you that Emma Breland will accompany you to the gala next Saturday. I spoke to her at the tennis club yesterday, and she's looking forward to it. Sweet girl. She's planning to wear pink, so maybe you could wear something that will match?

Is this woman for real? Does she think they're going to prom or something?

And the really insecure part of me is also wondering why the fuck Vaughn would make date plans with another woman if he really wants to be more than friends with me.

*He's your boss, not your boyfriend, you sad sap.*

I shouldn't be surprised, really. This is what these kinds of guys do. I saw it growing up, and obviously my dad was exhibit A in obscuring the truth and philandering. Vaughn said all the right things last night to break down my guarded exterior, and I fell for it.

Hook. Line. And sinker.

Do I really think Vaughn is the man-slut I originally imagined? No. I don't think he lied about that. But I don't like being made a fool of. I've experienced enough public humiliation to last me a lifetime. Don't tell me I'm what you want when you've got other girls lined up a few days from now.

I do think he is a twenty-eight-year-old man stuck under mommy's thumb though. It's one thing for her to keep setting him up with random women and another thing for him to keep humoring her when she does it. She might mean well, but when someone is continually putting you in a position you profess not to like, the onus is still on you to tell them you don't like it.

Vaughn has no backbone with his mom, and I'm not here for it. I've got enough mommy and daddy issues of my own to work out without taking on someone else's. I don't need another project in my life. He can figure it out on his own.

I pour myself a cup of piping hot coffee. Dark roast. Lots of cream. And I lean against the counter to take that first heavenly sip. No other sip tastes as good as that very first one in the morning. I close my eyes and savor it, sighing and steeling my backbone, preparing myself to be mature but removed when he wakes. I'm a big girl. I don't have any expectations after one night of fooling around. We're not getting married. He doesn't owe me shit. So I'll smile at the memory and carry on.

I feel good about my conclusion and satisfied with my plan going forward. We're just an employee and her boss who fell into each other in a moment of weakness. A moment that ran high on emotions and low on sleep. Now, back to professional Billie. The Billie who's going to win herself a Denman Derby with the little black horse outside.

By the time Vaughn comes down the wooden stairway, completely dressed but still looking like a sex-mussed god, I've fed DD, tracked my phone down, and fired off all the messages I need to. I have a full cup of coffee in me, and I'm feeling more like myself.

Like smart, self-sufficient Billie.

"Hey." The corners of his sinful lips tip up as he prowls

toward me, eyes roaming my body in a knowing way. In a greedy way.

Heat builds at the base of my spine in response.

I'm honestly pathetic. I can't even help myself around this guy.

"Hi," is my intelligent response when he cages me in against the counter with his arms. The scent of his skin wraps around me, plunging me back into the feel of him all over my naked body last night. The way he made me squirm and buck and beg.

His stubble brushes up against my jaw, and I shiver as he whispers in my ear, "Are you freaking out yet?"

I can't help the way my body responds to his. Especially now that I know what he's capable of. Which is why I overcompensate by smiling too cheerily and clearly state, "No! I'm great!"

His head tilts, assessing me. His intelligent dark eyes scan my lighter ones, clearly not buying my line.

"Billie..." His lips graze up over my cheek and brush against mine. "Don't lie to me."

He kisses me more firmly, and my traitorous body arches into him happily. I press one hand into the center of his chest and push him away, even though my body is screaming at me to pull him closer.

"I need to get dressed and head down to the barn. I'm meeting Dr. Thorne there in an hour." I brush past him, forcing my legs to move away from the sanctuary of his arms.

He turns to follow my retreating form with a confused look on his face. "Take the day off, Billie."

I wave him off from over my shoulder as I start up the stairs to get dressed. "Nah. It's all good. I'll sleep tonight. Your phone's on the counter. I found it in the chair." And then because I'm not as mature as I like to think I am, I toss out, "There's a text from your mom."

# CHAPTER 22

## Vaughn

Fan-fucking-tastic. A text from my mom. I reach for my phone, dread creeping up my spine as I read the message.

*Jesus.*

Her timing is impeccable. I have to hand it to her. I finally start breaking down the walls around one of the most closed-off women in the world, and my mom sends a text about setting me up on a date with another woman.

A date I have no intention of partaking in.

Especially after last night.

It's no wonder Billie shot out of here with that too-sunny, awkward smile on her face. She was totally freaking out, and that text was the cherry on top.

Unfortunately for Billie, I won't scare off that easily. Her wounded pride over a silly text will not be enough to deter me. I've had a taste, and I want more. *A lot more.*

I'm a levelheaded, patient man. A pragmatic man. I may

not be accustomed to being the one doing the chasing, but I've never been so set on any woman in my life. I'll play the long game with Billie.

She's worth it.

I poke my head into her room. "Billie, I'm running home to take a shower and change. And then I'm coming back."

"You don't need to do that! I'm all good. Bye!"

Her fake enthusiasm makes me roll my eyes. With her childhood laid out in the open, I'm on to her now. That bright, cheery facade is a cover, that much is becoming abundantly clear, and I'm going to pry it off, piece by piece. Get to the moody, temperamental woman underneath. That's the Billie who intrigues me. The Billie I want.

I'm barely buckled up before I'm barking, "Call Mom," at my Bluetooth system.

The loud ringing sounds through the speakers, followed by my mom's cheery greeting. "Vaughn! Such nice timing. I'm in the car with your brother. We're going for coffee. Want to join us?"

This is her new thing, intentionally ignoring the fact that I'm not living in the city anymore.

"Hi, Mom. Not today. I'm at the ranch, remember? I do need to talk to you though."

"Sure, honey. What's up?"

I opt to just blurt it out. "You're going to have to stop setting up dates for me. It's gone on long enough now. No more."

Awkward silence.

"I… Vaughn, I'm sorry. I was just trying to help."

I sigh. My relationship with my mother is strained at best. On one hand, I don't want to make her feel worse than she already does. I'm not oblivious enough to think that she doesn't live with intense guilt for handing me over to my grandfather and drowning herself in a bottle for few years in the wake of my father's death. But this making up for her years of absence by smothering me as an adult stunt has got to end. I have to confess, I'm worried that without it, we'll have no common ground. We'll be even more estranged than we already are. But that's a bridge I'll cross later.

"I know, Mom. But it's not helping anymore. Do you want me to call Emma Breland and cancel, or will you?"

I feel bad canceling. I've known Emma Breland for years. We've attended several events together as *friends*. It's not her fault my mom intrudes beyond what's normal. It's not her fault I've been too big of a pushover to put a stop to it either.

"You can't humor me one last time? She really is lovely, Vaughn. It's a good connection to make for the farm. I know you get along we—"

I take a deep breath. Is she serious right now? "Mom. Stop it. I said, 'No more.'"

I can hear my brother's evil cackle in the background.

"Am I on speakerphone?"

"Hello, brother," Cole responds, failing to hide the amusement in his voice.

"Mom, I have the perfect solution for you. Get Cole to take Emma to the gala. He's overdue for a date."

No chuckles this time. I smile inwardly, loving ribbing my older brother. He's made it through more than most people ever will, but he came back out the other side cool and removed. Unreachable. It's time he dips a toe back into the dating pond.

"Don't pick on your brother." And it's time my mom stops tiptoeing around him too. "I'll speak with Emma. I'm sure you'll see her there."

I roll my eyes. The woman is truly impossible. "Mom, I'm not coming."

"Why not?" She sounds truly aghast.

"Because I'm not ready yet. I'm busy. I'm happy out at the ranch. I need more time before I step back into the vipers' den."

She sniffles, not liking my answer but also trained to not ruffle feathers or make a scene. "Whatever makes you happy, darling."

"Great. Talk later," I say before hanging up and gunning it down the back roads to my house.

***

Billie has been avoiding me all week. Or that's how it feels, even though I know she's been spending her days driving to and from the track in Vancouver, training the horses we have down there now that the suspension has lifted.

I'm hiding out in my office at the farm. Totally failing at proving to her how badly I want her. That I'm serious about her. I had big ideas in my head about what I was going to do. Grand gestures I was going to make. But I realize I'm out of my depth here.

My feelings for her scare me. They've paralyzed me.

Basically, I'm a total pussy.

Close a high-stakes business deal? No problem. Fire someone? I'm your man. Talk to a girl I like and respect? I guess I'll just crumble instead.

People taking off on me when things go wrong is common. My mom. My brother. I've been here before. But somehow with Billie, it's worse.

I've seen her around the farm, always with that forced happy look on her face, but she's constantly armored up with someone else. Constantly with one of her sidekicks, Violet or Hank, and impossible to get alone. And I'm too chicken to just pull up to her house when she clearly doesn't want to be around me.

Short of groveling, I'm too inexperienced with relationships to know what to do next.

Plus, I don't grovel.

So when I get a text saying she has some things she wants to talk to me about, I breathe a sigh of relief. She's coming to me. *This* is familiar footing.

I fidget while I wait for her. Organizing my desk. Setting things just right. Running my hands through my hair. I'm nervous. Excited. Like a little kid.

*Knock, knock, knock.*

My head snaps up to meet her amber gaze as she stands in my doorway. Chestnut-brown hair and golden eyes. Everything about her is warm and sensual, like velvet.

"Come on in."

"Thanks for seeing me," she says formally, awkwardly.

"Of course," I say, like a total chickenshit. "What's up?"

"I've found a jockey for DD," is her reply as she comes to sit in a chair across from me.

"Okay." That's not what I thought we were going to talk about.

"It's Violet," she continues.

I take a minute to pivot, to realize we're talking about business rather than anything personal. Rather than *us*.

"Little country bumpkin Violet?"

"Don't be pretentious, Vaughn." She sniffs. "She's excellent with the horses. Gifted, really. And she's been working toward her license. All I have to do is sign off on her riding hours, and she'll be set."

Okay, she's got my attention now. I lean forward on my desk, steepling my hands beneath my chin. Trying not to be *pretentious*.

"Billie…she's…well, she's very young. Very inexperienced. Has she ridden in a single race? And you're just going to throw her up on a derby-contending horse to find her footing?"

"She is." She holds her hands up as though she's surrendering. "That's all true. But I've had her up on DD all week. He loves her. We can't take any chances with how sensitive he is. You know that as well as I do." Billie pierces me with a knowing look. "He's only got so many races in him. He's not a run-every-weekend horse. And she'll stay out of his way. Let him do his thing. You should see them together. It's… well, it's amazing."

I groan and rub my hands across my face, scrubbing, before pushing them back through my hair.

How did I end up here? Betrayed and abandoned by the man I admired most. Hiring a wild card of a trainer for his farm—his tarnished legacy. And now about to put a completely green jockey on my most valuable horse—this farm's only possible saving grace.

This is not the organized and logical approach I like to take to things. These decisions…they make little sense.

I am losing it.

"I…I don't know," I reply honestly.

She just stares back at me with determination painted all over her dainty features, and I know deep down that I won't deny her this.

"Do you trust me, Vaughn?" she asks with a quirk of her head.

Trust her? I more than trust her. Looking at her now, she's strong and resolved, saying what she wants and fighting for it. Not some giggling heiress amenable to everything I say or do. She's her own person. So thoroughly. So unapologetically.

I admire the hell out of her. Warm foreign feelings hit me like a ton of fucking bricks.

"Yes," I reply. My eyes search hers. It's true, but my mind is reeling with the realization that I would give this woman anything she wants, which is hilarious, because she might be the one woman I've ever met who wants absolutely nothing from me.

"Trust me with this. I won't let you down."

I remain silent, wanting to believe her but warring with my current frame of mind, which tells me people I love aren't always who I think they are. That they can't always be trusted.

I had my grandfather up on a pedestal. There's nothing I wouldn't have done for that man. Nothing I still wouldn't do for him to restore his reputation. And then he turned out to be so different from the idealistic image I created of him in my mind. I'd been so blindsided. How does one man misjudge one person so completely?

But Billie isn't him, and I don't want to spend my life wallowing in his betrayal. I don't want to be the sad, quiet guy with granddaddy issues.

So I leap and decide to trust the woman sitting in front of me, lit up with excitement. *I want that.* I want to feel like *that* again.

"Okay."

"Okay?" she asks, disbelief soaking through her voice.

How can I say no to her when my reward is *that* look on her face? That sparkly look, where she shines from the inside out. Where she glows. That special look she has that's reserved for all things horses. I want her to look at me like that. I want to bottle that up and drink it. Save it for the days when I'm feeling gloomy and generally unlovable.

She jumps up wearing a Cheshire cat grin on her face, doing small claps with her long elegant fingers. Fingers I want back in my hair and wrapped around my cock.

Fuck. Everything this girl does is a turn-on. *Her fingers, for crying out loud.* I mentally chastise myself. *Pathetic.*

She's like catnip for me. I lose my mind around her.

"Thank you, Vaughn," she singsongs, heading toward

the door. "I'll get to work on updating his entry papers for the next race. You won't regret it."

"I know," I reply, because it's true. In the months I've known Billie Black, I've seen her grit and determination. I've seen her hard work in action. When she sets her mind to something, she makes it happen.

Watching her leave, I scramble for something to say to make her stay and talk. "Billie…"

"Yeah?" Her brow quirks up as she grabs the doorframe and looks back at me.

"Do you have plans this weekend?"

The psycho fake mask slips over her cheerful face. I cringe inwardly, realizing how badly that one brief text must have stung after our night together.

"I do."

I take a deep breath, steeling myself, wanting to find my own date for the first time in a long time. Not just any date either. I want Billie.

"Do you…?" I thump my chest with a fist and clear my throat. "Like you're going out?"

Her body stiffens. "Yup. Like I said. Plans." She walks away without looking back.

I feel heat flourish across my cheeks and my heartbeat in my ears. How the hell did she go from writhing beneath me, begging me to fuck her, to having "plans" in a matter of five days?

Have I blown my opportunity with one thoughtless text that was completely out of my control? I feel like I know her better than that. She isn't that thin-skinned, but she is skittish about men. She made that much clear. Which leaves me with one obvious alternative: sweet Billie is lying to me. Trying to push me off her trail. Trying to cover her tracks.

But she's too late. If I am the predator, she is my prey, and I already had a taste I can't forget. I'm coming back for more, whether or not she realizes it.

I'm not tiptoeing around her anymore.

# CHAPTER 23

## Billie

I'M AN IDIOT.

Why did I say that? Of course I don't have any plans. All I do is fucking work at Vaughn fucking Harding's fucking farm. I have no social life to speak of.

And now I've backed myself into a corner.

Like a big fucking idiot.

I hide in an empty stall down the hall from his office, scrubbing my hands over my face and trying to catch my breath, because until now, I've been able to avoid the thought of him out with some gorgeous, suitable girl in pink.

I'm mad at myself for lying, for acting like a total chickenshit. And I'm mad at him for asking me what I'm doing, totally rubbing it in. He has some serious nerve taking me to bed and still planning a date with another woman. And he hasn't said a word about that to me since he left that morning. He *knew*, and he hasn't said shit. Not that it should surprise me. This is par for the course with spoiled man-children like Vaughn Harding.

If I'm being completely honest, I'm offended he hasn't gone out of his way to talk to me this week. I know I've been in Vancouver at the track until late most days, but still…

I secretly want him to drive up to my front door, press me against a wall, and kiss me breathless. I want to see that manicured facade slip. I want all that testosterone lurking beneath the surface to spill over. I want him to *choose* me. I want him to work for it.

I need him to man up, and he didn't. And now I'm disappointed. Which is stupid, seeing as how he's my boss and one of Vancouver's most eligible bachelors. I have no good reason to be disappointed, no right to it. But here I am, lying about having a date just to spite him. And I just shot myself in the foot because of course, there's no date to speak of.

I need help. Professional help. But for now, Violet will have to do. I fire off a text message to meet me at DD's paddock. By the time I arrive there, she's already waiting for me, a concerned look on her dainty face, twisting her hands.

"What's wrong?" she blurts out as soon as I'm close enough to hear her.

"What are you doing tomorrow night?"

"What? Nothing. Why?"

"Great. Let's do something."

"You sure you want to hang out with a lowly groom?" she quips.

My cheek quirks up. I love delivering good news. "I don't… but the new jockey for local sensation Double Diablo will do."

Her eyes are round like saucers as she stares back at me, her serious little cherubic face frozen.

"All righty then, Vi. That's not the reaction I was expecting."

"This isn't funny, B. Are you joking?" she whispers, color draining from her face by the second.

"Why on earth would I joke about this? I'm evil but not that evil. Congratulations! We have promoted you. Vaughn and I just need to sign your papers. And you need to submit for your license. And probably start obsessively weighing yourself leading up to race day."

Her mouth opens and closes, but no sound comes out. She looks like a precious little fish out of water.

"I mean, you're still my bitch," I joke, "which is why you have to be my date tomorrow night."

"I...okay," Violet responds breathlessly.

I throw my head back and laugh at her. "That's all you have to say?"

Her smile cracks open, huge on her small face, and both hands come up to cover her mouth, muffling her giggles. Her shoulders shake with the force of her disbelieving laughter as it pours out of her. She looks so damn happy; it makes my cheeks hurt with the intensity of my smile.

I open my arms, offering her a hug, and she's there almost instantly, squeezing me right back.

"Billie. This...this is too much. I don't even know what to say."

I push her back and grab her shoulders. Her eyes sparkle with unshed tears, which is making my eye sockets burn in response. "Violet," I say as I shake her gently, "you deserve this. You've worked so hard. You're unflappable and calm. Something that both the horses and I need."

She chuckles at that.

"It is not too much. You're here before anyone else, and you leave after everyone else. You've put more blood, sweat, and tears into this career than almost anyone I know. Never, never sell yourself short. Take it, own it, and don't for a second think you haven't earned every bit."

Tears leak out over her long lashes; they're shimmering on the tops of her round cheekbones as she regards me.

I squeeze her shoulders. "We stick together, yeah? Sport of kings my ass."

She splutters out a watery laugh and reaches up to wipe her face.

"Now, stop crying. It's only one date. And look at me. I'm hot. It won't be so bad."

She barks out a laugh and shoves me back. "Good god, woman. Can you even be serious for a minute?"

"Never," I call out.

"Seriously though. Thank you, Billie. I'll make you proud. I promise."

"You already do, little Vi."

"Drinks on me tomorrow night! We'll go to Neighbor's pub."

"You're on. I'll drive," I say, feeling excited I might finally get off the ranch for a while in a social capacity. With one more quick squeeze, she's hustling away, practically sashaying up to the barn.

I feel a pang of guilt at knowing I'm using her as armor against Vaughn, but I also know she'll forgive me when I come clean. Violet is good people like that. Plus, I need all the armor I can get.

I style my hair in long chestnut waves. I even put on makeup and a gray T-shirt dress. It feels good to wear something other than jeans and boots, and I'm actually looking forward to going out and doing something that has nothing to do with horses. I drive to the barn to pick Violet up from her small apartment above the stables. She looks beautiful and distracted when she hops into the black Gold Rush Ranch truck.

"You doing all right?" I ask as she buckles herself in rather violently.

She looks straight ahead through the windshield. "Yup. But I need a drink."

And she isn't kidding. That night, I lose track of how many paralyzers Violet drinks. I switch to water after a couple of beers as I listen to her make vague comments about some guy she's been seeing who is clearly super unavailable. I don't know where she finds the time, but by the sounds of it, she finally told him to hit the dusty trail. Hence the voracious speed of her drinking.

She ends up telling me more about her family and childhood in Alberta. Her parents and her brothers. How stifling and overprotective they are. How she basically moved out to British Columbia just to see the world on her own. The more she talks, the more sluggish her words get, and as much as I'm amused by listening to her talk my ear off, I eventually suggest heading back to the ranch.

I watch her totter up the stairs to her apartment, wondering if I should have helped her up there, and breathe a sigh of relief when she closes the door behind herself. Poor little Violet is going to be in a world of pain tomorrow.

When I pull up to my dark cottage, tiredness hits me. All the commuting this week, getting to know new people around the track, listening to Violet, thinking about Vaughn—I'm feeling a little tapped out.

Which is why I'm instantly agitated when I see Vaughn sitting on my darkened front step.

"What are you doing here?" I sigh as I hop out of the truck.

"I came to talk to you." There's a bite to his tone that I don't like.

I walk right past him, shoving my key into the front door. "Don't bother. I'm going to bed. You should head back to your gala or whatever it is you're doing tonight."

He stands and takes a long step onto the porch. "You are so totally infuriating," he barks, surprising me with the volume of his voice, before quieting to an angry growl. "I'm about done with you running away from me."

*He thinks he can talk to me like this?* I spin around in the doorway, blood pumping quickly through my veins. "Speaking of running, how about you run back to your date in the pink dress now?"

A deep, sardonic laugh rumbles in his chest as he stalks

closer. "If I didn't know any better, I'd say you were jealous, Billie. Where were *you* tonight?"

I rear back at that. "Are you fucking kidding me? I was out with Violet, for crying out loud! You, on the other hand, spent the night with me and then—"

"That mouth of yours," he cuts me off and presses his finger across my lips to silence me as he edges closer still. "I didn't go to the gala at all. I called my mom that morning when I left your place and told her to cancel it. I told her to stop trying to set me up, period. If you didn't purposely avoid me all week, you would know this by now."

I stiffen, and air whooshes through my lips. "Vaughn, you're my boss. I know we've blurred that line. But we need to define it again. I don't want this to be complicated. I don't want to keep tiptoeing around you. I just want to work and win races."

"I want the same thing." He growls and then pushes me back through the front door gently.

And locks it behind us.

# CHAPTER 24

## Billie

Vaughn yanks me to him, and before I know it, he has flipped me around and is pressing me back into the solid pine door.

His movements are confident, steady, authoritative, but his touch is gentle. I shiver as I watch him take total command of our interaction. He moves with the grace and surety of a mountain lion, and I stand before him panting and wide-eyed.

Like the most clueless prey.

My voice comes out shakier than I'd like. "I thought you just said you wanted the same thing?"

His hand glides up over my throat before he comes to grip my chin, forcing me to look at him, at his handsome face and his dark eyes searching mine, shifting between each of my irises, like he's reading an open book.

"I do."

Heat pools between my thighs at the deep rasp of his voice.

"Let me redefine that line you keep talking about. You are more than my employee, and I am more than your boss. I'm done giving you space that we both don't want. It's not at all complicated. You'll work with me during the day and underneath me at night. Every night. There will be no tip-toeing. There will be no running. There will be no one else."

Blood rushes in my ears. All my protests die on my dry tongue.

"I fucked up this week, backing off the way I did. What I should have told you is that I want *you* and to win races. I want it all."

He's nuts. So goddamn bossy. And he's never been hotter. My head spins with the weight of his confession.

"Tell me you don't want that, and I'll walk out this door. I'll pretend we never happened."

That last promise is like a spear to my heart. How could I ever pretend we never happened? It would be impossible, and the weight of that prospect is too much to bear.

My hands slide up the lapels of his suit jacket to grip the collar. It never fails to amuse me that he continues wearing suits while living and working in the middle of nowhere. He regards me silently, waiting for me to say something, to respond to his admission. My tongue darts out across my bottom lip as I scour his features, admiring him with no shame. His shapely lips, his strong brow, the sharp definition of his jaw, and the stubble that blooms out from there below his high cheekbones. His brand of beauty is harsh and overwhelming in its masculinity. He isn't smooth and shiny. His beauty *hurts*.

More than that, he's a good man. I know it in my bones. In my marrow. He's so different from what I expected. It makes my chest ache with longing, with the pain of my distrust.

I sound breathless even to myself when I blurt out, "This is such a bad idea."

His stubble rasps across my jaw as he presses a feather-light kiss just beside my mouth. Taunting me. Leading me down a path that I'm sure there's no coming back from.

"Lose the dress, and I'll prove to you otherwise."

He kisses me below my ear now, nipping gently there.

"But—"

"Billie, stop. Nothing else matters."

The man makes me crazy: hot, cold, excited, angry, comfortable, anxious, safe. He's chosen me, and I don't think that anyone in my entire life has truly chosen me or gone after me when I ran away. And here he is, invading my space in the most delicious way, demanding that I choose him back.

It seems like a small gesture, but to my twisted heart, it feels like everything. Right now, held by him, surrounded by his bulk and scent, all l I want to do is stop denying my feelings. To get out of my head for the first time in years and let his infectious heat thaw me out.

I'm *tired*. Tired of running, tired of planning, tired of pretending I don't want him. My resolve crumbles as my head races. He's right. Nothing else matters.

Trying to control my erratic breathing, I take a hold of

the hem of my dress. Vaughn still has my chin grasped in his warm palm; his thumb is rubbing circles on my cheek reassuringly, only stopping as I pull my dress over my head and drop it unceremoniously on the floor. It pools by my feet along with all my inhibitions.

His sharp intake of air is loud in the quiet room as his hawkish eyes devour my body. I stand before him, naked save for my black lace panties and bra and a pair of brown wedge heels.

"Fuck, Billie. You are exquisite."

His hands drag down to my breasts, squeezing and caressing them, pulling them out over the top of my bra before discarding it. He holds one in each big palm before his head drops down to pull each hard nipple between his sinful lips. The feel of his mouth on my body is new and familiar all at the same time. Like we've been here before, like he's known my body for years. Like we were made for each other.

My head tips back on a moan, and I run my fingers through his thick hair, whimpering. "Please don't ever pretend we never happened."

He slides back up to look me in the eye, cupping my head with both hands. "You're even more insane than I already thought if you think I could ever forget us."

His lips crash down onto mine, and he pours his frustration into the kiss. His intensity is almost palpable, like I could reach out and run my fingers through it. He possesses me with his expert mouth, leaving me breathless and writhing up against the door. Leaving me damp and wanting more when he pulls away.

His hands drift down the gentle curves of my body before lifting me up and walking across to the kitchen island. "Sit on the counter."

He nods at the butcher block island beside me, and for once, I'm not annoyed by him being domineering. Heat coils at the base of my spine as I move to do what he's requested. I shift over on wobbly legs, and with his hands on my hips, I sit on the cold counter.

He steps away, putting space between us, as he crosses his arms and leans back against the opposite counter. I want him closer. I want his hands all over me. I want him inside me.

"If we're doing this, there can't be any more secrets, Billie. I can't take any more dishonesty in my life. Please don't hide your past from me."

His voice cracks with emotion, and my heart lurches. He's such a noble man, and the sting of his idol's betrayal won't be easily erased. But my promise to be better is a start.

"No more secrets," I whisper back.

He nods with authority. "Good. Now pull those skimpy panties to the side and show me how you touch that pretty pussy when you're alone and thinking of me."

*Jesus Christ.*

My breath catches in my throat. Shyness overtakes me as I feel unfamiliar heat creep across my sternum all the way up and to my bronzed cheeks. Vaughn Harding is not the square he appears to be. And looking at him now, the way he regards me with his hungry eyes, his sharp cheekbones stained pink, and his broad chest rising and falling like he's out of breath, I want nothing more than to please him. To make him happy.

To dive into whatever this is between us. If he needs this to make him feel like I'm really here, wanting what he wants, then I'll do it. A thousand times over.

I look up from beneath my lashes, lean back slightly, and let my legs fall open. Peering down, I hook two fingers into the thin strip of lace at the apex of my thighs and drag it slowly to the side, eliciting a groan from across the room. I subconsciously praise myself for shaving and primping so thoroughly today. Vaughn's eyes are darting all over my form, like he can't choose which part of me he likes the most.

The corners of my lips tip up. Urged on by the plain desire I see all over his face, I circle my clit a few times with my opposite hand and let a small moan spill out over my lips, which makes his eyes settle on one spot. His posture is taut, and I see the bulge between his legs fighting against the fabric of his slacks.

While I have his attention, I drag two fingers through my glistening folds and then slowly press them in. I hum and close my eyes against the feel. The brazenness of what I'm doing, the arousal thrumming in my hips, makes me feel like I'm having an out-of-body experience. I put on a show, lazily pumping my fingers in and out of myself while he watches from across the room.

A growl tears out of his chest at the sight, and in three long strides, he's standing between my spread legs, towering over me, holding my sensitive inner thighs open. "Do you have any idea how hard you make me? How wild you drive me?"

"Show me," I huff out. And he needs no further urging.

His hands undo his belt, and mine attack the buttons along the front of his dress shirt in unison. I want to see everything that I've only been able to feel. I want him disheveled and undone under my hands. I want him to feel as out of control as I do.

His cock springs free from his briefs as he pushes them down. He fists the base of it firmly, pumping toward me a few times. I lick my lips and reach down to palm his steely length myself. Rock-hard, silky smooth, and warm in my hand. And Vaughn completely naked? He's an absolute vision.

"I…I want…" I'm speechless. I'm drunk on the smell of amaretto and the way he's looking at me. I want it all. I want him everywhere.

"Tell me what you want, Billie. Say it." His mouth lands back on the tops of my aching breasts, and the rasp of his facial hair tingles across my chest.

I grip his shoulders as I bring my head down toward his bowed one and place my lips and teeth right up against his ear. "I want you to fuck me."

He's upright and pulling a condom out of his jacket pocket like a flash of lightning, rolling it over himself like an expert.

"Of course you just happen to have a condom in your jacket."

His eyes flash at my jab. "I only brought it because I knew you'd be impaled on my cock before the night was through."

*Okay. Yes. More dirty talk, please.*

I roll my lips together and glower at him in response, loving his filthy mouth. He smiles back at me, gripping my chin again and running his thumb across my lips. His other hand lifts my thigh as he lines us up on the edge of the countertop.

I close my eyes, wanting to memorize this moment. The feel. The anticipation. I want to imprint it in my brain forever. So many months of longing, dodged advances, culminating in this. What could be better?

"Eyes open, Billie," he rumbles as he squeezes my chin and tips it down. "I want you to watch me fuck you."

He looks down, forehead leaned against mine, pressing into me, and I can't look away. Wouldn't want to even if I could. He fills me slowly, inch by inch, and I watch my body stretch to accommodate his girth. Our heavy exhales mingle between us as we hold each other's bodies and watch them come together in the most intimate way possible.

I feel impossibly full as he pushes inside, and once he's seated, I feel him throbbing within me. Seeing and feeling our bodies joined this way leaves me breathless.

He pauses there before he whispers, "Holy fuck."

My hands loop around his tense neck, and I shimmy my hips toward him. "Vaughn. Please move."

He thrusts slowly first, dragging himself out before sliding himself back in a few times, lost to the look and feel of our coupling. Then his lips find mine in a worshiping kiss while his fingers trail across my hip bones as we slowly move against each other.

But it's not enough. I want to *feel* it.

"I want more. Harder," I whisper across his skin, urging him on.

His feral eyes fly open, shining with approval. Hunger. Desperation. And that perfectly cultivated facade unravels right before my eyes.

*Finally.*

He unleashes on me. Each pad of his fingers presses into my ass cheeks as his hands grip me there. I wrap my legs around his waist as I cling to his muscled shoulders and latch on for the ride while he increases the intensity of his thrusts. His thighs slap loudly against the backs of mine as he plunders me.

He owns me. He possesses me. He *fucks* me.

His voice rasps desperately against my mouth, "Take it, Billie."

There's nothing gentle about the way our bodies clash. It's all teeth and nails. Sharp gasps and growls. Months of mounting emotions bubbling over. Pure, tangible passion.

We're explosive. Desire. Frustration. Longing. Anger. And something more that I can't bring myself to put a label on. My heart stutters at the thought, and my body shakes with the brutal force of his thrusts. Sensation overwhelms every corner of my body, the heavy thrum in my pelvis building with every delicious stroke.

*This is what I want.*

One of his hands slides down my body to land between us. His deft thumb brushes across my aching clit. Once. Twice. Three times.

"Come for me, Billie." His voice is deep and demanding.

The words fall from his lips like a direct order to my body. Heat builds in my core, making that spot beneath my hip bones pinch. The heat pools there, and my legs tremble with the intensity of it.

"Oh god. Vaughn, I'm going to—" My orgasm hits me like a tidal wave. It burns and tingles like a surge of electricity spilling over me. My body shakes as I break apart in his arms. I know he's watching me intently, my body, my facial expressions, so focused on my pleasure—and I don't even care. I'm so lost in the moment, so lost in him, that nothing could distract me.

"So. Fucking. Beautiful."

Aftershocks of the orgasm rack my body as I hold him close, nuzzling into his neck, soaking up that intoxicating signature smell. I feel all gooey and soft, putty in his hands as he continues to pump into me. Good lord. This man is... so much.

"I'm going to watch you come all night long."

His dark promise makes my body break out in goose bumps, and a shiver runs across my shoulders as his thrusts hit peak force and speed.

I wrap my hands up in his silky dark hair and run my teeth along his jawline before whispering seductively in his ear, "Give it to me."

"Billie—" He snarls and bites down hard on my shoulder as he shoves himself deep in my body.

His hands squeeze my hips in time with the pulsing of his orgasm. We stay there, our ragged breathing perfectly in sync. Holding on to each other for dear life.

I'm trying to wrap my head around the enormity of what I'm feeling, sitting on my kitchen counter in Vaughn's strong arms. My head is buzzing, and every inch of my skin is hypersensitive. I feel like he's pried me right open, exposed all my soft and vulnerable hidden corners. My first reaction is to tuck them back away, to zip that side of myself back up. After all, being soft hasn't ever gotten me anywhere in life. But here, in his arms, I feel safe. Like maybe it's okay to embrace those feelings. Like maybe I won't fall apart if I do.

He trails the tip of his tongue across where I'm certain he's probably left a bite mark. He dusts my neck and cheek with gentle kisses as he comes to face me.

His dark eyes bore into my honeyed ones as he says, "What should we christen next?" It's a question as much as a request.

I garner an eye roll and an affectionate smile when I nod eagerly. "Everything."

# CHAPTER 25

## Vaughn

I've barely slept all night.

For starters, Billie is an insatiable animal. Her wild-child streak and jokes laden with sexual innuendo should have prepared me. But then, I've never been prepared for anything about this woman.

We spent hours rocking into each other. Exploring each other. We christened this cottage in a way I'm sure it never has been before. She's so carefree, so adventurous, so ravenous for me. I've never felt more desired and masculine as I do with her in my arms.

I knew I wanted her, but this…this is so much *more*.

Just looking at her now, naked and sleeping serenely on her back, one hand thrown possessively over my stomach, makes my chest ache in an unfamiliar way. I press a palm to my sternum, rubbing absently, trying to ease the mounting pressure.

I should be asleep too, but I can't tear my eyes away from her, can't stop soaking up her every feature. I want to commit everything about her to memory. I'm terrified she's going to duck and run as soon as she wakes up. Like everyone always does. I'm terrified that if I put a toe out of place, she'll throw in the towel.

She's gun-shy, and I can't blame her.

But her unpredictability scares me. The only predictable person in my life died and threw me for a goddamn loop. It feels inevitable that I'll be left in the lurch again. She's so guarded and has spent so many years putting up walls to cover big secrets. Maybe I should be angry with her for concealing her identity, but I'm not. In fact, I feel like I understand her better than ever.

If I could start fresh without my family's scandal looming over me like an ever-present storm cloud, I probably would. I can't hold that against her. I won't. It doesn't matter what her name was a decade ago. I want who she is now. Like, *really* want her.

She snuck up on me, planted the seeds, and I let the roots take over, wrapping themselves around every pulse point, filling up my darkest corners, squeezing painfully at my heart. We are intertwined now, and the thought of ripping her out—it's too painful to bear.

She rolls toward me, her slender hand dragging over my chest, sliding it underneath my palm. "That's a lot of staring. You plotting ways to kill me or something?"

*Busted.*

Her eyes close again as she snuggles into my shoulder.

The weight in my chest is buoyed by the blooming heat her touch pours around it. "Nah. I tried to fuck you to death last night, and it didn't work."

A soft giggle spills from her lips. "That's probably the way to go out though." She wraps herself around me, one long leg resting over mine. I slide an arm under her neck and hug her close to me, loving the feeling of her naked body latched on to mine. "I'll be walking funny all day thanks to you and the monster in your pants."

I take a hold of her wrist and pull her hand between my legs. "This monster?"

"Jesus, Vaughn." She laughs as she palms my hard cock. "Good morning, Monster." Her confident grip slides up and down, and I swell even more, filling her hand.

I turn so that we're lying face-to-face, letting the tips of my fingers drift over the hills and valleys of her body, feeling the gentle dips and curves of her. Breast to waist to delicious round ass. I kiss her gently since her lips look puffy and pink from the way our mouths sparred all night. "I'm out of condoms. You're an animal, Mowgli."

Her hand continues to glide up and down my length as she whispers onto my cheek. "I don't need a condom for this…"

She moves over top of me and drifts down under the sheets, dragging her nails over the ridges of my abdomen. I feel her press a firm kiss into the crook of my hip before she drags her teeth along the line of my groin. My hips buck up as she licks her way across to the other side, sucking on a sensitive spot just beside the base of my cock.

Billie edges down farther, and I push up on my elbows to watch her. She holds my gaze with her glowing amber eyes and lets her lips brush against the tip of my cock. I groan and clench my molars. Her tongue darts out and swirls around the swollen head, lapping up the glistening drop of precum. *Does she have any fucking clue how sinful she looks right now?*

"Billie," I say, my voice thick with arousal, "what do you think you're doing?"

From between my legs, she gives me her best innocent look, lashes fluttering slowly across her cheeks as she licks my length brazenly from base to tip. "I'm trying to apologize to you for being… What did you call it? So totally infuriating?"

And then she takes my cock all the way into her mouth, straight to the back of her throat.

"Fuck," I rasp out, tangling my fingers in her chestnut waves, holding her hair back so I can watch her take me. Watch her cheeks hollow out as she bobs eagerly in my lap. "Best fucking apology ever," I growl, applying some pressure to the back of her head, feeling her go soft and pliant in my hands. Letting me move her how I want. So goddamn trusting, turning herself over to me this way. It feels like the ultimate victory. The ultimate gift. And it's like throwing gasoline on a wildfire. The animal instincts inside me buzz with pleasure, with wanting more. "Billie. I need to fuck you."

She pulls off me, wide eyes trained on mine as she daintily wipes a smudge of saliva off her bottom lip. "Okay," she breathes out. "I'm clean and on birth control."

I internally beat my chest like an absolute caveman. "I'm clean. I've never gone without a condom."

Her teeth press into that bottom lip, just like they did the first day I met her. So fucking distracting. "Good. I want you bare."

I jerk in her palm. Fuck me, this woman can talk about consensual safe sex and I'm raring to go. The thought of no barriers between us drives me insane. I pull her up to me and then roll her over so that she's underneath me. *Where she belongs.* My fingers swipe through her wet heat once.

*My girl is so ready*. I slide into her. Slow. Steady. Skin on skin for the first time. Wanting to be as close to her as possible. Moving together, we share feelings that neither of us can put into words yet. She got hard and dirty Vaughn last night, but this morning, I feel off balance. *Sentimental.*

We fuck lazily. We kiss slowly. We let our hands roam tenderly. I whisper in her ear and tell her how good she feels, how incredibly beautiful she is. I tell her that our bodies fit together perfectly. And she moans her agreement as she topples over into another orgasm, her limbs trembling around mine as I pour myself into her body.

After soaping each other in the shower, I offer to cook Billie breakfast. She sidles up to the island, looking fresh in an off-the-shoulder white shirt. Just the sight of her shoulder and elegant collarbone peeking through makes my mouth go dry. The implication of no bra is downright distracting. I focus back on the cutting board. Can't keep mauling her if I don't feed her.

I slide a cup of coffee across the kitchen island to her

waiting hands. She glances down into the mug, a small smile touching the corners of her mouth. I know she's checking the amount of cream I put in for her.

Her cheek twitches as a look of uncertainty overshadows the small smile. "What do we do now? What is this?"

My heart pounds in my chest. This is the conversation I've been dreading. The one where Billie the escape artist finds a way out of being *us*. I keep chopping vegetables for the omelet.

"We're together, Billie. I don't care what you name it. It's like I told you last night." I look up to her striking face. "You're what I want."

Her caramel eyes glisten with tears. "I want you too." Her voice is quiet. "But I'm concerned about how that works at the farm or around the track. It's hard enough dealing with douchebags like Patrick Cassel without being accused of banging my boss."

"You are banging your boss." I point at her. "And you love it."

She rolls her eyes, grinning. "I do. But can we just keep it quiet for a bit?"

I don't love the idea. I've never had a woman want to keep me hidden away. Usually it's quite the opposite. But Billie has a point. She's worked hard for her career, put a lot on the line to make it happen for herself, and I would never want to be the one to ruin that for her. Truth be told, I've become her biggest cheerleader. Whatever it takes.

"Of course," I say as I turn away to fire the stove up and hide my disappointment. It still stings, and I don't want her to see that it does. I don't want to push her too hard, too fast.

My phone rings on the counter, interrupting our conversation. Dread pools in my stomach when I see it's a call from a number I don't recognize. I never thought I'd be afraid to answer my phone, but this is my new normal.

"You gonna answer that?"

"I don't know who it is. I still keep getting calls from reporters asking about my grandfather. I'm tired of telling them I have no comment."

"Let me take one for the team then." She presses the answer button and turns it to speakerphone with a look of excitement on her face. Ever the shit disturber. Her fake sugary voice fills the room. "Helloo! Vaughn Harding's phone."

"Put me through to Mr. Harding." The voice is deep and sharp, slightly accented, as the man barks his order.

Billie is unfazed. "Unfortunately for you, I don't take orders from people whose mother didn't teach them to say please or thank you."

I cringe inwardly, stifling a laugh. She really has no filter. It's part of her charm.

"My mother is dead. Put him on. Now."

"I guess it's a blessing that she's not here to witness your bad manners firsthand then," Billie snipes back.

My fingers pulse and squeeze the knife in my hand. I don't want to police her behavior, but she is going to get me in trouble with that mouth one of these days.

"May I ask who's calling?"

"Stefan Dalca."

I pale. The man is an enigma, practically a recluse. A shady one who showed up in the area a year ago with too much money and no answers about who he was or where he came from. And in a small town where everyone knows everything about everyone else, his secrecy is downright suspicious. His land, his stables, his horses, he bought them all outright and then waltzed into the tight-knit racing industry in the Lower Mainland like he'd been a mainstay for years. Everyone in the community agrees, it's fishy as all get-out. I've intentionally avoided all connections to the man, which is easy to do when he's secluded on his property.

"Charming. You were far more polite last week when you were needling me for information at the track."

My eyes flash up to Billie. *Huh? She's met the man?* The line is quiet for a few beats too long.

Crazy Billie has left one of the area's most dubious businessmen speechless. If I weren't trying so hard to be quiet, I would laugh. I chance a look at her, assessing her profile. Yeah, she looks pleased with herself right now. She's just a cat playing with a mouse.

I shake my head. How did sensible Vaughn Harding end up with this smart-mouthed firebrand?

"Aha. Is this Miss Black? Or is it Miss Farrington?" His voice is more teasing now. It's almost like I can *hear* the smug look on his face through the phone. I want to punch it right off his slimy face.

"Miss Black," she replies, not giving away the momentary shock that flits across her face at him using her old name.

"Well, in that case," Dalca continues in his smooth voice, "Miss Black, may I please speak to Mr. Harding? I'd like to make him an offer on the black horse we spoke about last week."

Now it's Billie's turn to pale. Her whole body goes rigid, except for her mouth, which opens and closes without any words.

"Okay," she finally says, eerily calm. A lot calmer than she looks as her eyes dart to mine.

How the hell am I going to play this?

"Vaughn Harding speaking."

"Mr. Harding. My name is Stefan Dalca. We haven't officially met, but I had the pleasure of speaking with your"—he trails off suggestively—"trainer, Miss Black."

Billie turns away from me, looking out the window toward DD's paddock.

"This is a private number, Mr. Dalca. Care to elaborate on how you came to have it?"

"I have my ways." His tone is dismissive. "At any rate, as you know, I'm working hard to build an elite string of racehorses and thought we could work together as two of the big players in the area. I saw your black colt run last weekend, and I'd like to make you an offer."

Great. Just what I need. Another morally corrupt asshole trying to latch on to my business.

"My company email is listed on the website. You are always welcome to send me a written offer. Though I have to tell you, I'm not looking to work with anyone." Out of the corner of my eye, I see Billie's body relax on a long exhale.

His laugh is a deep rumble through the speaker, the kind of laugh you direct at a small charming child when they say something adorable. I don't like it. "Everything has a price, Mr. Harding. I knew your grandfather, you know."

Billie's head whips toward me now as I grind my teeth, making my jaw click.

"We had an excellent working relationship."

My voice comes out dark and dangerous. Now he's gone too far. This conversation is over. "How lovely. Thank you for your condolences. Have a nice day now."

"Keep your eyes peeled for my email. It's been a pleasure chatting with you."

I hang up, knuckles white, chest heaving, mind racing. *What a prick.*

"Well, that was...interesting," Billie muses.

I just grunt in response, not sure what to say.

"DD isn't for sale, right?" Her eyes are so clear and honest, focused right on my face. "I mean, I know horses come and go. I know it's part of the business but—" She cuts off, looking out the window and running her palm up over her throat like I had the night before.

"But you're attached to him?" I supply.

She clears her throat. "I mean, yes, I am. I'll be the first to admit I love that horse." Her voice cracks, but she continues. "Probably more than any horse I've had the pleasure of spending time with. But, Vaughn, he can win it all. I know he can. He's my—our—best shot at winning the Denman Derby. Hell, maybe even the Northern Crown. Horses like him come around once in a lifetime. You can't just replace that kind of prestige."

I give her hand a reassuring squeeze across the counter. "Don't worry about it. Dalca's the last type of person I plan to go into business with."

She places her other hand on top of mine, giving it a gentle squeeze, before she walks out of the house wordlessly to go feed her horse. A silent offering of her trust.

Stefan Dalca would have to make me one hell of an offer for me to ever even consider taking that horse away from her.

# CHAPTER 26

## Billie

THE RUBBER CURRYCOMB IN MY HAND MOVES IN SMALL aggressive circles over DD's dusty black coat. The little pig rolled around in the mud and looks like an absolute swamp monster. Which, for once, is fine by me. I need to work out some angst.

Last night was *a lot*, but the phone call from Stefan Dalca had been something else altogether.

Vaughn fucked my brains out, but not all of them, so I didn't miss the fact that he didn't actually confirm that DD isn't for sale. Which is exactly why I held myself from jumping into the deep end with the man.

As my boss, he owes me no explanation about selling horses. My job is to train them, make them as successful as possible. His job is to run the business side, crunch the numbers, make deals with buyers and so forth.

But as my whatever-the-hell-we-are, well, that muddies the waters a bit, doesn't it?

I'm not quick to open the cage around my heart, but I know Vaughn is close to getting there. If I'm honest with myself, he's consumed me since the day we met. I've gone out of my way to harass him. I accused him of being the little boy who pesters the girl he likes, but the truth is I am no better.

I constantly needled him, pushing the limits of his patience, all to see what he'd tolerate. To see if he'd snap. I've been hot and cold to the extreme. Because maybe, just maybe, if I couldn't scare him off, he'd be worthy of my trust. Maybe if I put my worst foot forward and he still stuck around, maybe then I could open up.

I need to sit down and explain this to Vaughn. I owe him an explanation. We probably should have talked about this already, but we were too busy giving each other delicious orgasms.

God, I've never had sex like that. Uncontained passion. Overflowing pleasure. There was no turning back. It's like something destined us to get that out of our systems. I don't know why I held back for so long, really. Vaughn is the perfect blend of gentle and domineering. Hot doesn't even begin to cover that first time on the kitchen counter.

He's addictive. Hazardous to my well-being.

I finish brushing DD to a shine and feeding him all the carrots I can find before heading to the stables to check in on the man I haven't been able to stop thinking about. The phone call with Stefan Dalca took the wind out of his sails, and while I was out with DD, he darted out of my house saying he was going to do a few things in his office. I'm intuitive enough to see that call rocked him to his core.

He said he was okay, but I'm not buying it.

I peek around the corner into his office, leaning against the doorframe. He's sitting at his desk, looking out the window with a thoughtful expression on his handsome face, fingers steepled in front of his chin. His body is tense, and I see the defined lines of concentration on his forehead.

"I recognize that look," I say as I tap gently on my temple. "You're hashing something out."

His chocolate eyes dart to mine, but his body doesn't move.

"Yes." He huffs out a sigh.

I move into the room and drop myself into one of the chairs facing him, the same one I sat in on the day of my job interview. "You're a slow processor, you know?"

He quirks an eyebrow at me like I've insulted him.

"No, no, hang on. Let me finish. It's like...I feel, and it slams into me with such force. I feel everything so intensely. So...instantly." I rub my hands over my thighs as he regards me, not interjecting a thing. "Whereas you're so adept at keeping up appearances, you don't even realize something is influencing you until much later. You've buried it, and by the time you get around to uncovering it, it's necrotic. Practically eating you alive."

He sits still, looking at me from over the tips of his fingers. Seconds stretch out as we stare at each other.

"Maybe."

Ugh. Men. Why do I keep coming back for more?

"Tell me what's wrong."

"Dalca sent his offer."

I stare at him, hearing my heart beating in my ears. I'm scared to ask. "I'm so sorry. I had no idea who he was when he started talking to me. Is…is it…?"

His shoulders slump as he scrubs his hands over his face. "It's a lot."

I feel myself pale. "How much?"

"Not enough. Especially considering the way he roped Dermot into the conversation like he has something on him. Not wild about that implication. I don't even know where to start."

"Okay. I'll start. I want to tell you about my childhood."

He shuffles papers around on his desk, avoiding eye contact with me. "You don't need to do that."

"I grew up in Toronto, in a painfully ostentatious neighborhood called the Bridle Path—also known as Millionaires' Row. And yes, it's exactly as pretentious as it sounds. And no, I have zero intention of heading back that way, which is why the West Coast is the perfect place for me. Same country, opposite side."

"Way better weather."

"Way hotter bosses." I wink at him and then continue. "I spent my youth being groomed to make someone a gracious wife."

That garners me a chuckle. "Have your parents ever met you?"

I smile sadly at him. "That's just the thing, isn't it? My parents were so focused on curating everything about me, about our family, my appearance, my education, my extracurricular activities, my friends, that they overlooked pretty much everything about who I actually am. I don't think they really cared. If they could have had two point five kids just to achieve that perfect statistic, I think they would have."

His jaw ticks and his eyes soften. "I'm sorry."

I shrug. "I take solace in imagining their faces when they find out I'm an unmarried racehorse trainer with no postsecondary education."

"You don't talk to them at all? They haven't reached out?"

"Not even once. I was seventeen when the videos of my dad surfaced. I'm sure you've seen them. Pretty, young escorts, a pile of cocaine, and Canada's favorite prime minister. Naturally, I was expected to fall into line and come to my father's defense like a good soldier." I shake my head as I feel my tear ducts burn. I blink my lashes, trying to push the swell of water back down. "Nothing will ever be as humiliating as having to stand by him through that, watching my mother smile and nod at people like everything was fine."

Vaughn reaches across the desk to hold my hand in his. "So you left?"

I take a deep, ragged breath. "Yup. On my eighteenth birthday. My trust fund swapped into my name, and I stormed out of there in an absolute blaze of glory. Took a bus out of town and ended up on Hank's doorstep. I knew, even as a teenager, I wasn't ever going to fall on my own sword to cover up another person's mistakes. I was done." I let that long-buried anger seep into my voice now. "When you make shitty fucking decisions, you'll probably end up in a shitty fucking situation, and you don't force the people you love to sacrifice themselves for your reputation. It's unforgivable."

Vaughn's long fingers trace over the veins on the top of my hand as he stares at me. Like really stares at me. It's unnerving. I feel like he's looking right into me, right through my skin and muscle. Right through my bones. Right into my patchwork heart.

"Poetic." A dimple on his cheek peeks out, and I can't help but laugh. This man has been making me laugh since day one, whether it was at him or with him. Vaughn Harding is amusing.

"On a lighter note, I have an older brother. His name is Rich. He's the only member of my family I keep in touch with, and you'd probably really like him. Sometimes he fakes a business trip to come see me…" I trail off, thinking about how long it's been since I've seen my brother, since I've hugged him. "I miss him."

"He stuck around?"

"Oh yeah. That schmuck was born to be a politician. He'll stay out east, though he's not terribly tight with our parents either."

"That's…" He trails off, looking for the right words.

"A lot?" I huff out a tired laugh as I squeeze his big warm hand. "Sure is. But now you know my whole sordid past. The point of the story is people almost always disappoint me, but horses don't."

Vaughn's eyes burn with determination and something more when he says to me, "I don't want to disappoint you."

I shrug in response, not ready to get my hopes up in that department. Not yet.

"Then don't."

★★★

I launch myself at Vaughn the minute we push through the front door of my little log house. I hear his breath leave his chest in a whoosh as I crash against him, wanting him to wash away the memories I just dredged up.

He rumbles against my lips, "Bed. Now." His palms grip my biceps as he gives me a gentle shove toward the stairs.

A telltale spark dances around in my pelvis as I walk across the room. I love this version of him.

I lift my shirt over my head, dropping it on the floor. I unclasp my bra, dropping it on the steps. At the top of the landing, I shimmy out of my jeans and look over my shoulder at him as I head toward the bed wearing only a thong. I feel like he's hunting me as he prowls behind me, covering the ground more quickly with his long strides.

With one hand on my shoulder, he spins me around to face him and palms my breasts. "This body is *mine*."

I stand at the edge of my bed as his hands slide all over me. His lips follow in their path. Down my throat, across my collarbones, onto my nipples where his tongue darts out as he sucks and nips. I can't stop the wanton moans that spill from my lips.

The man sets me on fire.

His mouth travels down my body as he drops to his knees before me. He looks up from where he's kneeling, and I run my hands through his silky strands, soaking in his handsome face. The sharp masculine planes, the deep, dark eyes dancing with sinister intentions. Just looking at him kneeling before me makes me squeeze my thighs together in anticipation.

He hooks two fingers into the strip of fabric covering me and pulls it to the side. "This time when you beg me to fuck you while I eat this pussy, I might actually indulge you."

My teeth drag across my bottom lip as I sigh out, "Fuck."

Vaughn moves in. His expert mouth tortures me with every swipe of his tongue, every graze of his teeth, every well-timed suck. From above my heaving chest, I watch his head move against me.

I pant and try to put off begging. I really do. But I'm weak. "Please." It comes out strangled. "Please, Vaughn, I want more."

He doubles his efforts as his fingers dig into my hips and ass.

"P-please fuck me."

He sucks hard on my clit, making me cry out. He is both impressive and forever infuriating.

"Vaughn Harding!" I scold him. "Get that fine ass up here and fuck me. Now."

His chuckle is dark as he rises to stand eye-to-eye with me. "That's not how I remember you begging that night."

"You're impossible." I close my fingers in his hair and pull his face to mine. I can taste myself on his lips as he kisses me back. It feels intensely personal, and all I want to feel is his skin on mine. "Please." I tear at his shirt while he grapples with his pants.

When we're naked, he turns me around, fisting my hair

and shoving me down onto the bed. Goose bumps bloom on my arms in anticipation.

His hard body covers mine from behind as he lines his bare cock up, whispering in my ear, "You're so wet for me, Billie."

"Yesss," I hiss out as he licks the spot on my shoulder where I'm sporting a red mark the exact shape of his teeth. I grind my ass back against his steely length, aching for him.

"Tell me what you want, baby. Hard or soft?"

"Hard."

He slams into me, fully seated in one thrust. Breath rushes out of my lungs in one breath as my body adjusts to his size.

"And then soft."

His dark chuckle rolls across my skin like static electricity, snapping at my nerve endings. "Whatever my girl wants, she gets."

We sink into each other, ravenous. Two broken people, damaged by the ones meant to love them the most, finding solace in each other's arms.

# CHAPTER 27

## Billie

Violet is already up on DD by the time I get down to the dirt track. She's in the saddle walking him around the grass infield. The sun has barely risen, but Violet is ready to go.

We already talked about testing the waters with him after his colic. Luckily, it wasn't very severe, and he's pretty much recovered. My hysterics may have been *slightly* over the top. But this horse is special, and I won't take any chances with him.

"Morning!" Her hand shoots up in a terse wave as I flip a leg over the white fence and sit on top of it. DD raises his neck and whinnies at me in greeting.

At least one of them is happy to see me. The duo walks toward me, and DD's petite head swings back and forth happily. He looks relaxed with his ears perked forward and back stretched long, and it warms my heart to see the anxious little horse looking so content. He just needed time and a gentle hand—and a metric fuck ton of treats. *Greedy little jerk.*

"Who pissed in your Shreddies, Vivi?" I ask as they approach me now.

"Har-har-har."

DD reaches his head out once he gets close enough, shaking me down for cookies. I blow a raspberry on his soft nose and boop him on the forehead. "After your workout, piggy." I lean back and take in Violet's wide blue eyes and the pinched expression at the corners of her mouth. "You okay?"

"Mm-hmm." She looks down and fiddles with the reins in her hands.

I swear, if it's that guy still, I'm going to kill him myself. "Don't quit this gig to become an actress."

"Don't tell her what she can and can't do."

I turn to see Vaughn walking down the gentle slope away from the offices. He's holding a steaming cup of coffee, and he gives me a knowing smirk as he approaches. My spine tingles at his heated look. Images of how I've spent the last couple nights flash through my mind. Filthy. And delicious. The man is turning me into a mindless bimbo. He's fully dressed, it's first thing in the morning, and all I can think about is dragging him back up to his office and locking the door.

Alas, I've got horses to train and races to win, so I ignore the blush that creeps across my cheeks as he leans in to hand me the cup of coffee and quietly says, "Should I make you beg for this too?"

"Prick," I huff out. I look down and see the perfect coffee-to-cream ratio in the hot mug and wrap my palms around it, letting the heat seep into my skin in the cool morning air. "Thanks, Boss Man. I'll keep you posted on how it goes at the track today."

He chuckles as he turns to leave, knowing I've just dismissed him. We're supposed to be keeping our relationship on the down-low around the barn, but when I look at the skeptical look on Violet's face, I have a feeling that we might already fail in that department.

I clear my throat and take a sip of coffee. "Planning on telling me what's up now that he's gone?"

She quirks an eyebrow at me and nods her head up toward the barn. "I don't know. You planning on telling me what's going on with you two?"

I lift my mug toward her to acknowledge her point. "Good talk. You ready to take that little psycho for a light breeze? See how he feels?"

She sighs and her shoulders relax. Her relief at me dropping that line of questioning is clear. "Yes. So ready."

"Good. Let's see what you've got."

DD breezes beautifully for Violet. She stands up in her irons and just lets him run. Her gentle squeezes on the reins hold him back, and her perfectly still torso allows him to move how he likes. When they round the top corner of the track, she presses the reins at him, and he shoots forward like a bullet. His stride lengthens, and he eats up the ground. Effortless.

If she can get him in position next weekend, the other horses won't stand a chance. And we'll be qualified for the Denman Derby, leg one of the Northern Crown. Bucket list, here I come.

Back at the barn, Hank is standing in front of a tack stall

chatting with one of the grooms who is prepping Brite Lite for her turn on the track. Her sweet friendly gray face turns to me as I approach.

"Billie girl!" Hank greets me with his warm smile. "How ya doing this morning? How'd DD run?"

I shake my head at him, grinning like a lunatic. "That horse will win it all, Hank. He's primed."

His smile grows to match mine. We both know horses well enough to know how exciting a horse like DD is, how infrequently they come along. His big hand squeezes my shoulder as I lean into him for a hug. "You've worked magic with that little black horse. I'm proud of you."

I rest my head on his shoulder and sigh. "All thanks to you, old man."

"I don't think I can take all the credit for the woman and trainer you've become. Hard work pays off, and I don't think I know anyone who has worked harder than you. You deserve this."

His approval makes my chest ache with what I've missed my whole life. The praise my own parents most likely will never give me.

"Thanks, Hank," I say, not trusting myself with any more words than that.

★★★

The weeks fly by. I spend mornings with the young horses on the ranch and afternoons at Bell Point Park in Vancouver. Hours are spent commuting between the two, but it's worth it when I fall into Vaughn's strong arms every night.

All I can think about is this coming Saturday, the race that counts for everything. If DD can pull off a win, he'll be qualified for the derby. Because we let him start slow, this is the final qualifying opportunity. The dream I've dreamt for years now is within reach, and in my gut, I know if I can just get him there, he'll pull it off. He's a competitor. He'll know what to do.

I'm nervous about keeping him healthy. I'm nervous about putting a completely unproven jockey on him. I have moments when I wonder if I'm qualified to do my job at all. Impostor syndrome is a raggedy-ass bitch, and I know I'm not doing a great job of hiding my anxiety.

In bed, under the shroud of darkness, I confess my worries to Vaughn. He listens to my fears. He soothes my body with his. He's the rock I need. The rock I've been searching for my entire adult life. He doesn't coddle me, but he doesn't let me beat myself up either.

To be honest, he's too good to be true. Which is why I'm here at his house, just down the road from the barn, snooping through his bathroom. I came in here to clean up after a marathon sex session and couldn't help myself.

I'm terrible, *I know*.

I quietly open the drawers. Toothpaste. Deodorant. Shaving cream. Razor. Condoms. I huff out a sigh. "Boring. Boring. Boring."

"Looking for something?" He's leaning against the doorjamb, toned arms crossed across his chest, chocolate hair all mussed—just the way I like it.

I make eye contact with him in the mirror. "Yes. I'm trying to figure out what's wrong with you."

"I'm sorry, what?"

"You heard me." I turn to face him now and wave a hand in his direction. "Ever since you got me naked, you've been *nice*. And just the right amount of dirty."

He smirks.

"And so fucking gentlemanlike."

"Okay. And this is a problem?" He looks incredulous.

"It's just—" My teeth dig into my bottom lip as I look back into his dark eyes. "I'm waiting for the other shoe to drop. People are notoriously good at letting me down, so if I can find some proof of you not being this…this perfect, of this being an act, then I can prepare myself for when shit will inevitably hit the fan. I'll know what's coming."

Vaughn's smirk fades, and he looks back at me softly, like I'm a cornered wild animal. "Billie. This isn't an act. We're not an act. I'm not going to let shit hit the fan." He steps into the bathroom and wraps me in his arms. One hand strokes my hair soothingly as he presses a kiss to my forehead. "Just focus on winning the races you need to. You've worked too hard to be distracted by me. You've got too much on your plate. I'll be here when you need me, waiting for you. I'm not going anywhere. I'm in this for the long haul."

I relax in his embrace and run my hands down his back. "See? It's not normal to know the perfect thing to say."

"Plus, I keep all the body parts in my freezer," he adds.

I can't help but laugh into his chest as I feel my anxiety melt away in the safety of his embrace. "You do have that handsome serial killer vibe about you."

"Speaking of handsome, tell me more about how I'm perfect."

I groan as he laughs and lifts me up. I wrap my legs around his waist as he walks me back to bed where, despite my doubts and fears, he holds me tight in his arms all night long.

★★★

Race day is here, and I'm a wreck. I've given up *everything* to get to this day. It's do or die. There are no other qualifiers, and next year, DD will be too old to qualify. The pressure is weighing on me, and I'm letting it get to me.

I could be sick. Everyone else seems fine, perfectly happy. Like they trust that I'm leading them down the right path. At my log house this morning, Vaughn told me as much. Hank is all chipper. Even Violet doesn't seem that nervous for her debut race—a qualifying stakes race, no less—which is probably because she knows she'll be sitting on the most horsepower out of the entire group. I've talked her half to death about strategy. I think I'm at the point where I'm annoying her now with the whole mother-hen vibe.

So I'm hiding from everyone in DD's stall, brushing him to a perfect shine even though I'm wearing a beautiful pantsuit. But it doesn't matter. Breathing in that comforting scent and trying to find my center while he munches happily on his hay is what I need right now.

Hank's head pops into the stall. "You should head up to the VIP lounge soon."

I don't look up; my hand continues brushing the rubber

comb in circles on the pitch-black coat. "I don't think I'm going to watch the race. I might just stay here at the barn. Can you record it for me? I'll analyze it after."

"You're not really going to send your baby out there alone, are you?" He strokes DD's forelock as I look into the horse's big intelligent eye.

My chest pinches at the thought of missing the race, but my head swims with the pressure of it all. "I'm freaking out," I whisper to the man who might as well be my father.

"I know you are, Billie girl. You don't have to go up to the lounge, but make sure you watch it. Find a quiet spot along the rail or in the stands where no one will know who you are. You will not want to miss the feeling of watching your boy win. What the two of you have is too special."

"Yeah," I mumble.

I know he's right. He just smiles and leaves, thank goodness. A hug would have had me falling to pieces in his arms.

I spend the next hour alone with DD, methodically getting him ready, wrapping his legs perfectly, placing all his tack just so. It's almost strange that no one talks to me, but I'm pretty sure Hank has warned them off bothering me, and to his credit, Vaughn knows me well enough to know I need to be alone right now.

It still unnerves me how easily he understands me, how he accepts me—my paranoia and colorful vocabulary too. He doesn't even try to change me. I'm thinking he might just like me for who I am. And the thought of letting him in completely terrifies me. I literally pinch myself sometimes to make sure I'm not dreaming.

Right now, I pinch myself to make sure this day is really happening. I step back to look at DD. His dishy head, his dainty legs, how handsome he looks in his yellow silks. He's getting antsy. He knows what's coming.

I press a kiss to his muscular neck. "I love you, DD. Be safe out there."

He's ready to go.

# CHAPTER 28

## Billie

THE GATES FLY OPEN, AND THE TEN HORSES EXPLODE ONTO the track.

The loudspeakers crackle to life. "And they're off!"

I'm standing at the far corner of the track facing the finish line. I'll see them through the first turn and then, if everything goes to plan, I'll have a head-on view of DD making his final move.

My heart pounds in my chest as I watch Violet execute our plan to perfection. She's light and still in the irons and gently holds DD back. He shies away from the pack all on his own, so this is a simple task off the start. They thunder toward me, and the ground trembles beneath my feet. The front-runners round the first corner, flying past, fighting for that coveted spot along the rail. Burning all their energy—exactly what I want them to do.

DD is galloping steady, not too far back but not crowded

either. Just the way he likes. He's a blur of shiny black and yellow as he passes the end of the oval moving into the clubhouse turn. Rounding out of the second bend, heading into the straight, I see his ears shoot forward. His head drops imperceptibly, and his ears flatten in that signature pissy fashion of his as he looks through the maze of horses ahead of him and realizes he's not winning.

*Attaboy.*

A lane opens up, and Violet moves in, easing into the middle of the pack. Exactly where DD doesn't like to be and exactly where he'll want to get out of as quickly as possible. They steadily move down the straight, passing the horses that are tiring.

Hours on the trails and trotting hills have given DD an edge where stamina is concerned. He's not at top speed yet, and he's got lots left in the tank. My fingers squeeze the rail of the fence as the pack moves into the far turn. He's dragging Violet now, leaning down into the bit—he knows what needs to be done. This is where they need to make their big move out of the middle of the pack. This is where they come from behind.

DD flies out of that final bend looking like a small and mighty warhorse. His face is vengeful, and his ears are so far back they're downright aerodynamic. But when Violet's arms press forward, his ears perk, and they're off.

In sync, they move up like they've just been shot out of a cannon. The other horses look like they're running in slow motion. All I can hear is blood thundering in my ears as I watch them move past horse after horse.

With only two horses ahead of them, Violet doesn't bother with moving close to the rail. She sets their sights on the finish line and pushes her hands at him, urging him on. I see her lips moving, talking to him, as dirt sprays up around them.

My hands move up over my mouth as they barrel down toward me. I want to scream, to cheer, but I can't tear my eyes off them as they eat up the soft ground and sail past the leaders. Right into first place and more. They blaze across the finish line easily six lengths ahead of the next horse.

It's not even close.

I feel wet heat on the apples of my cheeks as they gallop toward me, relaxing into a slower gait as Violet leans back a bit and murmurs at DD. He snorts and tosses his head, looking awfully pleased with himself.

I can't help but jump up and shout, "Violet Eaton, you are a rock star!" as they come into the bend where I'm standing. I swear one of DD's pointy little ears flicks toward me in recognition. Violet hears me too. I'll never forget the smile she gives me. So big it looks like it might hurt, like her cheeks are swollen.

I give her a matching one, and my heart soars with the reality of what's just happened. She leans down as DD slows in the bend and wraps her petite arms around his sweat-slicked neck, hugging him.

I can't believe it. We did it.

A no-name jockey, a freshman trainer, and a horse that no one wanted to handle.

We fucking did it.

I hustle to the winner's circle, not wanting to miss a moment of this. I'm going to soak it in. Revel in it. Kiss my little black horse. Shit, maybe even kiss my boyfriend. That's how crazy I am feeling.

People swarm the pen where they hand out the plate and take photos, and I push my way through. When I get close, I can see Vaughn's perfectly coiffed hair, a head above most of the people around him as he moves toward the circle.

"Vaughn!" His head snaps back toward my voice as I walk briskly his way.

He stands still, hands in his pockets, letting the crowd part around him. He's shaking his head at me, lips pressed together, trying to hold back a smile. When I get close enough to look up into his warm chocolate eyes, I squeal and throw my arms around his neck. He laughs into the curve of my shoulder and lifts me off the ground. He hugs me so hard, with so much pride.

He kisses my cheek and whispers, "You did it."

I feel like I could burst. I squeeze his biceps through his suit jacket and lean back to look at his handsome face. "No. *We* did it."

And then I kiss him. In full view of everyone around us, and I don't even care if they see. I don't want to keep us secret. *Us* feels too good. He grunts in surprise, but his palms cup my jaw, and he kisses me back. Sweetly. Stroking my cheek lovingly with his thumb.

My icy heart melts in his hands. Everything feels so right today.

After mauling DD with kisses, almost knocking Violet

over with the violence of my hug, and crying a few happy tears in Hank's comforting embrace, we pose for photos. Vaughn is presented with the trophy for the win, but he hands the trophy over to me almost instantly, and then they drape DD in the championship blanket. I feel Vaughn's presence beside me the whole time, like a rock, his hand often resting on the small of my back as people step forward to talk to me.

Cole shows up too, and despite my best efforts to ignore him and just enjoy the moment, I don't miss the way he gawks at Violet. The way he leans in toward her and whispers something. And the way her face drains of all color and excitement as she stares back at him slack-jawed. Violet doesn't look like a woman who's just been congratulated; she looks like a woman who's seen a ghost. Now *that* is something I'm going to have to come back to later.

I feel like I'm just spinning in circles, thanking people for their congratulations and answering their questions. Questions about DD, questions about my training methods, questions about how we chose Violet to get the ride.

One member of the press stretches her phone toward me. "Can you comment on the rumors that you were in a physical altercation with a well-known jockey here at the track?"

The pads of Vaughn's fingers press into my hips as I let a small smile touch my lips. "That doesn't sound very professional," is all I say before turning away.

Vaughn leans in, his voice rumbling across my neck and sending a shiver down my spine. "Sounds like word's gotten out about what a naughty girl you are."

I mutter under my breath, "I'll show you naughty tonight."

His hand trails down over my ass, and his voice is like silk against my skin. My cheeks heat as I look around. It's too busy for anyone to notice where my boss's hand is roaming.

"I'm holding you to that," he says, looking around now. "But I'm going to duck out for a sec and see if I can find Cole. Meet us up in the lounge for a drink when you're done here?"

"You bet," I say over my shoulder, already greeting the next person who's approaching me.

With a squeeze of my elbow, he's gone, and I turn my best smile back on the people hovering around, even though all I want to do is take DD home and fulfill my dirty promises to Vaughn.

***

Back in the quiet of our row at the barn, we dote on DD. He gets a cool bath, ice boots on his legs, and a lot of tender loving care from Violet, Hank, and me. We haven't used other grooms with him so far, and I'm not sure why we'd start now. Our ornery little champion only likes certain people, and I don't blame him one bit.

"He felt perfect out there," Violet says in awe as she towels him off.

"You guys *looked* perfect," Hank adds.

I smile. "He's right. You were both perfect. Beautifully ridden. Beautifully run. There isn't much more I could ask for."

Violet points at me. "It was your plan. Your training.

Your strategy. I just hopped on at the last moment and executed it the way you wanted."

"She's right." Hank squeezes my shoulder.

"That may be true, but we aren't going to have it this easy at the Denman Derby. We don't have much time to prepare. We'll have to be perfect *and* lucky to win that one."

Violet nods solemnly, but Hank just laughs.

"Girl. You are too serious for your own good. You just won! You're qualified. Get outta here. Go make moon eyes with Harding Junior."

I gawk back at him. *How the hell did he know?*

"Billie, for Christ's sake. I may be old, but I'm not blind yet. You two have been circling around each other for months."

"He's right," Violet adds as she tosses a blanket back over DD's damp coat.

"You couldn't have picked a better one," Hank says. "Go act your age. Have some fun for once."

"I don't—"

"Git," he cuts me off, waving his hand, dismissing me. "I won't leave your horse's side until you get back. Don't worry."

I give in and walk down the long alleyway, past countless other stalls, toward the grandstand and VIP lounge. I'd really rather share a drink in the barn with our staff who actually played a part in today's success, but I also know there's a time and place to schmooze. So here I am, ready to schmooze. For the business and for Vaughn, because I know he secretly likes this shit.

I round the corner but stop short when I hear Stefan

Dalca's cool authoritative voice. "I've been waiting for a response to my offer."

The voice that replies is icy, and I know it well. "I've already informed you that the horse isn't for sale."

I step back into the alleyway and peek my head around to see Vaughn's back to me as he faces off with Dalca.

"Everything has a price."

"So you've said. The horse just qualified for the derby though. He isn't going anywhere."

"You're right. It's probably worth more than the ten million dollars I offered last week."

*Fuck me*. Ten million? Is he serious? It's not unheard of for a stud who could go on to make a lot of champion babies. But DD is still relatively unproven.

Vaughn's posture is rigid as he faces off with the other man. He's not intimidated by Dalca's dangerous vibe. He's got a few inches on him, maybe a bit more, as he draws up and says, "I don't care what your offer is."

Dalca's smile is sly as his eyes dance over Vaughn with unbridled amusement. He's clearly enjoying this encounter, throwing his money around without a care in the world. He isn't the sunny media darling that Vaughn is. He is the shadows moving in the dark. Backroom deals and threats are his currency. He's wily, like a fox, not to be trusted. I want to jump in and tell him to hit the dusty trail, but this is Vaughn's battle, not mine.

It probably isn't appropriate for me to be listening in, but hey, no one ever accused me of being appropriate. Why start now?

"I almost get the feeling that you don't like me, Mr. Harding."

"I don't."

This is the Vaughn I met that first day when I pulled into the parking lot at Gold Rush Ranch. Cold and dismissive.

"Twenty million."

I cover my mouth to muffle the sound of me choking. That's an insane number, and the business side of me knows it's also not an offer to turn down. That amount of money could go a long way, buy a lot of nice horses. But the sentimental side of me? No, DD is too special. He could be worth one dollar, and I'd feel the same. He's priceless. The thought of him leaving makes my eyes sting.

"It's not about the number. It's about the future. The horse isn't for sale. End of story."

I am going to worship the hell out of that man tonight.

He turns to leave, but Dalca stops him in his tracks when he says, "The future, hmm?"

Vaughn angles his broad shoulders back toward the shady businessman.

"Twenty million and I go to the press with irrefutable proof that your grandfather wasn't involved in any illegal gambling schemes. I'll clear his name."

Everything goes still. I swear the birds stop chirping. The world feels like someone hits pause, save for the knowing grin spreading across Dalca's face. It's a calculated smile, like he saw the open chink in Vaughn's armor and aimed right for it.

It feels like a spear to my gut just watching it all play out.

"Are you telling me that my grandfather wasn't involved in your scheme?" Vaughn's voice is brittle, almost breathless, now. He still looks impenetrable, but his voice is a dead giveaway that Dalca just delivered an absolute knockout punch.

Dalca snorts. "It wasn't my scheme, Harding. And no, I'm just telling you I can make it look that way. He did what he's been accused of."

Vaughn goes white like a sheet, the truth of Dalca's words hitting him like a wrecking ball. The silence that follows is so heavy I feel it like a vise on my lungs and can't help the loud gasp that escapes my lips when Vaughn nods his head tersely and says, "Send me the paperwork."

That head of wavy dark hair, the one I love running my fingers through, whips around in my direction. Alarm shines in his eyes as he takes me in, the way I'm peeking out around the end of the building. I know that I'm intruding, but truthfully, I don't give a fuck. I stare back at him in absolute disbelief. The man I admire for his morals—his judgment—just sold off my hopes and dreams, his farm's redemption, all to salvage the reputation of a dead man who fucked everyone over.

I shake my head, begging to wake from what feels like a bad dream.

"Ms. Black, how nice of you to drop in." Dalca's voice drips with sarcasm. "No need to hide back there. I have a proposition for you as well." He waves me forward with a smug smirk.

I walk toward them on wooden legs, avoiding meeting Vaughn's eyes. I can't look at him right now. I'll either kick him in the balls or start crying. That's the tightrope I'm walking right now. *I wish I had that whip for both these assholes.*

"Congratulations on your big win today," Dalca says.

I make sure I don't stand too close to Vaughn, who is still staring at me.

"I've followed this horse since they started trying to make him run. I know what a challenge he's been. I also know that you've forged a special relationship with him. You're very talented, and you've done incredible work."

Now he looks earnest, genuine, but I just stare at him with no emotion. How could he possibly know all this? Am I supposed to swoon at his compliment?

*Fuck this guy.*

"When the horse arrives at my facility, I can assure you he'll be treated exceptionally well. Nothing but the best. That said, I'd like to offer you a position as his trainer. Head trainer. The compensation would be more than competitive."

*Double fuck this guy.*

I still say nothing. I pop a hip and cross my arms as I glare back at him, rage simmering in my gut. The *gall.* The absolute balls on this asshole to blackmail Vaughn into selling the best horse his farm will ever have and then turn around and solicit his employee right in front of him. It makes me want to rearrange his striking face.

Dalca's intelligent eyes skim my face, looking for an answer in my expression. But my face is an unreadable mask. I mastered this look as a teenager when my dad sold his family down the river to save his political career.

"Listen to me, Gangster Gary, and listen to me carefully."

My voice is almost a hiss, trembling with barely contained rage. "I'm well acquainted with macho sleazebags like you. Overgrown children who think they're smarter than everyone around them."

Vaughn cuts in now. "Billie, be caref—"

I hold a palm up and swivel my head in his direction. "Don't you dare interrupt me. I have some choice words to share with you as well, but I can only handle one spoiled asshole at a time, so you just wait your fucking turn."

He presses his lips together. Vaughn's no pushover, but he's also smart enough to know which battles are worth picking—and apparently this ain't it. *Smart boy.*

My attention whips back to Dalca. His strong features are set in what looks, remarkably, like surprise. "No one ever talks to me like this."

"Well, maybe it's about time they start."

He rears back with a small amused smile on his face. Which honestly just pisses me off even more.

"I've spent enough years of my life catering to powerful men with no moral compass, whose priorities are all jumbled, whose loyalty lies only with themselves, and I'm not about to jump into that pool again. Do I love that horse? With all my fucking heart." My voice cracks with the emotion of it. "But I'm also a professional. Horses come and go. It's all a part of the sport. I'm a big girl, and my life will go on. But I will never sacrifice my integrity for money. And I will never, *never* work for a man like you."

He tilts his head at me, like I'm a puzzle he's trying to piece together. I don't like it, not one bit. I turn to leave.

To my back, he says, "Among the Romani people, we would say that Double Diablo is your heart horse. Your equine soulmate. A horse you understand like no one else can."

Emotion clogs my throat. My chest burns. Leave it to this manipulative prick to deliver a fatal blow like that. I know I can't look back; I can't handle seeing the pity written all over Vaughn's face or the victory on Dalca's. So I just call back over my shoulder, "In that case, good luck at the derby with my heart horse."

# CHAPTER 29

## Vaughn

FUCK. *FUCK.*

I spin on my heel and take long strides after Billie. From behind me, I hear Dalca say something about sending the offer via courier this week. I don't know. I can't even focus on him right now. All I can see is the utterly broken look on Billie's face when she heard me accept his offer.

I've come to accept that Dermot was probably guilty of fixing races, of defrauding the sport. But hearing confirmation of that stung. But even so, it was an offer I had to accept. To clear my grandfather's name would mean so much, not only for the business but for my family. It could mend the rift he created with this whole scandal. I have to make her understand, make her see that this is the best way forward.

With twenty million dollars, I can buy multiple champions for her to train *and* restore the farm's reputation. Obviously, this is not how I wanted her to find out. I would have liked time to figure out how to put this to her gently. If I could just get Billie to sit down and talk to me, she'd understand.

My pulse thrums in my throat as I follow her down the bustling stable alleyway toward DD's stall. Her heels clack as she speeds away from me. I'm impressed by how quickly she can walk in her heels, but then I'm reminded that Wilhelmina would have had plenty of experience with that. She hasn't always been the casual horse girl I know and love.

Watching her walk away from me, feeling those ripples of rage pour off her, I realize I do in fact love her. I didn't want to piss her off or hurt her, but the offer Dalca made was too much for me to ignore.

"Is the trailer packed?" she barks into one of the stalls.

"Yes," Hank responds, looking confused as he pops his head out of the stall. "Why are you back already?" He looks beyond Billie to see me storming up behind her.

Having finally caught up, I grab Billie around her upper arm. "Outside. Now."

She spins and shakes her arm out of my grip. "Don't lay a fucking hand on me, Vaughn Harding. I'm working right now. I'll talk to you later."

"No, Billie. We're talking right now."

DD, Violet, and Hank all stare back at me wide-eyed. Billie looks downright wild with flushed cheeks and her chest heaving.

"Let's go have a celebratory drink, Vi." Hank ushers her under the rope across the stall doorway, giving me a stern look and Billie a fatherly rub on the shoulder as he leaves us to face off. Violet scampers along behind him, looking back over her shoulder with concern in her wide blue eyes.

"Very professional," Billie mutters as she ducks into the dark stall next to the little black horse.

"You think I care about being professional right now?" I lean against the doorway and watch her crouch down and wrap the fluffy shipping bandages around DD's dainty legs.

"No. I definitely do not." Her voice drips with sarcasm. "I think you care about yourself, and that's about it. Today, you made that abundantly clear."

"Are you kidding me right now? Taking that deal is what's best for everyone. It's *business*, Billie. Twenty million dollars and the farm's name out of the mud? Do you know how many promising horses we can add to the string for that amount of money? How much work we can do around the farm? It's a no-brainer."

She snorts. "No brain. That's for sure." Her hands flatten the cotton wrap over the pillowy base, every movement sure and quick and edged with agitation. She runs her palm up DD's leg and stands. Her fingers scratch at his withers, making him twist his neck toward her happily. Her smile in his direction is wobbly, and then she turns those feline eyes on me. "You really don't get it, do you? It's not about selling the horse. It's about *why*. This horse just ran his heart out for us and qualified for one of the most prestigious races in the world. He came out of nowhere and overcame a lot of shit to put your beloved farm on the map. But that's not enough, is it? Because this isn't about the farm's reputation. He just put you back on the map, and in return, you traded him away on a shady deal."

"So what if I did? Twenty million is twenty million, Billie."

"So what? If he keeps winning, he'll make you that in breeding fees in his first year at stud." Her voice is shrill as she looks at me in utter disbelief. "Time to face facts, Vaughn. Your grandfather *did* break the law. He did everything they have accused him of. That snake in the grass just confirmed it. Covering it up will not change a goddamn thing!"

"How about a little support? This is important to me. You know how hard this has been for me," I roar back, hating everything that she's saying.

She huffs a breath out as she rears back slightly. "So important that you're willing to trample all over my career? Violet's career? Our relationship?" Billie's head shakes back and forth, her disappointment almost tangible. "Imagine thinking that your desperate need to cover up a legitimate crime—one that undermines the respectability of our sport—trumps everyone around you. Real living beings are going to suffer for this. And that's all an acceptable sacrifice to polish up a dead man's reputation?"

I just stare back at her, grinding my teeth.

She huffs out an incredulous breath. "Unbelievable. Reality check, Vaughn. He was exactly as crooked as his reputation suggests. It's okay for him to have been both a fabulous grandfather and a shady businessman. Reconcile it. Deal. With. It."

I keep staring, at a loss for words. Deep down, I know that it's not an acceptable sacrifice. It sounds downright ludicrous when she lays it out like that. But I've spent so many months wishing and dreaming of a way to make the gossip and whispers stop. To make everyone see the wonderful man who I got to know. I can't turn my back on that goal, can't even fathom it.

Her eyes sparkle in the dim light of the barn, and tears build up over her honeyed irises. "You said you wouldn't disappoint me." Her chin trembles as she sucks air in.

Seeing her pain up close like this, it's killing me. I feel like my chest is about to crack open, like my beating heart might fall into the wood shavings in the stall right at her stiletto-clad feet.

"This is a business decision. I have to stand by my choices, even when employees don't like them."

As soon as the words leave my lips, I know they're the wrong ones. But my adrenaline is rushing. I'm pissed off that she doesn't understand, and I'm on an emotional crash course that I can't seem to stop.

"Employee?" she snaps at me.

"Yes, Billie. Trainers don't usually decide about the sale of horses they don't own. I know you feel like this horse is yours, but he's not. He's mine."

She draws herself up as a steel door slams shut over her face. All expression is gone as she stares back at me, lips pressed together in a thin line. "Thanks for the clarification, Mr. Harding." Her tone of voice is one I've only ever heard her use on people she's about to verbally eviscerate. "Hope that knowledge keeps you warm at night, because I definitely won't be." Her voice is cold as ice when she finishes by saying, "I'm not going to sit pretty on the arm of someone whose dubious decision-making skills are based solely on public perception again. I deserve someone who will choose *me*. We're done."

It's been almost twenty-four hours, and I still haven't heard from Billie. I miss her already.

After she told me we were done, I shrugged my shoulders coldly, spun on my heel, and stormed off. All I could hear as I walked away from the woman I love was the swoosh of blood in my ears. Rage simmered in my gut, but it coiled and intermingled with shame too. I knew I shouldn't have spoken to her that way. Even now, a day later, I know I sounded like a total asshole. Yet I can't bring myself to apologize. It's not my fault she doesn't understand.

I stare out my office window at the paddocks, at DD's empty one. Billie obviously kept him down at her house last night. She looked so broken at the thought of the little black horse leaving. I hate to think that I hurt her by making the decision I did, but it's not unusual for horses to come and go. Especially ones as promising as Double Diablo.

I'll give her time to cool down, and then I'll lay my line of thinking out more clearly. She'll come around. I know she cares about me, even if she's been reluctant to accept those feelings. This is just a bump in the road. Couples fight all the time. We'll work it out.

I have to work this out. I can't lose her.

A firm knock on my office door pulls me out of my head. Billie stands in the doorway, hip cocked and arms crossed. I let my eyes drink in the way her blue jeans hug every sensual curve of her body, but when I get up to her face, my breath hitches in my throat. Her silky chestnut hair is pulled up in a high ponytail, her pale skin is makeup free, and her typically bright whiskey eyes are dull, puffy, and red.

*You did that, asshole.*

My chest constricts at the sight of her. She's obviously been crying. A lot. Which is not what I was expecting. I thought tough, sunny, optimistic Billie would win out. Sure, she'd take some time to herself—I know she doesn't like to be smothered—and then she'd come back out swinging. But this…this is not what I saw coming. She looks devastated.

"Hi," I say.

"Hi." Her voice comes out soft and fragile. "Do you have a minute?"

I shift in my seat, immediately uncomfortable with how formal she's being. "Yeah, yeah. Of course." I gesture to the seat across from me. The exact seat where she sat across from me a couple weeks ago and told me about her family, about her father and what he'd put her through. The exact seat she sat in when I hired her.

"Thanks." She folds herself into the chair, avoiding eye contact with me as she drops a piece of paper between us.

I clamp my teeth together at the sight of it, leaning back in my leather chair and steepling my fingers beneath my chin. "What is that?"

She glances up at me nervously. "It's my two weeks' notice."

I blink at her slowly, trying to process what she's saying to me. "You're…you're quitting?"

"Yes." Her teeth clamp down on her bottom lip, and I can't help but remember what it feels like to suck that lip into my mouth while my hands roam her toned body.

"Why?" My shock bleeds into my tone. I know I upset her, but this is blindsiding me.

"I…" She looks away out the window, sucking in a deep shaky breath. "I just can't do this." We stare at each other wordlessly, a stream of emotions in our eyes. "It just hurts too much to stay. I'll find somewhere…less complicated to go."

Is she kidding? "That's it? You're just going to quit on me?"

Her eyes are watery, and her smile is sad when she looks at me. "You quit on me first."

I rear back. "Is that really what you think? You can't bring yourself to see my side of things at all?"

"Oh, I can see them just fine. I just don't like what I see."

I scoff, but she continues.

"If it's all right with you, I'd like to spend one more day with DD. After that, you won't see me around the farm. I'll finish out my two weeks down at the track instead and will move out once I have everything wrapped up. I don't know how things are going to proceed with DD and"—her voice breaks—"I can't be here when he leaves."

A lone tear slips out of her eye and trails down over the apple of her cheek. I want to wipe it away. Kiss it away. Fold my arms around her and absorb every hurt.

But I don't. Instead, I guard my heart and focus on the thread of anger building in my chest at the thought of her leaving. The least I can do is make it easy on her to go. I should comfort her, I should tell her I'm in love with her, but I'm not one to grovel. Instead, all I want to do is lash out.

"And us? I thought you weren't running anymore." My comment comes out snide, and I instantly hate the childish approach I'm taking. She deserves better than this type of behavior.

She pushes to stand and reaches a hand across the desk in my direction. "Thank you for the opportunities you've afforded me." Her long lashes are wet and clumped together as she gazes into my eyes. "I can't tell you how much I appreciate everything you've done for me. I hope you'll be happy."

Her meaning is clear. She hopes I'll be happy with my decision. And why wouldn't I be? All I've wanted for the last year is to clear my family name. This is something I had to do, and if she can't understand, then so be it.

I stand and wrap my hand around hers. Her handshake is just as firm as I remember, her eyes just as emotive. I can see everything there. Betrayal. Anger. Confusion. Sadness. Absolute devastation.

*You did that, asshole.*

I should feel good about my decision. Instead, all I feel is sick as I watch her turn and walk out the door.

# CHAPTER 30

## Billie

"Are you sure?" Hank is sitting at my kitchen island, eyes full of concern, while I lean on the counter across from him scrubbing my face with my hands.

Am I sure? No. I'm not sure of anything right now. Vaughn Harding rocked the very foundation of everything I thought I knew about myself.

I put him up on some sort of moral pedestal, so not only did he rip my heart out, but he also added insult to injury by stomping all over it. I knew I shouldn't have gotten involved with him. Workplace entanglements always end up being clusterfucks. And this was a clusterfuck to end all clusterfucks.

"Yes, I'm sure," I say from behind my hands. "Why did I do this, Hank?"

"Because I begged you to come work with me," he offers with a hesitant chuckle, trying to make me feel better.

I drop my hands and look up at the ceiling. "Not the job. This is the best job I've ever had. I mean Vaughn. What is it about me that is so undesirable? Why does no one ever choose me? Like really *choose* me. Even when there's nothing in it for them. Even when it's not convenient."

I hear the strangled grunt he emits as he moves to stand before me. He puts his palms on my shoulders, and I peer up into his kind, open face. Silent tears stream down my cheeks as he gives me a gentle shake.

"I chose you, Billie. And I'd choose you again and again. You're like a daughter to me. I'm so proud of you. And I can't speak to your family and the choices they've made. To be frank, they sound like a bunch of assholes."

I can't help the small hysterical laugh that spills out over my lips. He's not wrong on that front.

"But Vaughn." He sighs and looks up at the ceiling. "He's a good man who's making a misguided decision. He's had a hard year, but you're right that it's not your job to fix this for him. He has to figure it out on his own. If I know him at all, I suspect he'll come around. I just hope he's not too late."

I blink rapidly and press my lips together. "I don't know if I can forgive him for this even if he does."

Hank hugs me then, cocooning me in his big heavy body. Everything about him is soothing and warm, steady and sure.

"That's your prerogative, Billie girl. But don't forget that if you want people to choose you, you'll have to give them the opportunity. I know you've been burned, and I know you don't trust easily, but you'll never find what you're seeking if you're not at least open to being chosen." His big hand smooths the back of my hair down. "It's a delicate balance. You're an exceptional young woman, so don't sell yourself short, but don't lock yourself away either. Somebody worthy will earn your trust."

"Okay," I whisper into his shoulder.

"Promise me you won't let this make you gun-shy."

"I promise." I say as I sniffle and nuzzle in harder. I'm pretty sure I've soaked his shirt in this spot with my blubbering.

"Did you just wipe your nose on me, kid?"

I laugh now.

Hank has always had the ability to make me feel better while also setting me straight. He gives me the kick in the ass I need and rubs my back all at once, which is something you do for people you love. You're honest with them about their shortcomings, but you're still on their side. No matter what.

"I think I might have. But I'm done now." I pull back and give him a shaky smile. "I'm not going to cry anymore. I can't cry anymore. It's dehydrating. And exhausting." Major understatement. I'm positively dead on my feet. I didn't sleep at all last night, and the emotional toll of the last couple days is catching up with me, hard. "Both of which will lead to premature aging, which I just can't have." I wink at him, trying to lighten the mood a bit.

He grins back. "There she is. My little fighter. I sure missed you while you were traipsing around Europe." His fingers squeeze my shoulder reassuringly.

I roll my eyes at his description of me. "Missed you too, old man."

⁂

I lean on the fence of DD's paddock. His head snaps up from his hay net, and he greets me with a gentle nicker before plodding over for attention. And cookies, let's be honest. It's probably cookies.

"Hey, boy." I run my hand over the big round plate of his cheek as he blows warm air into my ear. His head goes right over my shoulder, like he's about to hug me, but instead, I feel the brush of his sneaky little lips at the back pockets of my jeans.

*Searching for cookies.*

"I'm just your meal ticket, aren't I, big fella?" I press a kiss to his shiny ebony neck and then hand him a cookie, because I'm a sucker like that. Wrapping my arms around his neck as he crunches happily, I whisper, "I'm going to miss you, DD."

My eyes well, and that telltale ache at the back of my throat springs up.

Images of Vaughn moving over top of me spring up into my mind. I can almost feel the way his fingers trail possessively up over my rib cage. The way the scratch of his stubble beneath my ear can shoot goose bumps across my chest. The way the arches of my feet ache when he pushes me right to the edge so relentlessly.

But I shake it off. Thinking about those days and nights isn't productive, and they're damn near impossible to escape. Every time I let myself wallow in those memories, it's like being tossed around in the surf during a storm. Grasping around for something—anything—to hang on to until the realization hits me that there's nothing to save me. That I'm destined to sink into the black water.

I get back to brushing. This will probably be my last day with DD before he leaves for Stefan Dalca's facility, and I won't waste it wallowing over a man.

Instead, I spend the afternoon exploring the trails around the farm, relaxing into the gentle sway of DD's rib cage beneath the saddle, soaking in the feel of the warm sun on my back, on my face, and marveling at how relaxed DD is as he strolls along the trails with his head slung low and tail swishing.

I scratch at his withers often. I lean down over his toned neck to hug him too. I do my best not to cry, but silent tears stream down my cheeks as we turn back up toward the barn. A heavy pit forms in my stomach as we get closer. This is it. *Goodbye.*

I've said goodbye to plenty of horses in my career, but this feels different. And it's only made worse because my relationship with Vaughn has blown up too. Everything between us was fast and new and exciting. When we were together, it felt promising. We spent months getting to know each other, talking, sharing secrets—sharing quiet moments. Our gazes held unsaid words, and our touches lingered just that little bit too long. It was no wonder other people saw what was happening while we were both still in denial.

We were a head-on collision that neither one of us saw coming.

I can't help but wonder if I'm making the wrong decision. Have I overreacted? Would it be worth looking the other way to keep at least one of them? At least then I wouldn't be left with nothing.

A sigh rattles out of my chest. No. My pride won't let me do that. I've compromised my dignity one too many times to cover up the scandal of a powerful man. It left me feeling dirty, bought…cheap. I'd take a broken heart over that feeling any day.

Even if it means losing the man I love.

I've spent an awful lot of time denying my feelings about Vaughn Harding. Shielding myself, cracking jokes, ignoring the telltale signs of losing myself in him. But here I am, living proof that I am very much in love with him. I didn't even realize it until I lost him.

Maybe I should have told him. I keep circling around in my head. Maybe he would have handled the whole thing differently if he knew. But then, if he loved me back, he wouldn't be doing this, would he?

If he loved me, he wouldn't be selling DD off to clear a dead man's tarnished reputation at my expense.

At DD's stall, I shower him in kisses and slide my hands across his silky coat. I cradle his head and look into his big black eyes, reminded of Vaughn's dark irises.

"You be a good boy for your new family." My voice cracks brokenly and tears rush out, unstoppable in their flow. I tap his forehead, making him blink quickly in confusion. "You win it all for me, little man. Do you hear?" His pointy ears tip forward, and I stand on my tippy-toes to whisper, "Run your little heart out. Leave the rest of 'em in the dust."

Then I sit down on the floor of his stall and let the sobs I've been holding back all afternoon rack my body.

The floral tang of gin spreads out across my tongue as I look around the busy patio. Neighbor's pub is the quintessential small town dive bar: grizzled bartender, suspect carpet on the floors, and filled with either locals or people stopping in on their way to or from Vancouver. The patio is basically just a parking lot filled with picnic tables.

I love it.

Violet decided that a girls' night out is what I need. Apparently, finding me crying on a dirty stall floor was too much, even for her. So here I am, at a small-town bar, sitting in the sun, sipping a gin and tonic with Violet and my favorite vet in town, Mira Thorne, both looking at me like I'm a ticking time bomb.

"So help me, if you bitches don't stop looking at me like I'm going to break, I'll waste my drink on your faces. I'm *fine*."

Mira, the ice queen, smirks. "You're entertaining."

Violet's big blue doe eyes bore into me, concern etched all over her dainty little face. "Billie, I just want to make sure you're okay. I'm sad you're planning to leave Gold Rush, but more than that, I'm worried about you. You're always the glass-half-full one. And now you're not. It's stressing me out."

"Vivi, don't stress about things you can't control. You're

about to be one of the most sought-after jockeys in the business. No way will Dalca switch up a winning combination. He's a lot of things, but stupid is not one of them."

Mira snorts as she takes a big glug of her cocktail.

I incline my head toward her. "Care to elaborate, Dr. Thorne?"

She smacks her lips and turns her cunning eyes my way. "The man is a goddamn snake in the grass. But you are right that he isn't stupid."

"I didn't know you had any experience with him."

"I'm a track vet. I know everything about everyone. Every rumor. Every hookup. Every backroom deal. He's been after me about coming to work at his farm exclusively."

I wrinkle my nose in distaste. "Gross."

Violet's cheeks go pink as she leans in and whispers, "Well, I mean, he's not *that* gross. He's actually pretty yummy."

"Yummy, Violet? Really? How old are you?"

Mira's eyes light with amusement. "You mean *fuckable*, Violet." Violet blushes, and Mira cackles.

As far as Stefan Dalca goes, I can't see past my pure rage to look at him that way. Never mind his physical attributes, I'd throw the whole man in the trash and slam the lid. "You're both fucked in the head." I turn to Mira. "Careful with that. He's scary manipulative."

"Don't I know it," she says, leaning back and sighing. "But I need to explore my options. I'm going to have to find something more consistent than just the track. Getting laid off during the offseason isn't ideal for paying back student loans. Or other things." She trails one dainty finger down the condensation on the glass before her. Head shaking, she adds, "Not nearly enough."

"Talk to Hank. We were literally just discussing hiring an on-site veterinarian. Ruby Creek doesn't have a local practice, and you know firsthand how bad DD's colic could have been if you hadn't been close already."

Mira strokes her chin as she muses. "You might be on to something. I'm dead sick of commuting downtown." She snorts. "And I'm dead sick of living with my parents on their dairy farm. I need a change."

I almost spray them both with gin as I struggle to contain my shock. "You still live with your parents?"

Pink smudges pop up on her round cheekbones. "It's a long story."

"This is great, you guys." I hold my glass up to cheers them. "Hearing about your fucked-up lives is actually making me feel better."

Mother hen Violet gives me a disapproving look, but Mira cracks a sultry smile and taps her drink against mine. I swear the woman just oozes sensuality out of every pore without even trying. Beauty and brains—what isn't to like?

Feeling the gin go to my head after not eating properly for days, I blurt out, "If I wasn't so into dicks, I'd be into you, Mira."

Violet chokes on her drink, laying her hand across her reddening chest, downright scandalized. But Mira just winks at me. "Don't knock it until you try it."

"Speaking of dicks, Vi…what's good with you and G.I. Joe?"

Mira quirks her head to the side in question.

"Vaughn's brother," I explain. "The two of them are weird as fuck around each other. I don't need a college education to figure that much out." I turn my gaze back on Violet, who is now taking very unladylike gulps of her drink.

Yikes. Looks like I struck a chord.

She takes a deep breath and then looks out across the busy patio, avoiding eye contact. "I plead the Fifth."

"Oh god. This has to be *so* good, Vi. You are killing me."

Mira smiles and pats Violet's shoulder. "Everything comes out in the end, Violet."

Violet looks like a deer in the headlights when she turns to the other woman and says, "In this case, it better not."

Our night continues much the same. Good laughs, good ribbing, and good company. On a lot of levels, I feel more settled than I have in years. But that could be the gin buzz too.

Later that night, when I walk into the empty cabin and look out at the darkened paddock, I don't even cry.

# CHAPTER 31

## Vaughn

I STARE AT THE COMPUTER SCREEN, NOT EVEN REALLY SEEING it. All I can see is Billie riding up to the barn, a devastating repeating loop that I can't escape.

Earlier, I watched Billie and DD walk to the barn. She looked achingly beautiful in the tack, so natural and at ease. There's nothing fake about her when she's with a horse. Her hips swayed in perfect sync with his languid gait, and the sun glinted off the long chestnut braid that's slung over one shoulder from beneath her helmet.

I stood entranced by the sight of them until I looked at her face. Tears. They glistened there on her defined cheekbones.

*I did that.*

I rest my head in my hands and rub at my eyes, hoping it might help me see the way forward. It's impossible not to ask myself if I made the right decision. I look back up at the screen in front of me and the contract Stefan Dalca sent over yesterday. The one I've been avoiding signing for almost twenty-four hours now.

*Twenty million dollars.*

An insane number, to be sure. But is it worth it? I know what Billie said about making that in breeding fees if DD were to win the derby is true. People pay a million dollars a dose for winning studs, and if he produced winners, possibly even more.

I know it's stupid, but at this moment, I don't care about the money. I have more than I need. I don't even specifically care about the horse right now. He's a good horse, but in my mind, there are lots of good horses.

There's only one Billie.

I *love* Billie, and I lost her by my actions. She spilled her guts to me about her family. About her feelings. She told me flat out what kind of behavior she couldn't abide. And then I turned around and did just that.

I keep hoping I can think of some way to make her understand, to turn her to my side. Some way to keep her *and* clear my grandfather's name. Some way to have it all. Usually, I can work these kinds of things out. I turn on the charm and present a plan that's appealing to all parties involved. But that's not working for me here. No matter which way I spin it, I'm coming up blank.

Billie doesn't fit into the box I can usually push people into. She's a psycho kangaroo that jumps all over the goddamn place. And I love her for it.

*What a fucking mess.*

Rather than sitting here like a lovesick creep, watching her through the window, I should have talked to her. But I didn't know what to say or *do* to fix this. I don't have experience with *this*.

Hank walks past my office door without stopping.

"Hey," I call out. "Hank, come back for a sec."

A moment later, he pops his head into my office, looking downright grim. "What's up, boss?" His hand taps the doorframe.

"I..." My resolve falters. What do I even say here? "I need some advice."

He grunts in response and narrows his eyes at me. "Let me stop you right there." He takes a few steps into the room and closes the door behind himself before pinning me with a frightening look. "Billie is the closest thing I've ever had to a daughter. And she's out there right now *sobbing* in that horse's stall. I know horses move on. Billie does too. But this isn't about the horse. It's about *you*."

His index finger jumps in my direction, and for a moment, I see Hank as the stereotypical farm dad sitting on the front porch rocker with a big gun on his lap.

*And I'm the poor fool who broke his daughter's heart.*

"Listen, Vaughn. I'm proud to work here at Gold Rush Ranch. I respect you. But I *love* Billie. So right now, watching my girl's heart break, I can't say that I like you very much. I'll get over it. So will she. But you..." He shakes his head solemnly and says, "Well, I'm afraid that it'll be too late when you finally come to your senses, and then she'll be the one you never get over. All you'll have left is more money that you don't need and the memory of a dead man who wanted nothing but the best for you."

My chair creaks as I lean back and run my hand through my hair. "Thanks, Hank," I say on a ragged exhale. He just knocked all the excuses straight out of my head.

He gives me a quick salute before leaving. "Anytime, boss."

I'm reminded of taking a baseball to the chest as a teenager. That's what this feels like. A sharp, deep ache that takes my breath away. Followed by shame. Shame that hits me hard and fast, like a wrecking ball. It threatens to knock me right off my feet. I grip the edge of my desk to keep myself upright. I swear I feel her pain lance right through me.

*I did this.*

But I'm out of my depth. I drop my head onto the desk and stare at the floor beneath my feet, trying to put the pieces together. I've been solely focused on fixing my family's reputation. I think of my mom, my brother... *my dad.* All people who deserve better than what my grandfather left us with. The ability to fix all that is within my grasp.

*But at what cost?*

I turn the music up loud and drive straight to downtown Vancouver, to my brother's office. I've been putting off going over financials with him for days, and it seems like the perfect mindless thing to do. And with the perfect person. Cole is a former soldier, so he isn't going to sit me down and talk about my feelings. He's going to talk numbers and respond to my questions in grunts and dirty looks.

Which is exactly what I need.

Pushing through the glass doors of the lobby, I give Mack, our longtime security guard, a wave and head up to the top floor.

Everyone at the head office is happy to see me—unlike at the farm. Smiles. Waves. Even a handshake or two, followed by a "Good to see you!"

Their kind greetings just make me uncomfortable.

*I don't deserve this kind of welcome. Do they have any idea what I've done? What kind of person I've become?*

My inner guilt rears up, and I try to shake it off as I stride through the modern office toward my brother's door.

I waltz right in without knocking, something I know will agitate him. Little brothers have to still be little brothers, you know? It doesn't matter that I'm twenty-eight. Poking the bear can still make me giggle like a child. Internally now though. Not out loud. Plus, I feel like shit. Have to get my kicks in where I can.

Cole's perfectly coiffed black head snaps up in my direction. "Sure, Vaughn. Come on in. It's not like I could be doing anything."

I flop into the comfortable chair facing the big imposing desk. A smile touches the edges of my mouth. "What could you possibly be doing in here that requires privacy?"

"Maybe my secretary is blowing me under this desk right now," he deadpans. Cole hardly ever makes jokes, and when he does, they're shocking and meant to make you feel uncomfortable.

That shit doesn't work on me. "Great. I'll let Mom know that her recluse of a son is one step closer to making her one of those grandbabies she wants so badly."

He shakes his head at me and stacks up the pages in front of him.

Knowing I've got him there, I press on. "Let's go over those financials you've been bugging me about."

Cole says nothing as he continues to organize the top of his desk with military precision. I swear to god he cleans this thing with a toothbrush or whatever it is they make them do there. Unlike my desk, which I sometimes like to refer to as a "creative space," his office is spotless and neurotically organized. Nothing out of place.

He's still giving me the silent treatment a couple minutes later, forcing me to sit here and watch him in silence. I can never tell if Cole is unbothered by the quiet or purposely doing it to give himself the upper hand. It's like he knows it makes me twitchy.

My knee bounces as I watch him methodically organize his space and ignore me. I hate it when he does this power trip shit. It makes me feel like I'm at the principal's office. I guess this is my repayment for not knocking.

With an exasperated sigh, I huff out, "Cole. We crunching those numbers or what?"

He gives me a disapproving look, but he doesn't look away this time. He really *looks* at me, and I swallow under the intensity of his gaze. His cunning gray eyes scan my face and trail down to my collared shirt and jeans. After enough ribbing from Billie, I've finally given up the dream of wearing a suit around the ranch, and Cole doesn't miss this change. He's analyzing me, and it's fucking unnerving.

"You know how I stayed alive in Iraq?"

"Bored your enemies to death?" I quip, trying to lighten the mood. He almost never even references his time in Iraq. But he doesn't take the bait.

"Attention to detail." His eyes narrow as he gives me a finger gun. "And you, brother, are acting and dressing fucking weird."

I scoff and look away. "I'm fine."

"You expect me to believe you showed up here willing and eager to go over financials? *In jeans?* I usually have to chase your pretty-boy ass down and force you to go over this stuff with me. Stop lying."

A breath I didn't even realize I was holding rushes past my lips on a deep exhale. I run my fingers through my hair and look up at the ceiling. "It's that fucking horse."

"The twenty-million-dollar one?"

"One and the same." I steeple my hands under my chin as I look back at my brother. "It's just proving to be complicated."

"Why?" Suspicion seeps into his tone.

"I may have failed to mention there was another condition of his purchase. One that Billie is aware of and…not impressed by. Now I'm all turned inside out and second-guessing myself." I shake my head. "Over a woman."

"Vaughn. We both know Dalca doesn't play by the rules. What's the condition?"

My heart pounds in my chest. Having to say it out loud

feels different from just knowing about it. Presenting the idea to one of the most moral men I know makes me feel greasy. Dirty. "Twenty million and he goes to the media with proof that Grandpa wasn't actually fixing races."

Cole gives me the glare he gave me when we were kids, the one he'd only pull out just before he beat my ass. The way his broad frame almost vibrates now makes me think he might do it again, and while I might have a couple inches on him in height, I still know I won't stand a chance.

His voice is quiet, and his words are sharp and perfectly enunciated when he finally speaks. "Why the fuck would you make a deal like that? With a snake like Stefan Dalca?"

"To clear Grandpa's name—our name."

"Your sense of duty is ass-backward."

I groan and lean back in defeat. Not a single person seems to agree with me, and when you're the only constant in an equation, consider the fact that *you* might be the problem.

And it's looking more and more like I'm the problem.

"Lose the rose-colored glasses, kid." His voice is louder now, rougher. "Time to stop living in pretty fairy-tale land where everything always turns up Vaughn. We all loved Dermot, but the man fucked up. He made poor decisions. Consciously. You think I spent years in special operations not to do a little research on what went down with him? He did it. Plain and simple."

"I know," I mutter.

He barks a disbelieving laugh. "You're telling me you know he's guilty, but you still dove headfirst into a shady backroom deal to fabricate his innocence? In exchange for a boatload of money and the only good thing that's happened to that business—and you—in years?" He's shaking his head at me now, incredulous at my confession. "I know you've spent years perfecting the shiny veneer of this family's reputation, but good god, Vaughn. This is real life, not a PR fix."

*Jesus.*

"When you put it like that…" I trail off. What the fuck have I done?

Cole must miss the shell-shocked look on my face, because he just carries on berating me. "You're going to blow the most genuine relationship you've had in your entire adult life to stage a cover-up?" He laughs cruelly, and in this moment, I hate him for how right he is. "Billie Black might be the most insane and annoying woman I've ever met in my life, but at least her moral compass is intact."

"Fuck." I lean forward and cradle my face in my hands. "Fuck, fuck, fuck."

"Yup." Cole leans back in his leather chair, still shaking his head at me, like he can't believe what an idiot I've been. He barks out a laugh. "I thought I had the market cornered on being emotionally stunted. Stop trespassing, little brother. You're supposed to be the sweet one."

"Funny. Like…hilarious." All I can hear is the sound of blood rushing in my ears. *What have I done?* "What do I do?"

"You tear that contract up, and you *beg*."

After Cole laid me out with that verbal ass-kicking, he still forced me to go through the financials for the farm with him, sadistic bastard that he is.

I venture into my downtown condo, thinking I might stay the night. But it feels too modern and sterile compared to the warm wood and dated appliances that fill the cottages on the ranch. It feels wrong. Too excessive for one person. I don't belong here anymore. So I leave. It's late, but I don't care. I have to talk to Billie. I have to apologize.

But not before I stop at the bank of mailboxes. It's been months since I've come here, since I started hiding out at the ranch, and there's a notice saying they've started leaving my mail with the concierge. I unlock the box and groan at how full it is.

Carrying the stack with both hands, I plop down on the tufted bench in the lobby to sort through it before I leave. There's junk mail, bills, a wedding invitation from someone I barely know, and then I pause. An envelope with my grandfather's neat, slanted script addressed to me is the last piece of mail left.

My hands tremble. It suddenly feels too heavy to even hold up and far too daunting to open. I rest my hands on my legs and bounce my knee as I stare back down at the envelope, frozen by indecision. Why would my grandfather send me mail? I talked to him on the phone all the time.

I consider throwing it away, cutting my losses, and forgetting it ever happened. And then I forge on, tearing at the envelope and shaking my head at myself for considering being such a goddamn wimp. I pull the folded paper out, and it shakes in my hand as I read.

*Vaughn,*

*I've always been better at explaining myself in writing. So here goes nothing.*

*Watching you grow up has been one of the greatest joys of my life, playing a part in your story—an honor. I cherish the years we've spent together, just the two of us, no matter the circumstances that got us there.*

*I admire the man you've grown up to be. I see a lot of your dad in you, all the best parts mixed up into an absolute blessing of a boy. When he died, becoming your caregiver was my salvation. And when your grandmother Ada passed, the ranch was my escape, my focus. A goal. She always dreamed of winning big prizes with her thoroughbreds. Derbies, cups, plates, and in her wildest dreams, she'd muse about winning the Northern Crown. I still remember the night we lay in the back of my old pickup truck and I promised her we would do it. That if we worked hard enough and stuck together, we could make anything happen.*

*But as you know, cancer had different plans. She didn't get to see her dreams realized. A damn shame if you ask me—a crime. And even though she was gone, I spent every day working to make her dreams come to fruition.*

*I was seeing my years fall away. My time*

*to deliver on that promise I made in the truck bed all those years ago was slipping through my hands like sand. I got scared, and what's worse is I let my fear steer me toward choices that have betrayed her memory more than honored it.*

*I guess that's why I couldn't think of a way to tell you this to your face. I guess I'm too big of a coward. I don't want to be there to see the disappointment in your eyes or hear it in your voice. Because what I've done is a betrayal.*

*In the coming weeks, you're going to see my name—our family's name—in the news. I've made some bad choices, Vaughn. I've been around too long, made too many connections, become too sure of what money can do for me. Of what it can fix. But I can't buy my way out of this one. And even if I could, it wouldn't be the honorable thing to do.*

*Trying to play god with the sport that I love, that my beloved Ada loved, is my crime. You'll find out soon that several big races in the past few years have been fixed. I made the play, and I benefitted. But not enough to make the moral lapse worth it. There is nothing that is worth sacrificing our family's dignity and reputation this way, and for that, I am deeply sorry.*

*I don't know if you'll ever be able to forgive me, but I ask that you take some time. Days, weeks, whatever you require, and then please come visit me at the ranch. I want to see you, to explain myself and my actions in person. To give you a hug if you'll still let me.*

*My door is always open.*

*I'll always love you, Vaughn.*

*Your grandpa,*
*Dermot*

★★★

Billie's little log house is dark when I pull up. She's either asleep or not at home, but I walk up to the front door and knock anyway.

I have to talk to her.

I knock again. "Billie! It's Vaughn." When a light turns on, hope bubbles up in my chest. In the quiet night, I can hear her footfalls as she makes her way down the stairs. But the door doesn't open.

"What do you want?"

That spot just in front of my armpits aches with the need to hold her. To fold her slender body into my chest. Because Billie needs protection. She's had too many assholes in her life, and I'm kicking myself for being one of them. Even for just a few days.

"Open the door, babe. I need to talk to you." My voice comes out strangled, and my fingers itch to touch her. I press a palm flat onto the polished pine door, wishing I could reach right through it.

She's quiet for a few beats. "You should go."

"Billie." I squeeze my hand into a fist and lean on the door. "I want to explain. I want to apologize. I want you...us."

She doesn't respond, but I hear her soft crying on the other side of the door and thump my fist on it again.

"Shit. Please. Open the door. I hate listening to you cry. I'm so fucking sorry."

"It's not enough. I can't do this again. I promised myself I wouldn't. You can't drag me into this now that I'm finally free." A broken sob bursts out of her like a gasp. "It's just cruel."

My urge to comfort her is so strong, I actually wonder if there's a way to rip the door right off its hinges to get to her. I crumple onto the deck, trying to stay with her even if we're separated by the slab of wood. "Tell me how to fix this. I'll do anything."

"You can't fix it. You broke my trust. I know this must be hard for someone like you to fathom, but sometimes when you break a toy, you can't just rush out and buy a new one."

"I just want a chance to prove how much I care about you, Billie."

She laughs sadly. "If you cared about me, you wouldn't be selling my horse. You wouldn't be making this deal. There's a reason they say that two wrongs don't make a right."

The lights shut off. I don't even know what to say to her parting words, so I just sit on the porch, looking out at DD's empty paddock.

She's a hell of a lot more than a toy to me. But she's also

not wrong; I'm absolutely unaccustomed to not getting what I want. Which is exactly why I'm not about to give up.

I fire Hank off a text as I jog back to my car.

# CHAPTER 32

## Billie

I'm being petulant, and I know it. Hank has been on my ass all week about going to the derby, and I keep brushing him off, refusing to go.

I haven't heard from Violet since yesterday. I imagine she's focused on prepping for the race of her life. And I haven't heard from Vaughn either, not since he showed up at my house almost two weeks ago.

I imagine he's rolling around in a twenty-million-dollar pile of cash.

A sneer touches my lips at the thought. I've officially moved out of the crying phase of our breakup into the bitter phase. I'm almost glad no one has been around me lately, because I'm not good company right now.

Mira called me once to check in. I was snarky on the phone, and she told me she wasn't cut out for motherhood and to please call her back when I was done acting like a child. Then she hung up. It was a comment that actually made me laugh and also send her a text message to apologize.

I was giving myself until the derby was over. Once DD won the race, I'd be able to put that dream away. The one where I was the trainer of a horse that won a leg of the Northern Crown, North America's most historic thoroughbred race series. I wanted to watch, to feel it slip away, to let the emotions course through me and then lay them to rest.

Then I could start fresh.

Again.

And I will. I'm not a quitter. I'm strong. I've made it this far, and I'm not about to let a pretty man in an expensive suit set me back. I'll land on my feet. I always do.

Except for right now. Right now, I'm sitting on the floor staring at DD's empty paddock, drinking coffee after coffee like an absolute sad sack. Pathetic.

Which is why when I hear knocking at the door, I don't even bother to get up. It's derby day. Everyone should be busy doing something else.

"Billie! Quit your cryin' and get that scrawny ass out here."

Except Hank. Fucking Hank is like an old bloodhound with a scent that he can't give up on. The man has no off switch. He doesn't know how to give it up.

Deep down, I appreciate him not giving up on me. But I'm still annoyed. I want to wallow by myself, not deal with his pushy ass.

When I open the door, I'm greeted with a smile, but that smile slips away as he looks me over. I'm in a sweatsuit.

Hardly derby ready, unlike Hank, who looks awfully dapper in his navy suit.

"Billie Black." His tone is scolding. "This is not the young woman I raised. And you know I pretty much raised you, so don't even start in on me. Your horse is about to run the biggest race of his life, of *your* life, and you're still moping around here like Eeyore personified."

I snort at the mental image and look down at myself. *I'm even wearing gray!* The thought makes me giggle, but Hank just looks at me like I'm a crazy person. Which doesn't matter. I've grown accustomed to people looking at me that way. I like to think it's part of my charm.

"Get. Dressed. Driving into the city on Saturday is a nightmare." Obviously, Hank isn't in agreement about my charms.

I begrudgingly trudge upstairs. Hank is a gentleman through and through, but I also know he's old school enough to pick me up and carry me out of here wearing my Eeyore-gray sweatsuit.

Twenty minutes later, I'm ready to go. I slide my feet into saddle-brown leather wedges at the front door, trying to tone down the dressiness of my outfit. I may not be the fancy girl my parents raised me to be, but this is a sport I love—a tradition I love.

You don't show up to derby day dressed like a slob.

In honor of that tradition, I paired wide-leg cream-colored dress pants with a lace blouse. Classy *and* sexy. You can see little peeks of my skin through the bare spots in the patterned lace. It isn't a dress, but this is as close as I'll get.

My hair is fresh, which feels like a feat this week. I only had time to dry it in loose natural waves, falling down past my shoulder blades, but it will have to do. My makeup is simple. I mostly used it to cover up the dark circles underneath my eyes, and whatever I didn't achieve with concealer, I'll fix with a nice big pair of aviators. It's a pristine, bluebird sunny day in Vancouver, so I can easily hide behind dark lenses.

It's the perfect day for a derby.

Hank parks near the Gold Rush Ranch bank of stalls, and I bolt away from there as fast as possible.

Childish? *Probably.* Necessary? *Definitely.*

I've been working at the track every day for the last week. I've kept my head down, shown up at the ass crack of dawn to breeze all the farm's horses that are stabled here, worked with our exercise riders, grooms, junior trainers, and shown up for every single race that one of ours has run in the in-between. I don't hang around to listen to track gossip and drama. I just do my job and then leave to mope around my house.

And that's another thing I'll have to address at some point. Hank informed me I'm welcome to stay there as long as I need. Presumably, Vaughn relayed that message to him. But I can't stay there much longer. The charming little log house is brimming with memories. Too many memories. When I look out the window, I see DD munching on a big bag of green hay in his private little oasis. Inside the house, I see Vaughn sitting at the kitchen island, barefoot and happy, peeling the label off a bottle of beer. Upstairs…

My eyes sting.

Upstairs, I see Vaughn's dark mop of hair between my legs. I still smell him on my pillows. I feel him sliding inside me.

No, there are too many memories in that little log house.

I've done my job to perfection throughout the last two weeks. No one could ever fault my professionalism on that front, even if most people think I'm a total basket case who quit over the sale of a horse.

Being here at Bell Point Park on the exact day I've spent the last several months working toward just feels…heavy. Like I'm being suffocated. I keep telling myself that heavy feeling is all to do with my dashed professional dreams. But deep down, I know it's more.

Deep down, I know it's Vaughn.

I feel his absence like a missing limb. Despite my best efforts at keeping him distant, he wriggled past my best-laid defenses. Looking back, I'm not even sure I realized I was falling in love with him. Did it happen when he purposely brought me coffee the wrong way? When we faced off in one of our verbal sparring matches? I mean, what kind of woman gets off on that kind of snarky bullshit?

Maybe it was one of those cozy nights that we cooked together and talked for hours? When he opened up to me about his father's death? His grandfather's death? Or was it the night he walked DD in circles for hours so I could rest?

I can't put my finger on when I fell in love with him anymore. It just feels like I've loved him forever. Like our hearts have been intertwined for so long that cutting his from mine is causing me to bleed out. So I hustle out of the barns, past the staging area, hoping I won't run into him, and then melt into the crowd gathering by the finish line. I want to be among the fans while I watch DD win, because I have no doubt he will. I want to dive right into that tension. That excitement. Lean into every turn with everyone around me. I want to enjoy this race like any fan would, not like someone who has a stake in it.

I want to feel something other than sad.

My mind wanders to Vaughn, who's probably schmoozing up in the VIP lounge. And Violet, who is probably looking like a nervous little fawn as she gets ready right now. My text to her yesterday was full of pointers and tips. I couldn't help myself. She responded with Thanks B. See u in the winner's circle.

I rolled my eyes when that text came through. I'm staying as far away from the winner's circle as possible. I'll celebrate with Violet on another day, in another place.

I push to the front of the crowd, standing my ground by holding on to the white banister before me. I wrap my fingers around the post and close my eyes. Buttery summer sunlight beats down on me. The ever-comforting scent of horses floats on the gentle breeze, mingling with the smell of fast-food stands and spilled beer. People talk animatedly around me, and old-fashioned horn music bellows from the speakers in the infield.

A smile touches my lips. Yup. This is race day.

The announcer's voice crackles over the sound system, droning on about the odds on each horse as the board in the infield reflects the changing numbers. I see Double Diablo up there. He's drawn number eight, which puts him in perfect position for a closer, the type of horse that likes to run at the back of the pack. The higher numbers would box him in along the rail; he'd get stuck exactly where he hates to be.

It's almost all too good to be true. Perfect weather. Perfect position. I can't help but shake my head. The universe is working in our favor today.

*Their* favor, I remind myself, right as the announcer's voice starts up again.

His odds are worse than they should be. Nine to two, which means for every two dollars someone bets, they're going to be paid out eleven dollars.

I shake my head. Not terrible, but not great either. They're still underestimating DD. An inexperienced jockey and a relatively unproven horse who likes to come from behind at the last moment—who could blame them, really?

But the punters are wrong. Someone ballsy is going to win a good chunk of change today.

The loudspeaker crackles to life above at the top of a pole. "Five minutes to race time!"

The horses file out onto the track. I press one hand to my stomach to calm the flapping butterflies and lean out over the fence, straining to try and see a small black horse trotting out onto the track. I catch sight of Stefan Dalca's colors, black and lime green. Perfect for a venomous snake in the grass like him.

But the horse is a flashy bay. Brown body, white legs. Does he seriously have more than one horse running today? Shady motherfucker.

Finally, I see DD being led out by a nice calm pony horse. Some horses like to go for a quick gallop before the race, but the name of the game with DD is keeping him calm and steady. He's got nerves enough for the lot of us and needs to preserve that energy for his final burst. He's so shiny that he looks like an oil slick, almost purple and blue in the sunlight.

And he's wearing black and yellow.

# CHAPTER 33

## Billie

I BLINK FAST, TESTING MY EYES, TRYING TO FIGURE OUT WHY Violet is sporting the golden Gold Rush Ranch silks, the silks that look so pretty against the coal-black horse, rather than the bright green.

The speakers buzz back to life. "Ladies and gentlemen, we've had a somewhat unconventional change to our lineup today."

The pulse point in my neck throbs, and I wrap my hand around my throat to feel it pulse beneath my fingers as I stare out at the track.

"Number eight, formerly raced under the name Double Diablo and owned by Gold Rush Ranch, has just submitted a change in name and ownership."

*What the fuck?* I thought this was done already.

"Please note in your programs that number eight is now registered under the name Mister Black."

My mouth goes dry, my tongue like sandpaper. That's what I jokingly told Vaughn I'd name him *months ago*. What the fuck kind of sick joke was this?

"And the colt is now both owned and trained by Miss Billie Black."

Despite all the noise and people around me, all I can hear is the sound of my breathing. All I can do is stand here, frozen in shock, while the world continues to spin around me. All I can look at is *my* horse heading toward his gate.

This has to be a joke.

The hand I have wrapped around my throat feels clammy against my sensitive skin as I turn to look around myself. I want to tell someone. I have *questions*. But no one here knows me. No one around me understands what just happened.

Turning back toward the track, I feel a familiar sting across the bridge of my nose as I sniffle and press my lips together.

*Owned and trained by Miss Billie Black.*

This must be a mistake. Because I sure as shit have not purchased any twenty-million-dollar horses lately. How could this happen? Even if I accessed my long-forgotten trust fund, I couldn't make this happen, not even close.

I feel hot, even though the air beneath the shadow of the grandstand is cool. I can't peel my eyes off the starting gate as the horses step in one by one. It feels like everything is happening in slow motion. Like this is some sort of insane dream that I will wake from any moment now.

Who am I kidding? My subconscious couldn't have come up with a scenario like this on its best day.

The crowd goes quiet, and I'm still in a confused daze when the bell rings out and the gates fly open. "And they're off!"

I stand rigid, gripping the white fence railing for dear life as I watch the black bullet I've spent the better part of this past year pouring my heart and soul into. He draws back off the line, like always, shying away from the sounds and rush of horsepower all around him.

All twelve teams thunder past, and I see Violet's gloved fingers offer a small reassuring scratch at his neck as they find their pace toward the back of the pack. She's cool in the irons, calm like a rookie jockey has no business being.

They're off to a good start.

They hang back through the clubhouse turn and move forward through the second stretch. But they get stuck. There's no path through the middle of the pack, and the horses are running wide, rallying for position down the straightaway.

"Fuck," I mutter. There's nothing open. Nowhere for them to go. Unless…

Violet stands taller in the irons, shifting her weight imperceptibly to the left. She wouldn't really take him in on the rail, would she?

DD's inside ear flits forward like an arrow in response to her change in balance. He sees the opening that she's shown him, and he's already heading that way. Picking up speed. Pushing in toward the rail.

I want to look away, but I can't. He's completely boxed in. Anxiety clogs my throat. There are no other options, but this isn't ideal. Far from it.

Heading into the far turn, there are four horses ahead of him, he's running three wide, and there's a whole pack behind him. I bite at my bottom lip and tap my fingers against the railing. He's going to be stuck there, right to the finish line. *Fuck.*

This isn't good.

But as soon as they start to round the second bend, Violet leans low and shoves her hands forward at him. She hits the gas. My instincts say it's too early, but nothing about this race has been perfect from a strategic standpoint.

DD flattens his ears like a small but mighty warhorse and launches out of that corner like a cannon, toward me.

My hand shoots up to stifle a small gasp as he blows past the horses beside him. Violet takes him wide around the four front-runners. It's cost her some ground to give him a clear lane to the finish line, but provided he doesn't run out of gas, he should be able to sprint down the final stretch.

My left hand joins the right, over my mouth, as I watch DD fly down the track.

Stefan Dalca's flashy bay horse is in the lead, but DD is gaining on him rapidly. Where the other horses are starting to tire, DD's fiery attitude is pushing him harder. Faster.

He smokes them all.

He and Violet fly toward the finish line in sync, both laid out flat, wild eyed and determined.

I feel the ground shake beneath my feet as they thunder past. The flash of the camera momentarily blinds me as I watch them blow past.

*They did it!*

The next closest horse is a couple seconds behind. Violet and DD outclassed the field in every way possible.

*My god. He won!*

My chest aches, and the sting in my nose comes back in full force. But this time, it's accompanied by wetness streaking down my face, over my hands that are still plastered over my slack-jawed mouth.

The crowd is loud, some cheering and some booing, but that doesn't stop me from hearing, "Congratulations, Miss Black."

I spin around to face that voice I know so well. Deep and smooth. The voice I've played in my head and that's haunted me in my dreams.

"Your horse ran beautifully," Vaughn continues, looking downright edible in a gray suit.

I drop my hands and hold them wide in shock. "But… how?"

"I sold him to you," he says, stepping closer. Like it's the most obvious thing in the world.

"I don't have that kind of money, Vaughn."

He smirks at me, looking cocky. "I found a dollar in your grooming stall. I took that in trade."

"You sold *me* a derby winner for *one dollar*?" Disbelief seeps into my voice. *Is he fucking crazy?*

He shoves his hands into his pockets and rocks back on his heels. "Yup."

I stand there, gaping at him, utterly bewildered. "Why on earth would you do that?"

He takes another tentative step toward me, coming

almost toe-to-toe. "You told me I couldn't fix this unless I didn't sell your horse. So that's exactly what I did…or didn't do. Whatever. The gist of it is he's yours." A tired sigh whooshes out of his chest. "I couldn't bring myself to sign the contract. I knew that while I had already broken your trust, I didn't have to break your heart by selling your horse." He reaches toward my waist before thinking better of it and snapping his hand back. His eyes dart down before meeting mine again. "I want *you*. And there's no price on that. The money. The horse. None of it matters so long as you give me a chance to earn your trust back."

I scoff, not prepared to let him off so easily.

He runs his fingers through his dark hair with that edge of agitation I get off on before he sighs. "I love you, Billie. And I'm an idiot. I obviously don't know much, but I know that both of those statements are true."

Did I just hear him right? "You"—I point at him—"love me," I say as I point back at myself.

He barks out a disbelieving laugh. "Yes. I love you. I'm pretty sure I've loved you since that day you marched onto my farm, dressed me down, and then demanded extra pay for having a great ass."

"Huh," I say, propping my hands on my hips. I'm honestly at a loss for words. We stare at each other in awkward silence for several seconds before I blurt out, "I can't believe you actually named my horse *Mister Black*. It makes me sound like a total nut."

He blinks once slowly. "That's…what you have to say to me?"

He's so good looking, and he looks so bewildered right now. It's an excellent combination, I think. I can't help the smile that touches my lips as I look away across the crowd and say, "Kiss me, Boss Man."

That hand that stuttered moments ago shoots out to palm my waist as he pulls me toward him. There's no hesitation now. And he's like the sun. I can't help but be pulled into his orbit.

His thumb strokes my jaw while his fingers grip my neck. I sigh and lean into the feel of his hands on my body. In public, with clothes on, it feels like sparks dancing across my skin no matter what.

When he drops his head toward mine, I lick my lips, wetting them, so I can feel his breath dance across my mouth as he moves in.

When he's close enough that it feels private, when his broad shoulders envelop me, I whisper my own secret against his lips. "I love you too, Vaughn Harding."

The edges of his shapely, wicked lips tip up in satisfaction. And then he kisses me. With one hand on my hip bone and the other gliding down over my throat, he pours all that love right into me. I can feel it in the way he moves against me. His lips tease mine in the most careful and delicious way. In a way that makes my cheeks burn and my thighs press together. In a way that sends shivers down my spine and tingles across my hips.

I hang on to the lapels of his jacket for dear life, letting his passion soothe my tortured soul like a balm. Like an antidote. Wishing we were somewhere more private right now. That we didn't have a winner's circle to get to.

Because *my* horse won the derby. Somebody fucking pinch me.

When he finally pulls back a bit, he holds me close and rests his forehead against mine. We're both a little breathless as he looks me in the eye and promises, "I'll always choose you, Billie."

And I smile.

Because I believe him.

★★★

After the whirlwind that is the winner's circle and never-ending interviews, I feel like I'm drunk. The kind of intoxication where your vision goes wonky and time flies because you just feel like you're spinning in circles meeting people and talking. I can't even tell you what I've said.

The entire day has officially broken my brain. I am mush.

Which is why when Vaughn slides his warm hand down my forearm and then grips my trembling fingers in his, I don't protest. I let him lead me away from the media circus, away from the throngs of people and reporters loitering around. I expect him to take me up to the stuffy VIP lounge, but he turns left and heads toward the Gold Rush Ranch bank of stalls. His thumb draws small reassuring circles on my palm as he walks me down the aisle toward where DD usually stays.

He pulls a rectangular hay bale down off a stack of them and plops it right in front of *my horse's* stall and then points at it. "Sit."

I'm too dumbstruck from the day to even argue with

him. I take a couple of steps on wooden legs before sitting on the bale and exhaling. I put my head down low between my knees and try to take some cleansing breaths, try to get my bearings a bit. I feel like I'm in the fucking twilight zone.

"Here." I look up to see Vaughn holding out a folded piece of paper to me. His hand shakes slightly as he does.

"What is it?"

"Just read it." His voice is soft and vulnerable, even though he looks like pure masculine power towering over me in an expensive suit.

I press my lips together and take it from him, gently unfolding it on my lap. And then I read.

One hand falls across my chest as I read the letter from Dermot Harding. Basically, a love letter to his family. Intensely personal and intensely reflective. My throat feels thick, and my lashes go wet as my eyes trace the beautiful words the man penned to his grandson, the intense tragedy of his life almost more than I can take while I'm already feeling so vulnerable.

"Vaughn…" I look up into the eyes of the man I love and run my hand up over my throat.

His jaw ticks as his eyes blink quickly, trying to shut down the emotion building there.

I stand up, going toe-to-toe with him, placing one palm on each stubbled cheek and then looking him straight in his deep chocolate eyes. "Vaughn. I know I never got to meet your grandfather, which is a damn shame, but I can tell you two things." I give his head a reassuring little shake. "Dermot Harding was a good man, and he loved you deeply. How incredibly lucky are you?"

Vaughn doesn't say anything. His glistening eyes search mine, like he might find the answers to the world in me. Like I'm precious beyond compare.

"I love you, Billie Black," he says and then wraps me in his arms. A tight, bone-crushing hug, like the handshake he gave me on the first day we met. Like he'll never let me go.

We're still holding each other in the busy barn alleyway when Hank, Mira, and Violet walk up leading a freshly bathed DD.

"Back off, Harding. I need a turn," Hank quips as Vaughn chuckles and nudges me toward him.

Hank congratulates me and tells me he's proud, Mira gives me a full report on DD's postrace health before offering me quick congratulations, and when Violet and I hug, we basically just squeal and then cry like the emotional messes we both are right now. I see Mira roll her eyes, which just makes me laugh.

I put DD into his stall, showering him in praise and kisses while the others talk. I cradle his pointy little ear in my hand and lean in toward him so I can whisper, "We did it, boy. We showed them all." He nickers and shakes his head before pushing his head around my side to check my pockets for treats. *Some things never change.*

When I step out of the stall, Vaughn has procured a bottle of champagne and some red plastic cups. He pops the cork and pours each of us a cup of the celebratory bubbles before dragging me down onto the hay bale beside him.

I tilt my head toward Vaughn's ear, not wanting to interrupt the story Hank is telling now, and I whisper, "We're going to deliver on that promise your grandfather made, you know. We're going to win it all."

He squeezes me closer to him, letting the corner of his mouth quirk up as he responds, "I know. You'll do anything you set your mind to." He lifts my hand and drops a gentle kiss on the back, like a seal on the promise we just made.

I lean into the heat of his body, resting my head on his shoulder and sipping my champagne, as I listen to my friends—no, family—recount the race. Everyone is grinning ear to ear. Everyone is beyond happy. And I realize I am too. The happiest I've been in a long time, possibly ever. Maybe I've finally found what I've been searching for.

These people. This place. That horse. Sitting together on a hay bale beside the man I love. What could be better?

# EPILOGUE

## Vaughn

Billie woke me up by crawling on top of me and whispering, "I need your cock, Boss Man," in my ear before dragging her teeth down my neck and fisting my length roughly. I have a real love-hate relationship with that nickname.

But this morning, it's working out well for me.

She's straddling my waist, hips rolling seductively. Golden morning sunlight fills the room, highlighting the matching streaks in her chestnut hair like a halo. I watch her body move, her hands roaming her breasts wantonly.

*Fuck.* She's looks so good touching herself while she rides me. Like an angel. A pain-in-the-ass angel with a trucker mouth, who I love.

"Come here, baby," I rasp out, urging her to lean forward. When she does, I wrap my hand around her throat, and she moans, letting her eyes flutter shut.

I can't help but smirk as I squeeze lightly around her slender neck. My dirty girl loves this.

She slams herself down harder on my length, and I feel a bead of sweat roll down the back of my neck as I strain to watch her.

When I reach my other hand up to circle her sensitive nub, her panting starts to sound more like mewling. "Oh god, Vaughn. I'm going to come."

I thrust up into her wet heat, swirling my fingers, excited to watch her come apart. It never gets old. This woman can crawl on top of me for the rest of my life, and I'll never tire of it.

When I squeeze that delicate bundle of nerves, she cries out and writhes on top of me. Her lips part, and her loose hair sticks to her damp forehead. The view paired with the way she's pulsing around me is too much, and I roar my orgasm into her body and growl, "Take it all, baby. Every drop."

"Yesss," she hisses out before falling forward onto my heaving chest.

We lie together, letting our breathing slow, letting our heart rates return to steady beats, for several minutes. Our quiet moments together are still some of the most intimate we share.

She eventually presses a gentle kiss right over my heart. "Thank you. Now coffee, please."

I laugh as she rolls off me and flops onto the mattress with a satisfied smirk on her face. "That's all you want me for. My cock and my coffee."

She bites down on her bottom lip with a mischievous glint in her eye. "Don't forget your tongue."

I shake my head as I toss on a pair of sweats, shooting her a wounded look over my shoulder as I jog down the stairs. If my girl wants coffee, she gets coffee. With cream. Just the right amount. Exactly how she likes it.

Down in the kitchen of the log house, I hit the button on the coffee maker and then slide on a pair of shoes to head outside.

DD nickers at me when he hears the back porch door open. I imagine that he's saying something like, "Bring my hay, peasant!"

So that's what I do. What the king wants, the king gets.

I shove a few flakes of our best into a net and toss it over the fence to him before giving him a few sound pats and shaking my head.

*The little horse that could.*

The horse that nobody wanted to work with. The horse that saved me—who brought Billie back to me. I'd never be able to repay him. So the best hay that money can buy and the odd peppermint for the rest of his life it will be.

Back up on the porch, I realize I missed the newspaper that someone left there. Hank or Violet, hard to say which. Stepping into the house, I shake the paper out and read the headline.

LOCAL STALLION TAKES THE NORTHERN CROWN IN ANOTHER STUNNING WIN

Pride bubbles in my chest. I can't take credit for any of this. It's all Billie, and I couldn't be more proud of her. Her work ethic, her drive, her passion. I've always known she's an inspiring woman. A force to be reckoned with.

A force I have every intention of locking down for the long haul. I pat my sweatpants to make sure the little black box is still there, where I planted it last night.

Coffee in hand, I head back upstairs. Billie is lounging in the sunny bedroom wearing my T-shirt in the charming little house we've both come to love and call home over the last several months. My city apartment is a glorified closet at this point.

Setting the coffees down on the bedside table, I drop a kiss on her forehead, trying to hide the shaking of my hands. "Coffee for my love. Just the way she likes it."

She giggles happily and sits up, propping pillows behind herself. "I'm amazed you didn't bring it black just to piss me off."

"I would never do that," I deadpan.

"Mm-hmm." She looks at me with accusation in her eyes.

I place one hand across my chest like I'm about to take an oath. But with the other, I pull the velvet box out of my pocket and hold it out to her. "I promise to make it just the way you like it for the rest of your life."

She shakes her head like she's testing her vision and then points at my outstretched hand. "Is that…?"

I drop to my knees beside the bed. "Billie Black, I choose you. Over and over again. Every time." My voice cracks with emotion, but I forge ahead. "Will you marry me?"

Her eyes are glassy and her cheeks are the prettiest pink

as she stares back at me with earnest intensity on her face. It feels like minutes pass when it's really only seconds.

"Vaughn Harding, I'll choose you back every damn day."

"Is that a yes?"

One tear spills out and trails over her cheek as she whispers, "That's a hell yes."

I launch myself at her on the bed, wrapping around her, soaking up her feel, her smell. Our joy.

I can hardly believe it. I get *this*.

*Forever.*

How the hell did I get so lucky?

She sniffles and nuzzles into my neck. And then she says, "Do we have to name DD Mister Harding now though?"

I can't help but laugh as I lean back to look at her. "You're insane, you know that?"

She tilts her head and smiles shyly. "Yeah, but you love it."

And I smile.

Because it's true.

# BONUS SCENE

## Billie

DD's slender back bumps and sways beneath me. I close my eyes and relax my back and hips to let his motion lull me into a temporary place of calm. His black coat makes touching him like sitting on a big black rock that has been soaking up the sun's warmth all day.

His inescapable dusty horse smell mingles with the coconut scent of the moisturizing spray I use on him. His aluminum-clad hooves make a dull *clip-clop* sound against the lush grass, and the birds sing sweetly overhead as he plods along the path we take home every day.

This is peace. This is happiness. This exact moment is pretty much heaven. Who needs therapy when you can have this?

DD is like me in that way. We like the simple life. He'll be much happier away from the hustle and bustle of the track, away from the other horses and trainers and all the unspoken tension that inevitably floats around places like that.

Horses are simple to understand if you're listening. If something scares him, he tells me. If he's busy eating, he tells me. If he doesn't like someone, he tells me that too. He is honest, direct, and reliable. There are very few surprises with a horse's personality once you get to know them.

After spending every day together for almost three months, I have come to know DD very well. I know his body language, his moods, and I know that he can feel my inner turmoil right now when he stops and looks back at me to gently nibble the boot of my toe. I lean forward and give him a little ear scratch behind the leather strap of his bridle. My "What a sweet boy" comes out so much weaker than I want it to.

But it doesn't matter. DD won't judge me.

Not like Vaughn, who must currently think I'm totally erratic. Okay, more erratic than he already did. My reaction smacked me up the side of the head, like a dodgeball I didn't see coming. I sure as shit didn't dodge. And then I ran away from him like a huge crybaby. Like he owed me something. Talk about an overreaction.

He canceled our regular Saturday night dinner to go to some glitzy fundraiser. That's allowed. And he's probably got some smoking hot date to take with him. That's allowed too. Even though the mere thought makes my chest pinch painfully.

I blow a raspberry out through my lips.

My emotional control is somewhat lacking. I'm aware

of that character flaw. But this. *Yikes.* This was new. I should not be disappointed over one missed casual dinner where I make boring small talk with a person I barely even like.

And since I don't like him, I definitely shouldn't care that he's probably going to spend the night with a completely different type of woman than me. She'll be beautiful and glamorous and probably not avoiding her family name and her gigantic untouched trust fund. No, Saturday's girl would probably be perfectly at home in that lifestyle rather than hiding out with her temperamental equine boyfriend.

It's his loss. My plan was to make the best asparagus risotto. I'll still make it. I'll just force Violet to hang out with me. I don't have to be a lonely hermit if I don't want to be.

And who Vaughn bangs in his free time is less than none of my business. In fact, I don't even want to think about it. It makes me feel a little bit nauseous to let my mind wander over to that image. *Why would it make you feel nauseous, Billie?* Because he's gross and all wrong, that's why.

He's a quintessential trust fund baby, exactly what I fled. He cycles through women like I cycle through trashy paperbacks. He's uptight and has a terrible sense of humor. And he's my boss at a job that I love and value and don't want to lose. Essentially, he's good enough friend material and terrible anything else material. I hardly notice his dark brooding eyes, defined jaw, and toned shoulders.

I'll admit to noticing his exceptional work ethic and his butt, and that's it. Because I'm only human and that butt is glorious. I get the best view of it when I piss him off and he storms away. Double win.

Basically, other than that ass, I am so not going there. I've got horses to train and races to win.

★★★

I start prepping dinner early so I'm not still cooking while Violet is here. Housing is limited in Ruby Creek, so she lives in the apartment over the barn.

I've been in a funk since Vaughn canceled on me, and the sting of not having any long-term friends or family around hurts more than usual. Which is why I'm calling Rich while stirring my risotto for the next few minutes.

"Hey, Little Willie!"

I roll my eyes at my brother's greeting even though he can't see me.

"Shut up, Dick."

He cackles. This has been an ongoing point of amusement for us throughout our lives. How two people as proper as Victor and Miranda Farrington managed to name both their children names with penis-themed nicknames would forever be beyond me.

"How is slumming it going for you?" my brother prods. He's such a priss.

"I'm not slumming it, princess. I'm living life like a normal person does. And it's great, thank you very much."

"I know, B. I'm just bugging ya. You know how proud I am of you."

His approval makes me feel all warm and gooey inside. A flash of guilt hits me for not being a better sister to Rich after everything he's helped me do. "I'm sorry I haven't called lately. The new gig has been keeping me busy," I say guiltily.

"Figured as much. Don't stress it. Busy around here. More of the same. Dad wanted me to ask if you were good for money. Your accounts are all still here. He says you haven't touched them."

He always has to go and ruin a perfectly nice conversation with this shit. "Don't plan to," I bite out.

"Okay, okay. Don't shoot the messenger. Just thought I'd ask. They worry about you, you know."

I snort. "Little late for that, don't ya think?"

"Yeah, yeah, B. I know. How about a visit sometime this summer? I'll come play cowboy for a few days or whatever."

"Never want to see you in chaps, bro. Never. But yes, absolutely. Let me know when you're thinking, and I'll take a peek at my work calendar. I'll be down at the track in Vancouver a lot more by then, so maybe we can keep you in your natural concrete habitat." I pause, hating that I even have to ask him my next question. "They don't know where I am, right?"

His responding sigh is an exhausted one. "No, B. They don't."

"Okay. I'll talk to you soon."

"Don't be a stranger," he says right as my timer goes off.

I hear the line click and look around the empty house, feeling a little less alone after talking to Rich.

With dinner prepped, I take a quick breeze through the house to make sure it's up to snuff for company and then I hit the shower. Violet will probably appreciate seeing me without sweaty helmet hair for once. With time to spare, I decide to style my hair for the first time in, I don't know, possibly years. It's too long right now. I haven't had it cut since I was in Ireland. Not enough time and not enough reason. Usually a braid or a bun is sufficient, especially when most of my days are spent with a helmet or cap on.

But today, I use a large-barrel curling iron to create some loose shiny waves. The nostalgia of primping like this hits me like a ton of bricks. These are things that mattered before I left my parents' home. High-society pressure told me that it did. That I represented my family reputation in some way, and the care I took in getting ready was somehow a reflection of my pride in that.

My parents would have had something to say if I tried to walk out of the house looking anything short of put together. I'd spend over an hour every morning getting ready for school, like how I looked mattered while I was trying to get an education. And the unspoken part of it all was that it did matter in those circles. No one cared what kind of professional I could become or how smart I was. They cared about what connections I could make through marriage.

*Welcome to the 1800s!* What a joke.

I pair my shiny chestnut locks with something plain and casual, a silent middle finger to my upbringing. Torn light denim jeans and a thin white crop sweater are just lowbrow enough to do the trick. I'm just finishing up with a quick spritz of perfume when I hear light tentative rapping on the door.

Ha. Violet. So predictably timid. If Vaughn thinks I'm a

bonkers, then I'm pretty sure Violet must believe I've escaped an insane asylum. But we work well together. She has become the yin to my yang. The horses love her, our gentler handling methods align well, and even though she's softer than I am, she isn't a pushover. Which is also good because this industry will eat a flaky woman alive.

I swing the door open to find diminutive little Violet standing there with a bouquet of flowers in one hand and a bottle of white wine in the other.

"You're already the best date I've had in years."

Her shoulders rise up to her ears, and she squeezes her lips together to avoid smiling.

"Vi, has anyone ever told you how adorable you are?" I say, grabbing the flowers from her outreached hand and taking them to the kitchen to find something that could pass as a vase.

"Yeah, you. Almost daily." She snorts sarcastically.

"There she is! Violet the paradox. Never change."

"Yeah, yeah. Where's your wine opener? I need a drink."

I eye her speculatively and hand her a corkscrew.

"Something you want to share?"

"Nope," she replies, popping the *p* in an ultra-sassy way so I know that she's lying.

"Is it a guy?"

Her bright blue eyes assess me from over the wineglass she has already filled and is all but chugging from.

"Yikes," I say, forcing my lips back into a toothy grimace. "Would you like to speak with the resident therapist? His office is just out that door." I point to the back corner of the kitchen. "He's the strong, silent, dreamy one with shiny black hair."

Her cheeks suck in to keep from spitting out her full mouth of wine.

"Made you laugh!" I cry out, pointing at her.

She giggles and daintily dabs at her lips. I think I successfully made her lose a few drops of wine. "No, I think I'm good to just drink and chill out for tonight…unless you want to go over that hair-pulling episode with Mr. Harding yesterday?" Her brow quirks up quizzically.

"All right!" I reply a little too brightly, rounding the corner of the island and slinging my arm over her miniature shoulders. "Come sit with me on the patio, and we can talk about not-guys all night long."

★★★

The asparagus risotto is delicious, just like I knew it'd be, and when we're finished, we lean back in our patio chairs, looking out over the back field and rubbing our overly full stomachs. We're polishing off another bottle of wine, because why the fuck not?

"I think I have a food baby," Violet groans.

"Just make sure you tell everyone that I'm the daddy," I quip back. Leaving out the part where I too feel like I might have a food baby.

She groans. "Seriously, Billie. Why did you feed me so much?"

"Trying to make you grow, Vi. It's like you're stunted. You should become a jockey really."

"That's the plan."

My eyes shift over to her at that, but I'm too full to actually move to look at her.

"Really?"

"Yup. All my hours right now count toward the licensing requirements."

"I had no idea," I say thoughtfully. "Why haven't you asked to do any riding?"

"I don't know," she says, stretching out her sprite-like little legs and sighing. "I just haven't wanted to step on any of the exercise rider's toes, you know? I have to sort of wait my turn."

I muster the energy to sit up, turn toward her, and look at her intensely. "No, Violet. I don't know. Life doesn't just happen to you. You make it happen for yourself. Especially as a woman in this business. Say what you want. Say it every damn day. Step on those toes. Bathe in their tears. Achieving your goals"—I give her a good, firm, somewhat tipsy poke in the middle of her chest—"through hard work, dedication, and natural talent is not crossing a line. Take what you want. Do it honorably, but do it unapologetically."

She stares back at me, all big blue eyes and mop of silvery hair, and gives me a forceful nod. It's like I can see the determination flicker in her chest and blaze up across her facial features.

"That's some deep advice for someone who seems like they're joking around all the time."

"I'm two speeds. You just haven't seen me angry yet, little Violet," I retort with a wink, trying to keep my facade up, not wanting to show how solemn I'm feeling beneath it all tonight.

She shudders at that. Like she already knows she probably doesn't want to see me angry. *Smart.*

"Go get some sleep," I say, waving my hand at her dismissively. "You start riding some of the young horses on Monday."

"But who will groom for you?" she responds, looking alarmed.

"We'll tag team it. I didn't get to where I am by not knowing how to take care of my own horses. I can do grunt work just as capably as you."

She looks shocked, pert pink little mouth hanging slightly ajar. In her defense, most trainers wouldn't ever consider doing a groom's job. But then plenty of them don't even get on their own horses. They just set the program and have exercise riders do the work while they critique on the sidelines. I'm not saying that kind of system can't work, but it's not my style. If I'm not willing to get my hands dirty, how can I expect Violet to want to do it for me?

I cough out a laugh. "Violet, stop giving me that look. You're going to catch flies in your mouth, and then I'll have to start calling you flytrap, and everyone will want to know why."

She slams her mouth shut and rubs her hands down the tops of her thighs as she pushes up to stand.

"Okay, Boss Woman." She says it so quietly that I'm not even sure if I heard her correctly.

I tip my head all the way back and groan very dramatically. "Violet. Don't ever say that again."

She's full-on laughing at me now. "I think I will. And then I'll bathe in your tears over it."

"Jesus. What have I done?" I chuckle into her hair while wrapping her tiny frame in a tight hug.

"Thank you, Billie," she says earnestly.

I step back and look her in the eye, holding her shoulders at arm's length with a faint smile tugging at the corners of my lips. "You're welcome, Violet."

She beams back at me and then turns to leave, walking through the field toward the stables in what is not a very straight line. I'd be willing to venture a guess that my little Violet isn't in the habit of polishing off an entire bottle of white wine. So I stand there, chuckling to myself and watching her traverse the hill in the fading light.

With Violet gone now, it's just me, myself, and my thoughts again. And sometimes I hate living in my own head. I fixate on my past, I grapple with self-doubt, and I overanalyze the future. I feel tired of myself tonight. I need a holiday from my own brain.

So I open another bottle of wine.

## Vaughn

I don't know what I'm doing here. It's a magnificently bad idea.

My night has been a typical represent-the-family sort of schtick. Smile for a few pictures, answer some reporter's soul-sucking questions about my grandfather and Gold Rush Ranch, and then make meaningless small talk with a bunch of strangers.

The only thing out of the ordinary is that I actually had the gonads to tell my mom I'd be attending alone. She grumbled about it, but I didn't care. I wasn't in the mood for women or entertaining one or whatever else came with a night out on the town with a date.

I'd be lying if I said there weren't nights over the last several years when I hadn't at least sampled the goods. When I was in the mood, it felt good, and it was convenient. That sounds cruel, but I was always very up-front with my dates. One night. No strings. Back to work. Long-term entanglements just aren't for me.

Which is why showing up at Billie Black's cottage at 10:00 p.m. is a terrible idea.

I cut out of the fundraiser early and started the long drive from Vancouver to Ruby Creek. I want to say that I couldn't tell you why I was doing this, but deep down, I know that I could.

Watching Billie's face fall yesterday afternoon was a punch to the gut. She'd been ecstatic after her ride. Positively glowing. Seeing her then was like looking at the sun too long and then trying to look elsewhere but having those big bright spots marring your view.

I waltzed in and tarnished her glow.

She's a tough cookie. She covered the slip of her features quickly but not quickly enough. I saw it. And then she marched off with this fake ultra-perky persona that didn't suit her at all. I liked it better when she was giving me hell. At least I knew where I stood then. For her to be frank, cheerful, amenable Billie creeped me out.

So maybe I could say I'm only driving out here to make sure she's still herself. To have her dress me down, swear like a sailor, prove that she's okay in her own unique way. But then I'd have to admit that I missed having dinner with her.

Sitting at a big round table full of people I only know in passing and don't really like has always been an easy sell for me. But tonight, knowing that I could instead have been perched on a stool enjoying a cold beer at Billie's kitchen island made it almost unbearable.

I pull up, relieved to see that there are still lights on in the cottage. I have no idea what I'm about to do or say, but I stride up to the door and knock swiftly three times. And then I wait.

But I don't hear or see any movement. I knock again a couple of times and then splay my fingers against the wooden door, leaning closer.

"Billie? It's Vaughn," I call out, hoping that she'll hear me.

I soak in the quiet for a few beats before I hear, "Sorry, I'm busy with my therapist!" from around the side of the house.

I follow the sound of her voice around to Double Diablo's paddock and find her lying flat on her back on a blanket beside his paddock.

"Is this where you sleep now, Mowgli?" I venture apprehensively, not sure her response was really an invite to join her.

Standing above her, in an area only lit by the dim warm glow of the exterior cabin lights, I can see that she looks more introspective than usual. I gaze down, drinking her in. Her skin glows against the brightness of her white shirt. Riding outdoors has left her looking kissed by the sun. Her chestnut hair is splayed out around her feminine face, styled in waves reminding me of the ripples you see in the sand at the beach.

She hums quietly, as though she's actually contemplating sleeping here. And then she shivers almost imperceptibly.

"Are you cold?"

"No," is her simple response as she continues to gaze up at the stars.

I shrug off my tuxedo jacket and lay it over her body like a blanket, as though I'm tucking in a small child, and take an apprehensive seat on the grass beside her, not wanting to invade her space but not wanting to leave either.

I sit quietly, taking in the stillness of the night, and watch her reach up to run one long finger across the collar of my jacket. I'm entranced and realize I have no clue to what to do or say next.

"Your jacket smells like perfume" is how she breaks the silence.

I don't want to have to explain myself—it's probably from my mother anyway—so I try to resort to our comfort zone and come back with, "You smell like wine."

She snorts at that before retreating into her head and looking all contemplative. I decide that giving her some space to sit in silence is the kind thing to do, not to mention I'm still not sure what to say to her or how to explain why I'm here in the first place. The moments stretch out, and I can feel my eyelids start to droop, forcing me to lie back. The dampness of the grass seeps through my white dress shirt, and I contemplate leaving when Billie whispers, "Do you ever feel like you're lonely even when you're in a room full of people?"

*Jesus.* I turn my head to look at her and let my eyes linger on her profile. Her face is serene, but her eyes look turbulent under those long lashes.

"All the time," I say on a sigh.

"Huh" is her only response.

"Are you lonely, Billie? If you need time off to visit family or something, you just need to ask."

She lets out a loud "Pfff!" before turning her head to look back at me. "I'm not in contact with my family."

"Why not?"

She closes her eyes gently for a beat before looking back into mine. "They disowned me. Or I disowned them. Probably depends on who you ask."

"How come?" I ask, open curiosity on my face now.

"Snoopy, snoopy," she says with a small curl to her lips as she reaches forward to boop me on the nose.

A laugh rumbles in my chest. "Billie Black, you are drunk as a skunk."

"Your date smells like she was sprayed by a skunk," is her very witty retort.

I scoff and shake my head at her. I interlock my hands behind my head to gaze up at the stars. They're so clear out here. Away from the neon glow of the big city, they aren't dulled at all.

She's still staring at me when she says, "You're so obedient. Do you ever just want to shirk your responsibilities? Stir the pot a little? Do things your own way rather than constantly worrying about how it will reflect on your family name or what people will think?"

*God.* Why does drunk Billie have to be all deep and full of questions? I know she's talking about my mother's well-meaning but bizarre fixation on matchmaking me. I know being married to my dad was the pinnacle of happiness for her, and that's what she wants for me. But she's never really stopped to ask me what *I* want. The whole schtick makes me feel sleazy enough as it is without having to discuss it with someone whose respect I value.

"I've never said that I worry about that."

She follows my line of sight, looking up at the night sky. "I can tell you do."

Am I really that transparent? Most of my employees, coworkers, and dates have compared me to Fort Knox in some way, shape, or form. A ragged sigh escapes my lips. "It would be hard for you to understand."

"The only thing that's hard for me to understand is why you put up with it," she replies with a bit of bite.

We turn to look at each other then. Really look at each other. I soak in her wild untamed beauty, trying to ignore how intensely I feel her gaze. It's like a weight on my ribs. I can see her chest rise and fall with each breath. Her typically upturned mouth is pinched with tension, and her intense amber eyes are glassy from a few too many drinks. She looks more broken than usual, and the urge to fix her is overwhelming.

Seeing her all laid out and tortured looking like this makes my cock swell and breath quicken. I lick my lips—I can't help it. The forlorn authenticity of the way she looks right now speaks to my primal side, the one that wants to comfort her in the most primitive way possible. The one that wants to press her cheek against the grass and claim her. The one that wants her riding me so I can watch every emotion play out across her face when I slide into her. So I can watch her head tip back in ecstasy while I roll her nipples between my fingers until she cries out and shatters with me inside her.

I want Billie Black. And it's the worst fucking idea I've ever had.

"You should go," she whispers hoarsely, yanking me from my reverie.

I blink a few times before pulling myself together. She's right, of course.

"I'll get you some water before I go," I say, shooting back up to my feet and heading quickly toward her back patio, adjusting my swollen cock now that I'm facing away from her.

I stop in my tracks as I take in the outdoor dinner table where we usually sit together on Saturday nights. Except I wasn't here tonight, and there are still two wineglasses sitting out beside the bottle of wine. Through the back window, I can see a big bouquet of white roses on the counter.

Suddenly I feel like I've intruded on something that wasn't meant for me. A night that wasn't meant for me. I've intruded on an employee, on a *friend*, by showing up completely uninvited to say absolutely nothing. And I blew off an important networking event to do it. All I had to show for my night was a raging boner and a harsh reminder that romantic entanglements were an unnecessary distraction from my career goals and a potential threat to the family reputation.

Billie was an especially bad idea. She couldn't possibly understand my world and the pressures that go with being a Harding. Tonight was proof of that. The woman basically had a personality for every occasion. Hot, cold, indifferent—*complicated.*

So in what I will admit is not one of my bravest moments, I walk around the other side of the yard, get into my car, and drive away.

Billie can get her own water.

# Acknowledgments

I did it! My first novel. And I would not have made it to the finish line without the help of so many people.

First, my husband, who patiently listened to me hash this story out (and okay, sometimes cry about it) even though it doesn't include any dragons or lightsabers. My son, who is the best reprieve from writer's brain. Nothing like playing dinosaurs when I can't shake that fog. And my parents, who have been telling me that I should write for years now. Love you guys. And look! Skipping most of high school English worked out all right after all.

Paula, my editor and fairy godmother, you turned a pumpkin into a princess-worthy carriage. I would be lost without your keen eye and thoughtful critique. I pretty much live for your notes in the margin. It's hard to believe that this is the very first book we did together, who could have known that we'd go on to do another eight or nine? And more to come, because you are stuck with me!

My agent, Kimberly, who believes in me so thoroughly, and who's so good to me even when I'm not at my best, I'm so fortunate to have you on my team.

My editor at Bloom, Christa (and all the other amazing members of team Bloom!), thank you from the bottom of my heart for loving my books and for giving my debut series this kind of love. When I wrote this book I *never* thought this is where it would end up and it is truly such a thrill to be working with you all.

Lastly, Melanie Harlow, I don't know how I'll ever really repay you for your kindness, generosity, and feedback. Your truth bombs always land in just the right place, at just the right time, and I could not be more grateful for you.

Thank you, everyone, for reading. I really can't believe I published a book.

Someone pinch me.

# OUT OF THE GATE

A Gold Rush Ranch Prequel Novella

*For all the girls whose best use for flowers was braiding them into their horse's mane.*

"Why are you so sad?"

"Because you speak to me in words and
I look at you with feelings."

—LEO TOLSTOY

# CHAPTER 1

## Ada

I HIT THE HARD DIRT WITH A LOUD THUD THAT ECHOES through my bones. My teeth rattle at the impact and I feel a small rock pressing into my right shoulder blade. I close my eyes and groan at the sound of galloping hooves rumbling across the ground.

*Again.* She tossed me again.

I'm a farm girl; we're raised hardy. But good lord—my eyes flutter shut—this filly is going to be the death of me. All I want to do is spend my summer break away from university, training my new project horse. I want to be the one to sit on her for the first time, maybe walk around in a small circle. My expectations are pretty low. But she is not having it.

Footsteps approach and I still don't open my eyes. I know all the ranch hands think my project is a great joke and, frankly, I don't want to hear about it.

I'm probably fine. Bruised to hell and sore tomorrow,

but fine. Right now, if I don't move, nothing hurts. So maybe I'll just stay here? Live out my life lying in the field.

A noisy sigh rushes past my lips as I take an inventory of my aching body.

Toes and fingers still wiggle.

Head still turns side to side.

"You alive, Goldilocks?"

Heart stops beating.

Eyes squeeze shut even harder.

That voice. I'm pretty sure my blood stops pumping and pools in my beet-red cheeks.

"Coulda sworn I taught you better than that."

My lungs empty painfully, all the air rushing out in a gasp.

Dermot Harding.

My heart slams back into action, rioting behind my ribs as I lift my hands to scrub my face. Not wanting to even look at him, because I know what I'll see. The single most attractive man I've ever known, older and out of my league. The man I've spent the last three years trying to get over. The childhood crush I've never outgrown.

The man I've loved since I was a ten-year-old girl.

When I finally decide to pry my eyes open, he's looking down over me, blocking out the direct sun but wearing its rays like a halo. Smirking.

My body melts into a pathetic, speechless puddle of a lovestruck girl right at his feet. I forget about my horse. I forget where I am. I just stare at him, thinking that I could probably just lie here under his glow and be happy.

And then the anger hits. *Three long years.* Not a letter. No word. *Nothing.* I latch on to that feeling, knowing I'll need it to maintain my strength. That inner fire and fury will be the only thing that keeps me from falling down the same rabbit hole as before. I haven't worked this hard at moving on to end up there again.

"You're back." *Obviously, Ada. You idiot.* I blink like I can't quite believe he's here. Standing over me, in the flesh, after so long. "When did you get back?"

He reaches one broad palm out to help me up. "A couple months ago."

I place my hand in his and struggle to swallow a small whimper when we make contact. Instead, I just make an awkward gurgling noise. I swear my entire body comes alive when he's around; it's like an electric current shoots up my arm. Touching him is akin to resting my finger on one of the live fences around here—it always has been. For me anyway.

His eyes widen imperceptibly as he pulls me to standing and then he yanks his hand back, as though I'm diseased or something. Like he can't stand touching me. Like *that* night all over again.

Clearing my throat, I dust my jeans off and roll my shoulders back, then jut my chin up proudly. I refuse to crumble around him. I have nothing to be embarrassed about. I'm an adult now, a university student—I've lived my life. Had boyfriends. Grown up. *Moved on.*

We all make regrettable choices when we're lovesick teenagers.

From the corner of my eye, I see my filly, Penny, grazing

happily by the fence. Not feeling the least bit bad about bucking me off. Apparently, she's glad to be rid of me and *that's* the exact energy I need to channel too.

He's been home for months and hasn't thought to come see us? Feelings of inadequacy sour my voice when I finally respond with, "And you're just stopping by now?"

Dermot shoves his hands in his pockets and kicks at the ground. "I needed some time to get right after my tour. To unwind."

The gravel in his tone has my eyes snapping up to scour his form before me. Here I am acting like a petulant child, not even considering how his time in the army may have impacted him.

I drink him in like a cold soda on a hot day. Annoyingly, he's just as delicious as I remember. With a dropping sensation in my gut, I'm forced to admit he might be even more stunning than ever. He looks more densely muscled, broader, more mature—he must be thirty-one now. Dark shadows move behind his fathomless eyes, like a man who's seen too much.

But that doesn't matter, because he's more painfully irresistible than ever before. Hawkish dark brown eyes and even darker hair, strong masculine features that still somehow manage not to look too coarse. The perfect dusting of scruff over shapely lips.

Lips that didn't move at all beneath mine that night.

Big hands that could circle my entire waist. Dermot is tall and imposing, a farm boy through and through, and I feel like a delicate little bird next to him. A bird that has been chirping around his head, seeking attention for years.

A bird that he batted away three years ago before leaving the ranch—the country.

I stood on his balcony, eyes shrink-wrapped in tears at the knowledge he'd be leaving, and a voice thick with longing. I told him I'd miss him. I told him I loved him. And then I stood up on my tippy-toes, slid my hands over his muscular shoulders, and pressed my lips against his while he stood there completely frozen.

"Ada, you can't do this, you're too young," he said with pity in his eyes as he gently pushed me away.

The memory still makes me cringe. Makes my throat feel hot and dry. It could still make me cry, if I let it. But I finished crying over Dermot Harding a long time ago. I've moved on.

"Why are you here?" My voice sounds wobbly even to my own ears, and I cross my arms to hide my shaking hands.

"Your dad asked me to come down and break some youngsters for him." He grins at me, melting my panties. *You're still pathetic, Ada.* "He says no one starts a horse better than I do."

I scoff with forced amusement, meeting the warmth of his eyes. A soft, alluring brown, like the saddles I spent hours oiling on a fence while watching him break the young horses every summer. The perfect contrast against the bright green valley of Ruby Creek that leads out to the steep North Cascades mountain range.

"And after watching you just now, I have to say…I might know why he thinks that." He winks, always cocky and joking. Like nothing monumental ever happened between us.

"Yeah, yeah." I shake my head as I turn to walk toward Penny. "It's great to see you too, Dermot," I add from over my shoulder, not able to look at him any longer.

"You want help with the filly?" I stop midstep, surprised by the offer.

"Do you have time?" I call back, trying to act casual as I continue my approach toward the beautiful copper-colored filly.

"Spending a few weeks, so yup."

My breathing goes shallow. *A few weeks?* I'm going to have to deal with my haywire hormones, years-old embarrassment, and fluttering stomach for *a few weeks*? "Okay, great!" It comes out a little too brightly, making me wince.

"You're a twenty-one-year-old woman, Ada, get your shit together," I mutter to myself as I grab a hold of Penny's bridle and turn back toward where Dermot is still standing, looking at me quizzically.

"Tomorrow afternoon? I'll work the others in the morning." He nods toward Penny. "Then you can tell me all about Big Red here."

I just give him an awkward thumbs-up and turn back toward the barn, feeling his eyes roam my retreating figure like a spray of warm water across my back.

Time alone with Dermot Harding? Lord, help me.

★★★

"Your very own racehorse, huh?" Dermot drawls, the river babbling quietly behind him.

I trail my fingers over Penny's silky forehead, nodding

and admiring her intelligent eyes—maybe a little too intelligent for my own good. I know deep down it will all be worth it when I can convince her to give me a shot. My daddy didn't raise his only child to be a quitter. But hitting the dirt day in and out is demotivating, not to mention painful.

Dermot chuckles. "Can't fault you for knowing what you want. You've been on about wanting to get into racehorses since you were a little kid. Picked yourself a hell of a challenge to start with."

"That's what everyone keeps telling me," I say, unable to tear my eyes away from where he's tightening the cinch on my saddle. The way his tanned forearms ripple and flex as he ties the leather off there is like dirty talk for the most primal parts of my brain. My tongue darts out, wetting my bottom lip as he pats the filly's neck and I let my eyes trail the veins that run down the top of his firm hand.

*For crying out loud, Ada. You're lusting after a man's veins.*

I promised myself I was going to play it cool today. But I obviously lied, because I'm not playing it cool right now, and wasn't first thing when I woke up this morning and imagined him moving over top of me, inside of me. Our movements jerky, hard, and fevered in my mind's eye.

Yeah, I imagined hate sex with Dermot Harding for the first time in a long time and now I'm a nervous wreck around him. Knowing he's sleeping across the driveway in the little laneway house after all this time apart? It's almost too much.

We left so much unsaid between us, and now everything feels awkward and strained. For me, anyway. He seems completely unaffected. Like the same easygoing, unflappable

Dermot I've always known. But that's probably how most responsible adults react to an eighteen-year-old girl kissing them. For him it was probably a funny, teenaged blip in the radar. The bubbling over of wild hormones for a young girl stuck on a ranch for too long.

But for me it was the memory that still had the power to make me blush, the hot lance of disappointment that kept me up at night to this day. One of my greatest mistakes.

His hand lands on my shoulder, and I startle. "You ready? I'm going to hop on Solar and then pony Penny into the water. Once I get her knee-deep in the river, you can get on. In the water she won't be able to turn into a bucking bronco, and hopefully having an experienced horse beside her will help her stay calm."

The heat from his body seeps into mine, making me almost too hot under the high summer sun. I give him a terse nod, steeling myself. We lead Penny and my dad's favorite ranch horse, Solar, down to the river behind the small guesthouse where Dermot lives when he stays on the ranch. His family farm in Merritt is just far enough away that staying on-site makes the most sense.

I take a deep breath, determination clear on my face as I approach my thoroughbred filly. Dermot swings one powerful leg over Solar's broad back with Penny's rope tight in his hand and coaxes her into the gentle current. Once they're deep enough, I walk in, feeling the cold bite of the mountain water against my ankles. "Hey, little girl." I rub my hand along her flank reassuringly. "How about we try this again, huh? I'll be good to you if you're good to me."

Dermot snorts and my eyes narrow.

"Something funny?"

"Yeah. You're going to spoil this horse even if she's not good to you."

Does he even realize what he just so casually implied? I shake my head and turn away, chest searing with indignation. "I guess you'd know," I bite out as I lift my boot into the stirrup at her side.

"Ada..." He trails off, but I ignore him and step up, leaning against Penny's back. I feel her go rigid beneath my weight, anticipating my leg swinging up through her peripheral vision.

"Easy, girl," Dermot coos now, his voice all deep and soothing as I run my hand up her neck, just waiting a few moments to let her hopefully relax a bit. When I hear her loud snort, I decide to take my chances and ever so slowly lift my leg over the saddle.

I squeeze my core, trying to sit down as gently as possible. Letting my body hover before I come to rest on her back, softly. I feel her start and then go still.

I lift my head slowly, not wanting to break the tenuous agreement we seem to have come to, and look up at Dermot as a wide genuine smile takes over my face. It's been at least ten seconds and I'm still sitting on her. Her ears are flicking back and forth uncertainly, and her body is tense—but I'm still here!

Dermot's perfectly white teeth glint back at me as he gives me a proud shake of his head.

And then, with a squeal, Penny rears straight up. Her

neck fills the space in front of me as she stands on her back legs. Her reflexes are so quick that I don't even feel it coming.

Before I can even grab her mane, I'm unceremoniously dumped into the freezing river water.

# CHAPTER 2

## Dermot

"ADA!" AT FIRST, I WANT TO LAUGH. HER FACE WENT FROM shit-eating grin to unadulterated shock so damn fast. But then she toppled backward into the water. And now all I can feel is pure panic coursing through my veins. She has to be okay.

I tie the filly's rope around the horn of the saddle and jump off my horse, the sound of her scream still lingering in my ears. My steps feel heavy and awkward as I trudge through the river toward the other side where she fell.

"Fuck!" Her open palm lands on the water with a loud slap, and I see the horses startle behind me.

Ada is kneeling on the riverbed, chest-deep in the water that's surrounding her petite form. She's soaked from head to toe, her golden hair dark with wetness and slicked down against the elegant curve of her neck.

"Are you okay?" I keep moving toward her. I have to

make sure she's all right. Much like yesterday, I can't force myself away from her—even though I should. I can't stop scanning her doll-like face, comparing it to all the nights I lay on my cot and tried to recall the way she looks. Imagining Ada's face, every curve, every freckle, was like therapy—a distraction from the much more violent images running through my mind every night.

Ada's fresh face, replaying that kiss; it all became my only lifeline to the real world during a time when I was knee-deep in blood, gore, and depression.

"I don't think I've ever heard you swear before," I say, falling onto my knees in front of her and resting my hands on her shoulders.

She scrubs her hands across her face and back over her head. "That's because you haven't known me since I was eighteen! And yeah, I'm *fucking* sick of falling off."

Okay. So, she's mad. Even someone as emotionally numb as I am can figure that much out. "Does it hurt anywhere?" My eyes dart all over her body, looking for signs of distress. My hands flutter down over her toned arms, feeling for possible broken bones. *Mr. Wilson will kill me if she's injured.*

"I'm fine." She sighs. "I mean, I hurt everywhere. That's what falling off every damn day gets you."

I grip her by the ribs. I can feel the thick strap of her bra through her thin wet shirt as I pull her toward me and stand us both up. She comes to stand easily and everything seems to be in working order. I rake my gaze up over her curves, prepared to make a smart remark about how if she doesn't want to be sore, she should stop falling off, but I stop when I get to her soaked tank top.

The one plastered onto her body, leaving absolutely nothing to the imagination. The taper of her waist, the swell of her breasts, the hard points of her nipples so clear through the wet fabric.

My throat goes dry and I groan, squeezing my eyes shut and looking away. Nothing good can come from admiring Ada like this. That kiss three years ago woke a sleeping giant inside my mind, opened my eyes to possibilities I *never* considered. Ada had always been just another farm kid to me—until she wasn't.

I've been almost constantly reminding myself that she's still the young daughter of a man I've known and respected for years. A man who has become my friend, almost family. She's still the girl all of Ruby Creek knows and loves. A girl that same town would whisper about if something were to happen with the older ranch hand who's been hanging around since she was a child. There is absolutely no way around how inappropriate that would seem, and I refuse to torpedo her reputation like that. I've had three years to mull over the options, and the only feasible one is that I need to stay the fuck away from her.

Plus, a woman like Ada deserves better than me. So I tear my eyes up and away from her body, only to be met with the equally tempting heart shape of her slightly parted lips, the spray of soft freckles across her bronzed cheeks, and those wide emerald green eyes.

The green eyes in which I watched a heart break three

years ago. The green eyes that have haunted my dreams every night since. The green eyes that have looked at me like I hung the moon for years.

And now? A look full of longing and promise that a man like me shouldn't get used to.

*Ada Wilson out of bounds.*

I trail my hands down over her hips, relishing the feel of her body in my grasp. Wanting to pull her closer. I settle with inclining my head in toward her, seeking that signature scent that I've spent three years trying to commit to memory. My fingers pulse, squeezing her waist, and my words come out rough. "Are you sure you're okay?"

"Yes." Her voice is soft and slightly breathless. A raspy whisper that feels like silk on my skin.

She stares up at me with a fire that wasn't there before, like she can't decide between mauling me or drowning me. Her eyes twinkle as she drinks me in. And I let her—because fuck, does it ever feel good to have a woman like Ada Wilson look at you like *this.* Her hand comes up, and she trails her dainty fingers delicately over my cheekbone like she might break me or spook me. *Like last time.*

"Dermot…I—" Her voice cracks a little, and damn if I don't feel a guilty pinch in my chest at her show of emotion. I should put a stop to this, I really should.

"Ada. You shouldn't look at me like this."

She presses a finger to my lips to silence me and quirks one shapely brow up in challenge as she bites back, "Why would you care how I look at you?" The pads of her fingers brush up over the bridge of my nose and then across the peak of my brow, as though she's reading braille. Like my features might tell her a story, give her some answers. She drags her nails across my scalp, sending a spray of goose bumps down the back of my tense arms. "You've made it very clear how you feel about me." Her hands fall away and she looks me straight in the eye as she delivers her killing blow. "And anyway, I've moved on."

Then Ada pushes off of me as she moves past my immobilized form. I feel the heavy thump of my heart against my sternum. *Made my feelings clear?* Of course that's what she thinks. I've never told her otherwise. Nor will I.

In the months since I got home, I've tried to prepare myself for eventually seeing Ada again. I've worked hard at talking myself into believing that the chemistry I keep recalling from that night was all in my head. A shocking memory riddled by my intense longing to be back somewhere safe, away from the sounds of whizzing bullets and pained screams. My plan was to be cool, calm, slightly removed. But then I laid eyes on her, flat in the grass like a flower in the sun just begging to be picked, and my resolve started to crumble.

Now I'm constantly reminding myself that she's the ranch owner's daughter, and that I'm just the ranch hand who comes by to break his young horses every summer. *That's it. That's all.*

"Let's go," I grumble, and it comes out more harshly than I intend. But a rough tone is going to hurt her a lot less in the long run than thinking a man like me will ever be able to give her what she needs. What she deserves.

She unwraps her filly's reins and takes off up the riverbank, her stride stiff and her head held high.

"You can't be doing this, Dermot." I mutter as I grab Solar's reins and follow in her footsteps, lost in thought. It's safe to assume she's not listening by how far ahead she is. At the very least, she doesn't look back. Which is a good thing, because I know I've got desire written all over my face.

I shake my head and kick a rock as I forge ahead. I'm too old, too set in my ways, and after the things I saw on tour, I've retreated too far into myself to ever truly share my life with someone—especially someone as vivacious as Ada. She deserves to see and do it all, not be stifled by someone who hits the ground when he hears a loud noise.

I need to stay away from her. For her, and for myself. I've got a habit of sending people running. My parents could hardly wait for me to turn eighteen before they packed up and moved somewhere warm. They never visit and barely call. Girlfriends never last. And even friends I made in the army have either fallen out of touch or just plain never made it back. Everyone leaves, and Ada would eventually too.

Gold Rush Ranch is a slice of heaven. The Wilsons' vast swath of land here in Ruby Creek sits in a picturesque little valley where tourists visit to seek a hairy mythical creature on Sasquatch Mountain. It's bright and sunny here, just like Ada.

My farm up in Merritt is cold and stark, and the mountain peaks are so high that I feel almost claustrophobic sometimes, especially when the place gets snowed in. It's what my parents left me after they retired and moved south. None of my siblings wanted it. Apparently I'm a sentimental sap, because even though I'm not actually doing anything with the land, the thought of handing it over to someone else is more than I can bear.

And it's definitely not the place for Ada.

Which is fine, because I'm definitely not the man for her either. No matter how she looks at me or how my cock twitches against my jeans when she touches me.

After storming to the barn, we untack wordlessly beside each other. I sneak looks at Ada as she moves around the filly, brushing her a little more vigorously than necessary. It almost makes me chuckle. Leave it to Ada to want a race-horse when her dad has fields full of top-end ranch horses. She always was one to want something she shouldn't.

I pull the saddle off of Solar and manage to bite out, "Same time and place tomorrow. I'll get on her though."

She bristles and rolls her shoulders back. "Take a hike, Dermot. She's my horse. I'm breaking her. Help, don't help, I don't care. But you sure as hell will not waltz in here and take over *my* project." Her hand flails up above her head. "I've had it up to here with people telling me what I can and can't do." She spins on her heel then, and storms off with the fiery little filly prancing along beside her.

As I watch her leave, I realize that Ada Wilson is not the same girl I left on that porch three years ago.

***

"Okay, give me a leg up," Ada says, turning her ass toward me. I take a deep swallow, feeling my Adam's apple bob in my throat. Giving someone a leg up onto their horse isn't special, but it doesn't fall squarely into my *Don't Touch Ada Wilson* plan either.

I step up behind her, breathing in the scent of her tangerine lotion. It suits her, bright and citrusy—intoxicating. She lifts one leg and waits for me to help her. Bending down, I wrap my palm around her slender calf, willing myself not to trail my hand up further.

She looks back over her shoulder at me, probably wondering what the holdup is, and for a moment our eyes lock. I take a deep dive into the emerald depths of her irises. So wide and expressive, and for once since I got back they don't look angry. I hold them with my gaze, just enjoying looking at her.

*Bad idea.*

I shake my head and clear my throat. "One. Two. Three." On *three* I toss her up, but am slow to let go of her leg. I can't seem to tear my eyes away from the way my hand looks on her. The contrast, the compliment. Soft and hard. Sunny and dark. Young and old. *Older.* I refuse to consider myself old at thirty-one.

Either way, nothing about us matches. Ada and I are a dichotomy, opposites, like two ends of a magnet that can't seem to stay away from each other no matter how fucked up it is.

"Dermot?" she asks, her expression quizzical. "You okay?"

I yank my hands off her leg and step back abruptly, offering an, "All good," over my shoulder as I duck out of the round pen and turn to lean on it as casually as I can manage.

Ada ignores the awkward moment and gets to riding. She looks so damn pleased with herself as she trots around on her leggy filly, and pride swells in my chest. This girl is tough as nails, not a quitter's bone in her body. We've spent the rest of the week working on Penny—a chestnut mare through and through. She pulls out an awful lot of acrobatics, but Ada sticks on every time, and after one week she's got her walking and trotting in the round pen unassisted. Not half bad.

Where the filly has flourished, interactions between Ada and I are strained. She can barely look at me since that day in the river and I'm so busy trying not to stare at her body, the way her hips sway in the saddle, that I feel like all I do is make things more awkward by staring at her face instead.

The way her tongue darts out to wet her lower lip, the ways she purses her mouth when she's concentrating, the small genuine smiles she gives Penny that make the corners of her eyes crinkle.

Everything about her is downright distracting. Maybe I'm better off only looking at her ponytail? I stare at it, watching it sway. I could wrap it around my hand, give it a good hard tug, and…

My forehead falls onto the top fence panel in defeat. *I am fucked.*

I've known Ada since she was a buck-toothed, knobby-kneed ten-year-old. She used to burn around here on her bike, getting messy and getting into trouble. A true ranch rat in every sense of the word. The only child of one of the most hard-working, loving, and respectable couples I've ever known. It didn't surprise me at all when I came back summer after summer and saw her growing into a remarkable young woman.

I would have expected nothing less. But she was still just little Goldilocks to me. I still saw tangled blond hair and cheeks smudged with purple from feasting on wild blackberries when I looked at her.

Sure, her obvious crush was a running joke around the ranch when she was little. She'd follow me everywhere, make excuses to do things with me. Chat my ear off about horses, so full of questions. I was a twenty-year-old man, and I was awkward as all get out, especially when the other staff and even Mr. Wilson would rib me about it. It was endearing, really. But eventually everyone stopped talking about it, and I assumed she'd outgrown it. A childhood crush to look back on fondly.

Until she kissed me.

She shocked me into stillness when she cupped my jaw and pressed her plush, heart-shaped lips against mine. Clearly, with age, she'd just gotten really fucking adept at hiding her feelings.

"Be safe, Dermot. I love you," she said. And I pushed her back from me like it meant nothing and told her she should go. The look in her eyes that night? The way they welled up as she traced her fingers across the bow of her top lip? *Fuck.*

That look haunts me to this day. I can feel it like a weight on my chest.

I never wanted to hurt Ada. In fact, I've always known I would kill anyone who did. But that night, she planted a seed of possibility in my mind. And its vines grew fast and reckless, altering my sense of right and wrong, warping my memories, and changing everything I was supposed to feel about Ada Wilson.

That seed has left me battling myself for the last three years. Battling against wishing I'd fisted her hair and kissed her back. Hard. Shown her what a man could do, what a man could make her feel.

But I couldn't. Ada belongs firmly in the *My Friend's Daughter* column and also in the *She's Way Too Fucking Young for You* column.

Which is why, as we're wrapping up on Friday afternoon, I try to make casual conversation after a week's worth of tension between us. "She's looking good, Ada. You should be proud of yourself. Penny's not an easy horse."

She smiles as she strokes the filly's forelock lovingly and muses, "The payoff on something easy never feels as sweet though, does it? I like a challenge."

I clear my throat. I must be obsessed, because everything this woman says sounds like a metaphor to me.

"Next week we gallop?"

She turns and grins at me. "Next week we gallop."

And then I'm down on the ground. A loud bang flattening me almost instantly. I drop so quickly that I barely remember getting here. I wrap my arms around the back of my head, waiting for another bang to come. Another explosion. More screams. The *tch-tch-tch* of bullets spraying everywhere. All I know is that I have to protect myself so that I can get home safely.

It's only when I feel a soft hand stroking soothingly between my shoulders and Ada's soft sugary voice saying, "I'm right here. It was just a truck backfiring. You're okay," that I start to realize where I am and what I've done. The flashes like this come hard and fast. There's no predicting them. And there's no avoiding them.

"Dermot?" Her hand moves up to massage the back of my neck as I pant into the dusty earth beneath me, trying to calm the erratic beating of my heart. "What can I do for you?"

"Nothing," I whisper raggedly, still unable to move. "Just give me a couple of minutes."

I expect her to walk away, but instead she ties her filly up and then lies down right on the ground beside me, going back to stroking my back quietly. She doesn't ask me questions, she doesn't rush me, she just stays with me.

After a few minutes, the anxiety of the moment passes, and I feel my breathing normalize again. I peek over at her, facing me with her head propped in her hand, wide green eyes regarding me carefully. She might be acting calm, but she looks scared. *This is why you're no good for her.*

"I'm okay."

"Are you sure?" Her brows knit together in concern.

"Yes." I roll onto my back to look up at the sky, remind myself of where I am. Ada does the same, but reaches between us to wrap her small hand around mine. She squeezes it tightly. Once. Twice. Three times. A simple enough gesture, but one that has a line of electricity buzzing up my forearm into my inner elbow. An ache. A dangerous current flowing between us.

I pull my hand away, resting both of them on my stomach, and try to lighten the mood. "We've got to stop meeting like this."

She chuckles, but it's a little brittle. A little forced. So I look over at her and try again, not wanting to talk about what just happened. "Friday night. Big plans, Goldilocks?"

She presses her lips together. "Actually, yeah. Meeting up at Neighbor's pub in town."

"Meeting up?" I waggle my eyebrows jokingly. "Like a date?"

She turns her head, eyes like beams straight into mine. Something sad shining in the sage-colored highlights of her irises. "Yes, Dermot. Like a date."

And then she gets up and walks away. Leaving me alone with an entirely different and unfamiliar type of green-eyed monster.

Maybe it's time to catch Ada up on the torture she's put me through for the last three years.

# CHAPTER 3

## Ada

My date sucked.

I buckle my seat belt and turn the key in the ignition. Shaking my head as I pull out onto the road that heads home. Ready to berate myself the whole way back.

I spent the entire time thinking about Dermot, wishing it were him I was out with but also wanting to kick him in the balls for ditching and then coming back like nothing happened. And then wanting to wrap him in my arms and fend off all the demons he's been living with. Just thinking about Dermot, strong and proud, cowering on the ground makes my eyes well with emotion—makes my chest ache for him.

I still want him, demons and all. And I hate it.

What's worse: that day in the river, he didn't even deny that he's made his feelings about me clear. He's supposed to feel nothing for me, except maybe some sort of brotherly love. But I'm not a virginal teenager anymore, and I didn't miss the way his eyes burned across my skin, the way his firm hands pulsed around my waist as he drank me in. This desperate little part of me thought he'd maybe change his mind and spill words about how badly he wants me, like in one of those books my mom hides under her mattress. *Talk about tragic.*

I've been telling myself that I'm over him, that I've moved on. But apparently my heart missed the memo. I've tried. I've had boyfriends at university. But they never last, and they never make my heart pound. They never keep me up at night, thinking about how their hands would feel gliding over my fevered skin. And even when we get to that point, it's fun but…lacking. There's no fire. No passion. No knocking the art off the walls. I want that messy, desperate, gasping-for-air kind of sex.

Travis, my date from tonight, is a nice enough guy, but we've been friends since before we could talk and we still feel like just friends now. We've been out a few times, but I know it's not going anywhere. Pickings are slim in a small town like Ruby Creek, and as I drive back to the ranch, I find myself wishing I could settle for a guy like Travis Bennett. Wishing I could be interested in cattle ranching. It's the family business, after all.

But instead, I spend my days dreaming about Dermot Harding and thoroughbred racing.

My parents drive us in to Vancouver every summer for the Denman Derby. A full day to watch the races. I look forward to that one special day every year, to the anticipation

I feel when the bell rings and the gates flash open. To the rumble of hooves that shake the ground as the horses thunder past. There's just *something* about the whole sport.

I want to be a part of it.

And I want Dermot Harding. Stupidly, obsessively, pathetically—the feelings are seeping out through the seams of the carefully constructed box I tucked them away in. For the past three years, I've easily contained them in the *Never Gonna Happen* section of my brain. But that was before he touched me, before I knew what his calloused palms felt like sliding across my arms. Gripping my waist.

Before he hit me with a look so full of tortured longing that it took my breath away and made me flee. A look that has been living in my head for a week, bouncing around like a pinball in a machine. Giving me a goddamn headache.

So I went on a stupid date. Thinking I could clear my head, but boy was I wrong. Now all I am is agitated that I wasted my own time and possibly gave a friend false hope for something more. "Great work, Ada," I mutter as I pull into the ranch and park in front of the main farmhouse. Slamming the door harder than I should, I round the back of my car toward the path that leads to the front door.

Which of course takes me right past the small laneway house that my parents built for guests. The one that Dermot stays in when he's here. The one with *the* porch.

"You trying to injure that car, Goldilocks?"

He's sitting on the weathered swing that looks out toward the mountains with a glass of amber liquid in his hand. The mellow glow of the outdoor lights highlights the strong planes of his masculine face, the inky shine of his hair, and the brightness of his fresh white T-shirt. I imagine the shirt wet like in the river earlier this week, remembering the way it clung to the defined lines in his chest and hung suggestively over the deep V that disappeared beneath his waistband.

My mouth goes instantly dry at the memory.

I stop and face him, sick of holding my tongue. *Sick of feeling so lovesick.* "Better than injuring you, wouldn't you say?"

"Ada—"

"No. Don't *Ada* me. I'm not in the mood."

I move to keep walking, wanting to put distance between us before I say something I'll really regret, but he stops me in my tracks when he says, "Okay then. How was your date?"

There's a bite in his words that I don't entirely appreciate, not considering the way he's all but disappeared for the last three years. Now he's going to waltz in and act like he has some sort of claim on me? Nah. He's not entitled to that tone where I'm concerned.

I storm up the two steps toward him, hand gripping the railing so hard that I feel the edges of the wood bite into my fingers almost painfully. "It was great." I lie through my teeth with a confidence that doesn't match my inner turmoil. "Travis is great."

Dermot swaggers across the porch, all confidence and maturity, while I feel like I'm shaking in my boots, holding myself up on the railing like a crutch. So I step up, refusing to back away and give him the win, pressing myself against the vertical beam for support, gripping the railing that carries on around the deck.

Braced and ready for battle.

He comes close, too close, invading my space and stealing all the surrounding oxygen, like he just absorbs it with his presence alone. "Travis…" He rolls the name around in his mouth like he's tasting it, examining the flavor. He's close enough that I feel his breath fan across my collarbones, a small reprieve from the heavy mugginess that pervades the night air.

I watch him swirl his drink casually, ice clinking against the heavy glass. "Does Travis send goose bumps up your arms just by coming close?"

I glance down to confirm what he's talking about. *Dick.* I jut my chin out defiantly. "Travis is good for me."

"Anyone would be better for you than me."

An unladylike snort escapes me. "No shit."

He chuckles, stepping forward again, eyes searching my face as I press my back into the timber post behind me. "You weren't nearly this mouthy when I saw you last."

Rational thought flees my mind at his proximity.

"Things change." My voice comes out soft and raspy as I soak him in. His imposing frame, the way his Adam's apple bobs in his throat as he swallows. Suddenly I feel very young and very out of my depth. I squeeze my thighs together, noting that telltale spark at the base of my spine, that deep thrum in my pelvis.

"They do." Dermot grips my chin firmly and my breath leaves me in a quick exhale. I stand stock-still, chest rising and falling in time with his, not wanting to break whatever tenuous connection we have right now. He places his drink on the porch railing behind me and trails his index finger over my lips possessively. The top one, and then the bottom one as he muses, "You're too young for me."

I swallow audibly in response, and smirk with a confidence I don't feel. "Guess that makes you too old for me, something you've made very clear now."

His intelligent eyes dart around my face, analyzing me. Like he's making a tactical calculation. "I'm not sure I made myself all that clear, actually." He leans toward my ear to whisper, "Not very clear at fucking all."

I can feel the hard points of my nipples rasping against my bra as his toned body moves in, completely invading my space. His chest presses against mine as we face off, making me feel competitive. Or cornered. Like I want to lash out at him. "What the hell is that supposed to mean?"

"It means nothing should ever happen between us. It would be a mistake."

Good god. This man gives me whiplash.

"Thanks for clearing that up," I spit out. "Now get your hands off—"

"And yet..." He cuts me off abruptly, his hold on my chin tightening as he does. "Fuck it."

His lips crash down onto mine and this time he moves against me almost frantically. Hungrily. I moan into his mouth, trying to kiss him back, but he just holds my head in place, taking what he wants. What he *needs*. The kiss is brutal, primal, like a punishment more than a reward. Like a volcano that's been waiting to erupt. And this lava? It's probably going to burn us both.

But I must have a death wish because I arch my back toward him, pressing into his hard chest. I fist his shirt, wanting to pull him even closer. Wanting to crawl into his embrace and never leave, wanting to memorize the feel of his arms around me and the clean soap smell on his skin. The taste of whiskey on his tongue and the rasp of his stubble against my skin is a combination I'll never forget.

His kisses turn languid, reverent almost, as he cups my head and trails his thumbs over my cheeks. His mouth moves in their wake, peppering kisses over my earlobe, into the crook of my neck, and across the base of my throat. Shooting arousal straight between my legs. I turn to putty in his arms.

This. *This* is what I've spent years dreaming about. But no dream could do the real thing justice. Dermot Harding is powerful, exacting in every touch, experienced in a way I didn't anticipate, in a way that makes jealous feelings bubble to the surface as his hands roam my body and his mouth lays claim to mine. You don't learn how to own a woman this way without an awful lot of practice. He just didn't want to practice with me.

The realization is like a cold bucket of water over my head. Everything that was molten and hot quickly turns to brittle stone.

I freeze in his arms and panic comes rushing in. Memories of him turning me away in this exact spot—something I refuse to feel again. He tries to pull me back in, resting his forehead against mine. "Ada..." His lashes flutter shut, and he shakes his head. "What am I going to do with you?"

His eyes bore down on mine, burning with need as he rocks into me. I can feel his hard length through his jeans against my hip bone, a torturous teaser of what I could have had. Of what I want.

"Nothing." I almost don't recognize my own voice, so cold it's downright arctic. But what I do recognize is the survival instinct flaring inside of me. Doing *this* with Dermot is dangerous for my heart. Maybe it's easy for him to walk away and waltz back in. But for me? This is torture. Borderline cruel.

He sighs and steps away from me, almost trembling with the self-control it takes. "I'm sorry, Ada." His eyes are earnest and gentle as the heat of his body leaks away from mine. "This is just…" His hands rest on his hips and he looks toward the sky, as though he might find guidance up there. "I don't know how to explain what I'm feeling. I don't know if I should—if I can." He laughs sadly. "It's been three years and I still can't make sense of it myself."

His voice is kind, but his words feel like the cruel lash of a whip. I can't believe we're here *again.* Except this time, it's worse. This time he kissed me back, practically knocked me over with the weight of his desire. This time I know the feelings aren't one-sided. And him pushing me away now because he's too scared to talk to me? It teaches me something I never knew about Dermot Harding.

I spew venom, not the shy teenager I was last time this happened. "Never took you for a coward, Dermot."

I know my blow lands with force because I see the hurt in the depths of his dark eyes. I feel bad for him momentarily until the humiliation hits. I spin on my heel, needing to get away from him and whatever the hell that just was.

Away from that goddamn porch.

I avoid Dermot the next day, opting not to do any work with Penny. I sulk around the house and offer to help my mom with prepping dinner. Which seems like a great way to clear my mind until she says, "Oh perfect! I could use some extra hands. Your father invited Dermot for dinner tonight so we can catch up with him."

*Great, just what I need right now.* I can't even bring myself to respond.

"Nice to have Dermot back, isn't it? I hear he's been a big help with Penny," she supplies lightheartedly, trying to stir some response out of me.

I just grunt.

"You always had the sweetest little crush on him as a girl. Like his shadow around this place." She chuckles good-naturedly, "I think you'd have followed him to the ends of the earth for a while there."

"Sounds creepy," I mutter, not looking up from the tomatoes I'm dicing.

"Aw, no." A wistful smile touches my mom's round face, and her eyes glaze over as she recalls the past. "Dermot was a good boy then, and he's a good man now. One of the best I've known. I think you could sense that even as a little girl."

I feel an aching twinge in my chest because as much as I want to throw this tomato at his stupid handsome face right now, I know she's right. Sighing, I let my shoulders fall on an exhale. "I know, Mom. He's been a big help with Penny. I think we're going to head out into the fields and gallop next week. See if I can stay on." I wink at her, trying to prove that I'm not sulking as badly as it might seem. Plus, everyone seems very amused by how often Penny has turfed me.

She claps excitedly, so genuine in her response. "I just know you're going to do great things with that little spitfire. She's the start of something new and exciting for you. I can feel it in my bones."

We sit around the dinner table that night making small talk. My parents love having Dermot around; they've always had a soft spot for him. I know they took him under their wing when he had no one else around. I also know they'd have had more children—they'd have filled this whole place up with a herd of Wilsons to take over the ranch for them one day.

Instead, they got me. Just me. One girl who has no interest in cattle ranching. But they don't care, just want me to be happy. My cheek quirks in amusement. It's an ongoing joke that maybe I'll marry a rancher to keep the tradition alive. My dad says it and then winks. Yes, Thomas Wilson knows he broke the mold with me, and he loves me for it.

"So, Dermot," my dad starts in, "what are your plans for your land? Do you have anything going on up there?"

"I'm not sure, sir. A company that wants to buy it contacted me, actually. They seem to think the area is rich in mining resources. But I don't think I can bring myself to sell the family farm, no matter what's on that land."

My father stares down at his plate, spearing a piece of chicken and chewing exaggeratedly, like he's really mulling something over. "Don't sell it, son." He sits up and looks at Dermot seated across from him, next to my mother. "That land is valuable, and if they're out hounding you about it, they know there's something good on there. Might be the perfect opportunity for you start something for yourself."

Dermot looks genuinely shocked, like starting his own business isn't something he's ever considered. His dark heavy lashes flutter across his cheek bones rapidly as he tries to process what my dad has just said to him. "I—"

Tom holds a hand up to stop him. "Just think about it. You know that Lynette and I want to see you succeed. As much as I love having you down here every summer, I also know you're destined for bigger things. You've been through a lot, so if we can help you in any way—connections, financials, whatever—you just say the word. We'd be happy to help."

He looks at my mother now and she nods in agreement, eyes shining with emotion. An unspoken agreement, like they know each other so well there's no need to use words. That the two of them still look at each other like this after thirty years never fails to blow my mind. It used to gross me out, but I've come to realize how special what my parents have is. How precious.

*I want that.*

When I look back at Dermot, he's pressing his lips

together, assessing my dad. His voice is rough, full of emotion, when he looks down shyly and says, "I'll look into it. Thank you, Tom. But first I'm helping Ada get that filly to the races."

I pipe up now, excited by the prospect of his help. Because past drama aside, Dermot is one of the best horsemen I've ever met. His help would be invaluable. "Really? You promise?"

He stares back at me sincerely, quieting the room with the intensity of his look. He nods once, decisively. "I promise."

"Good!" my dad barks, breaking the spell. He tosses his napkin down on his plate and leans back in his chair as he turns toward where I'm sitting beside him, like he's totally oblivious to the current between Dermot and I. "So, Ada, what are your plans for Saturday night in Ruby Creek? You going to paint the town red?" He winks.

I know that *moping and drawing hearts with mine and Dermot's initials in them* isn't an appropriate answer. But really, I have no plans. Which sounds far too lame to say out loud in front of everyone. Why couldn't he have just let me skulk upstairs after dinner without flinging me into the spotlight? Sitting across from Dermot, watching his easy smiles, his hands flexing as he cuts through his chicken, his softly mussed hair flopping across his forehead—this entire dinner has been torture enough.

I suppose that's why I blurt out, "Probably going to head into town for a drink or something."

"With who?" *Why is he doing this?*

I bulge my eyes in agitation. "I don't know, Dad. There's almost always someone I know there. It's a small town, I'm not too worried about it."

He just grunts in response and I look down, fiddling with the edge of the tablecloth in my lap. Dad's obviously not wild about the idea of his little girl going to the bar by herself for no good reason. I wish I could tell him I don't really want to go either, but now I've backed myself into a corner.

"I'll go with her." My head snaps up. Dermot just shrugs casually, not looking at me. "I could use a little civilization. Haven't been out much since I got back."

"I don't need a chaperone," I seethe. This is not what I want, and I don't care if I sound like a petulant child. I want to be alone, or at the very least just not anywhere near Dermot.

Lately all he does is make me angry and then horny. It's a terrible combination, and I need some damn space, but he's around every corner, his voice echoes around the stables all day long, and I swear I get whiffs of his clove-scented aftershave when he's not even nearby. The man is driving me to distraction, which is why I hid out in the house today. I'm fed up with his hot and cold behavior. *I'm over it.*

Or at least I thought I was until he came waltzing back onto the ranch and tossed me right back into the deep end of my obsession.

"Ada..." my mother scolds me. I know she's going to make some comment about manners and me being better than this.

But Dermot cuts her off. "Of course you don't. I'll just give you a ride and then leave you to your devices with your friends."

I glare at him before shoving my chair back and storming upstairs.

# CHAPTER 4

## Dermot

ADA PULLS HERSELF UP INTO MY COBALT BLUE PICKUP, HUFFing out a breath as she slams the door much harder than necessary. She shoves her seat belt into the buckle roughly before leaning back and crossing her arms, eyes trained straight out the windshield.

Okay, so she's pissed. Again. I guess I can't blame her. I'm a mess. I've *made* a mess.

"Are you going to drive or just sit there staring at me?" Her tone is biting and her jaw is set stubbornly. She still refuses to turn her eyes my way.

Shaking my head, I shift the truck into reverse, looking over my shoulder as I back out onto the long driveway. "You used to be cute, but now you're a mouthy pain in the ass, you know that?"

I swear she almost growls in response. Her mouth purses like she's eaten something sour, the tip of her dishy nose twitches, her chest flares an angry red, and she literally turns her entire body away from me to look out the window. "Good. That's what you deserve."

Her words don't hurt. I'm a grown man. It takes more than a shot-from-the-hip insult to wound me, but the physical act of her turning away from me, that she can't even look at me—that aches like a rusty lance to the heart.

My poor behavior, my inability to control my urges around her, or really even just communicate, has hurt one of the few women I've ever truly cared about. The woman I've spent the last three years dreaming about, writing letters to that I never had the balls to send. The woman I feel *more* for, but can never pursue.

Agitation blooms within me as I run through the last week in my head. Every time I've put my hands on her body when I should have kept them to myself. All the words that have spilled from my lips, that I should have shoved back down when I felt them bubbling up.

The last thing I ever want is to hurt Ada. Which is why I make a pact with myself, right here and now, as we drive in tense silence along the quiet dirt road.

I need to talk to her. I need to explain. I need to show her the letters so that she doesn't go on thinking that this thing between us is one-sided.

Impossible? Yes. But one-sided? Definitely not.

She jumps out of the truck almost before I've put it in park, like the cab is on fire and she can't get far enough away, and takes off through the heavy wood door of Neighbor's pub. The only watering hole around Ruby Creek.

I sigh heavily as I lock up and then trudge toward the entryway of a bar I don't really want to be at. I'm tired. I only volunteered to go out tonight because I could see the worry etched on Tom's face over his only daughter going out by herself. And I couldn't blame him, or at least that's what I was going to tell myself.

That's right—I'm only here tonight to do a friend a favor. It has nothing to do with the fact that I'm obsessed with his daughter and can't stand the thought of her out with another man.

Striding into the dark little bar, it takes my eyes a moment to adjust. Ada has already found herself a spot at a table just next to the bar with a few friends. Two guys and one other girl. It gets my hackles up that it looks like they're on a double date now. I have no right to feel this way, and yet I pull out a stool up at the bar, near their little square table, pathetically hoping that if I listen hard enough, bits of their conversation might filter over to where I'm sitting.

That's where one week around Ada Wilson has gotten me, a thirty-one-year-old man. Trying to ignore the frequent boners I get from just watching the way her ass fills out a pair of jeans as she walks around the farm and hoping I can eavesdrop on her conversations with friends. *Pathetic.*

Someone slaps the glossy bar top in front of me and I startle before looking up into the kind, wide face of the man behind the bar. "What can I get ya?"

I clear my throat as I look down the back shelf, full of glass bottles. "Just a beer is good."

The man grabs a pint glass and steps over to the taps,

cranking the handle toward himself to let the golden liquid spill out. He's got a big farm boy build about him, and dark blond hair. I'm willing to bet he's only a year or two older than Ada. "You new around here? Don't think I've met you before." He drops a coaster down in front of me, plunking the frothy beer on top, and then offers me his hand. "Hank Brandt."

I squeeze his hand back. "Dermot Harding. Nice to meet you. I live up near Merritt but come down in the summers to help Tom Wilson with some colt starting."

He claps his hands as he leans against his side of the bar, making himself comfortable. "Right on. The Wilsons are good people."

I glance over at where Ada is sitting, nursing a bottle of beer and staring off into space. Clearly not interested in whatever conversation is happening at her table. "The best," I say absently.

"You bring Ada out tonight?"

I scoff and shift my attention back to Hank. "Yeah. Tom wasn't wild about her coming out alone, so I offered to join. Don't think she much appreciated my offer."

The young man waves his hand dismissively. "No need to worry about Ada. She's a good girl. If a little oblivious."

I quirk my head. "What do you mean?"

His lips tip up and he shrugs. "I mean…look at her."

I do, and this time she's glaring at me. Trying to incinerate me with her gaze, burn me to the ground. She might be a good girl, but right now she looks about ready to kill me.

"Every eligible guy in town is interested in Ada, but she doesn't notice. She comes in here, has a polite drink or two with friends, gently turns down offers for dates, and then goes home. I've heard some guys say she's had boyfriends at university, but here at home? I think this is the first time I've ever seen her hang around someone."

"Hm?" I ask as I tip my beer back. The cool fizz spreads across my tongue, soothing the fire I want to breathe at the thought of Ada having plural boyfriends at university.

Hank points. "Travis there"—my chest tightens—"the one with his arm around her chair. They were in together the other night too."

I sneak a look out of the corner of my eye, and sure enough, the lanky, sandy-haired boy has his arm slung casually over the back of Ada's chair. My first thought is that I want to break his arm, which is swiftly followed by intense shame. Shame that I, for even a moment, would think I have a right to feel that way.

She deserves that. Someone young and vibrant, not brimming with baggage, who can keep up with her and not worry about the implications of his relationship with her. Someone promising and carefree. Unlike me.

I just grunt, hunch myself low over the bar top, and take a big swig of my beer. More people filter in around me, and Hank moves on quickly to help the other patrons. I'm grateful to be out from under his assessing stare. The man may be young, but he was looking at me like he had me all figured out. He was making me squirm.

I'm not alone for long though. A shrill squeal assaults

my eardrum from the same side as Ada's table. "Dermot Harding! Is that really you?"

My body goes rigid as I feel long nails drag across the blades of my shoulders and a body press against my side. Tara Bennett, a few-nights fling from just before I left, rubs herself up beside me. "It is! How are you, honey? It's been too long!"

"Hi, Tara," I say graciously, "long time no see."

I don't need to look at Ada to know her attention is on me now. I can feel the weight of her stare like a fiery brand on my bare skin. Like a heavy pulse in my bloodstream.

Tara trails her hand over the small of my back and I try not to cringe. What felt good three years ago feels downright wrong now. I turn toward her on my stool so that she's forced to remove her hand. But she just drops it onto my knee and steps toward me. She's wearing a Neighbor's pub T-shirt with a jean skirt and a black apron. "You working here now?"

"Sure am." She smiles proudly, eyes searching my face excitedly. "I'm off in a couple of hours if you want to catch up. You can buy me a drink." She winks flirtatiously. "For old times' sake. We had some good times, didn't we?" She slides her palm up my thigh boldly, and all I want to do is recoil.

Tara is a pretty girl, no doubt. But all I can think as I stare back at her is that she's not Ada. That's not the face imprinted on the backs of my eyelids. Lips a little too thin, hair a little too blond, makeup a little too thick, scent a little too sugary. Ada is soft and natural; she smells like the marmalade she has for breakfast every morning mixed with freshly cut grass—that sweet and fresh smell. I love that smell. I love… *Don't even think it, Dermot.*

The loud screech of a chair against the floor crashes through my awareness. I turn toward the sound, startled, to see Ada shooting up out of her seat. Face bright red like a perfectly ripe apple. Like a poisonous apple.

She marches up to me, swipes my keys off the bar top before I can connect the dots, and storms out the door like a twister on a path of destruction. Through the window, I watch her jump into the driver's seat of my beloved blue truck, crank the ignition, and gun it out of the parking lot. Leaving a spray of gravel behind her while everyone looks on in utter confusion.

Except for me. I'm not confused at all. She just overheard every word Tara said.

# CHAPTER 5

## Ada

I TRY TO SLEEP, BUT THE FARMHOUSE IS TOO HOT, MY BODY and mind too restless. The air coming in through my window provides no reprieve, and even if I could get comfortable, my overactive brain won't give me any peace. It makes me miss the air-conditioning at my university residence hall. I switch the bedside lamp on and look at my clock. *Midnight.*

I heard the crunch of tires on the gravel driveway a couple of hours ago. I heard Dermot when he said, "Thanks for the ride." And as much as I wanted to run to the window to see who drove him home, I was too chicken. I couldn't bring myself to do it. If it was Tara, I didn't want to know. Having to watch her paw him so boldly, so publicly…well, that was more than enough torture for one day. Her suggestive words were the catalyst for my eruption.

I was ready to scald them both before I decided the safest course of action would be to just leave. And ditch Dermot.

He deserved that. He had to know that letting another woman do that right in front of me would hurt. And I mean *hurt.* The ache in my lungs was very real. The mental images racing through my mind…god, I'm not sure I'll ever be able to erase them. Suspecting and seeing are two very different things.

I know I'm being immature. Dermot is a grown man, with years of experience on me. Logically, I know it's not like he's been chaste. He's tall, dark, and handsome in the most mouthwatering way. He's funny. He's a perfect gentleman. What woman *wouldn't* turn into a puddle at his feet? But seeing it firsthand was something else. I didn't want to face what his years on me really meant.

Worse than that, I like Tara. Correction: I *liked* Tara. In this moment, I'm not sure I'll ever be able to forgive her for having had a taste of what I want. The unfairness of it burns in my throat and lurches in my stomach.

My fist slams into my soft mattress. I'm far too keyed up to sleep. Too angry. Too *irrational.* I'm tired of feeling like this.

Sighing in frustration, I grab a towel off the back of my door and creep down the creaky old stairs, trying not to wake anyone. I've been doing this for years when I can't sleep. A quick dip in the cool river when it's this hot never fails to help me find peace. I know it's just the mental reset I need right now.

I slide my feet into a pair of sandals and walk across the backyard toward the riverbank, shooting Dermot's laneway house a dirty look as I walk past. The sound of crickets fills the air like a small symphony over the rush of water in the distance. Everything is so perfectly peaceful. It's dark and clear but the moon is full, shining like a spotlight over the entire valley.

I drop my towel in my usual spot. A deep bend in the river where the current is almost nonexistent, where the water is still and deep and cold.

Standing on the towel, I scoot out of my sleep shorts and rip off my tank top, dropping them both on the rocky ground. This is the best part about living in the middle of nowhere—no prying eyes.

I walk to the edge of the water, talking myself into making the plunge. Even though I know how it's going to feel, it takes a lot of internal convincing to throw myself into the icy water, every damn time.

With a small smile, I turn away from the water toward the walls of the riverbank, spread my arms wide, close my eyes, and fall backward into the deep pool.

I hold my breath and tread water below the surface, turning myself over to the rush of cold and the breathlessness that follows. The weightlessness of my body and the silty taste of the water that slips past my lips refreshes me. It's peaceful down here, dark and quiet, like time stands still. Like everything about my world is so inconsequential when the river and the rocks around me have been here for centuries. Weathering the storm.

My problems feel like a speck of dust when I think about the vastness and timelessness of the surrounding land.

Noise filters in, warped by the water around me. "Ada!" I

kick my legs toward the surface to see what's going on. "Ada!" The voice is louder as I breach the water. "Ada! Oh my god! Are you okay?"

Dermot is perfectly illuminated by the bright silvery moonlight, calf-deep in the water, shirt torn off on the rocky bank, eyes wild and chest heaving like he's about to rescue me. From what, I'm not sure.

I smooth my hair back off of my face as I tread water. "What are you doing, Dermot?" I ask coolly.

He fists his hands on his tapered hips as he regards me, eyes scanning me clinically as if to confirm I'm actually okay. "I was sitting outside, heard a splash." He still sounds out of breath.

I take a moment to admire him, to weigh my response. Where he was still lanky and boyish three years ago, he's filled out now. I let my eyes follow the trails of his defined abdomen, his cut chest, the tempting hollows just above his collarbones, and the way his biceps bunch into a tight ball beneath his broad shoulders. I lick my lips, tasting the earthy river water that's dripping down my face.

*Dermot Harding is a boy no more.* He's now a clear and present danger to my heart. To my sanity.

"Okay. That doesn't explain what you're doing here." I try to keep my voice even, removed. Wanting him gone. "I'd like some privacy, please."

"You scared me. I thought you were—" He scrubs one broad palm over the dark scruff adorning his jaw. "I don't know. Not thinking straight. In trouble."

My jaw falls open as I realize what he thought I was

doing. Shock, followed by indignant fury. "You think I would kill myself over your dumb ass, Dermot Harding?" I shout breathlessly as I move my limbs beneath the dark water, bringing me closer to the shore, just to where my feet can touch.

"I—"

"You're an idiot. That's what you are." I scoff before launching back in. "I mean the gall. The absolute gall. Get over yourself."

"I know you're mad about Tara," he says sheepishly, unmoving on the moonlit shore.

I bark out a laugh. "Well, hey, at least you know something. Hope she gave you an eventful ride home."

"What was I supposed to do, Ada? Be rude to a perfectly nice girl? And the bartender drove me back, because *you* stole my truck."

He had me there. The tiny petty voice in my head wanted him to be rude to her. But I also know he wouldn't be the man I've loved all these years if that was something he'd do. Dermot is brimming with integrity, which unfortunately, I like—even though it keeps biting me in the ass.

"Ugh." I look away, toward the shadowed stand of trees down river, not wanting to meet his eyes. Not wanting him to see how badly I want him. An urge that's only gotten stronger the more time I spend around him. The beat of a drum that started out quiet and is now so loud I can hardly think over the overwhelming rhythm of it. It isn't fair, wanting something this badly that you can never have.

"That was three years ago, Ada. She means nothing to me."

I think he's trying to be kind, but his comment just angers me instead. "So you can only fuck women who mean nothing to you?"

He doesn't like that comment; his voice changes, and so does his posture. Where before it was gentle and coaxing, it's now hard and commanding. "Get out of the water, Ada. You must be freezing. And we need to talk."

I stare back at him, letting the corners of my mouth tug up just slightly as our eyes meet in the dark. I'm not following his orders. "Why don't you come in for a swim, cool off a bit?"

"I don't have a swimsuit," he bites out, voice trembling with barely contained agitation.

I can tell his control is hanging on by a thread. I can almost feel the heat of the fire growing inside of him as I stand there weighing my next move. I can either throw gasoline on that fire, take a chance, push him to the edge. Or I can drench it with cold water and retreat again, preserving my pride.

Maybe it's the heat, maybe it's my exhaustion, but I go for the gasoline.

"Neither do I," I say as I take a deep breath and lie out flat, letting my body float on the surface of the river. Letting the soft white light from the moon illuminate the shape of my body against the black water, letting it highlight the hard points of my nipples and the gentle swell of my breasts that lie exposed for his eyes.

It feels like long minutes drag by as I stare up at the twinkling stars against the dark blue sky, schooling my breathing, trying to play it cool even though my heart is rioting beneath my ribs. Really, I'm sure it's mere seconds before I hear the steady sloshing of water. Sloshing that fades into quieter swishes before I feel the press of a finger pad on my chin.

"Ada..." The finger trails down the front of my throat gently, like a whisper, pausing momentarily at the dip between my collarbones. I suck in a ragged breath, scared to burst whatever bubble Dermot and I are in right now.

I chance a look at him; the water doesn't come up as high on him and his eyes are locked on my body. Burning across my skin, I swear I can feel the heat of his gaze, the weight of it as he takes me in for the first time. His other palm flattens against the small of my bare back under the water, easily keeping me suspended before him as his finger moves again.

He drags it through the valley between my breasts, sending shots of electricity to my core. Even the cool water between my legs feels like a caress; the way it sways and laps at me under the quiet blanket of night feels downright erotic. Every nerve ending is firing under Dermot's attention.

His lips press together in concentration and I see his jaw tick before his eyes flit up to mine. I can see the desire in his eyes, the indecision. The fire. And it almost knocks me over with its intensity.

It's so obvious. How I ever convinced myself this man didn't want me is beyond my comprehension right now. It's written all over his beautiful face.

His hand flattens and his fingers splay out over the lower curve of my breast. Our breathing goes ragged, heavy, and my mind goes blank. It's like all I can hear is our mingled breaths and the rasp of his skin against mine as he palms my breast, squeezing firmly. When he rolls my aching nipple between his thumb and forefinger, I arch up into him, letting my head tip back, like offering myself to him is the most natural thing in the world.

I can't even stop the guttural sigh that tears itself from my throat. Years of longing packaged up in one needy noise.

His hand presses harder into my back as he drops his head to my opposite breast. Latching his lips onto my pebbled nipple while squeezing the other one. *I can't believe this is really happening.* I whimper at the feel of his tongue circling there, before nipping at me—sending a wave of tingling goose bumps across my chest.

I feel hot and wet between my legs as I try to squeeze them together against the ache building there. It's a lost cause, of course. The ache is only starting. It's on the upward trend of a crescendo. If he stops, I'll probably sink to the bottom of this river, devastated and unfulfilled.

But that's all before he slides his lips across my wet skin and cups my cheek possessively. "Do you know why Tara means nothing to me?" he whispers roughly.

"N-no," I stammer out, not wanting to talk about her.

And then he steals my breath with his admission.

"Because no woman has meant a single fucking thing since that night you kissed me."

My heart pounds erratically as I'm lifted out of the water and into his arms. Chest to chest. Pelvis to pelvis. Mouth to mouth.

Dermot's lips claim mine and his fingers dig into my bare

thighs as I wrap them around his waist. We pulse together, like one heart beating in tandem. I can feel the erection straining against his wet jeans. I grind my naked sex against the rough denim desperately—wanting more—before tangling my hands in his thick hair and challenging him.

Even if this is just for tonight, I want it all.

"Prove it."

# CHAPTER 6

## Ada

WE CRASH THROUGH THE FRONT DOOR AND TUMBLE INTO the small laneway house. Dermot's fingers are digging into my ass with the strain of keeping me close while carrying me here from the river. There will probably be bruises tomorrow. I *hope* there are bruises tomorrow.

He doesn't struggle. All that military training is really paying off where carrying me is concerned. "Hang on, Goldilocks," he said as he gripped me and marched us back to his quarters.

My mouth hasn't left his skin. I'm going to take my liberties while his hands are busy holding me. The heady scent of his aftershave surrounds me as I trail my tongue over his shoulder and up over the hollow of his throat. He kicks the door shut behind us and groans when I bite down and suck on his neck. *Hard.*

I want to leave a mark.

He turns us and grips my jaw as he pushes my head back against the door. "Ada, you're playing with fire, showing your teeth like that."

"Good. I want to get burned." I watch his eyes widen and nose flare in the dim light of the small house. I lick my lips, soaking up the dangerous look on his face. He looks almost feral. Wild. Like a man who's lost control.

"I don't want to hurt you." His fingers pulse on my face.

"You already have."

His chest rumbles with a deep growling noise. "I mean with all the things I'm about to do to you. Are you…?"

I smirk, knowing he will not like the answer to this question. "You're not the only one who's spent time with people who mean nothing to them. I'm not a little girl anymore, Dermot."

His face darkens and his hips thrust forward into me roughly. Pinning me. "That's done now." He lets go of my chin and looks down between us, where my naked body wraps around him, where he stands between my spread thighs, as he trails his fingers through the folds of my pussy. "This is mine."

I nod absently, alarmed by his words but unable to look away from the sight of his fingers on me. I'm entranced.

"Say it, Ada. Tell me you're mine."

My top teeth press into my bottom lip almost painfully as I watch his fingers circling over my aching core. My legs tremble anxiously, but my voice comes out clear and sure. "I'm yours, Dermot. I've always been yours."

My confession seems to be his undoing. He sinks to the

floor right where we are, taking me with him. Lying back on the hardwood floor as I hover over him, shock coursing through my system over the fact that this is really happening right now. This man I've longed for—for as long as I can remember—stretched out before me, saying that I'm *his*. It's almost more than I can process.

When he angles his hips up, I grab his wet jeans and drag them down his legs, discarding them beside us, exposing muscular thighs and the outline of his rigid cock straining against the front of his boxers. My tongue darts out as I peel those off too, mouth going dry at the sight of him bobbing before me, impossibly thick and ready.

He's pushed up on his elbows, looking wide-eyed and uncertain, cheeks pink with arousal, dark waves disheveled from my fingers. I pause, soaking up every glorious inch of his body. Every line, every scar, every freckle. I want to memorize it all. Stamp it into my mind. I want to remember this moment for the rest of my life.

My chest aches with the beauty of him laid out before me. The sizzling burn of anticipation covering my skin. I push my knuckles to the floor, feeling the bite, wanting to make sure this is real. The words spill breathlessly from my mouth before I can stop them. "I've wanted this for so long."

His length jerks in response and he reaches for his jeans, pulling a condom out of his wallet and offering it to me. "Show me."

Our fingers touch as I take the wrapper, that same electricity I've always felt coursing through my veins like a storm. "I'm on the pill. Are you clean?" He nods once, his eyes wide and honest and totally heart-melting. I can almost feel my anger at him seeping away, dissolved by the droplets of water sprinkled around us. The intensity of my desire taking its place. I toss the foil wrapper across the floor and swing one leg over his body to straddle him. "Good. I want to feel you."

He groans and drops his head to the floor with a thud. His hands trail up over my hip bones to circle my waist. "You're going to be the death of me, Ada Wilson."

*Good,* I think to myself. *A little taste of your own medicine.* I reach down between us, fisting the smooth, steely length of him. Loving the sensation of it in my palm, feeling supremely powerful, like for once I might have the upper hand in this game of push and pull between us.

I line the swollen head of his bare cock up with my slick entrance. I should be cold, but instead my skin is burning. The feeling of him notched just inside of me sends a tremor down my spine. And after years of waiting, I drop myself down onto him. I impale myself on his girth and tip my head back on a strangled whimper.

"Fuck, Ada. Fuck…" He trails off, sitting straight up and pulling my breasts flush with his chest. The rasp of my nipples against the dusting of hair there has me mewling in his arms. It's all so much. So many emotions. So many sensations. I feel like I'm puffing more and more air into an already overfull balloon, like if I keep going, it's going to burst right in my face.

But I don't care, I can't stop.

I circle my hips on him, grinding down, loving the stretch of him inside me. Dermot's big, and I've never felt so deliciously full. He growls against the skin of my neck, the scrape of his stubble only adding to the blend of sensations coursing through my hypersensitive body. His fingers comb through my wet hair roughly, ending in a gentle tug at the base of my skull as he pulls my face right up to his. It forces me to look into his eyes, which somehow feels more personal in this moment than the knowledge that his bare cock is throbbing inside of me.

"Ada..." His thumb brushes reverently across my lips. "Do you have any idea how fucking good you feel? How many nights I've dreamt of this? The months I've spent trying to stay away from you? To convince myself this was all in my head? Fuck." He dips his chin and squeezes his eyes shut. "The things I want to do you..."

Tears spring up in my eyes. This confession...the time away, the years between us, the reasons this can't go anywhere, they all melt away in the wake of his confession. All the years I've spent feeling embarrassed, thinking I was the crazy one.

None of it matters.

Here. Now. Joined with the man I've always wanted. *Always loved.* This is all that matters.

I cup his cheek tenderly and echo his words. "Show me."

And then his lips are on mine, but it's different this time. It's leisurely and sensual, rather than hard and frantic. Our hands roam and we rock together in a steady rhythm. I feel every ridge and vein as he slides in and out of me, the rasp against my clit just adding to my frenzy with every thrust. My hips ache with the pleasure, that electric ball of tension building at the base of my spine with every thrust, with every brush of his fingers, with every lingering look.

*God, the look in his eyes.*

I grind down on him harder, moaning into his mouth. Whimpering against his skin. And when I'm bucking and writhing on top of him, lost to the sensations of having him inside of me, he lies down flat. His thumb goes straight for my clit, and he says, "Ride me, Ada. Come for me."

The words alone are almost enough to do it. I slam myself down on him hard a few times, taking his full length, feeling the bite of it and loving it. His thumb circles lazily, slick with the wetness of my arousal. And suddenly that building ball of tension snaps.

"Dermot!" I cry out as I grind on him harder. A single bead of sweat trickles down between my breasts like an arrow for the hot lance of pleasure surging through me as I ride the waves of my orgasm. And he doesn't stop touching or thrusting as I come apart around him. In fact, he picks up the pace, pushing me even further until my feet cramp and my thighs shake. Relentless in his taking until he joins me with his own release.

I feel him go rigid beneath me and growl possessively as he spills himself inside me. I feel my heart swell inside my chest, knowing that nothing has ever felt more right.

I fall forward onto his dampened torso, and he pulls me tight against him. Kissing my hair and trailing his hand up and down the indent of my spine. Our breathing is heavy and perfectly in sync, the only sound in the quiet house. I twirl a finger absently in the splash of hair on his chest, suddenly feeling like a little girl who finally got the thing she's always wanted.

Speechless. Breathless. Sated.

*Overwhelmed.*

But that's before Dermot whispers into my ear, "Time for a shower. I'm going to wash every inch of your body. And then I'm going to make a mess of you again."

An excited tremor courses through me, and I smile into his chest. "Let's go get messy then."

I fall back into the plushy feather pillows with a satisfied sigh. Dermot has spent the last several hours between my legs in one fashion or another, and I am positively boneless. I can die a happy woman now.

In my fantasies we'd been good together, but this was beyond. The chemistry. His skill. My hunger. It made for better sex than I've dared to dream about. If I'd known it could be like this, I would truly have lost my mind when he turned me down three years ago.

Saved by my own obliviousness.

But then I get to wondering if it would be like this at all if we hadn't been forced apart. If we hadn't had years to simmer and stew and *imagine*. I still can't believe that he's thought of this with me—that this might not be completely one-sided after all. And if I hadn't tried a thing or two in the dark, under the covers, with inexperienced boys at university, would I even be able to fathom the enormity of the last few hours with this man?

I don't think so.

I reach out to interlace our fingers as we lie beside each other, staring at the ceiling, watching shadows take form across the wood-beam ceiling as the early morning light reaches into the room. Snatching the safety and cover of night from us, or at least from him.

"You should get going."

My heart stutters and I go still. "I'm sorry, what?"

He rolls onto his side to look at me, head cradled in his palm. "I just mean back to the main house so that your parents don't find out."

I blink rapidly. Trying to catch up. Trying to wrap my head around what he's saying. "Dermot, I don't care if my parents find out."

He stares down at me intensely, with a sad smile on his face. "Ada…your dad—your parents—they've become friends to me, family almost. Taken me under their wing. Provided me with good, consistent employment. I can't just walk out my door in the morning with their only daughter on my arm. And everyone here, or in town, what would they think? I've known you since you we're a child. I never thought of you like this until that night on the porch, but no one else will know that."

Dread coils in my stomach. I hate the idea of keeping us a secret. Like there's something dirty about us being together somehow. But I also don't want to scare Dermot off. I need to figure out a way to strike a compromise.

I gaze back at him as I pull the sheet up over my naked body, uncertainty buzzing in my head now. "Okay but are we…? Is this…?" I groan and roll onto my stomach, burying my face in the pillows. I hate how I sound even asking. I hate needing him to reassure me that this is *more*.

The heat of his body presses beside me and I feel the drag of his teeth across my bare shoulder as he pulls the sheet back down. "Don't hide from me, Goldilocks. I told you. You're mine. I just… We need to think about this. I want you to be sure you know what you're getting into with me. I have a hard time believing you'll want me if you realize how fucked up I am."

"Are you talking about when the truck backfired the other day?"

His eyes go distant, to another place, as he carefully mulls my question over. "It's more than that, Ada. I'm not the same man I was when I left. I've seen too much. Been left behind too many times. I don't even think I like this new version of myself."

My heart thuds heavily and my chest aches, struck by the deep sadness in his voice. I don't know what to say to his assessment of himself. I wish he could see himself through my eyes. Strong and patient, with a wicked and addictive mouth. I feel safe when I'm around Dermot and all I know is that I want him any way I can have him. Walking away after last night would be… I can't even think about it. So instead, I lean into his broad chest and press a kiss right over his heart. "I like every version of you, Dermot Harding."

And then I wrap myself in a sheet and scamper back to the main house.

# CHAPTER 7

## Dermot

I'M DRAGGING TODAY. WHICH IS SAYING SOMETHING, because I haven't slept a full night since my tour. Usually, colt starting gets my adrenaline pumping; it's exciting to see the young horses get a good foundation. I live for long days on the ranch. It's where I feel most like myself—most at ease. But after a stressful first half of my night followed by a very active second half of the night, all I want to do is crawl back into bed.

With Ada.

There's no denying my feelings for her anymore. What I was convinced was merely a broken man's fixation on something innocent and unsullied, a comforting memory, is clearly so much more. I shouldn't have let things go that far, should have stuck to my plan and kept my distance. Because after last night, all my carefully built walls are mere rubble scattered at her feet.

I scoff at myself as I pull the saddle off the tired buckskin colt. I crashed through those walls like a goddamn bull in a china shop without considering the consequences of our relationship. What would people think of me? A man in his thirties, who's known this girl since she was little. Who's taken a vow of honor, promised to protect people. Now…it feels wrong when I run through the scenario in my head. It feels worse when I consider how betrayed her parents might feel. How her reputation in this small town might suffer.

But when I'm with Ada, everything feels right. Last night, my mind felt quiet for the first time since I left the army. With her, I wasn't just going through the motions. I was *present.*

And I want that every day. At what cost though?

Since my parents took off, Tom and Lynette have become like family to me. I don't want to lose them. But now I've put myself in an impossible situation. Keep Ada and fess up to her parents—who I love and respect, but who will no doubt want to castrate me. Or give Ada up and…well, I can't even bear the thought of it now.

*You are so royally fucked, Dermot.*

I give the young quarter horse a light brush before walking him back out to his herd. Taking deep, calming breaths of the warm summer air. Until my eyes land on Ada's jean-clad ass, and then the wind is knocked out of me all over again.

She's walking out toward Penny's paddock, spinning the lead rope in her hand and humming tunelessly as she goes. She doesn't look worried at all. And like she can feel my gaze on her, she turns her head back over her shoulder, looking directly at where I'm standing.

I'm immobilized. I just stare back, slack-jawed, unable to process the fact that an angel like her would ever choose a damaged man like me. How could she possibly know that she likes every version of me? She saw me crumple that day when the truck went off. How can she throw caution to the wind like that? How can she forgive me so easily for pushing her away, for breaking her heart? It all seems impossibly naïve on her part.

*That's why it's my job to warn her off.*

And how the fuck am I supposed to get anything done with her around when all I want to do is strip her down and bend her over?

She's practically glowing, and the smile she gives me now? It's like looking into the sun—downright blinding.

A hard clap on the back knocks me right out of my daydream, and I try to will the swelling sensation in my jeans away as I turn to face…Tom Wilson.

"Morning, sir." I tip my head nervously, color draining from my face, hoping he didn't notice me ogling his little girl. Hoping he doesn't notice my uncontrollable erection.

"For crying out loud, Dermot. Why do you insist on still calling me sir? It makes me feel old."

I chuckle. "Sorry, Tom."

"That's more like it." He waves me along as he turns to walk back toward the barn. "Tell me how the horses are coming along before I head into town."

I give him a brief rundown of how each horse is doing,

assuring him they'll all be broke and safe to sit on by the end of the week.

"You've always had a special way about you, Dermot. The horses know it, and so do people. It's hard not to love you."

My throat drops into my stomach like a stone. *If he only knew what I was doing to his daughter last night, he might not feel so sentimental.* "Thanks," I choke out awkwardly, looking away, unable to hold his gaze.

He barks out a laugh as he hops up into his pickup truck. "Hell of a mosquito bite you've got there, kid." I look back at him in confusion, realization only dawning on me when he smirks and taps his neck.

Ada's teeth left a bruise.

★★★

I'm trying to help Ada with Penny, but everything about her is driving me to distraction. The way her breasts bounce while she rides, the way her golden hair trails in the wind behind her when she gallops, the way she swung her leg over the saddle like she swung it over me last night.

Essentially, I'm a horny mess who can't stop envisioning all the ways I could corrupt a perfectly sweet twenty-one-year-old girl. *I want to corrupt her and only her for the rest of my life.*

Which is an alarming thought, a monumental realization, and truthfully more than I'm equipped to deal with.

"We galloped!" Ada singsongs from ahead of me as she slides down Penny's sweat-slicked flank, her entire body vibrating with contagious excitement.

My boots hit the ground as I step down off of Solar, grinning back at her. "You look excited."

Her emerald eyes rake down over my body suggestively and one eyebrow quirks up when she gets past my oval belt buckle. My body won't stop reacting to her mere proximity, no matter how much my brain begs it to stop. "So do you."

"Not here, Ada," I chide her, turning away, not wanting to hurt her feelings. But also not wanting to get caught by the other staff around the ranch. I hate that I have no control where she's concerned. I thought if I waited a few months after getting home, that if I could force myself to stay away from Gold Rush Ranch even though it was only a couple of hours away, that I'd be able to resist her draw—the imaginary connection I built up in my head overseas.

I didn't even last a full week. And god knows I didn't keep my hands to myself in the days leading up to last night either. For a soldier, my self-control is truly atrocious.

Back in the barn, we tie up and untack our horses silently. There's an unspoken tension between us. I know Ada doesn't understand my resistance and I can see the agitation in her every movement as she takes care of her little red mare. Even Penny seems nervous in Ada's presence. Like she can feel the storm brewing beneath her innocent-looking exterior.

We're walking past the hay shed after turning the horses out when she unexpectedly grabs me by the elbow and drags me into the darkened building. Before I can even protest, she's fallen to her knees and is grappling with my belt buckle, yanking my jeans down and fisting my cock like she's out for revenge.

"Ada—"

"Shut up, Dermot. I don't want to hear your excuses. Being around you has always been painful, but being around you and knowing what it's like to have you? It's downright unbearable."

She flattens her tongue, licking the head of my cock like a lollipop, and my mind goes blank. All my rational reasons to protest what she's doing fly right out the window. My hips buck toward her face when she wraps her lips around my girth, and when she slides her head toward my pelvis, I grab hold of the old plywood wall beside me to keep myself upright. Her tongue swirls and her cheeks hollow out as she works me, running her hands up over my thighs, squeezing my ass. Rolling my balls in her petite hand until I feel like I might lose control and finish right here and now.

But I'm not done. As much as I'm enjoying this, I want more.

I fist a chunk of her hair and pull her off of me, reveling in the way her eyes go wide and her lashes flutter as she looks up at me from the dirt floor of the shed. Reaching down, I scoop her up and turn around, sitting her on a stack of square bales as she squeals in surprise.

"Three bales high, the perfect height to taste what's between these thighs."

"Oh god." Her cheeks are stained the prettiest pink as she shimmies her hips to help me get her skin-tight jeans pulled off.

I toss them to the ground but put her beautifully stitched leather boots back on. "This is a good look for you, Ada,"

I murmur as I take hold of her thighs and spread her open before me. "You look fucking edible."

Her only response is the silent parting of her lips in the sweetest little *O* shape. She may have experimented with other men, but I can tell she doesn't have that much experience, and I am thriving off the quiet but needy way she reacts to me. I like that I can shock her with my mouth, and I know she does too as I watch her body tremble under my gaze.

I swipe a thumb through her folds and watch it come back glistening. I pop it into my mouth with an audible "Mmm," as I taste her, watching her eyes go wide and doe-like in response. "Tastes like..." I lift her legs higher before I growl, "Mine."

And then I dive in. Starting off slow and gentle with my tongue but ending up hard and fast. Urged on by her writhing and moaning, by her fingers raking through my hair.

Her legs shake, and she clamps them around my neck, but I don't stop. I add a finger, sliding into her wet heat while I continue to work her with my tongue. "Oh my god, Dermot. Please don't stop," she murmurs as I coax the orgasm from her body.

When it hits, her back arches and her hands turn to fists in my hair, yanking rhythmically, lost to her own pleasure. And I grin, loving making her fall apart like this. For me.

"Thank you," she sighs, breathlessly.

I pull away and quirk an eyebrow at her. "Oh, baby, I'm not done with you yet."

She just smiles as I pull her down off the stack of hay bales. Grabbing the twine of the top one, I chuck it onto the ground beside us and then spin her around. One hand on her hip and the other flat between her shoulder blades, I lean forward and whisper into her ear. "Two bales high, the perfect height to bend you over."

She moans as I press her chest down onto the bale of hay and add, "Legs wide, honey." I watch her step each boot-clad foot further apart, loving her eagerness. Groaning at how she looks bent over, bare legs disappearing into her boots.

It's fucking criminal.

I lean over her back while lining myself up, feeling her flutter against the contact. "You love this, don't you, Ada?"

And I slide into her.

"Yes!" she cries out, clenching around my girth and rocking her hips back toward me.

I tut at her playfully as I pull all the way back out. "Needy girl," I growl as I slide back in to the hilt. Pumping into her with a steady rhythm now, hearing my thighs slap against her bare ass, smelling the musky hay around us in the quiet shed, feeling her soft body moving beneath mine.

This—us—it's everything.

I stand up tall to watch from above and am struck by the depth of my feelings for her. By the enormity of them. How they've crept into my mind over the years no matter how hard I've tried to keep them at bay. I grip her hips, thrusting harder, driven wild by the fact that this woman wants *me,* when she could pick any man in the world. My control has gone up in a puff of smoke where she's concerned. And in this moment, I don't even care.

When she spasms and cries out my name beneath me,

a blush spreading across her lower back, hitting that high for the second time, it's almost more that I can take. And knowing that she's been taken care of means I can chase my release with abandon.

"My turn," I say gruffly, just as sensations and emotions collide, shoving me right over the edge after her. As the tension between us ebbs, I lean back down to cover her body with mine, to press a kiss just below her ear. To tell her we're going to make this work. That I'm *never* going to give her up.

But then I freeze. The shed door swings open, and a voice growls through what was previously a private, safe space.

"What the fuck is going on here?"

I scramble to cover Ada. I don't even care that my jeans are around my ankles; she doesn't deserve this. Prying eyes. I recognize the voice as one of the farmhands, Gord. It's not news to me that these guys are ultra-protective of Ada. They always have been. But being righteous enough to announce yourself this way takes some serious balls.

I know I'm in trouble.

"Get out!" I bark angrily. Mind spinning with what this means for me. For her. For *us*.

When I hear the door close, I stand up and mutter, "Fuck!"

Ada stands and spins to face me, reaching for her jeans. She's still flushed from her orgasm, but her eyes are wide and alarmed. She rubs my arms as I do up my pants. "It's okay, it's okay…"

"No, Ada. It's not." I scrub a hand over my face. "If he tells anyone before I get a chance to explain… You don't understand."

"Explain it to me then."

"I've been around here as an adult since you were a lanky little kid with a rat's nest for hair. The things they'll say about us… People won't understand that I never thought of you this way even once until that damn kiss." I rake my hands through my hair and look up at the corrugated tin roof.

She tips her chin down to button her jeans before hitting me with the most innocent, trusting look. Like a shot to the heart. "We're both adults now, Dermot. Who cares what people will say?"

"Your parents are more than just friends to me, they're the family I never had. My own took off and haven't come back to see me. I can't do this to them. Disappoint them like this."

"Why would making me happy disappoint them?" She sounds genuinely confused.

I knew this would happen. I knew this was a bad idea. I've known all along that I should stay away from Ada Wilson. That giving in to my confused and fucked up day-dreams borne of an innocent kiss years ago would only lead to trouble. I should have been stronger, because now this will hurt more than just me.

I grasp her face and kiss her forehead reverently before turning and walking out of the shed. If Ada doesn't care about her reputation—her future—I'll have to be the one to do it for her.

Gord's leaning up against the far corner of the building, a big wad of tobacco tucked into his lip, picking at his nails. He barely spares me a glance as I walk up. "The way I see it, one of us tells him or you just hop in that truck and head back up to the mountains."

I sigh. Hating the decision but refusing to be the thing that messes Ada's life up. I can give up the Wilsons if it means that Ada gets to go on and live life without a black mark against her name.

"I'll leave."

# CHAPTER 8

## Ada

I RUSH UP TOWARD THE OLD FARMHOUSE, LOOKING FOR Dermot. Needing to find him. That kiss on the forehead felt different. It lacked the heat and grit of our past several interactions.

It felt like goodbye.

He finally comes into view, jogging down the front steps of my parents' house. His shoulders are tense and tall as he marches across the driveway, that military training peeking out like it does sometimes now.

"What are you doing?" I ask, dread coiling in my gut. It's like my body already knows what my mind refuses to accept.

"I just went to let your mom know that I'm leaving. She'll pass the message on to your dad." He continues walking right past me, toward the little laneway house. Alarm bells ring in my ears.

"Where are you going?"

"Back home, up to Merritt."

I chase after him, like a sad little puppy on his heels. "For how long?"

He swings the front door open and I follow him through before he finally turns to look at me. His eyes are all steel. Cold and determined. The way he looked at me the night before, while I straddled him, right in this exact spot? All that warmth is gone.

"For as long as it takes." His words are like ice on my skin.

"For as long as *what* takes?"

"Sorting myself out. I can't do this to you."

I gasp, but he just turns and starts shoving stuff into his duffel bag. "Seriously, Dermot?" Anger bleeds into my voice, making it wobble. "You're going to run again?"

"I didn't run, Ada. I joined the army, served my country. Learned some tough lessons about life and myself. It's time you did the same."

"Oh yeah? Tell me, Dermot, what lessons am I supposed to be learning right now?" I cross my arms, digging my nails into my skin so hard it will leave marks.

He looks up at me. Dark eyes boring into mine, not unkindly, as he says, "That girlhood crushes are just that. Best left in the past."

I rear back as though he's just slapped me. This man made love to me, right here, last night. And now all of that is just a girlhood crush? I'm speechless. Frozen. All I want is for the floor to open right here and swallow me whole, but he continues talking as he drops his bag by the door and straightens the kitchen.

"I'm too old for you, Ada. I'm too broken. I've never had a long-term relationship, don't even know if I can manage one. I haven't slept through the night even once in almost three years. Loud noises scare me. I've seen things I can't get out of my head. I'm a mess, and you have the entire world in the palm of your hand. You deserve so much better than to be stuck limping along with me." His voice cracks with emotion and he tips his head up to stare at the ceiling.

My chest aches, the kind of ache that shoots right into my throat and threatens to transform into that all-consuming type of nausea. My cheeks feel hot and my eyes sting, but I refuse to cry. Dermot doesn't need me to feel bad for him. He needs a swift kick in the ass.

My finger shakes as I lift my hand to point at him accusingly. My voice comes out steely and eerily calm. An absolute bluff. "I have a dad, Dermot. He teaches me lessons, not you. You're just an asshole who's too self-absorbed to realize what he's got staring him in the face. You'll never be happy because you're too busy feeling sorry for yourself."

His jaw ticks, like he's swallowing words he wants to say. I hope the taste of the apology he owes me is bitter. I hope it turns his stomach.

"You should go," is all he manages to bite out.

The finality of his words lands like the lash of a whip. I try not to flinch, but I fail.

"So should you," I say, turning on my heel and storming out of the house.

I've been here before. I should have known better.

I don't want to face my parents and I don't want to face the staff. So I go to the only place where I know for a fact I won't face any judgement: Penny's field.

I duck through the wooden fence and head toward where she's grazing. The summer sun is beating down on her slender back, and her tail is swishing back and forth, keeping any bugs at bay. She looks shiny and healthy, bright copper—like a brand-new penny.

She's come along so quickly with Dermot's help, and the realization that I'll always have to attribute some of her progress to him stings like whiskey on an open wound. There's not a single place, or thing, on this farm that won't forever remind me of him. This is *my* home, *my* safe haven. And he waltzed in and stomped all over it. *Again.*

How could I have been so gullible?

I get close enough that Penny's head snaps up. She knickers her greeting, wide, intelligent eyes blinking back at me innocently—like I don't already know that this little chestnut mare has a devilish streak. I smile at her sadly. I like her sassy side; I wish I could be more like her. Tougher.

Because right now, I feel downright fragile.

And when I finally run my hands up around her silky neck, when I feel her warm, damp exhale on my shoulder, my carefully curated game face melts. The ache in my chest breaks through every barrier I've erected, hitting me with full force.

Taking my breath away as I burrow my face in the filly's neck and break down.

I don't know how long I stand there crying. But Penny's

patience with me wears out, and she eventually steps away, a wet spot on her neck, to get back to her grass.

I don't know what to do. I feel like I'm living in a waking nightmare. The sky is perfectly blue, the fields are bright green, the birds are chirping happily, and yet my world is crashing down around me. How can such a perfectly pretty day feel so utterly ugly?

How did I come so close to having everything I've ever wanted, only to be left here with nothing in the blink of any eye? How am I supposed to come back from knowing what having him felt like?

I plunk down on the grass, lying out flat, feeling too dizzy to go anywhere else, finding the sound of Penny's teeth ripping at the grass rather soothing. The puffy white clouds above me float peacefully, and I'm taken back to my days as a child on the ranch. Playing in the dirt all day long, jumping onto horses with no saddle or bridle, cloud gazing and daydreaming of Dermot Harding. I'm pretty sure I even pulled petals off of daisies. *He loves me, he loves me not, he loves me…*

Now all I see in the clouds are meaningless white blobs. A manic giggle erupts from my chest. Talk about a grim outlook for a twenty-one-year-old woman with her entire life ahead of her.

"Should I be worried about you?"

My dad's voice wraps around me like a warm hug. I hear him give Penny his signature loud pats on her muscled shoulder. "No."

"Ada, you're lying sprawled out in the field, staring at

the sky, laughing. I've been watching you. I don't even think you've blinked. I love you, but this is creepy."

I smile at the image he just painted. It is pretty creepy when he puts it like that. "Love you too, Dad," is all I can think to say back right now.

"Your mom's been looking for you. It's dinnertime." How could it be dinnertime? How long have I been lying here for?

"Oh, sorry," I mumble, still fixating on the fact that I've been lying in the field for hours now.

He mumbles something that sounds an awful lot like, "I'll fucking kill him," before taking a seat on the ground beside me.

He picks up a blade of grass, eyes it warily, and then places it in the corner of his mouth. A rancher through and through. "You all right, my girl?" he asks without looking at me.

I sigh. I don't want to lie to my dad, he's been a pillar of support in my life. My biggest fan. I don't want to think he'd be disappointed in me now. But Dermot has planted a seed of doubt with the intensity of his shame.

So I settle on something truthful that also gives nothing away. "I will be."

He just grunts and picks at the soil between us.

"Of course you will. You're my daughter."

# CHAPTER 9

## Dermot

I'VE ALWAYS FOUND THE MOUNTAINS THAT SURROUND MY family farm to be oppressive. But these past two weeks they've become downright depressing. Too tall, casting too long of a shadow, and way too fucking cold.

I miss the warm sunshine and rolling hills in Ruby Creek. I miss the camaraderie of being around other people at Gold Rush Ranch.

I miss Ada.

The further I drove away from her, the less my reasons for leaving seemed to make sense. Last time I *had* to leave. The army was waiting for me. But now? There is absolutely nothing waiting for me. An empty farm and a traumatized mind are all I have for company.

With nothing else on the horizon, I finally got an independent geologist out to check my land for mining deposits. It appears I've hit the literal gold mine in that department.

My reward for being the last Harding standing on this farm. When everyone else had the good sense to leave and start something new, I hunkered down. Too sentimental to part with it.

Too sentimental to do anything—to even move, apparently. Which is why I've spent my last several days walking and mapping the perimeters of my land. Checking the fences in the morning and then sitting on the front porch of the run-down house, staring out at my land in the afternoon. With over eighty thousand acres, I should be able to keep busy for a while.

The cows are long gone, sold before I left on tour. The chickens, too. No crops to speak of. The only signs of life here are the wildlife that passes through, the wildflowers that have taken over the valleys in my absence, and the squirrels that I'm pretty sure are now living in the attic.

And me. But I'm not living. I'm going through the motions. I sleep in fits and starts, often woken up by flashes of my time overseas—but that's not new. What is new is being woken up by deep regret over leaving Ada, rather than sweet dreams about one innocent kiss.

The memory of what we could have had under different circumstances haunts me. The way her ears went red and the tip of her nose twitched to hold back the tears when I told her I was leaving again.

The way I held her heart in my hand and crushed it into dust. All because I'm too big of a coward to fess up about how I feel and face whatever the repercussions might be. And maybe even more so because I'm fucking terrified to need anyone who might leave me. Who might move on. Every person in my life has been so impermanent. My parents, my older siblings, the friends I made in the army. Why would it be any different with Ada?

She's young. She's at university. She's going to run a racehorse business one day; I know it in my bones. Because Ada Wilson is smart, and strong, and an absolute go-getter. The last thing she needs is a broken-down man holding her back.

This is the best course of action for both of us. Even if it doesn't feel that way right now. Or at least that's what I keep telling myself.

I take a deep swig of my beer and rest my head on the back of the porch swing, giving it a good shove, hoping that maybe it might rock me off for a few minutes of peace. Where I could let myself remember the feel of Ada's silky skin beneath my fingertips, the press of her tongue into my mouth, the sound of her moans as I moved inside her.

*This* is a good dream.

I can feel myself drifting until the sound of tires rumbling over gravel cuts into my consciousness. Cursing without opening my eyes, I feel my body go rigid. I just want to be alone right now.

When the hum of the engine gets close enough, I open one eyelid.

And when Tom Wilson steps out of his truck, I open the other and straighten myself. Alarm courses through me. *Why the hell would he drive all the way up here?*

I sit up, blinking at him, rubbing my eyes to make sure I'm not seeing things. His truck is parked beside mine, except he's got a two-horse trailer attached to his, and by the way it's swaying, I'm thinking there's probably a horse or two in there as well. I'm so damn confused.

"You look like hell, son," he says good-naturedly as he climbs the steps up to the front porch.

"Wasn't expecting any visitors." My voice cracks after days of not speaking to anyone.

"Wanted to come for a visit. Felt like a trail ride in the mountains." He looks out over my land appreciatively.

I just blink at him in confusion. "You could have called."

He waves me off. "We both know you wouldn't have answered."

I just grunt. *He's not wrong.*

"You gonna offer an old man a beer, or just keep sitting there like a sulking bump on a log?"

"Sorry." I shoot up off the swing, realizing how rude I've been in the wake of his arrival. *Way to welcome a man you profess to love and respect, Dermot.* "Here." I point at the swing. "Take a load off and I'll grab you a cold one."

He gives my shoulder a brief squeeze as I slide past him into the messy house. In the kitchen, I hold the edge of the counter and bow my head, trying to figure out what the hell Tom Wilson is up to. If he knew about Ada and me, and was angry with me, well, I couldn't tell. But there's only one way to find out.

With two fresh beers in hand, I step back out onto the deck. "Beautiful farm you've got up here, Dermot. I can see why you didn't want to let it go."

I hand him his beer and take a seat in the big

Adirondack chair across from him. "Seems like I made the right choice."

Tom takes a long pull of his beer and looks back at me inquisitively.

"I did what you said and had somebody out to survey the land, drill some holes and all that."

He leans forward to rest his elbows on his knees, his watery blue eyes regarding me with a knowing look. "And?"

My eyes scan the scrubby, rocky land around us. "We're basically sitting on a gold mine. Seems that big mining company was sniffing around for good reason." I shift my eyes back to Tom. "Thanks for pushing me to look for myself."

His eyes twinkle, and he shakes his head, leaning back to look out at the craggy landscape. "How much?"

"A lot. A metric fuck-ton."

"Well, I'll be… What are you going to do with it?"

"Start a business, I suppose. Though I have no idea how to do such a thing." I look up at him, properly meeting his eyes for the first time since he pulled up. "Your offer to help still stand?"

"You've been through a lot for a man your age, Dermot."

I don't respond. What is there to say to that?

"I want to see you succeed. So yeah, of course the offer still stands. Some startup capital and my support for five percent of the company. What do you say?"

I feel a pinch across the bridge of my nose, a thickness in my throat that I will away. "I don't know why you've always been so good to me."

The sad smile he gives me barely touches his eyes. "Had

a soft spot for ya since that first summer you came to work for me. Twenty years old and a total idiot. Good with the horses though."

I bark out a laugh. "To be honest, Tom, I'm not sure much has changed. I think I'm more jumbled than I was then."

He just nods at me knowingly, tipping the brown bottle back and swallowing. "Nothing a night out on the range can't fix. Let's pack up and hit the trails so we can set up camp before it gets dark."

"We can just go for a ride in the morning, Tom. We really don't have to do the whole shebang."

He slams his empty beer bottle down on the small table beside him. "You never used to complain about campouts. Plus, I can see the inside of your house through the window. I'm too old to sleep in a messy bachelor pad."

I look through the window. *Messy* doesn't even begin to cover it. I've been a zombie living in a war zone; the place is a disaster. It makes me want to take a match to the old house, burn it to the ground and start fresh.

"Okay, give me ten minutes."

I settle into my sleeping bag, feeling more relaxed than I have in days. Fresh air, a change of scenery, a few sips of whiskey with an old friend. I feel like I'm twenty all over again.

My eyelids feel heavy instantly, and under the bright stars, beside the crackling fire, I drift off into a dreamless sleep.

When my eyes finally crack open, it's already light out and Tom is up making coffee over the fire. "Good morning, Sleeping Beauty."

I scrub my hands over my face and sit up, shocked that I slept through the night. "Sorry. I haven't been sleeping much lately."

"How long is lately?" he asks, forehead crinkled in concern.

A ragged sigh pries itself from my chest as I look up at the pillowy clouds drifting in the bright blue sky. "It's probably been almost three years."

"Oh, Dermot…"

I hold a hand up to stop him. I don't want his pity, and I don't deserve it after what I've done to his daughter. "It's okay, Tom. I don't need you to rub my back over it. I'll get better, eventually. It's always worse up here. It's too quiet. Too much time to think about…everything."

"Well, come back down to the ranch then. The laneway house is yours for as long as you need it."

I rake my fingers through my hair, tugging at it in frustration. "I can't."

He pours me a cup of strong black coffee and hands it over. "Why's that?"

"I just…" Shame coils in my gut. *If he only knew.* I take a sip of coffee to fill the silence.

"I know about you and Ada."

And all that coffee gets sprayed over my sleeping bag as I look at him. One side of his mouth quirks up, but he doesn't look all that amused.

I blurt out the first thing I can think to say. "I'm sorry."

His wise eyes narrow as he takes a deep inhale of his own coffee. "For what?"

"For betraying your trust." My heart is pounding in my chest. Anxiety coursing through my veins. *He's known all this time and acted like we were just going to hang out?*

"The only person you've betrayed is Ada. Me?" Tom lifts his shoulders and then drops them dramatically. "I'm just confused."

I feel my entire face go red. *Betrayed Ada?* Just the combination of the words makes me angry with myself. That's the very last thing I ever wanted to do. "Confused about what?"

"How the man I know could leave behind the woman he loves."

I startle. It feels like he's punched me in the gut. "Did she…?" I stare into the inky black liquid in my tin cup. "Did she tell you that?"

Tom just snorts. "You weren't kidding about still being an idiot." We sit in silence for a few moments, both lost in thought before Tom adds, "Any old fool with two eyes can see that you love that girl. And her?" He scoffs, shaking his head in disbelief. "She's always loved you. Right out of the gate. She never stopped. Not even for a minute. And that"—he wags his finger at me—"that is a gift most men will never know."

His words hit me like a wrecking ball. They knock the air right out of the valley, like the mountains have finally succeeded in suffocating me. I feel hollow.

"So you…don't care?"

Tom stands and starts packing the camp up, clearly agitated by my line of questioning. "Why? Because you're older than her? Because you've been around for years? I don't care, Dermot! And if you love her like I think you do, what other people think shouldn't matter either!" His voice is quiet, simmering with protective rage as he huffs out a deep, centering breath. "I love you like a son. I want you happy, just like I want Ada happy. And if that's together, then as far as I'm concerned, it's just the best of both worlds."

He shoves our things into bags, obviously done with our campout. I hear him mutter something like, "Ya'll are thick as bricks," as I stand to help him silently. Properly chastised.

Our ride back to the house is quiet. But not awkward. Maybe it should be, but I can't help but feel like Tom shed a lot of light on the situation. I also feel like a dog with his tail between his legs, like I should have known better, like I should have trusted myself.

Like I should have trusted Ada.

And now I'm going to have to prove to her she can trust me again. Knowing Ada, it won't be easy.

When we arrive at the homestead, I help Tom pack his trailer up. Years of working together have lent us knowledge of one another, meaning we move around in sync. Getting shit done quietly and efficiently.

When he pulls his truck door open, he turns around to look at me, holding his arms wide. I step into his fatherly hug, feeling his big, comforting slaps against my back—unable to stop the small smile they elicit. This man pats everyone like they're cattle.

When he pushes me back, he looks me dead in the eye, hands on my shoulders. "I can't make personal life decisions for you. But you promised that girl you'd help get her filly to the races. And I know you're a man of your word."

I offer him a decisive nod in response. "See you soon."

I'm going back to Gold Rush Ranch, and I'm going to get the girl whether I deserve her or not.

# CHAPTER 10

## Ada

I REGARD MYSELF IN THE MIRROR, MAKING SURE MY MAKEUP is perfect. Today is the Denman Derby and I'm going to enjoy myself, like I do every year. I've got a new floral print dress on, I've curled my hair and painted my nails—you wouldn't know I'm a total ranch rat unless I told you.

Feeling satisfied with the girl looking back at me, I take a deep breath. "Time to woman up, Ada," I murmur to myself, rolling my shoulders back. "This is your favorite day of the year. Who needs Christmas?"

The girl staring back at me looks beautiful and strong, totally ready to take on the world. And I am. As painful as the last two weeks have been, I've also learned a lot about myself. I feel like I walked through the fire and came out the other side, turned over a new leaf, realigned my vision for my future. I'm sure of myself, of my strength, in a way I never have been.

I think I'll always love Dermot Harding, but I have other dreams I need to achieve, and I know his dumb ass wouldn't want me to sit around moping. I think I've come to know that Dermot loves me in his own way.

In a way that's not good enough for me.

Because Dermot needs to love himself first. He's so paralyzed by what everyone will think of him, by feeling like nothing is ever permanent, that he can't give himself over to anyone or anything.

The realization hit me one night during a midnight swim in the river. He can't put himself first because he doesn't love himself enough to make it a priority. That was the night my tears switched from being for myself to being for him. A man too scared to accept the love I wanted to give him.

An absolute shame. And not something I can fix for him. Lucky for me, I don't suffer from that same insecurity.

So this is the new Ada, forged in fire, soon to be a university graduate and future owner and trainer of Canadian racehorse champions. Dermot Harding had a chance to get on board, and now he can get out of my way.

I trot down the stairs toward the front door, sliding my feet into the strappy heels I picked for today with a small smile on my face. I feel *good.* In fact, I feel great. Until I step out onto the front porch and see a metallic blue pickup in the driveway. Dermot is sitting on the tailgate, swinging his legs, with a bouquet of roses laid across his lap.

His head snaps up at the sound of the door slamming behind me. "Ada—"

Butterflies flap in my stomach, but I cut him off. "No. I don't want to hear it." I march toward my dad's truck as I hear my parents lock up behind me.

"Five minutes, Ada. I brought flowers."

I bark out an incredulous laugh. "Do you know me at all, Dermot Harding? Flowers? Try harder." I pull myself into the back of the cab and slam the door on anything else he has to say. Today is *my* day.

My mom gives him an apologetic pat on his knee and my dad tilts his head and shrugs as if to say, "Women." But within moments, my entire family is loaded up in the truck and Dermot is nothing more than a slouched-over figure in the rearview mirror.

★★★

Our day down at the track is a dream, as usual. The buzz of Derby Day never fails to stir something inside of me. I want to be there, with a horse of my own, running in the Denman Derby. I know now, more than ever, that it's what I'm meant to do with my life.

We had a beautiful dinner, wine, placed some bets—came out even. And now on the drive home we talk about all the horses we saw.

"I want to buy another one, Dad."

"Another what?" he asks, eyes flitting back to me through the rearview mirror.

"Racehorse."

He just chuckles, the apples of his cheeks all round with the width of his grin. "One thing at a time, Ada. Maybe as your graduation present. You only have one year left at university."

I look out the window, into the darkening landscape, and press my lips together to hold back the huge grin threatening to break across my face. I can't wait to get started.

The closer we get to the farm, the quieter we all become. No one dared to bring up Dermot's appearance when we drove off, but now the unspoken weight of his arrival is filling up all the empty space in the truck.

"Do you think he's still there?" my mom asks as we turn off the highway.

I just shrug and look away. Probably not. Staying power isn't exactly his forte.

"You know that boy is head over heels in love with you, don't you, Ada?" she presses.

I roll my lips together, trying not to bite back too hard. My mom means well, and I know they both figured out what happened between us too easily for them to not have been on to us before. I knew they wouldn't care. Why couldn't Dermot have just believed me?

"He's not a boy, Mom. He's a grown-ass man."

"Ada Wilson! Watch your language!" My mother sounds scandalized, but my dad just laughs. He knows me well.

"It's a fact. He's an adult. And if what you say is true, he's got a funny way of showing it," I add before staring back out the window.

No one can argue with what I've just said. And when we pull up to the house, the truck is dead silent as we peer out into the darkened driveway.

Until my dad groans. Dermot is still here, sitting on the back of his truck. Waiting. It doesn't look like he's moved all day, and even though I just went off about him being an adult…right now? Looking at him? He looks like a lost little boy.

I feel a tug at the center of my sternum, that invisible string that's always drawn me to him, trying to pull me toward him again. The accompanying pinch in my chest makes me want to hug him, to soak up all his pain and disappointment. To lend him my strength.

But I can't yet. I'm still too pissed off. Too hurt. "Don't let him stay here," I say as I hop out of the truck, sniffling. I give him a once-over, then dart into the old farmhouse. Knowing that if I stare at him too long, if I get lost in those dark eyes, my resolve will disintegrate completely. The man is like a big vat of acid for my willpower.

I kick my shoes off and head up to my room to get ready for bed, not wanting to talk to anyone. Ditching my dress, I slip into pajamas and then scrub my face clean until it hurts. I'm about to crawl into bed when I hear the front screen door creak open. I'm up and looking out my window so fast it's embarrassing.

Pulling the lace curtain back ever-so-slightly, I watch my mom walk out to Dermot's truck with a pillow, a blanket, and a sandwich. *Traitor.* Then I hear her say, "She'll come around." *Double traitor.* She pats his shoulder before she turns to walk into the house and I fall into bed, squeezing my eyes shut hard until I finally drift off into a fitful sleep.

★★★

When I wake up in the morning, I'm dreading looking out my window. If I see Dermot sleeping outside my house, I'm going to fall apart. I wanted him to come back for me, and he did. So why isn't it enough?

The only thing I can think of is the fact that he thought he could just waltz out here with a handful of roses and I'd run back into his arms. It showed a total lack of understanding—of reflection. The only thing I've ever done with flowers is braid them into my horse's hair.

I drag my feet across the oak floors toward the bathroom but am stopped short by loud metal clanging. *What the hell?*

I pull back the curtain, just like last night. Dermot's truck is still there, but he's moved out into the field next to the barn and is using a mallet hammer, jamming what looks like a bunch of metal fencing together.

I have to admit, he's piqued my curiosity, so I shove on some jeans and head out.

He doesn't look up when I approach the paddock fence. He just keeps working calmly and steadily. I admire him openly, the way his hands flex with each strike, the sweat beading on his forehead. I imagine running my tongue along the bead of it that slips down over his defined cheekbone. And then, realizing where my mind has wandered, I start to get antsy with how long he's been ignoring me.

"What are you doing?" I blurt, unable to take it any longer.

He just smiles and runs his arm over his forehead,

brushing away the perspiration. "Woulda thought you'd recognize this, Goldilocks."

My eyes scan the combination of bars he's put together, but I must be thick because I can't tell what it's supposed to be. "Okay," I huff out, agitated at not being able to pass this test. "Pretend I don't recognize it."

He chuckles, the dimple on his cheek peeking out playfully, and turns back toward his project. "It's a present."

"For what?"

"For you."

I rear back. I know I didn't want flowers, but I'm not sure I want this either. "Okay…why?"

He comes back to the fence and leans his forearms against it as he regards me. I can't help but look down at the way this position tugs his jeans tight over that very round ass. Being this close to him? It's like being offered water for the first time after spending two weeks in the desert.

He notices. And his cheek twitches, but he has the good sense not to comment. Instead, he says, "Because I made you a promise."

I just tilt my head, a silent signal for him to continue.

"To get Penny to the races. This is your new training gate. You only have a couple more months to race her as a two-year-old. And apparently the gate can be a challenge."

I look back at the gate. My mouth is moving, but no sound comes out. *This* is what I was talking about. I don't want flowers. I want *this.*

"Ada, you look like a fish dropped into a dry bucket. Go get your horse. I'm almost done here."

I nod mutely and walk away on wooden legs. What does this mean? Is he only back to help with Penny? Or is he back for me?

I'm standing beside Penny's shiny, coppery coat without even knowing how I really got here. Like my mind has been somewhere else entirely. She drops her head into the halter and we walk back toward Dermot, who is shifting the panels around so it's finally looking like a sort of chute.

"There are more attachments, but apparently the key is to get her comfortable in there. Walking through so she trusts you enough when you eventually box her in."

I raise an eyebrow at him, wondering if he's talking about Penny or me, but carry on anyway. We spend the morning working together. It's torture, feeling him so close to me and yet thinking he might only be back at the ranch on a professional basis. His body heat seeps through my clothes, and his form hovers close to mine as he moves around me, showing me the gate, breaking down how it works, but he never touches me. Not so much as an accidental brush of the leg or nudge of the elbow.

And after a few hours, I'm going insane. I want him to touch me. Kiss me. Throw me against this stupid gate and have his way with me. My entire body is thrumming with need and he's hardly looked me in the eye.

I know I need to leave. I've embarrassed myself far too many times by throwing myself at this man, and I can't let myself go there again. So I busy myself around the farm and Dermot goes back to sitting on his stupid truck. Like a lost puppy. A sexy lost puppy I want to kick and then kiss.

When I'm about to head into the house for dinner, I

catch sight of him sitting there, casually looking through some sheets of paper, and my patience snaps. I storm toward him. "What are you doing?"

He looks genuinely shocked by the bite in my voice. "I wanted to show you these."

"Not that!" I knock them right out of his hand and watch them flutter to the ground. "I mean *here*. What are you doing here? You gave me the gate. If that's all you wanted, you can now go."

But then I look down and catch sight of the papers near my feet.

*Dear Ada…*

I bend down and pick up the closest sheet. Feeling the beat of my pulse stronger in my throat.

*Dear Ada,*

*Just got to basic training and everyone here has someone to write to. I'm not sure who else I could send a letter to that might actually want to hear from me, so I guess you're stuck with me.*

*Yours,*
*Dermot*

*P.S. I should have kissed you back.*

I look at Dermot, his face completely unreadable where he sits. My hands start to shake and I sink to ground, right on the gravel driveway, desperately grasping at the other loose sheets. *Good god. There are so many.* The papers rattle in my hands as I lift them up.

*Dear Ada,*

*You know that feeling at the end of a long day on the ranch? You've been up early, worked your ass off all day, your legs feel like jelly, and you just crash into bed and have the best sleep? I'm so much more tired than that and I still can't sleep.*

*Instead, I avoid replaying my days by lying awake thinking about the night you kissed me. Analyzing it every which way I can. Trying to commit it to memory. Why did you do that? Plant a seed in the mind of a man you knew was leaving? A man who never saw you that way even for a moment? Now I don't know what to think about it, about myself, about you, and I don't even have the balls to ask. It's better this way anyhow.*

*Yours,*
*Dermot*

*P.S. I should have kissed you back.*

A ragged whimper bursts out of my chest as I riffle through page after page. Letter after letter. "Dermot…"

*Dear Ada,*

*Everything here is dark, and sad, and depressing. The days blend into each other and the only thing that ties me back to home is you. Your sunny blond hair, your carefree smiles, the scent of your tangerine body wash that wrapped around me that night when you stood closer than you ever have. The way your hands felt on my shoulders when you leaned in. What I wouldn't give for a simple gentle touch right now.*

*The longer I'm away, the more I remember things differently. The more I think that maybe there is a connection between us. Is it new? Has it always been there? I don't know. You're so fucking young. You're better off without me.*

*Yours,*
*Dermot*

*P.S. I should have kissed you back.*

A tear falls onto the letter in my hands, drawing my attention from the pages. "Dermot," I say, coming to stand. "I...I never got these letters."

"That's because I didn't send them. Never quite worked up the courage." *All these letters. All this time...*

His jaw ticks as his eyes sear across my body, pausing momentarily on my heaving chest before moving back up to my face. "That's not all I wanted. To give you the gate, I mean."

I come back to standing and hold the pages out wide in tearful exasperation. "Then for crying out loud, Dermot, use your words and tell me what you want."

He doesn't even hesitate. "I want you. I want us. I'll sleep in this truck for as long as it takes. If I'm relegated to being your assistant trainer for the foreseeable future, I don't even care. I just want to see you succeed, to see all your dreams realized. And I'll do anything in my power to make that happen for you. I'll love you even if you don't love me back."

My heart riots in my chest. Almost ready to burst with years of unspoken truths and unfulfilled wishes. I almost can't believe what I'm hearing. *Did he just say he loves me?*

I step in closer to him, grasping his knee with both hands and looking up into the depths of his chocolate eyes. "You're a fool, Dermot Harding." The muscles in his thigh tense beneath the tips of my fingers. "Don't you know?" I say more quietly now, feeling him lean down closer to hear what I'm about to say, his breath fanning across the sensitive skin below my ear. "I can't remember a time in my life when I haven't loved you. It's always been you."

Dermot's throat bobs with emotion as one calloused hand comes up to stroke my cheek. I see his eyes sparkle in the late summer sun as a secret smile touches his shapely lips. Lips that are moving closer to mine, lips that I can't wait to feel against my own again.

So I stand up on my tippy-toes and kiss him as his broad frame leans down over me, as he grips my head possessively, protectively. We kiss, and the world stands still, and everything feels so suddenly right. So hopelessly fated. Like no matter what either of us did, we'd have ended up here, today, in each other's arms.

I'm breathless when he pulls back and smiles at me, his thumb stroking my cheek softly. "I'm never leaving you again. If you'll let me, I'm moving into the laneway house."

I just wink through the tears spilling over my lashes, my voice tearful but happy. "I'll think about it."

Much later that night, we lie out in the bed of his truck on a blanket. For the last hour I've made Dermot read me his letters out loud. I've cried, we've kissed, he even stopped at one point to strip me down and show me how much he loves me. And now I'm tucked safely under his arm with my legs slung over his as we look up at the stars. They shine like a string of twinkle lights over the farm, not at all diluted by the glow of the city. It's almost like looking at a painting, never quite the same depending on the day. And today there's a meteor shower.

"Right there." Dermot's hand shoots up to point out the falling star. "Make a wish, Ada."

An airy laugh floats out from my lips as I snuggle in closer. "What am I supposed to wish for? I have everything I've ever wanted."

He presses a sweet kiss to my temple and whispers, "Pick something."

"Okay. I want to win the Denman Derby. I want to win it all. Maybe even the Northern Crown. Doesn't that sound crazy?" I shake my head, grinning.

"No, Ada. It doesn't."

"Oh yeah? You going to promise to make that happen too?" I laugh, nudging his ribs with my elbow, thinking he'll laugh along with me and my lofty dreams.

But instead, he's completely sincere when he looks down at me and says, "I promise."

Then his lips find mine, and I know deep in my bones that the world has a funny way of making wishes come true.

# EPILOGUE

## Dermot

BELLS RING AND THE HORSES SURGE OUT OF THE GATE. I FEEL Ada's nails digging into the palm of my hand. Her entire body is vibrating with anticipation—with nervousness.

This is Lucky Penny's debut race, and we both know we're out of our league. Two country bumpkins pulling up with one lone little racehorse. But everyone has to start somewhere, and Ada is determined.

Tom had to call in some pretty serious favors to convince a jockey to take the ride on Penny. But here we are, close to the end of the season, watching her blaze across the dirt track in the black and gold Gold Rush Ranch silks that Ada made. I wrap my opposite hand over the top of hers, feeling the center stone of the ring I put there a week ago dig into my palm. She smiles faintly but doesn't tear her eyes away from the track.

Ada and I happened fast, and yet we didn't. We both had

three long years to be sure about one another. And when you know, you know. I wanted Ada, and I wasn't about to wait any longer. Or give her time to come to her senses and pick someone better. We're planning a spring wedding at the ranch, and her parents are over the moon.

Almost as over the moon as when I showed Tom his five-percent ownership contract for Gold Rush Resources. I swear the grizzled old rancher teared up at me extending the name of his beloved ranch to our new venture. Ada rolled her eyes, but I didn't miss the way she wiped at her them either.

"Oh god." Her voice is shrill, snapping my attention back out to the track. Penny is in the middle of the pack but is slowly losing position. Her ears are flicking all over the place. The poor little thing looks nervous. Most racehorses end up living at the track during the season, so the competition is desensitized to the sights and sounds here today in a way that Penny isn't.

But we knew all this coming in. Ada doesn't care if Penny wins; she just loves that lanky, sassy mare and everything she represents. The catalyst that brought us together on more than one occasion. Our very own lucky penny.

"Dermot," Ada laughs, "I don't think we're going to win." Her voice is light and amused, and she's shaking her head lovingly as she watches Penny fall to the very back of the pack.

I pull her into my side, hugging her and dropping a kiss on the top of her hair. "No, Goldilocks. I don't think we are. Not today."

But one day we would. After all, I made her a promise.

Read on for a sneak peek of the next book in the series,

**A PHOTO FINISH,**

featuring the youngest Eaton sibling in the fan-favorite Chestnut Springs series.

# Violet

DID I REALLY JUST WIN THIS RACE?

Everything around me moves in slow motion. The pointy black ears ahead of me leading to the shiny black mane down the neck that rocks in a steady rhythm beneath me. My fingers tangle in that mane, holding on for dear life.

I look over my shoulder to ensure I actually crossed the finish line. That I didn't just black out and miss a chunk of the race. Maybe there's another lap left? Maybe I've absolutely blown it like the total rookie I am.

But all around me, other horses and jockeys are slowing, pulling up. Pony horses go around us to grab excited racehorses. I even hear congratulatory words coming from my competitors. Which is nice because I have no business being here on a horse like this, winning such a prestigious race.

This is my first race *ever*, and I just qualified for the Denman Derby. That's pure dumb luck. That's unheard of.

I shake my head, trying to clear my thoughts, and the sounds from around me come rushing back in. Cheering from the stands, horn music over the loudspeakers, the number on our saddle pad flashing across the board in the infield.

*We really did it.*

I flop down onto his shiny black neck, wrapping my arms around him and nuzzling into his sweat-slicked coat. My throat clogs with emotion, and my eyes water as I murmur, "Who's the best boy?"

When I sit back up, we slow to a walk. Once the race is over, he doesn't stay keyed up for long. DD is a big old teddy bear, though he hasn't always been. It wasn't so long ago that nobody wanted to go near him. But his new trainer, Billie, brought him around, and somehow, I lucked into getting the ride on him.

I sit back and give DD some rein as we walk casually off the track toward the winner's circle. I think that's what I should do. Alarm courses through me as I realize I don't really know what to do here. I know my way around Bell Point Park, but I've never won a major stakes race before.

A moment later, Hank, the barn manager at Gold Rush Ranch, is at my side, patting my leg and looking up at me with pure, contagious joy. His heavily lined green eyes twinkle with emotion. "Congratulations, Violet. I could not be more proud of you."

I blink rapidly and look away. Hank has that quintessential dad vibe going on. Or grandpa vibe? I'm not sure really. He's old enough he should be retired, but here he is working on the farm every day like he's some sort of spring chicken.

The smile I return is watery. The reality of everything is sinking in, and it's overwhelming. "Thank you, Hank."

He reaches up and grabs the reins close to DD's bit. "Whoa, boy." He pulls us off to the side under the shade of a tree. "You two just take a moment before you head up there. A few deep breaths to get your bearings."

I could hug Hank at this moment for knowing what I need right now, even though I'm too shell-shocked to realize it.

"Thank you." I smile down at him and then close my eyes to take those deep breaths he recommended.

Until just recently, I was a groom at Gold Rush Ranch, sometimes an exercise rider when my friend and head trainer, Billie Black, would ask me to help. Imagine my surprise when she announced I would be the new jockey for one of the most talented racehorses I've ever seen. One bad race with local favorite Patrick Cassel as jockey was all it took for her to blacklist him and replace him with me.

So I dumb-lucked my way into this and am now certain everyone will notice and call my bluff.

When I feel like I've stopped spinning, I roll my shoulders back and jut my chin out. DD's breathing has slowed, and I can hear him chewing on the bit in his mouth, a sure sign he's feeling more relaxed as well.

*Fake it till you make it, Vi.* It doesn't matter how I got here. I rode that race, and it wasn't an easy one. DD and I deserve this win, and I'm going to accept it with grace rather than beat myself up about not deserving it.

"Okay. I'm ready."

With a sure nod, Hank clucks, urging DD forward, and we head for the circus that is the winner's circle.

Billie is there, big sunglasses on to cover what I'm sure are tear-stained eyes. Vaughn, one of the two brothers who now own Gold Rush Ranch, is there too, arm snaked around her waist possessively.

I can't help but grin. Obviously, something is happening there. I shoot Billie a wink right as she rushes forward to hug DD and me. She blubbers something about loving me and being proud of me. And I'd be lying if my eyes didn't start to sting and water furiously too.

"Thank you for this," I whisper into her mess of chestnut hair as I lean down to return the hug.

Vaughn steps up next, opting for a firm handshake in lieu of a hug. His smile is wide and genuine, his chest puffed out proudly. "Congratulations, Violet. Beautifully ridden."

"Thank you for the opportunity," I say, grinning back like a total maniac. Because seriously, who puts a completely unproven twenty-six-year-old groom on a horse like *this* for a race like *this*?

My eyes dart over as someone else steps up to us just beside Vaughn. I feel my eyes widen as he does and scold myself internally. My poker face leaves something to be desired. This is something I know and still can't control. My feelings are constantly written on my face. Like a big flashing neon sign. And right now is no exception. The man is clearly Vaughn's older brother, Cole. I've heard plenty about him, mostly Billie ranting about what a dick he is and making jokes about him being a robot, which I can kind of see, looking at him now. Where everyone else is elated—celebratory—he looks downright murderous.

Murderous and delicious.

I don't know if the endorphins coursing through me right now are making me giddy or if being this happy kills brain cells, but I can't look away from the gorgeous man. Even though he's scowling at me, I drink him in like the champagne I can't wait to guzzle when this crazy day is over.

He looks like Vaughn yet totally different. Harder, more imposing. Where Vaughn is tall and lean, his brother is strong and broad. His shoulders push against his suit jacket, like they might tear through it if he flexed hard enough. My eyes trail down to his trim waist and powerful thighs. *Pull yourself together, Violet. You're practically panting.*

When I imagined the reclusive brother who spends all his time at their downtown office, the one who never sets foot on the farm, *this* is not what I envisioned.

"Hi!" I say a little too brightly. *Cringe.* "I'm Violet." I stick my hand out toward him while people and cameras crowd in around us.

He doesn't return my smile though. His shapely lips stay pressed into a flat line, and his gray eyes sear me from where I still sit on DD's back. When his hand wraps around mine, I can't help but realize how big the man really is. My hand and wrist practically disappear in his grip. The warm rasp of his palm starts softly, then he squeezes and steps close to the saddle. His opposite hand rises between us, and he crooks his index finger.

A silent order to move closer.

I feel my heart rattle around in my chest as I lean in like a total sucker. Like a moth to a flame.

I expect him to congratulate me.

What I don't expect is for him to send me reeling into past mistakes.

"Nice to see you again, Pretty in Purple. I almost didn't recognize you with your clothes on."

All the air in my lungs rushes out in an audible gasp as I jerk back away from him.

*No.*

I peer down at him, scouring his features, feeling all the blood drain from my face as I try to reconcile my memory of a man I've worked so hard to forget.

*No fucking way.*

There is only one person in the world who would ever know to call me that, who would ever have the gall to say it that way. My cheeks heat as memories from the last year come at me rapid fire.

That youthful experimentation part of my life was supposed to be a bump in the road on my way to total independence.

That part of my life was supposed to have stayed anonymous and in the past.

When I ghosted him without a word, he was supposed to stay where I left him.

He wasn't supposed to matter to me.

But as I drown in his gray eyes while the circus rages around me, I realize he still does.

# Acknowledgments

This story is short and sweet, but boy were there a lot of people behind the scenes helping me get this together (holding my hand). Melanie Harlow, without you this book would have had a mafia romance cover and a paranormal romance blurb. How freaking lucky am I to have someone like you in my corner? I seriously pinch myself. Casey, your eye for design and unflappable patience with my nonstop questions is admirable. You're the real MVP. And Kylie, thank you for your time and seriously detailed feedback—this story would be very different without your keen eye. It's a special skill! I'm telling you.

Finally, a big thank-you to my husband, for keeping me sane and being the best cheerleader a girl could ask for. You look cute in that skirt, babe. And to my son, for helping me choose the cover photo. ("Who is dad kissing in this picture?")

# About the Author

Elsie Silver is a Canadian author of sassy, sexy, small-town romance who loves good book boyfriends and the strong heroines who bring them to their knees. She lives just outside Vancouver, British Columbia, with her husband, son, and three dogs and has been voraciously reading romance books since before she was probably supposed to.

She loves cooking and trying new foods, traveling, and spending time with her boys—especially outdoors. Elsie has also become a big fan of her quiet 5:00 a.m. mornings, which is when most of her writing happens. It's during this time that she can sip a cup of hot coffee and dream up a fictional world full of romantic stories to share with her readers.

Website: elsiesilver.com
Facebook: authorelsiesilver
Instagram: @authorelsiesilver
TikTok: @authorelsiesilver